PRAISE FOR IRIS JOHANSEN'S
THE UGLY DUCKLING

"Recommended . . . fast-moving."

—*Cosmopolitan*

"Iris Johansen knows how to win instant fans. . . . Many will add her name to their list of favorite authors. . . . [She] does an outstanding job of mixing . . . a love story and an action-thriller into a real page-turner."

—*The Associated Press*

"A well-executed story that deftly provides chilling suspense."

—*Library Journal*

"A successful hardcover debut . . . As Johansen quick-cuts back and forth between the good guys and the bad, in tried-and-true Sheldonesque style, the plot eventually delivers just deserts to all—thanks to inventive surprises."

—*Kirkus Reviews*

"Don't miss this page-turner!"
—Catherine Coulter, *New York Times* bestselling author of *The Cove*

"Crackling suspense with a brilliant roller coaster of a plot."

—Julie Garwood, *New York Times* bestselling author of *For the Roses*

BANTAM BOOKS BY IRIS JOHANSEN

Iris Johansen

THE UGLY DUCKLING

BANTAM BOOKS
New York Toronto London Sydney Auckland

This edition contains the complete text
of the original hardcover edition.
NOT ONE WORD HAS BEEN OMITTED.

THE UGLY DUCKLING
A Bantam Book

PUBLISHING HISTORY
Bantam hardcover edition published May 1996
Bantam paperback edition/January 1997

ISBN 0-553-56991-0

Published simultaneously in the United States of Canada

Bantam Books are published by Bantam Books, a division of Bantam Doubleday
Dell Publishing Group, Inc. Its trademark, consisting of the words "Bantam
Books" and the portrayal of a rooster, is Registered in U. S. Patent and Trademark
Office and in other countries. Marca Registrada. Bantam Books, 1540 Broadway,
New York, New York 10036.

PRINTED IN THE UNITED STATES OF AMERICA

OPM 28

THE UGLY
DUCKLING

Prologue

Greenbriar, North Carolina

"I didn't mean to break it." Tears were running down Nell's cheeks. "Please, Mama. I was holding it and it just fell."

"I told you never to touch my things. Your father gave me this mirror in Venice." Her mother's lips were tight with anger as she looked at the broken handle of the pearl-encrusted mirror. "It will never, never be the same."

"Yes, it will. I promise." Nell reached out and tried to take the hand mirror. "I didn't break the mirror, just the handle. I'll glue it. It will be exactly the same."

"You've ruined it. What were you doing in my room anyway? I told your grandmother never to let you in here."

"She didn't know. It wasn't her fault." The sobs were choking her. "I just came to—I wanted to see—I made this wreath of honeysuckle from the fence and—"

"I see you did." Her mother disdainfully touched

the flowers in Nell's hair. "You look ridiculous." She held the mirror up before Nell's face. "Is that what you wanted to see? How silly you look."

"I thought I'd look . . . pretty."

"Pretty? Look at yourself. You're plump and plain and you'll never be anything else."

Mama was right. The girl in the mirror was plump, her eyes swollen and bloodshot. The bright yellow blossoms Nell had thought so beautiful looked limp and pitiful tucked in her untidy brown hair. By wearing them, she had made even the flowers seem ugly. She whispered, "I'm sorry, Mama."

"Was that really necessary, Martha?" Her grandmother stood in the doorway. "She's only eight years old."

"It's time she learned to face reality. She'll never be anything but an ugly little mouse. She has to deal with it."

"All children are beautiful," her grandmother said quietly. "And if she's a little plain now, that doesn't mean she'll stay that way."

Her mother snatched up the mirror again and held it before Nell. "Is she right, Nell? Are you beautiful?"

Nell turned her head to avoid her reflection.

Her mother turned to her grandmother. "And I don't want you filling her head with stories and fantasies. Ugly ducklings don't become swans. Plain children usually grow up to be plain adults. She'll have to be content with being neat and clean and obedient to be accepted." She took Nell's shoulders and looked directly into her eyes. "Do you understand, Nell?"

She understood. By accepted, Mama meant to be loved. She would never be beautiful like Mama, so she must make them all love her by doing whatever they wished.

She nodded jerkily.

Her mother released her, grabbed her briefcase from the bed, and moved toward the door. "I have a meeting in twenty minutes, and you've made me late. You must never, never come into this room again." She glared impatiently at Nell's grandmother. "I can't understand you not watching her more closely."

She was gone.

Her grandmother held out her arms to Nell. She meant to comfort, to ease the hurt, and Nell wanted to go to her, to bury her face in her shoulder. But there was something she must do first.

She turned back to the dresser and carefully gathered the pieces of the broken mirror. She would glue every piece with great care so that no one would ever know it was broken. She must work hard and be very clever and very good.

Because she was an ugly duckling.

And she would never become a swan.

One

Tanek wasn't pleased.

Conner could tell as he watched Nicholas Tanek stride out of customs. Tanek's expression was impassive, but Conner had known him long enough to read his body language. Tanek's power and presence were always evident, but not the impatience.

It had better be good, Tanek had told him.

It wasn't good, but it was all Conner had.

He ambled forward and smiled with effort. "Pleasant flight?"

"No." Tanek walked toward the exit. "Is Reardon in the car?"

"Yes, he arrived from Dublin last night." He paused. "But he can't go to the party with you. I could wangle only one invitation."

"I said two invitations."

"You don't understand."

"I understand that if it's a hit, I'm without a backup. I understand that I pay you to do as I tell you."

"The party is for Anton Kavinski and the invitations were issued three months ago. He's the president of a Russian state, for God's sake. It cost me a fortune to get even one." He added hurriedly, "And you may not need Reardon. I told you the information may not be accurate. Our man only found a computer message at DEA headquarters that indicated this party on the island of Medas *might* be hit."

"That's all?"

"And a list of names."

"What kind of list?"

"The names of six guests. No one that we can identify as players except one of Kavinski's bodyguards and Martin Brenden, the man who's giving the party. One name was circled for special attention. A woman."

"What makes you think this is a hit list?"

"Blue ink. Our man has a theory that Gardeaux's orders are color-coded to define action to be taken."

"Theory?" Tanek's voice was dangerously soft. "I've come all this way for a theory?"

Conner moistened his lips. "You told me to let you know anything that came up about Gardeaux."

The mention of Philippe Gardeaux had the desired effect of tempering Tanek's annoyance, Conner saw with relief. He had learned that no effort was too great, no action too minor, if it concerned Gardeaux.

"Okay, you're right," Tanek said. "Who sent this computer message?"

"Joe Kabler, the head of the DEA, has a paid informant in Gardeaux's camp."

"Can we get the informant's name?"

Conner shook his head. "I've been trying, but so far no luck."

"And what's Kabler going to do about this list?"

"Nothing."

Tanek stared at him. "Nothing?"

"Kabler thinks it's a list of bribery targets."

"He doesn't believe in the 'deadly blue ink' theory?" Tanek asked sarcastically.

Conner drew a breath of relief as they came abreast of the Mercedes. Let Reardon deal with him; they were two of a kind. "Reardon has the list with him in the car." He hastily opened the back door. "You can talk to him while I drive you to the hotel."

"Howdy, cowboy." Jamie Reardon's Irish brogue was blatantly at odds with the assumed western drawl. "I see you left your boots at home."

Nicholas Tanek felt a little of his impatience ebb as he climbed into the car. "I should have brought them. Nothing like boots to kick ass."

"Mine or Conner's?" Jamie asked. "Must be Conner's. No one would want to damage my venerable ass."

Conner gave a nervous laugh as he pulled out of the parking space.

Jamie's long face lit with mischief, his sly gaze on the back of Conner's head. "But I can see how you'd be displeased with Conner. It's a long flight from Idaho for no good reason."

"I told you it might be nothing," Conner said. "I didn't tell him to come."

"You didn't tell him not to," Jamie murmured. "Isn't silence assent, Nick?"

"Knock it off. I'm here now." Nicholas wearily leaned back on the leather seat. "Is it for nothing, Jamie?"

"Probably. There's no sign the DEA is taking it seriously. Kabler's certainly not spending government funds to get an invitation to Medas."

Another blind alley. Christ, Nicholas was tired of it.

"But getting away from those wide-open spaces is good therapy for you," Jamie said. "Every time you come back from that ranch, you look more like John Wayne. It's not healthy."

"John Wayne has been dead a number of years."

"I told you it wasn't healthy."

"It's healthy spending your life in a pub?"

"Ah, Nick, you never understood. Irish pubs are the cultural center of the universe. Poetry and art flourish like roses in summer, and the conversations . . ." He half closed his eyes, savoring the memory. "At other places people talk, in my place they have conversations."

Nicholas smiled faintly. "There's a difference?"

"The difference between deciding the fate of the world and buying a new video game for the kid." He lifted a brow. "But why am I wasting my time describing such beauty to you? You have only steers to talk to in that savage Idaho."

"Sheep."

"Whatever. It's no wonder cowboys are reputed to be strong and silent. Their vocal cords are atrophied from disuse."

"They have the usual verbal skills."

Jamie snorted.

"The list," Conner prompted.

"Ah, he wishes his summons to be validated," Jamie said. "He's afraid of you, you know."

"Nonsense." Conner's laugh was a little too hearty.

"I tried to tell him you're no longer in the business, but I don't think he believes me. I did hope you'd wear the cowboy boots. They're so wholesome and unthreatening."

"Stop it, Jamie," Nicholas said.

Jamie chuckled. "Just a bit of humor." He added in a tone inaudible to Conner, "I've no liking for the shifty rabbit. Every time he jumps, he makes me want to skin him."

"You don't have to like him. He has an inside man with the DEA."

"For all the good it's done us so far." Jamie reached in his pocket, drew out a folded piece of paper, and handed it to Nicholas. "And this looks like another blank."

"Who's giving this party?" Nicholas said.

"A banker. Martin Brenden, vice president of Continental Trust. Continental Trust is going after Kavinski's overseas investments. Brenden's rented this palace on Medas for the weekend and is throwing the party in Kavinski's honor."

"And what connection does Brenden have with Gardeaux?"

"None that we can trace."

"Kavinski?"

"Possible. Since Kavinski was elected president of Vanask he's become a major deal maker above and under the table. He may have offended Gardeaux by refusing to let drugs into Vanask." He paused. "But his name wasn't on the list."

"Then I'd bet on Kabler's interpretation. Bribery. He's been head of the DEA long enough to sift the chaff from the grain, and he's a shrewd bastard."

"Does that mean you're not going to Medas?"

Nicholas thought about it. It was probably a waste of time if Gardeaux's message was just a payola list. He had gone on too many wild-goose chases on the chance of finding the key to nail Gardeaux.

But if it was a hit list, then one of the intended victims might know something he could use. Besides, if Gardeaux wanted them dead, then Nicholas damn well wanted them alive.

"Well?" Jamie prompted.

"How do I get to this Medas?"

"There are boats bringing the guests from the dock at Athens. They start leaving at eight tonight. You just show up with an invitation."

"And I wonder how many of Gardeaux's men bought invitations as I did."

"I checked out the guests," Conner said. "Everyone who accepted is legitimate."

Maybe. "Any other way to get on the island?"

Conner shook his head. "It has a rocky coastline that's accessible only by the one dock. Medas is postage-stamp size. You can walk around the entire island in under an hour. Besides the mansion where the party's going to be, there's only a few other outbuildings."

"And Kavinski's security men will be guarding the dock," Jamie said. "It doesn't seem to be a situation Gardeaux would choose to rid himself of enemies." He smiled. "On the other hand, Kaifer seemed an impossible target, too, and we managed it."

"We were lean and hungry," Nicholas pointed out. "These days Gardeaux is a fat cat who prefers to wait outside the mouse hole for his prey. But I suppose I'll go and check it out."

"I could go. Or you could send someone else."

"No, I'll do it myself."

"Why?" Jamie's gaze narrowed on his face. "Could it be that you're growing restless in the wilds?"

God, yes, he was restless. Restless and impatient and wanting this over. He was no closer to bringing Gardeaux down than he was a year ago.

"You're too used to walking on the edge," Jamie said lightly. "And you'll never be anything but lean and hungry, my lad. I admit I miss it, too, at times." He sighed. "Unfortunately, it's deplorably true that one can have only so many conversations."

"I don't miss it. I just want Gardeaux."

"If you say so."

"I'll need a report on all the names on the list."

"It's already on the desk in your hotel room. As you'll see, there doesn't seem to be any common thread connecting the names."

No, Medas was going to be a snarl of inconsistencies and guesses and maybes.

But the circled name on the list that Conner had mentioned might indicate something; prime prospect or prime target. Either way, she merited attention. He unfolded the paper Jamie had given him.

The name that topped the list was both circled and underlined.

Nell Calder.

June 4
Medas, Greece

"I saw a monster, Mama," Jill announced.

"Did you, love?" Nell placed a white hyacinth to the left of the lilac in the Chinese vase and tilted her head appraisingly. Yes, perfect. She reached for another lilac as she glanced at Jill standing in the doorway. "Like Pete, the magic dragon?"

Jill looked at her in disgust. "No, that's a pretend monster, this was a real one. A man monster. With a long gray nose and eyes like this." She formed a circle with her thumb and forefinger, and then, judging the circle too small, used her other hand to make the eyes larger. "And a humped back."

"Sounds like an elephant." One more delphinium and the arrangement would be finished. "Or maybe a camel."

"You're not listening to me," Jill said. "It was a man monster and he lives in the caves."

"The caves?" Fear leapt through Nell. The flowers instantly forgotten, she whirled to face her daughter. "What were you doing there? You know Mr. Brenden told you that you weren't to go into the caves. The real estate agent told him the sea rushes in, and bad tides could sweep you away."

"I just went in a little way." She added virtuously, "And then Daddy called me and I came right back out."

"Daddy took you there?" Dammit, Richard should have watched her more closely. Didn't he know that an island posed all sorts of dangers for a four-year-old? Nell knew she should have gone with them when they all decided to take that stroll along the beach. Richard always became distracted when he was surrounded by Brenden's coterie. He always had to be the best, the most charming, the funniest, the cleverest in any group.

What was she thinking? Nell wondered guiltily. Richard didn't have to be the best; he *was* the best. Jill was her responsibility and she should have gone with them and taken care of her instead of hiding back here and playing with the flower arrangements for the party. "You mustn't go into the caves. It's not safe. That's why Daddy called you back."

Jill nodded. "Because of the monster."

"No." Jill was a sensitive and imaginative child, and this particular fantasy had to be nipped at the start. Nell dropped to her knees on the Aubusson rug and gently grasped Jill's shoulders. "There was no monster. Sometimes shadows look like monsters, particularly when you're in a spooky place. Remember when you wake in the middle of the night and think there are bogeymen under the bed? Then, when we look, there's nothing there?"

"There *was* a monster." Jill's lips set stubbornly. "He scared me."

For an instant Nell was tempted to let her continue to think the monsters existed if the idea would keep her out of the cave. But she had never lied to her daughter before and she would not start now. She would just have to never let Jill out of her sight while they were on this dratted island.

"Shadows," Nell repeated firmly, and for reinforcement added, "Isn't that what Daddy said when you told him about the monster?"

"Daddy didn't listen. He told me to hush. He was busy talking to Mrs. Brenden." Jill's eyes filled with tears. "And you don't believe me either."

"I do believe you, but sometimes there's—" She couldn't go on with Jill looking at her with those reproachful brown eyes. She gently stroked back the straight, silky brown bangs from Jill's forehead. His China doll, Richard called her, because of her straight, short bob. But there was nothing fragile about Jill. She was sturdy and as apple-pie American as Nell could make her. "Suppose we go down to the cave tomorrow morning and you can show me this monster and we'll chase him away."

"You won't be afraid?" Jill whispered.

"There's nothing to fear here, baby. It's a good place for children. The sea and the beach and this lovely house. You'll have a wonderful time this weekend."

"You won't have a good time."

"What?"

Jill's gaze held hers with an oddly mature shrewdness. "You never have a good time. Not like Daddy."

Never underestimate the wisdom of children, Nell thought wearily. "I'm a little shy. Just because I'm quiet doesn't mean I'm not having a good time." She gave her daughter a hug. "And we always have a good time together, don't we?"

"Sure." Jill's arms slid around her neck. She cuddled

closer. "May I come down to the party tonight? Then you'll have somebody to talk to."

Jill smelled of sea and sand and Nell's lavender soap she had begged to use in her bath last night. Nell's arms tightened around her for a moment before she reluctantly released her. "It's a grown-up party. You wouldn't like it."

And neither would she. She had grown accustomed to her duties as Richard's wife and could usually fade into the background, but that would be difficult to do this weekend. A plain wren would stick out like the proverbial sore thumb among the socialites and celebrities Martin Brenden had invited to the island to meet Kavinski and dazzle him into signing with Continental Trust.

"Then stay with me," Jill coaxed.

"I can't." She wrinkled her nose. "Daddy's boss wouldn't like it. This is a very important night for Daddy, and we both have to help him." She saw her daughter's face begin to cloud again, and said quickly, "But I'll bring you up a tray of goodies before you go to sleep. We'll have a picnic."

The anxiety immediately vanished. "And wine?" Jill asked eagerly. "Jean Marc's mother lets him have a glass of wine every evening for supper. She says it's good for him."

Jean Marc was the son of the housekeeper who reigned supreme in their apartment in Paris, and Nell was hearing a good deal about the rascal. "Orange juice." To stave off an argument, she added quickly, "But if you eat all your supper, I'll see if I can find a chocolate eclair for you." She stood up and pulled the little girl to her feet. "Now, go run your bath while I take this flower arrangement downstairs. I'll be back in two minutes."

Jill gazed solemnly at the Chinese vase and then

smiled luminously. "It's pretty, Mama. Even nicer than when they were in the garden."

Nell didn't agree. She always thought it was a shame to pick flowers. Nothing was more beautiful than a garden in bloom. Like the garden of the bed-and-breakfast she had painted when she was going to school at William and Mary. Mists and rich colors and all the textures of morning . . .

She felt a sharp pang and quickly shied away from the memory. She had no reason to pity herself. Richard had never denigrated her paintings as her parents had done. After they were married, he had even encouraged her to continue with her work. She just had no time. Being the wife of an ambitious young executive seemed to occupy every hour of the day.

She made a face at the vase as she picked it up. If she had not been forced to spend all afternoon doing Sally Brenden's flower arrangements, she could have sketched that beautiful shoreline. But that would have meant going with the Brendens and Richard for that walk along the beach. She would have had to smile and chat and bear Sally being gracious to her. Sally's subtle tyrannies were a welcome alternative to her company.

Nell brushed her lips across Jill's brow. "Lay out your pajamas and don't go near the balcony."

"You've already told me that," Jill said with dignity.

"I told you not to go into the cave too."

"That's different."

"No, it isn't."

Jill started toward the bathroom. "Caves are neat. I don't like balconies. I get dizzy looking down at the rocks."

Thank heaven for small mercies. She couldn't believe Sally had given them, a couple with a small child, a suite with a balcony overlooking that rocky shore. Yes, she could believe it. Richard had told Sally years before that he loved the view from a balcony, and Sally always tried to please him. Everyone tried to please the golden boy.

"You should see the boatload of security men Kavinski sent ahead. You'd think he was Arafat." Richard blew into the suite like a strong breeze. He glanced at the flowers. "Pretty. You'd better get them downstairs. Sally mentioned there wasn't a bouquet in the foyer."

"I just finished it." She was making excuses again, she realized with annoyance. "I'm not a professional. She could have had someone come out to the island from Athens to do them."

He kissed her cheek. "But they wouldn't be as pretty as yours. She's always saying how lucky I am to have such an artistic wife. Be a love and hurry them down to her." He headed for the bedroom. "I have to shower. Kavinski should be here within the hour, and Martin wants to introduce me to him over drinks."

"Do I have to go? I thought I'd show up just for the party."

Richard thought about it and then shrugged. "Not if you don't want to. I don't think you'll be missed in the crowd."

Relief flowed through her. It was much easier to fade into the background during a party. She turned toward the door. "Jill's running her bath. Will you keep an eye on her until I come back?"

He smiled. "Sure."

He was dressed in white shorts and shirt, his brown hair rumpled and his lean cheeks flushed by the sun. He always looked wonderful in a tuxedo or a business suit, but she liked him best like this. He was more approachable, more *hers*.

He made a shooing motion with his hands. "Hurry. Sally's waiting."

She nodded and reluctantly left the suite.

She heard Sally's sharp, birdlike voice before she started down the curving marble staircase. She had always thought that tiny voice incongruous in a woman almost six feet tall and lean and sleek as a panther.

Sally Brenden turned away from the servant she had been scolding. "There you are. It's about time." She took the vase away from Nell and placed it on the marble table beneath an elaborately gilded mirror. "I'd think you'd be more considerate. It's not as if I don't have enough to worry about. I still have to speak to that little man who's going to shoot off the fireworks, talk to the chef, and I'm not even dressed yet. You know how important this night is to Martin. Everything has to be perfect."

Nell felt the heat flush her cheeks. "I'm sorry, Sally."

"An executive's wife is important in advancing his career. Martin would never have become vice president if I hadn't been there helping him. We don't ask much of you, do we?"

Nell had heard this self-laudatory lecture many times before. She felt a ripple of annoyance but quickly smothered it. "I'm sorry, Sally," she repeated. "Is there anything else I can do to help?"

Sally waved a beautifully manicured hand. "I've invited Madame Gueray to the party. Make sure she's comfortable. She's deplorably awkward in public."

Elise Gueray was even more shy and out of her element at a party than Nell. She didn't mind that Sally usually gave all the misfits to her. She received a deep satisfaction from making their way easier and less painful. God knows, she'd have been passionately grateful to anyone who'd have eased her way during those first few years after she had come to Europe.

"I don't know why Henri Gueray ever married her." Sally glanced at Nell with guilelessness. "Yet you so often see these powerhouse men with meek, inadequate wives."

A swift jab and then a turn of the knife. Nell was too accustomed to barbs to give Sally the satisfaction of reacting. "I found her very pleasant." She turned away and moved hastily toward the staircase. "I have to get back to Jill. She has to have her bath and dinner."

"Really, Nell, you should get a nanny."

"I like taking care of her myself."

"But she does get in the way." She paused. "I spoke to Richard about it this afternoon, and he agrees with me."

Nell went still. "Did he say that?"

"Of course, he realizes that the higher up he moves in the company, the more duties will be expected of you. When we get back to Paris, I'll contact the agency I used when Jonathan was a child. Simone made sure he gave me no trouble at all."

And Jonathan was now a thoroughly obnoxious and rebellious teenager hidden away in a boarding school in Massachusetts. "Thank you, but I'm not that busy. Perhaps when she's a little older."

"If Kavinski can be persuaded to give us his foreign investments, Richard will be in line to manage them. You'll be expected to travel with him. I think he's quite right to break in a nanny before she becomes a necessity." She turned away and moved toward the ballroom.

Sally was acting as if it were already settled, Nell thought frantically. She could not give her daughter up to one of those serene-faced women she had seen walking with their charges in the park. Jill belonged to her. How could Richard even consider taking her away?

He wouldn't consider it. Jill was everything to her. She did everything he asked of her, but he couldn't expect her to—

"Don't let the old witch bother you. She just wants to see you squirm." Nadine Fallon was coming down the steps. "Bullies always pounce on the gentle ones. It's the nature of the beast."

"Shh." Nell glanced over her shoulder, but Sally was already gone.

Nadine grinned. "Want me to spit in her eye for you?"

"Yes." She wrinkled her nose. "But somehow she'd find out and then Richard would be upset."

Nadine's grin faded. "Then let him be upset. He should know you're no match for her. He should be the one spitting in that barracuda's eye."

"You don't understand."

"No, I don't." She passed Nell and continued downstairs in a cloud of Opium perfume and Karl Lagerfeld chiffon—red-haired, beautiful, exotic, totally confident. "I learned a long time ago back in Brooklyn that she who doesn't fight back gets squashed."

Nadine would never get squashed, Nell thought wistfully. She had fought her way from Seventh Avenue to be one of the top runway models of Paris and never lost that earthy humor and boldness. She was invited everywhere, and Nell had run into her more and more frequently of late. Richard called her "designer window dressing," but Nell was always glad to see her.

Nadine glanced back over her shoulder. "You look great. Lost a few pounds?"

"Maybe." She knew she didn't look great. She was as plump as when Nadine had seen her last month, her slacks were rumpled, and she hadn't had time to comb her hair since that morning. Nadine was just trying to soothe her after that malicious savaging by Sally Brenden. Why not? Size six could afford to be kind to size twelve. She felt a rush of shame at the thought. Kindness should always be valued and never looked at askance. "I have to see Richard right away. I'll see you later at the party."

Nadine smiled and waved.

Nell took the stairs two at a time and ran down the long hall. Richard wasn't in the sitting room. She could hear him humming in the bedroom. She paused outside to steel herself and then threw open the door. "I don't want a nanny for Jill."

Richard turned away from the mirror. "What?"

"Sally said you were considering a nanny. I don't want one. We don't need one."

"Why are you upset?" He turned back to the mirror and straightened his tie. "It was just an idle discussion. It's not good to smother children with attention. All our friends have help. A nanny is something of a status symbol."

"You *are* considering it."

"Not without your consent." He put on his tuxedo jacket. "What are you wearing tonight?"

"I don't know." What difference did it make? She always looked the same anyway. "The blue lace gown, I guess." Her hands clenched at her sides. "I don't smother Jill."

"The blue is a good choice. That scalloped neckline makes your shoulders look wonderful."

She crossed the room and laid her head on his chest. "I want to take care of her myself. You're gone so often and we're company for each other." She whispered, "Please, Richard."

He stroked her hair. "I want only what's best for you. You know how hard I work to make sure you and Jill have a good life. Just help me a little, Nell."

He was going to do it, she realized in despair. "I try to help you."

"And you do." He pushed her away and looked

down into her face. "But I'm going to need more from you." A flicker of excitement lit his face. "Kavinski's the key, Nell. I've been waiting for six years for an opening like this. It's not only the money, it's the power. There's no telling how far I can go now."

"I'll work harder. I'll do everything you tell me to do. Just let me keep Jill."

"We'll talk about it tomorrow." He kissed her on the forehead and turned away. "Now I'd better get downstairs. Kavinski will be here any minute."

She stared numbly at the door after it closed behind him. They would talk tomorrow and he would be gentle and firm and a little sad that he couldn't do what she wanted. He would make her feel guilty and helpless and, when they returned to Paris, he would buy her favorite yellow roses and take care of the interviewing of the nanny himself in order not to distress her.

"Mama, my bathwater's getting cold," Jill said reprovingly. She stood barefoot in the doorway, wrapped in a huge pink towel.

"Is it?" She swallowed to ease the tightness in her throat. She would enjoy this precious time with Jill and try not to think of tomorrow. Maybe they wouldn't get the Kavinski accounts. Perhaps Richard would change his mind. "Then I guess we'd better warm it up and get you in it."

"Yep." Jill turned on her heel and vanished into the bathroom.

"You look like a princess." Jill rocked back and forth in her bed, hugging her knees.

"Not likely." Nell gently pushed her down on the pillows and pulled up the blanket. "Now, don't try to stay awake. Take a nap and I'll wake you when I bring our picnic. One of the maids will be right outside in the sitting room." She teasingly ruffled her daughter's hair. "Just in case you see any monsters."

"I did see him, Mama," Jill said gravely.

"Well, you won't see him again." She kissed her forehead. "I promise you."

She had reached the doorway when Jill called, "Remember the wine."

Nell chuckled as she shut the bedroom door. Jill would never suffer from either shyness or inability to assert herself.

Her smile vanished as she passed the mirror in the hall. Only her daughter would see anything princesslike in her appearance. She was a little over five seven but definitely plump rather than Junoesque. Plump and boring and plain as grass. Her features were nondescript except for a nose that turned up instead of fading into the boring sameness as the rest of her face. Even her short brown hair was boring, the same pale acorn shade of Jill's without childhood's sheen. Plain.

Well, Jill thought she was beautiful, and that was enough for her. Not that Richard didn't think she was attractive. He had once told her she reminded him of a country quilt—enduring, traditional, and beautiful in its simplicity. She wrinkled her nose ruefully at her reflection before moving quickly toward the door. She didn't know one woman in the world who wouldn't rather be a glamorous silk sheet than a country quilt. But plain women had one advantage; no one ever noticed when they entered or left a room. She would have no trouble escaping the ballroom with Jill's picnic supper.

She stood at the top of the marble stairs, looking down at the crowded foyer.

Music.

The scent of flowers and expensive perfume.

Laughter and conversation.

Dear God, she didn't want to go down there. The tall, carved doors leading to the ballroom were thrown wide open, and she could see Richard standing in a corner, talking to a tall, bearded man with a ribboned chest. Kavinski? Probably. Martin, Sally, and Nadine were also crowded around him, and Sally's expression was almost fawning. Nell would be expected to meet Kavinski later, but she would only be in the way now.

Her gaze searched the room, and she finally spotted Madame Gueray in the shadow of the French doors. Elise Gueray was fiftyish, thin, and trying desperately to blend into the white velvet drapes. Nell felt a swift rush of sympathy. She knew that frozen smile and hunted expression; she had seen it in her own mirror.

She started down the stairs. Let Richard charm Kavinski and wheel and deal with everyone else in sight. Helping Richard by making that poor woman less miserable was much more to her taste.

"*Mon Dieu,* the man should have a rose in his teeth," Elise Gueray murmured.

"What?" Nell put a lemon tart on the tray. She had promised Jill a chocolate eclair, but she couldn't see any on the buffet table.

"You know, like Monsieur Schwarzenegger in that movie where he played the spy who could do everything except fly?"

She vaguely remembered the movie and huge Schwarzenegger tangoing with a rose in his teeth. *"True Lies?"*

Elise shrugged. "I never remember titles, but Schwarzenegger is hard to forget." She nodded at someone across the room. "And so is he. Do you know who he is?"

Nell glanced over her shoulder. The man Elise was

indicating did not have Schwarzenegger's height or
bulk, but she could see what Elise meant. Dark-haired,
middle thirties, with a face more arresting than good-
looking, he exuded total self-confidence. He would
never be caught in a situation he could not control. No
wonder Elise found him fascinating. For people like her
and Nell, such assurance was as appealing as it was un-
attainable. "I've never seen him before. Perhaps he's in
Kavinski's entourage."

Elise shook her head.

She was right, Nell realized. This stranger would not
travel in anyone's wake.

"Are you that hungry?" Elise's gaze had shifted to
Nell's tray.

Heat scorched her cheeks. "No, I thought I'd take
a selection up to my daughter."

Elise looked stricken. "I did not mean—"

"I know." Nell made a face. "I don't exactly look
underfed."

"You look very nice," Elise said gently. "I did not
mean to hurt you."

"You didn't." She grinned. "It's my predilection for
chocolate cake that hurts me. It's as comforting as a
security blanket."

"And do you need comforting, my dear?"

"Don't we all?" she evaded, then said more firmly,
"No, of course not. I have everything I could possibly
want." She added softly, "If you have time, I'd like you
to meet my daughter tomorrow."

"I would enjoy that very much."

"Oh, there are the eclairs. She loves eclairs." She
added the pastry to the treasures on the tray before turning back to Elise. "Will you excuse me? I'd like to take
these up to Jill. I told her to take a nap, but she's probably still awake."

"Certainly. I've taken too much of your time. You've been very kind."

"Nonsense. I've enjoyed it. I should be the one to thank you." It was the truth. Once her shyness was dispersed, Elise Gueray revealed herself to possess both humor and wit. She had made the past few hours pass pleasantly enough. Nell picked up the tray. "If I don't see you later this evening, I'll call you after breakfast tomorrow."

Elise nodded, her gaze going to her husband across the room. "I doubt if I'll be here when you return. Henri will be ready to leave soon. He only thought it important he meet Kavinski."

Nell edged around the crowd, her brow creased in a frown of concentration as she balanced the heavy tray.

The wine.

She stopped short outside the ballroom doors.

Oh, why not? A few sips wouldn't hurt Jill; Europeans fed it to their babies all the time. She wanted Jill to be happy tonight. Who knew how many more opportunities they'd get to just be together?

She ducked back inside the ballroom. Champagne. Even better. As she grabbed a glass of champagne from a passing waiter, the tray she was balancing in her other hand wobbled.

The tray was taken from her. "May I help you?"

Arnold Schwarzenegger. No, at closer range he resembled no one but himself. Very high-impact. That confidence was overpowering and she instinctively wanted to escape it. She pulled her gaze away from his. "No, thank you."

She tried to take the tray, but he held it out of her reach. "I insist. It's no trouble." He strolled out of the ballroom and she was forced to hurry after him. "Where is this assignation to take place?"

"Assignation?"

He glanced down at the tray. "He must have a hearty appetite."

She felt the heat sting her cheeks. Twenty-eight years old and she was blushing. She muttered, "It's a treat for my daughter."

He smiled. "Then I assume the assignation is still to take place in a bedroom, and you'll never make it up the steps with the champagne *and* the tray." He moved across the foyer and started up the staircase. "I'm Nicholas Tanek, and you are . . . ?"

"Nell Calder." She found herself running after him. "But I don't need help. If you'll give me—"

"Calder? Richard Calder's wife?"

He was surprised. They were always surprised Richard had chosen her. "Yes."

"Well, he appears too busy to help you. Permit me to substitute."

He was clearly not going to be dissuaded. She might as well let him have his way. It would be the quickest way to rid herself of him. She followed him up the steps and found herself watching the smooth flexing of his shoulders and buttocks. Both were sleekly muscled and extremely admirable.

"How old is your daughter?"

Her gaze guiltily flew upward, but he was still looking straight ahead, she realized with relief. "Jill's almost five. Do you have children, Mr. Tanek?"

He shook his head. "Which way?"

"Right."

He asked, "Are you with Continental Trust too?"

"No."

"What do you do?"

"Nothing. I mean—I take care of my daughter." When he didn't comment, she found herself continuing on. "I have quite a few social duties."

"I'm sure you're very busy."

But not like the women in his world. She was sure they were all sleek and gifted and as confident as he.

"You're American?"

She nodded. "I was raised in Raleigh, North Carolina."

"That's a university town, isn't it?"

"Yes, my parents taught at Greenbriar University just outside Raleigh. My father was president of the college."

"It sounds like a very . . . secure life."

He meant boring. She bristled. "I enjoy small towns."

He glanced back over his shoulder. "But, of course, it can't compare to the life you lead now. I'm told Continental Trust's European headquarters is in Paris."

"Yes, it is."

"And it must be pleasant being able to visit places like this. Luxuries can be very important."

"Can they?"

"I was speaking to your husband earlier in the evening. I'd judge permanent life in a palace would suit him very well indeed."

"He works hard to earn any luxuries we enjoy." His idle probing was beginning to annoy her. He couldn't really be interested in either Richard or her. She changed the subject. "Are you in banking, Mr. Tanek?"

"No, I'm retired."

She stared at him, puzzled. "Really? You're very young."

He chuckled. "I had enough money and decided not to wait for a retirement party and a gold watch. I now own a ranch in Idaho."

He had surprised her again. She would never have thought he was the type to wander far from the urban life. "You don't seem—"

"I like the solitude. I grew up in Hong Kong, surrounded by people. When I was in a position to choose, I opted for wilderness."

"I'm sorry, it's none of my business."

"No problem. I have nothing to hide."

She would wager he had a great deal to hide, she thought suddenly. He was a man who buried everything beneath that smooth surface. "From what business did you retire?"

"I dealt in commodities." He asked, "Which door?"

"Oh, the last one on the left."

He moved swiftly down the corridor and stopped before the suite.

"Thank you. It wasn't necessary, but I—"

He had opened the door and was striding in, she realized in astonishment.

The Greek maid hurriedly sat upright in the chair.

"That will be all," Nicholas Tanck said in Greek. "We'll call you when we need you."

The maid walked out of the suite and closed the door.

Nell stared at him, stunned.

Tanek smiled. "Don't be alarmed. My intentions are above reproach." He winked. "Well, unless you call avoiding a very boring party reproachful. I saw you bolting out the door and I needed an excuse to get away for a while."

"Mama, did you bring—" Jill stood in the doorway, her gaze on Tanek. "Who are you?"

He bowed. "Nicholas Tanek. You're Jill?"

She nodded warily.

"Then this is for you." He presented the tray with a flourish. "Mead and ambrosia."

"I wanted eclairs."

"I believe we have those too." He swept toward her. "Where will we dine?"

Jill studied him for a moment and then capitulated. "Mama and I are going to have a picnic. I put a blanket on the floor."

"Excellent idea. You're obviously ahead of us." He started setting the paper plates down on the blanket. He said over his shoulder, "You forgot the napkins. We'll have to improvise." He disappeared into the bathroom and returned a minute later with a pile of tissues and two embroidered hand towels. "May I, madam?" He draped the hand towel around Jill's neck and tied it in the back.

Jill giggled.

Nell felt a ripple of resentment as she saw that Jill was enjoying the novelty of attention from a stranger. This was supposed to be *her* time with her daughter and he was spoiling everything.

"Thank you for helping me with the tray, Mr. Ta-nek," Nell said formally. "I know you want to get back to the party."

"Do I?" He turned to her, and the smile faded from his lips as he searched her face. He nodded slowly. "Yes, perhaps I should return." He bowed to Jill. "But I'll wait to take back your tray, madam."

"Don't bother," Nell said. "The maid can get it in the morning."

"I insist. I'll wait in the sitting room. Call me when you're ready." He strode out of the bedroom.

"Who is he?" Jill whispered, her gaze on the half-open door.

"Just a guest." She was surprised that Tanek had given up so easily. Well, he had not given up entirely. It was clear he didn't want to return downstairs and was using the suite as a haven. Whom was he avoiding? A woman, probably. He was the kind of man who would have women chasing him. Well, she didn't care as long as he stayed out of the way and didn't bother them.

"I like him," Jill said.

Nell didn't doubt it. Tanek had made sure Jill felt like an empress in those short minutes.

Then Jill's gaze fastened eagerly on the crystal goblet, and she instantly forgot about Tanek. "Wine?"

"Champagne." Nell dropped to the floor and crossed her legs. "As you commanded."

Jill's radiant smile lit her face. "You brought it."

"It's a party." She handed her the glass. "One sip."

Jill took a huge swallow and then made a face. "Sour. But it's kind of warm and bubbly going down." She lifted the glass again. "Jean Marc says that—"

Nell snatched the glass from her. "Enough."

"Okay." Jill reached for the eclair. "But if it's a party, we should have music."

"Right." Nell crawled over to the nightstand, reached for the music box, and wound it. She set it down on the blanket, and they watched the two panda bears spinning slowly on the lid. "Much better than the orchestra downstairs."

Jill inched closer, lifted Nell's arm, and fitted herself beneath it. As she munched on the eclair, pastry flakes fell on Nell's blue lace gown, and Nell knew that before Jill was through, chocolate icing would be all over both of them.

She didn't care. To hell with the gown. Her arm tightened around her daughter's small, warm body. Moments like this were rare and precious.

And might become even rarer.

No, she couldn't let them do it. Richard was wrong and she must convince him that Jill needed her.

But what if she couldn't convince him?

Then she would have to fight him. She felt panic and despair rise at the thought. Richard always made her feel as if she were being both unreasonable and cruel when she disagreed with him. He was so certain of everything and she wasn't sure of anything.

Except that it was wrong to make her give up her daughter to a faceless stranger.

"You're squeezing me too tight," Jill said.

She loosened her hold but kept Jill close. "Sorry."

"S'okay." Her mouth full of pastry, she rubbed against Nell forgivingly. "Didn't hurt."

She had no choice. She would find the strength somewhere. She must fight Richard.

He had come for nothing, Nicholas thought in disgust as he gazed down at the surf crashing on the rocks below. No one would want to kill Nell Calder. She was no more likely to be connected with Gardeaux than that big-eyed elf she was now lavishing with French pastry and adoration.

If there was a target here, it was probably Kavinski. As head of an emerging Russian state, he had the power to be either a cash cow or extremely troublesome to Gardeaux. Nell Calder wouldn't be considered troublesome to anyone. He had known the answers to all the questions he had asked her, but he had wanted to see her reactions. He had been watching her all evening, and it was clear she was a nice, shy woman, totally out of her depth even with those fairly innocuous sharks downstairs. He couldn't imagine her having enough influence to warrant bribery, and she would never have been able to deal one on one with Gardeaux.

Unless she was more than she appeared. Possibly. She seemed as meek as a lamb, but she'd had the guts to toss him out of her daughter's room.

Everyone fought back if the battle was important enough. And it was important for Nell Calder not to share her daughter with him. No, the list must mean something else. When he went back downstairs, he would stay close to Kavinski.

> *"Here we go up, up, up*
> *High in the sky so blue.*
> *Here we go down, down, down*
> *Touching the rose so red."*

She was singing to the kid. He had always liked lullabies. There was a reassuring continuity about them that had been missing in his own life. Since the dawn of time, mothers had sung to their children, and they would probably still be singing to them a thousand years from now.

The song ended with a low chuckle and a murmur he couldn't hear.

She came out of the bedroom and closed the door a few minutes later. She was flushed and glowing with an expression as soft as melted butter.

"I've never heard that lullaby before," he said.

She looked startled, as if she'd forgotten he was still there. "It's very old. My grandmother used to sing it to me."

"Is your daughter asleep?"

"No, but she will be soon. I started the music box for her again. By the time it finishes, she usually nods off."

"She's a beautiful child."

"Yes." A luminous smile turned her plain face radiant once more. "Yes, she is."

He stared at her, intrigued. He found he wanted to keep that smile on her face. "And bright?"

"Sometimes too bright. Her imagination can be troublesome. But she's always reasonable and you can talk to—" She broke off and her eagerness faded. "But this can't interest you. I forgot the tray. I'll go back for it."

"Don't bother. You'll disturb Jill. The maid can pick it up in the morning."

She gave him a level glance. "That's what I told you."

He smiled. "But then I didn't want to listen. Now it makes perfect sense to me."

"Because it's what you want to do."

"Exactly."

"I have to go back too. I haven't met Kavinski yet." She moved toward the door.

"Wait. I think you'll want to remove that chocolate from your gown first."

"Damn." She frowned as she looked down at the stain on the skirt. "I forgot." She turned toward the bathroom and said dryly, "Go on. I assure you I don't need your help with this problem."

He hesitated.

She glanced at him pointedly over her shoulder.

He had no excuse for staying, not that that small fact would have deterred him.

But he also had no reason. He had lived by his wits too long not to trust his instincts, and this woman wasn't a target of any sort. He should be watching Kavinski.

He turned toward the door. "I'll tell the maid you're ready for her to come back."

"Thank you, that's very kind of you," she said automatically as she disappeared into the bathroom.

Good manners obviously instilled from childhood. Loyalty. Gentleness. A nice woman whose world was centered on that sweet kid. He had definitely drawn a blank.

The maid wasn't waiting in the hallway. He'd have to send up one of the servants from downstairs.

He moved quickly through the corridors and started down the staircase.

Shots.

Coming from the ballroom.

Christ.

He tore down the stairs.

Explosions.

Firecrackers, Nell thought absently. Sally had told her there would be a fireworks display to crown the evening. She must have stayed upstairs longer than she had thought. Sally would not be pleased.

The stain wasn't too bad. Thank God for the miracle of carbonated water. She had been afraid she would have to change. She dabbed carefully at the chocolate smear.

She heard a door shut in the sitting room.

The maid. What was her name? Hera. "I'm in the bathroom. I'll be leaving in a moment, Hera. I managed to smudge my—" She looked up.

A face in the mirror—pale, shimmering, distorted.

"What—"

The glimmer of steel, an arm lifting.

A knife.

She whirled as the knife descended.

Pain.

The knife was wrenched from her shoulder and plunged down again.

He must be a thief. "No—jewels. Please."

The dagger entered her again, this time carving her upper arm. She could see the attacker's lips drawn back from his teeth through the stocking mask. Not a thief. He was enjoying this, she realized in horror. He was toying with her. He liked to see her pain and helplessness.

The blood was running down her arm and the pain was so intense it was making her sick.

Why was he doing this?

She was going to die.

Jill.

Jill was in the next room. If she died, she couldn't keep him from hurting Jill.

He was raising the knife again.

She kneed him in the groin.

He grunted in agony and doubled over.

She pushed past him. He felt strange, rubbery against her body. She staggered into the sitting room. Her knees were shaking. She was going to fall.

"Bitch." He was right behind her.

She had to have a weapon. No weapons.

She yanked out the cord of the lamp on the table beside her. She threw the lamp at him.

He deflected it with one arm. He kept coming.

She backed away from him. Didn't they tell you your best defense was to scream?

She screamed.

"Go ahead. No one will hear you. No one will help you."

He was right. The firecrackers and cries from downstairs were too loud.

She was standing by the French doors that led to the balcony. She tore down the beige silk drapes and tossed them over his head. She heard him cursing as she darted past him.

Almost past him.

He freed himself in time to grab her arm and jerk her to her knees. He raised the knife again.

She lunged upward, her head striking him in the stomach.

His grasp loosened and she wrenched free.

"Mama."

Oh, God, Jill was standing in the doorway of the bedroom.

"Stay away, baby."

The balcony. If she could lure him out onto the balcony, Jill might be able to escape.

Her fist lashed out and connected with his cheek. She whirled and ran out onto the balcony.

He followed her.

"Run, Jill. Go to Daddy."

Jill was crying. She wanted to comfort her. "Run, bab—"

The knife. Stabbing. Pain.

Fight him.

Weak.

Strike out. Hurt him.

Give Jill time to get away.

Run.

No place to run.

The balustrade stone hard and cold against her spine.

Make him fall. Make him fall over the balcony. Her arms clutched desperately at his shoulders as she tried to turn him.

"Oh, no, you stupid whore." He broke free and shoved her over the balustrade.

She was screaming.

Falling.

Dying.

Nicholas fought his way through the panicked guests pouring out of the ballroom into the foyer.

He grabbed Sally Brenden's arm as she ran past. "What happened?"

"Let me go." Her eyes were glittering with terror. "Crazy. They killed them. Crazy."

His hand tightened on her arm. "Who fired the shots?"

"How should I know?" She turned to a heavyset man who had emerged from the ballroom. "Martin!"

Martin Brenden was pale and sweating. "Kavinski's down. And two others. And I saw Richard fall. They shot Richard."

"How many are they?" Nicholas asked. "Where are the shots coming from?"

"Outside through the window," Martin said. "Kavinski's bodyguards are after them." He grabbed his wife's arm. "Let's get out of here."

"How could this happen?" Sally asked dazedly. "My wonderful party . . ."

"They'll be found." He patted her arm. "Kavinski had two men posted at the dock. They'll never get away from the island."

She let him lead her away. "My party . . ."

Nicholas pushed through the crowd to the front door.

Two men running, their bodies lean and darkly gleaming in the moonlight. Wet suits.

They weren't heading for the docks but toward the far end of the island.

Of course, not the docks. Gardeaux would have found a way to avoid that trap after the targets were hit.

Target.

Nell Calder.

He whirled and ran back into the palace.

Two

"Christ. Look at her face. She's a monster."

Nadine's voice.

I saw a monster.

Jill had said that. Everyone was seeing monsters.

"Goddammit, don't just stand there. Get that doctor who's tending Kavinski. She needs help more than he does."

Richard? No, the voice was rougher, harder. Tanek. Strange that she would recognize his voice in the darkness.

She tried to open her eyes. Yes, Tanek. No longer elegant, blood-spattered, coatless. Was he hurt?

"Blood . . ."

"Be quiet. You'll be fine." His gaze held hers fiercely. "I promise you. You're not going to die."

Nadine was crying. "The poor thing. Oh, God, I have to throw up."

"Then go and throw up," Tanek said coldly. "But get the doctor for her first."

She must be the one who was hurt.

Falling.

Dying.

Shouldn't Richard be here if she was dying? She wanted to see Jill.

"Jill . . ."

"Shh," Tanek said. "You'll be fine."

Something was wrong. No, everything was wrong. She was dying and there was no one here who cared.

Only this stranger. Only Tanek.

"I've been watching the telly," Jamie Reardon said as soon as he picked up the phone. "You seem to have been having a busy evening, Nick. So Kavinski was the target?"

"I don't know. The bodyguard was hit too. Maybe Kavinski was an accident."

"How did they manage to get on the island?"

"Through a sea passage that empties out into the caves at the far end of the island. They anchored a few miles offshore and used wet suits and scuba equipment to swim into one of those caves. What's the news report?"

"That terrorists from Kavinski's country staged a raid and an assassination attempt, and five innocent bystanders were killed."

"Four. The woman is still alive. Barely. She was stabbed three times and fell from a balcony. She's smashed all to hell and on her way to a hospital in Athens. There was a doctor at the party and he says she'll probably survive if shock doesn't kill her. I need you to arrange for a private plane. We're taking her back to the States for treatment."

Jamie whistled. "Kabler isn't going to like that. He's going to want to talk to her."

"Screw Kabler."

"And what about next of kin? Can you get permission?"

"Her husband was one of the innocent bystanders. He's on his way to the morgue. Get Conner to falsify documents to prove you're her brother and get Lieber to call the hospital. Someone there will have heard of him."

"Why Lieber?"

"It'll seem the most logical. She looks as if every bone in her face is smashed."

"Why was Richard Calder killed? He wasn't on the list."

"Neither was his four-year-old daughter."

"Jesus."

Nicholas shut his eyes to close out the vision that had met him when he had looked down from the balcony. It didn't help. It was there before him anyway. "I fouled up, Jamie. I thought it was a wild-goose chase."

"You're not the only one. Kabler decided to pass too."

"I didn't pass. I was here. I could have stopped it."

"By yourself?"

"I could have warned her. She was crazy about the kid. She might have listened."

"And she might have thought you were nuts. You'll never know. If she was mixed up with Gardeaux, any blame lies with her." He paused. "Do you need help getting off the island?"

"Not if I leave now. Kabler's not here yet. I've already talked to the local gendarmes and I'm free to go. I'll meet you at the airport." He hung up the phone.

June 5
Minneapolis, Minnesota

Joel Lieber met them at the airport with an ambulance and a scowl. "I told you I didn't want to become involved with this business, Nicholas. I'm too busy to deal with men like Kabler. They interfere with my— Be careful!" He turned toward the paramedics who were unloading the stretcher. "No jarring. How many times must I tell you that there must be no jarring." Following the stretcher to the ambulance, he tossed back over his shoulder, "Go to my office. I'll see you there after I've examined her. Has she regained consciousness?"

"Only once right after we found her. The knife wounds aren't deep, but she has a broken arm and clavicle. The emergency room in Athens set those breaks, but I told them to leave her face alone."

"So that I could have that dubious honor," Joel said sarcastically. "Along with all the grief from Kabler that goes with it."

"I'll stand between you and Kabler."

"You mean you'll try. He's already called me twice today. It seems he didn't approve of me aiding the illegal transporting of a material witness."

"She needed you, Joel."

"The whole world needs me," he said with a sigh. "It's the bane of being brilliant." He got into the ambulance. "Unfortunately, I'm only Superman, I'm not God. I'll let you know later today if I can help her."

"I think the only degree he doesn't have is for veterinary surgery." Jamie's gaze was fixed on the diplomas and awards on the wall of Lieber's office. "I wonder how he missed that one."

"He knows enough to get by. He set Sam's leg once when it was caught in a coyote trap."

"You mean he leaves all this adulation to visit you in the backwoods?"

"Even Superman gets tired of being stroked."

"Only occasionally." Joel Lieber strode into the office, tossed his briefcase on the desk, and dropped into the leather executive chair. "Worship is the food and drink that nourishes genius. I prescribe a daily mega-dose of it for myself."

"I can understand that," Jamie said.

"How's business at the pub?" Joel asked.

"Flourishing."

"Then you should have stayed in Dublin and away from Nicholas."

"Ah, but what we should do and what we do so seldom coincide." He smiled. "We see a problem, a challenge, and we go for it. Isn't that right, Joel?"

Joel grimaced. "I may not pick up this particular challenge."

"Bad?" Nicholas asked.

"There are no cuts, but her entire face will have to be reconstructed. I can do the initial surgery in one operation, but then there will be psychotherapy and checkups and—Do you realize how much work that will take? I'm booked up for the next two years. I don't have the *time*."

"She needs you, Joel."

"Don't lay that guilt trip on me. I can't solve everyone's problems."

"Her husband and child were murdered in that raid."

"Oh, shit."

"She's lost everything. Are you going to tell her that she's going to have to live the rest of her life looking like a gargoyle?"

"I'm not the only surgeon in the world."

"But you're the best. You tell me so all the time. She deserves the best."

"I'll think about it."

"I met her. She's a nice woman."

"I said, I'd think about it, dammit," Joel said through his teeth.

"You do that." Nicholas stood up and moved toward the door. "I'll bring her dossier tomorrow and we'll talk. Come on, Jamie, let's get some dinner." He paused. "By the way, how's Tania?"

"Fine." Joel scowled. "She'll want to see you. I suppose you can come to dinner at my house."

"It's difficult for me to refuse such a warm invitation, but I think I'll pass." He smiled. "Why don't you get Tania's opinion on whether you should commit yourself to helping Nell Calder?"

"Damn you," Joel said.

Nicholas was smiling as he closed the door.

"Who's Tania?" Jamie asked as they passed through the reception room.

"His housekeeper. Tania Vlados is a mutual friend." He jabbed a button at the bank of elevators.

"Will she help persuade him?"

"I doubt if he'll discuss it with her. Tania would make him too uncomfortable. She's a bit of a bulldozer. Besides, we don't need her. He's already wrestling with himself. He grew up poor as dirt and it's always difficult for him to put the quest for wealth behind human kindness."

Jamie looked back through the glass doors into Lieber's luxurious office. "He seems to do all right."

"But he also donates his services one day a week to help abused children." The elevator stopped and he entered. "And it won't be the kids he'll drop if he takes on Nell Calder."

"You could offer him enough to sweeten the pot."

"Not now. It would insult him. Once he's committed, I assure you he'll make me pay through the nose."

"You're going to a hell of a lot of trouble."

"So?"

"You're not to blame for this."

"The hell I'm not." He wearily shook his head. "And don't give me that bull about her being responsible because she was dealing with Gardeaux. I don't think she did."

"Then why did he want to take her out?"

"I don't know. None of it makes sense. There has to be some reason." He paused. "She and the kid were both stabbed, when a bullet would have been quicker and more efficient."

"Maritz?"

"Probably. He was a Seal and he's the only one of Gardeaux's men who's in love with a knife. Nell Calder must have been his sole target. Her husband and the others were killed in the ballroom, but he stalked her."

"Prime target." Jamie nodded. "Which makes your innocent-bystander premise distinctly suspect."

"Then prove me wrong. It would make me happy as hell to find out she was working for Gardeaux. If you're going to trace any connection, we'll need more information than the dossier Conner's compiled on her. I want to know what she had for breakfast when she was six years old."

"And when do you want me to start?" He held up his hand. "Never mind. After dinner, right?"

"I can get someone else. It's donkey work, and I'm not sure it will bring us any closer to Gardeaux."

"Well, the pub's a bit slow right now. I might as well do it myself. Anything else?"

"A guard on her hospital room. Gardeaux might not

like the fact that she's still alive." He made a face. "Better make him unobtrusive, or Joel will have a cow."

"Not easy. Those medical types are very territorial." He thought about it. "Maybe a male nurse. I could call Phil Johnson in Chicago."

"Whatever. Just have him in place by tomorrow morning."

"What about tonight?"

"I'll be with her tonight."

"You didn't sleep on the plane."

"And I won't sleep tonight. I'm not going to make another mistake."

Tanek again.

He looked different, and for a moment Nell couldn't realize why.

The green sweater. He wasn't wearing a tuxedo. And he no longer looked angry and tense, only tired.

She could understand that. She was tired too. So tired she could barely hold her eyes open. She seemed to be floating. . . .

That's right, she was dying. If this was what it was like, it wasn't so bad.

She must have whispered, because he leaned forward. "You're not dying. You're fine." He grimaced. "Well, not fine, but you're not going to die. You're in a hospital back in the States. You have quite a few broken bones but nothing we can't fix."

She felt vaguely comforted. No, there was nothing he couldn't fix. She had known that the first time she had seen him.

"Go back to sleep."

But she couldn't go back to sleep. There was something wrong. Something to do with that dark horror before she fell. Something she had to ask. "Jill . . ."

His expression didn't change, but she felt a ripple of panic. Yes, something was wrong.

"Go to sleep."

She quickly closed her eyes. Darkness. She could hide there, hide from the hideous truth she sensed behind Tanek's impassive face.

She let the darkness carry her away.

"You do not eat my soup," Tania said as she sat down at the table. "Perhaps you think it unworthy of you?"

Joel Lieber scowled. "Don't start that. I'm not hungry."

"You work from dawn to dusk and your secretary says you seldom have lunch. You must be hungry." She calmly met his gaze. "Which means you think my soup unworthy. But I don't see how that can be, when you haven't tasted it."

He took up his spoon, dipped it into the soup, and brought the spoon to his mouth. "Delicious," he growled.

"Now the rest. Hurry. Before my roast gets cold."

He put his spoon down. "Stop giving me orders in my own home."

"Why? It's the only place you will take orders. You're a very arrogant man." She sipped delicately at the soup. "But you can be forgiven your arrogance in the operating room, since you probably know best. Here, *I* know best."

"About everything under the sun. You've made my life a torment since you moved in with me."

She smiled serenely. "You lie, you've never been so contented. I give you fine food, a motherly shoulder to lean on, and a clean house. You would be lost if I left you."

Yes, he would. "Your shoulders aren't at all motherly." They were straight and square and always looked as if she were going forth into battle. Sadly, she *was* accustomed to battle. She had been born and raised in the hell Sarajevo had become. Nicholas had brought her to him four years before, half starved, wounded, and scarred from shrapnel. Eighteen years of age, with the eyes of an old woman. "And I got along very well without you for a number of years."

She snorted. "So well, Donna divorced you because she never saw you. A man must have a home as well as a career. It's good I came in time to save you." She took another sip of soup. "Donna thinks so too. She thinks I'm the best thing that ever happened to you."

"I don't appreciate you conspiring with my ex-wife."

"I don't conspire. I talk to her. Is that conspiring?"

"Yes."

"I'm here alone all day. I need to practice my English, so I talk on the phone." She said with satisfaction, "My English is getting much better. Soon I will be ready to go to the university."

He went still. "You will?"

"But don't be frightened. I will still stay with you. I'm very happy here."

"I'm not frightened." He glowered at her. "I'd be glad to be rid of you. You're the one who marched into my house and took over."

"I could do nothing else," she said simply. "You would have grown old and sour as an unripe olive if I hadn't come to you."

"And you're here to keep me young and sweet?"

"Yes." She smiled. "Young, I can do. Sweet is a greater challenge."

She had a wonderful smile. Her face was angular and strong, with wide, mobile lips and deepset eyes. It was not a pretty face until she smiled, and then Joel felt as if she had given him a special gift. He had taken away the scars, but God had given her that smile.

She said calmly, "Though it would help if you would take me to your bed."

He looked down and hastily took a sip of soup. "I told you, I don't jump into the sack with teenagers."

"I'm twenty-two now."

"And I'm almost forty-one. Too old for you."

"Age means nothing. People don't think that way anymore."

"I do."

"I know, you make it very difficult for me. But we won't argue about it now." She rose to her feet. "You're already upset and you'll blame the indigestion on my soup. We'll finish dinner and then you can tell me what's wrong over coffee in the library."

"Nothing's wrong."

"You know you'll feel better talking about it. I'll get the roast."

She disappeared into the kitchen.

"Drink your coffee." Tania curled up across from him in the big Chesterfield, tucking her long legs beneath her. "I put a little cinnamon in it. You'll like it."

"I don't like sweet coffee."

"Spice isn't sweet. Besides, how do you know? I bet you've not had anything but vile black brew since medical school."

"It's not vile." He added, "And you don't let me have caffeine anymore."

"You still have it at the hospital."

"I suppose your spies report back to you? I'll drink what I please." He deliberately set his cup on the table beside him. "And I don't want to have any coffee at all now. I have to get back to the hospital and check on a patient."

"The patient you're so worried about that you can't eat?"

"I'm not worried."

"Then why are you going back to the hospital? Is it one of the children?"

"No, it's a woman."

She said nothing, only waited.

"Nicholas brought her," he added reluctantly.

"Nicholas?" She sat upright in the chair.

"I thought that would pique your interest," he said sourly. "But it doesn't make any difference. You can't persuade me to take this case just because Nicholas wants me to do it. The breakage is too severe to reconstruct her face exactly the way it was. I'll turn her over to Samplin."

"I wouldn't try to persuade you. I owe a debt to Nicholas and it's mine alone to pay." She frowned. "Who is the woman?"

"Nell Calder. She was one of the victims at the Kavinski massacre."

"No, who is she to Nicholas?"

"You needn't be jealous. I think he barely knows her."

"Why would I be jealous?"

Her surprise was genuine, and Joel felt a ripple of relief. He tried to shrug casually. "The two of you are close as peas in a pod."

"He saved my life and he brought me to you." She gazed at him thoughtfully. "Nicholas and I want nothing from each other except friendship."

"Nicholas seldom does anything for nothing."

"Why are you talking like this about Nicholas? You like him."

He did like him. He was also jealous as hell of the

bastard. He had a sudden memory of a scene in *Casablanca* when Ingrid Bergman stared wistfully after Humphrey Bogart while Paul Henreid looked noble and boring in the background. It hadn't mattered to her that Henreid was a heroic resistance fighter; black sheep were always more interesting.

"You don't understand him," Tania said. "He's not as hard as he seems. He's on the other side now."

"Other side?"

"He's led a rough life. Things happen to scar and twist you until you think you'll never believe in anything, that there's no evil you couldn't commit to survive. Then you go beyond it." She looked down into her coffee cup. "And you become human again."

She was not only talking about Nicholas. She had been through that hell and come out on the other side too. He wanted to reach out and comfort her, to tell her he'd care for her and treasure her always.

He picked up the coffee cup and took a drink. "It's good," he lied.

Great, Joel. Nicholas saves her life and you compliment her coffee.

She smiled brilliantly. "I told you so."

"You're always telling me so. It's very irritating."

"So why does Nicholas want you to help this woman?"

He shrugged. "I think he believes he's partially responsible. So he brings her to me to absolve his guilt. I'm not buying it."

"I think you are. You feel sorry for this woman."

"I told you, I can't give her back what she's lost."

"You can't put her face back exactly the way it was," she said. "But you can give her a new face, right?"

"I thought you weren't going to try to persuade me."

"I'm not. It's entirely your decision. But, since you'll

probably do it anyway, I think you should give yourself a challenge to make it more interesting." She smiled teasingly. "Have you never wanted to experiment with your own Galatea?"

"No," he said flatly. "That's not plastic surgery. It's fairy tales."

"Ah, but you need fairy tales, Joel. No one needs them more than you." She stood up and took his cup away from him. "You hated this coffee, didn't you?"

"No, I thought it—" He met her gaze. "Yes."

"But you did it for me." She brushed his forehead with her lips. "I thank you."

She carried the tray out of the library.

The room seemed suddenly dimmer without her vibrant presence.

She had said the debt to Nicholas was hers alone.

It wasn't true.

Nicholas had brought Tania into his life. It was a debt he would never be able to repay even if the bastard continued bringing him his wounded strays for the rest of his life.

"Oh, what the hell."

Think Galatea.

"What are you doing here?"

Nicholas looked up as Joel came into the hospital room. "I could ask the same of you," Nicholas said.

"I belong here."

"Plastic surgeons don't make rounds at eleven o'clock at night."

Joel was glancing at the chart. "Did she wake?"

"For a minute or two. She thought she was dying." He paused. "She asked for her daughter."

"She doesn't know her husband and daughter are dead?"

"Not yet. I thought she had enough to contend with."

"Too much. Surgery and the psychological adjustment." He grimaced. "And then you mix in traumatic loss. It can trigger a breakdown if she's not strong enough. What kind of woman is she?"

"She's no powerhouse." He had a sudden memory of Nell Calder's face when she had left her daughter's room. "Soft, gentle. She was crazy about the kid. You could see her world revolved around her daughter."

"Great." Joel wearily ran his fingers through his curly brown hair. "Does she have any other family?"

"No."

"A career?"

"No."

"Shit."

"She studied art during her first three years at William and Mary. Then she transferred to Greenbriar and switched to education. She met Richard Calder, who was studying for his master's in economics at Greenbriar. It appears he was a prime catch—brilliant, charismatic, and ambitious. She married him three weeks after she moved back home and quit college. She had Jill a year later."

"Why did she drop art?"

Nicholas shook his head. "I don't know. I'll try to fill in the blanks later."

"It's not going to be easy."

"But you're going to take her on?"

"You may wish I hadn't. The work I did on Tania is child's play compared to the surgery required here. I think you may pay for my new lake house."

He grimaced. "That steep."

"She must suspect something's wrong, and we can't keep putting off telling her. You'll have to break it to her that she no longer has a family."

"Why do I have the honor?"

"I don't want her identifying me with it. I have to represent hope and a new life. Tell her and then walk away. She won't want to see you again in the foreseeable future."

"Bad cop, good cop?"

His brow rose. "You'd know more about police procedure than I would, but you've got the general idea." Joel was becoming more cheerful by the minute. "We can't have Superman's cloak tarnished. Tomorrow I'll lessen the sedation so that she's alert enough to understand and you can talk to her."

"Thanks."

Joel's smile faded. "Be gentle, Nicholas. It's going to be a hell of a shock."

Did he think he was going to try to hurt her? Nicholas thought. He nodded curtly. "Not that it will do any good. She won't care if I'm gentle as Jesus Christ once she realizes what I'm telling her."

"I'll come in later and give her a sedative."

"And take away the pain?"

"That's what the good guy does. That's why I became a doctor. Ugliness and deformity can bring a lifetime of pain. I can change that." He turned and headed for the door. "Of course, the big bucks don't hurt." He gave Nicholas a sly smile over his shoulder. "Well, maybe they'll hurt you. Yes, I believe I'll make sure your wallet cries out for mercy."

Nicholas heard him begin to whistle as he strolled down the corridor.

"Go to bed." Tania stood in the doorway of the library.

"Soon," Joel said absently. He studied the measurements he had scrawled on the oval diagram on the pad.

He always liked to work on the pad first before transferring the image into the computer.

"Now." Tania strode forward and stopped at the desk. She was barefoot and wearing only one of his old T-shirts. Why did women look so damn sexy in men's clothes?

"It's after midnight," she said. "You can't operate tomorrow if you don't sleep."

"I don't operate until tomorrow afternoon." He wearily shook his head. "And then I have to go and tell Nell Calder that for the next few weeks she's going to have to lie in bed with a minimum of movement. Nice, huh? She'll have plenty of time to think of her husband and kid."

She looked down at the oval. "This is her face?"

"I'm checking the measurements to see what's possible. I need to have something to tell her. Everything else has been taken away. She needs something to hold on to."

"You'll give it to her." She put her hand on his shoulder and added softly, "You're a good man, Joel Lieber."

He leaned forward and fastened his gaze on the pad. He said gruffly, "Then go to bed and stop bothering me. I have work to do."

"Two hours." She stepped back, and her hand dropped away from him. "And then I'm coming back to get you."

His gaze lifted to watch her stride toward the door. She never strolled, she always looked as if she knew exactly where she was going.

"I have nice legs, yes?" She smiled at him over her shoulder. "That is lucky. Donna said you were a leg man."

"Actually, I'm not. I told Donna that only because she had breasts like a boy."

She clucked reprovingly. "You lie now, not then."

She left the study.

Joel forced himself to look back at the pad. She would be back in two hours and he must not be here. She deserved more than a workaholic twice her age who had already failed at one marriage. He must not think of those long legs or that smile.

Yeah, sure.

Well, he had to try.

Think Galatea.

The face was not Tanek's this time.

A young face, broad cheekbones, a nose that had once been broken, blue eyes, blond crew cut. "Hi, I'm Phil Johnson, Mrs. Calder."

"Who?"

"I'm your nurse."

He looked more like a linebacker, she thought. The white hospital tunic stretched over shoulders that rippled with muscle.

"You feeling better? They've cut down on your medication, so some of the fuzziness should be gone."

She was thinking more clearly, she realized. Too clearly. Panic was beginning to ice through her.

"Don't worry about all the bandages." The smile he gave her glowed with warmth. "You're going to be fine. The wounds aren't serious and you've got the best surgeon in the business to take care of the rest. People come to see Dr. Lieber from all over the world."

He thought she was worried about herself, she realized incredulously. "My daughter . . ."

His smile vanished. "Mr. Tanek's outside. He asked me to call him when you woke."

Tanek's expression when she had asked about Jill came flooding back to her. Her heart was beating so hard, she thought it would choke her as Tanek walked into the room.

"How do you feel?"

"Scared." She hadn't known she was going to blurt out the word. "Where is my daughter?"

He sat down in the chair by the bed. "Do you remember what happened to you?"

The knife, the pain, Jill standing in the doorway, the tinkle of the music box, falling. She began to tremble. "Where is my *daughter*?"

His hand closed on hers. "She was killed the same night you were attacked."

She jerked as the words struck her. Dead. Jill. "You're lying. No one could kill Jill." Her words rushed out feverishly. "You saw her. You met her. No one would hurt Jill."

"She's dead." He said roughly, "I wish to hell I were lying."

She would not believe him. Richard would tell her the truth. "I want to see my husband. I want to see Richard."

He shook his head. "I'm sorry."

She stared at him in shock. "What are you saying?" she whispered. "Richard wasn't even in the room."

"There was an attack in the ballroom. Your husband and three others were killed. Kavinski was wounded."

She didn't care about Kavinski.

Jill. Richard. Jill.

Oh, God, Jill . . .

The room was whirling, darkening.

Up, up, up, we go, into the sky so blue . . .

Was that Jill singing? But he had said Jill was dead. Richard was dead. She was the only one alive.

Down, down, down we go . . .

Yes, go down into the darkness. Maybe there she could find Jill.

"Joel, get the hell in here," Nicholas called out. "She's fainted, dammit."

Frowning, Joel strode into the room. "What did you do to her?"

"Not a thing but tell her she doesn't have a life anymore. No reason why she should be upset."

"In your usual tender, diplomatic manner, I assume." Joel checked her pulse. "Well, it's done now. I don't think you've done too much damage."

"She fainted, dammit. Do something."

"It's better if I let her come out of it on her own. You can go. She won't want to see you when she comes out of this."

"So you told me." Nicholas didn't move, his gaze on Nell's bandaged face. Her eyes . . . "Don't worry. I don't want to see her either. She's all yours, Joel."

"Then let go of her hand and get out of here."

He hadn't known he was still holding it. He released her hand and stood up. "I'll be in touch. Keep me informed."

"And get Kabler off my back. He called again this morning."

"What did you tell him?"

"Nothing. I didn't talk to him. Why do you think I have a secretary?" Joel sat down in the chair Nicholas had vacated. "But I can't have him questioning her. It would be too traumatic."

Nicholas had been thinking about Kabler. He didn't want him questioning Nell either, and Phil's presence wasn't a cast-iron guarantee she was safe from Gardeaux. "Can you move her to your clinic in Woodsdale?"

"You mean for her recovery?"

"No, now. You have operating facilities there."

"I don't use them often."

Only when a famous movie star or head of state wanted complete privacy and anonymity. Woodsdale had all the amenities of a luxury hotel and the privacy of a confessional. "It would be difficult for Kabler to reach her there. Your security people are top notch."

"You should know, you hired them all for me." His brow wrinkled in thought. "It would be inconvenient. Woodsdale is over a hundred miles from here."

"It would be more inconvenient having to deal with Joe Kabler."

He sighed. "I may still have to deal with him."

"And you may not. It depends on how much else he has on his plate and how badly he wants her. How soon can you move her?"

"I didn't say I was going to." He shrugged. "But it would probably be best. This afternoon, I suppose."

"She'll take the nurse I hired with her." He thought about it. No, there was something else he needed Phil to do. "He'll follow her to Woodsdale tomorrow."

"He's one of yours? He looks too young."

Nicholas didn't answer directly. "His qualifications are impeccable and he has excellent references."

"If they're authentic."

Nicholas grinned. "The majority of them are. And your nurses seem to like him. You'll find you do too."

"Well, he's better than that Junot you hired for Woodsdale. The man looks like a Renaissance assassin. I can't let him near the patients when they first come out of anesthesia. They'd go into shock." He frowned. "And he won't let me fix him."

"Poor Joel. How frustrating for you. Junot is no fool. Sometimes looking like what you are can be an advantage."

He went still. "Is that what he is?"

"What difference does it make? He does his job and

causes no trouble. Are there ever any disturbances when he's around?"

"Not likely. But I don't like the idea of harboring criminals."

"He's not a criminal." He smiled. "Anymore. But you'll find Phil much more reassuring." He left the room and started toward the nurses' station, where Phil was chatting with the head nurse.

Same room, another face.

Jill.

Jill wasn't here. Nell quickly closed her eyes. Go back to the darkness.

"I'm Dr. Joel Lieber. I know you've had a great shock, but I have to talk to you," he said gently. "I'm going to have to operate very soon in order to bring about the best results, and I can't do that without your permission."

Why wouldn't he go away? He was holding back the darkness.

"You don't want to talk? All right, just listen. Your face is badly shattered. I could try to put it back the way it was, but it would still not be quite the face you saw in the mirror every day. But I can give you a new face, probably a more attractive face. Since it's the bones that are damaged, only one operation would be required. I'd go in through the upper mouth and push up and repair the—" He stopped. "No details. You don't want to hear them right now." His hand closed around hers. "But I'm good, very good. Trust me."

She didn't answer.

"Do you have any preference? Is there anyone you'd like to resemble? I can't promise, but I might be able to manage a fleeting resemblance."

He kept talking. Why wouldn't he let her go back to the darkness?

"Nell, open your eyes and listen to me. This is important."

No, it wasn't important. Everything of importance had vanished. But his tone was so compelling, she opened her eyes and stared up at him. He had a nice face, she realized numbly. Square and strong with gray eyes that should have appeared cold but managed to be intelligent and compassionate instead.

"That's better." His hand tightened. "Did you understand?"

"Yes."

"What do you want me to do?"

"I don't care. Whatever you want to do."

"You want me to do what I think best? What if you don't like what I do? Help me."

"It doesn't matter," she whispered. Why couldn't he understand that?

"It *does* matter." He shook his head wearily. "But evidently not now. I hope it does later." He stood up. "I'm moving you to my clinic this afternoon. I want to operate the day after tomorrow. I'll be out to see you tomorrow evening and I'll show you the possibilities."

He was troubled. He seemed like a nice man. It was too bad she couldn't help him.

He was moving toward the door, she realized with relief. He had released her. Her eyes closed.

She was asleep again in minutes.

This wing of the hospital was almost deserted. Strictly nine to five, Phil Johnson thought as he strolled down the corridor.

A pretty LPN was coming toward him. She had a fresh face, dark, curly hair, freckles. He loved freckles.

He smiled.

She smiled back and stopped. "Are you lost? This is the administration wing."

"I was told to drop off these insurance forms."

"The record office closes at seven."

He made a face. "Just my luck. Do you work here?"

She nodded. "I'm interning in records now." She made a face. "I fainted in the emergency room. Personnel thinks I may be suited more to numbers than sutures."

"Tough," he said sympathetically. He looked down at the folder he was carrying. "I guess I'll have to return these to pediatrics and bring them back tomorrow."

She hesitated, then shrugged. "I'll let you in. You can put the folder on Truda's desk."

"That would be great." He smiled as he watched her pull a key ring out of her pocket and insert a key into the lock. "I'm Phil Johnson."

"Pat Dobrey." She flipped on the light and took the file from him. "I'll put it in Truda's in box."

He watched her from the doorway as she moved across the room. Cute, definitely cute.

She came back toward him and turned out the light.

He took the keys from her. "I'll do it." He locked the door, rattled the knob. "That does it." He handed the keys back to her. "Thanks a lot, Pat. Let me walk you to your car."

"That's not necessary."

He smiled. "No, it's a pleasure."

Ten minutes later he was waving a regretful farewell as Pat roared off in her Honda. Sweet girl. Too bad he wouldn't be here to follow up. He turned and jogged through the parking lot to the hospital.

A few minutes later he let himself into the record office and silently closed the door.

He didn't bother to turn on the light but moved quickly to the desk and turned on the computer. The screen would furnish all the light he needed and wouldn't be seen under the door.

The keyboard felt smooth and familiar under his fingers. Too familiar. It was like touching the body of a lover who was always new, always exciting. Get to the job, he told himself.

Since he didn't have the password, it took him a few minutes to hack his way into the file. No challenge.

Nell Calder.

Her transfer to Woodsdale had already been entered.

Good. He deleted the entry, went to the file cabinet, and pulled the entire paper record on Nell Calder. Not that it would be necessary unless the records were subpoenaed. Computers ruled the world, and a clerk would more likely print out a record from the computer file than dig in the paper files and copy it. But Nicholas had said to be sure.

If the paper file turned up missing, it would only be thought to be misfiled. People made mistakes, not computers.

He returned to the computer, typed in the necessary lines, and exited the program. He sat there, staring at the blank green screen, more alluring than any woman to him. Hey, he was here, surely it wouldn't hurt to pop into one of the databanks and see what was—

He sighed and turned off the computer. It would hurt. Why else had he gotten rid of the computer in his apartment and taken up nursing? Nicholas had given him a chance and he wouldn't foul up by giving in to temptation.

He stood up, put the Calder file under his arm, and moved toward the door. He carefully removed the strong transparent tape he had slid over the lock while Pat was putting the file in the box. It had been a lucky break running into her. Otherwise he would have had to try the collection of master keys in his pocket and - run the risk of someone noticing what he was doing.

He turned and took a last wistful look at the computer before he shut the door.

It wasn't so bad. After all, it wasn't as if he didn't like his job. He liked people, and helping them gave him a good feeling. He hoped he could help Nell Calder. Poor lady. She must be in deep hot water, or Nicholas wouldn't have ordered the entry he had typed into her record.

Patient succumbed to wounds 2:04 P.M. Body released to John Birnbaum Funeral Home.

Three

"Is this her picture?" Tania picked up the photograph on top of the open dossier on Joel's desk. She studied it and then nodded. "I like her. I think she has heart."

"And how do you come to that conclusion? Her eyes?"

Tania glanced at Nell Calder's wide-set brown eyes before shaking her head. "Her mouth. It looks . . . sensitive. Don't change the mouth."

"It's too big for perfect symmetry."

"Symmetry is cold. If I were her, I would not like to look cold."

No danger, Joel thought. "I thought I was going to create this Galatea?"

"Do you wish me to go away?" she asked, disappointed.

"No." He smiled and pulled up a chair for her at the desk. "You might as well help me. I'm not getting any input from her."

"Poor lady. The first pain is the hardest. When my parents and little brother died, I wanted to die too."

It was the first time she had talked about the death

of her family. He turned to face her. "Did they die together?"

"No, my father was a soldier. My mother and brother were killed in the streets by snipers a year later. They were on their way to fetch water for us." She looked down at the picture of Nell. "It's the loneliness and helplessness that are worst. When everything is taken away, it's hard to find a reason to live."

"And what reason did you find?"

"Anger. I wouldn't let them have the satisfaction of killing me too." She smiled with an effort. "And then I found you, and my life had purpose again."

He was too moved. He hastened to back away. "Saving me from the sins of caffeine?"

"Among other things." She tapped the picture with her forefinger. "You must find a purpose for her."

"First I have to find a face for her." He pulled up the image program in the computer and Nell's face appeared on the screen. He picked up the computer pen and bent over the computer drawing tablet beside the screen. "Cheekbones?"

"High."

His pen stroked upward on the pad and on the screen Nell suddenly acquired higher cheekbones. "Enough?"

"A little more."

He moved the cheekbones higher.

"Good." She frowned. "That turned-up nose must go. Personally, I like it, but it doesn't go with the cheekbones."

He got rid of the nose and inserted a delicate Roman nose. "Okay?"

"Maybe, we'll see."

"The mouth . . ."

"I want to keep the mouth."

"Then we'll have to square the jaw." He adjusted the line of the jaw. "The eyes?"

She tilted her head. "Can we slant them upward just a little. Like Sophia Loren?"

"It will require stitches."

"But it would be very interesting, yes?"

His pen changed the shape of the wide-set eyes. The change was enormous. The face on the screen now appeared strong, cleanly molded, and vaguely exotic. Yet the wide, mobile mouth gave a look of vulnerability and sensuality. It was not a classically beautiful face, but it fascinated and arrested.

"A little Sophia Loren, a little Audrey Hepburn . . ." Tania murmured. "But I think we must work on the nose."

"Because I did it without your input?" he asked dryly.

"Because it's a little too delicate." She leaned forward, her gaze on the computer screen. "We are doing well. This is a face to launch a thousand ships."

"Helen of Troy? Our Nell doesn't look like a Greek goddess to me."

"I never thought Helen of Troy looked like a goddess. I think she had a face that was unforgettable, that made people want to never look away from her. That's what we must do here."

"And what happens after we give her this face?" He turned to look at her. "A change that dramatic can traumatize."

"From what you tell me, she's already traumatized. I doubt if turning into Helen of Troy will do any more harm to her, and it may help her." She said, "If she has no purpose, she will at least have a weapon. This is important."

"Is that why you let me operate on you?"

She nodded. "The scars did not matter to me, but I knew it would matter to the people around me. I have my living to earn, and people shy away from ugliness."

He smiled. "I suppose I could make her look like you. It's not such a bad face."

"It's a very good face, but it would cause problems when I get you to admit that you cannot live without me. You're confused enough as it is. No, we will give her this wonderful face to smooth her way." She nodded at the pen. "Now, let's see if we can make the nose just a *little* thicker."

Nicholas met Joel as he was exiting Nell's hospital room the next evening.

"Don't talk to me," Joel said curtly. He waved the clipboard. "The permission-to-operate authorization."

"She didn't sign it?"

"She signed it. I told her precisely what I was going to do. I showed her a computer readout of exactly what she would look like. I'm not sure she heard a word I said. I know she didn't care." He ran his hand through his hair. "You know that she may sue me when all this is over?"

Nicholas shook his head. "She won't sue you."

"How do you know? She's a zombie, dammit."

"I promise you. I'll protect you from all ramifications, legal or personal."

"Really? Kabler called again today."

"Next time have your secretary refer him to the St. Joseph's administration office."

"Why?"

"Because Nell Calder died yesterday afternoon."

"What?" Joel stared at him, stunned. "My God, what have you done?"

"Nothing for which you can be blamed," Nicholas said. "Just continue to refuse to talk to Kabler. If he checks with administration, he'll find that she died of wounds and was removed to a local funeral home."

"And if he checks with the funeral home?"

"They'll have record of her cremation. Her obituary will appear in the paper tomorrow."

"When I told you to take care of it, I didn't mean— You can't do things like this."

"It's already done."

"And what do you think Nell Calder will say about her demise?"

"When it's safe, she can say that 'reports of her death were greatly exaggerated.' "

"Safe?"

"She wasn't one of the innocent bystanders. She was targeted. She may still be in danger."

"Christ. I don't suppose you considered telling me what I was getting into?"

"I considered it, but it would only have made your decision harder." He smiled. "And the decision would still have been the same, wouldn't it?"

"So you kept me in the dark to save me from undue worry," he said sarcastically.

"Well, and to save myself from hearing your arguments. Isn't a fait accompli much simpler?"

"It is not."

"Of course it is."

"The records show I was the attending physician. I'm the one who will be blamed for falsifying them."

Nicholas shook his head. "I have the original authorization of transfer signed by you. If you need it, I'll produce it."

"If it suits your convenience."

"No." Nicholas met his gaze. "I promised to protect you. I'll keep my word, Joel."

Joel stared at him moodily. He knew Nicholas would keep his promise, but it didn't improve his temper. "I don't like to be manipulated."

"I didn't manipulate you. I manipulated the records." He glanced at the clipboard with the permission slip. "And you're not really angry at me, you're worried about your patient. She's no better?"

"She's close to catatonic," Joel said. "I can do only so much. What the hell good is a new face going to do her if she ends up in an institution?"

"We won't let that happen to her."

"You bet your ass we won't." He stabbed a finger at Nicholas. "And I won't be alone in this. You're not running back to Idaho. You're staying right here on call. Do you understand?"

"Perfectly." A smile tugged at his lips. "Do you mind if I stay at a hotel in town? I'm allergic to hospitals."

"As long as you're on call."

Nicholas held up his hands in surrender. "Whatever you say."

"Yeah, sure." Joel strode away from him down the corridor.

Bellevigne, France

"You blundered," Philippe Gardeaux said softly. "I don't like mistakes, Paul."

"I didn't expect her to fight so hard." Paul Maritz scowled. "And I thought the fall would kill her."

"You wouldn't have had to rely on the fall if you had done your job correctly. One stroke should have done it. You indulged yourself, didn't you?"

"Maybe," he said sulkily.

"And you killed the child. How many times must I tell you that you never kill children or animals? For some reason, it arouses more anger than if you slaughter a hundred adults."

"She ran at me after her mother fell. She was hitting me."

"And you had to defend yourself against a four-year-old," Gardeaux said dryly.

"She might have recognized me. It was the second time. She saw me that afternoon in the caves."

"You had goggles and a mask on," Gardeaux said. "I don't like excuses. Now, admit that you were frustrated and needed to strike out at something, and I'll forgive you."

"I guess I . . . maybe I was mad," he mumbled.

"Now, wasn't that easy?" Gardeaux leaned back in his chair and lifted his wine to his lips. "Just admit your faults and everything goes well. The child was a mistake but not a consequential one. The woman has been taken to a hospital in the States and will live. You'll have to rectify that prognosis if you think she may recognize you now." He paused. "She was taken there by Nicholas Tanek. I hardly think it a coincidence that he was there on Medas. Which leads me to the conclusion that we might have an informant in our midst. Do you suppose that you could seek out and eliminate that informant without making another blunder?"

Maritz nodded eagerly.

"I hope so," Gardeaux said gently. "This is very distressing to me. If you should disappoint me again, I'd have to find a way to distract myself." He covered a yawn. "How do you think your knife would fare against Pietro's sword?"

He moistened his lips. "I'd carve him to pieces."

Gardeaux shuddered. "Hand weapons are so brutal. That's why I prefer the grace and romance of a sword. I often think I must be the reincarnation of a Medici. I fear I was never meant for this age." He smiled at Maritz. "And neither were you. I see you riding behind Attila the Hun."

Maritz was vaguely aware this was an insult, but he was too relieved to complain. He had seen what Pietro had done to the last man Gardeaux had ordered him to fight. "I'll find him."

"I know you will. I trust you, Paul. All you needed was a little clarification."

"And I'll go after Tanek too."

"No! How many times must I tell you that Tanek isn't to be touched?"

"He gets in your way," Maritz said sulkily. "He causes you trouble."

"And will be disposed of in time. My time. You'll not touch him. Do you—"

"Daddy, look what Mama gave me." Gardeaux's youngest daughter ran out on the terrace, waving a pinwheel. "The wind turns it and it goes faster and faster."

"I see, Jeanne." Gardeaux lifted the six-year-old to his lap. "And did she give one to René as well?"

"No, René got a puppet." She nestled closer. "Isn't it pretty, Daddy."

"Almost as pretty as you, *ma chou*." He set the pinwheel spinning.

The little girl had shining brown hair and looked a little like Nell Calder's daughter, Maritz thought. But then, most kids looked alike to him.

"Go away, Paul," Gardeaux said without looking at him. "I've already robbed my wife and children of too much time. Come back when you can give me good news."

Maritz nodded. "Soon. I promise you." He ran down the steps that led to the garden. Gardeaux never liked them to go through the house. He was afraid they would run into his wife or children and dirty them, he thought sourly. In fact, he never liked them to come to Bellevigne at all except as security during one of his highfalutin parties. That was why Maritz had been surprised when Gardeaux had called him when he had returned from Medas and told him to come.

Surprised and frightened.

He crossed the drawbridge and looked back at the chateau. He didn't like being scared. He couldn't remember when he'd last felt that panicky terror. When he was a kid, maybe. Before he'd found his talent, before he found the knife. After that, everyone had been afraid of *him*.

They were still afraid of him. The woman had been afraid. She had fought but she had been terrified.

The woman. He would have another chance at her, a chance to do something that would put him back in Gardeaux's good graces.

He was being like all the rest, he realized in disgust. Crawling, whining, afraid that Gardeaux would raise his hand against him.

He crossed the drawbridge and looked back at the chateau. A king in his castle. Sometime he'd like to see if the king could be toppled.

A shiver went through him as he remembered Gardeaux's eyes when he had threatened him with Pietro. It wasn't Pietro, it was the sword that chilled his blood.

His pace quickened as he headed for his car. First the informant, and then the woman. That would make everything all right with Gardeaux.

"Get here. *Now*," Joel said.

Nicholas flinched as the phone was crashed down at the other end. He turned to Jamie.

"I have to go to Woodsdale. Something's wrong."

"I thought you said Lieber told you the operation went well," Jamie said. "It's been over a week, too long for a relapse, right?"

"Maybe. I don't know." He pulled on his suit jacket

and closed the new dossier Jamie had gathered on Nell. He had been going over it when Joel called. "Anyway, I have to go. Want to come along?"

"Why not? I haven't seen Junot in a long time." Jamie rose to his feet. "Did you know that I offered him a job as a bouncer in my pub when you broke up the network?"

"Big mistake."

"I always liked Junot." He followed Nicholas from the hotel room. "But he's better off at Woodsdale. Less chance of confrontation."

"I thought so."

Junot met them at the gate that led to the underground parking garage at Woodsdale. He was not wearing a uniform. Nicholas had persuaded Joel it would not be needed.

"I'll park the car. Dr. Lieber wants you to go right up. Fourth floor." Junot smiled slightly as he saw Jamie. "How you doing?"

"Good enough. Thought I'd let you show me the grounds while Nicholas was busy."

"Great alarm system. You'll be impressed. Even you'd have trouble."

"Ah, stabbed to the heart. You doubt me?"

Nicholas left them and strode quickly down the ramp. The front entrance of Woodsdale was located in the concrete bunker of the parking garage. Totally secure and private so that no celebrity would be seen entering or leaving after they had surgery.

Joel met him as he exited the elevator on the fourth floor a few minutes later.

"She's your responsibility," Joel said grimly. "Fix it."

"What's wrong?"

"What's been wrong all along. She's withdrawing more and more every day. I've had a battery of psychiatrists in there with her. I even called in a priest. Nothing does any good. She doesn't eat. She doesn't talk. I started intravenous feeding yesterday."

"Are you saying she's going to die?"

"I think she's willing herself to die, and she has a surprisingly strong will. I can probably keep her alive if I put her on machines."

Nicholas had a sudden memory of Terence begging him to turn off the respirator. "No machines."

"Then you find a solution." He gestured. "Third room on your left."

Nicholas moved down the corridor.

"Tania says she needs a purpose," Joel called after him.

"And I'm supposed to supply it."

"You're supposed to make her want to live so that all my work won't be wasted."

"You may not like my methods."

"I won't like it if she dies or has to be institutionalized either," Joel said. "As long as you don't escalate either of those possibilities, you'll get no argument from me. I've done everything I can."

And Nicholas was supposed to perform the miracle Joel couldn't. Great. He pushed open the door.

Nell's face was still bandaged, and she looked smaller, slighter than when he had last seen her. She stared straight ahead and gave no sign she was aware that he had come into the room.

Purpose.

Oh, yes, he knew all about that subject. He could give her purpose.

Nicholas Tanek.

She had thought he had gone from her life, Nell thought dully. She wanted him gone. He was the one who had told her about Jill. . . .

She tried to block his presence from her mind; she had grown very good at that. No, he was too strong. Her uneasiness increased. She quickly closed her eyes.

"Stop pretending. You're not asleep," he said coldly. "Just gutless."

A ripple of shock went through her.

"Are you enjoying yourself lying there, pitying yourself?"

He didn't understand. She wasn't pitying herself. She just wanted everyone to go away.

"I'm not surprised. You've caved in and run away from everything all your life. You wanted to be an artist and your parents snapped their fingers and you dropped everything and came running. Your husband molded you into what he wanted and you let him do it."

He was talking about Richard. Cruel. Richard was dead. You didn't talk ill of the dead.

"Did anyone tell you how Jill died?"

Her lids flew open. "Shut up. I don't want to hear it. Go away."

"She was stabbed."

The knife. Oh, God, the knife.

"He enjoyed doing it. He always enjoys it."

Yes, he enjoyed it. She remembered the smile behind the mask as he had stabbed at her.

"He's out there, free. He took away her life, all the joy, all the things you planned for her. You let him steal that from her."

"No! I tried to stop him. I drew him out to the balcony and—"

"But she's dead and he's free. He's walking around remembering how he killed her. It's so easy to kill a child."

"Stop it." His words were ripping, tearing at her. Why wouldn't he leave her alone? She had not imagined anyone could be this brutal. "Why are you doing this?"

"Because I don't care if you're suffering or not. She's dead and you're betraying her. You're going to lie down and let this roll over you just as you've done everything else your entire life. She was a nice kid, she deserves better than a mother who won't even rouse herself to wonder if the man who killed her would be punished for it."

"She's dead. Nothing I could do would—"

"Excuses, qualifications. Don't you get sick of backing away from life? No, I guess not." He leaned forward, his gaze boring into hers. "Here's something to remember while you're lying here, thinking about your daughter. She didn't die easily. He never lets them die easily."

She felt something explode inside her. "*Damn* you."

"But I guess you don't care about that. You'd rather go back to sleep and forget all this unpleasantness." He stood up and moved toward the door. "Well, go ahead. You probably couldn't do anything about it anyway. You've never taken an effective action in your entire life."

Her voice vibrated with intensity. "I hate you."

He looked at her without expression. "Yes, I know."

He left the room.

Her nails dug into her palms as her hands clenched into fists. She wanted him back so that she could strike at him as he had struck at her. Cruel. She had never known anyone so cruel.

Except the man who had killed Jill. The monster.

He never lets them die easily.

The words stabbed through her with more pain than the knife that had ended Jill's life. She had not allowed herself to think of Jill suffering, Jill dying. She had thought only of the loss, the emptiness of life.

Life would not have been empty for Jill. She was a child who loved every facet of life. She would have run toward it with both arms opened wide.

And she had been cheated of it by a monster who killed helpless children.

The knowledge was twisting, hurting, burning inside her. He was out there, free, while Jill was dead.

"No." She wouldn't have it. She felt as if the thought were searing away the past, the present, the future.

You've never taken an effective action in your entire life.

Lies.

No, truth.

It was so easy to see the truth now that none of it mattered.

Do what I say or I won't love you anymore.

The unspoken threat had always been there. First with her parents, and then Richard, and she had scurried to obey in terror of losing that love.

But now the fear was gone because there was nothing to lose. Everything of importance was already lost.

Except the memory of Jill.

And the man who had killed her.

"Well?" Joel asked as Nicholas walked out of the room.

"I don't know. Have everyone stay away from her for a while and let it simmer."

"Let what simmer?"

"She had an open wound and I cauterized it with a red-hot poker." He added, "And without anesthesia."

"I'm not even going to ask what you mean."

"I wouldn't. You'd disapprove." He moved down the hall toward the elevators. "But I think I can go back to Idaho for a while. There's no question she'll want to see me after this. Call me when you think she's semi-normal again. I need to ask her a few questions."

Nell did not sleep that night. She stared into the darkness while Tanek's words pounded at her.

Jill.

Growing up, going to school, first party, first dates, first child. So many firsts she'd never know.

Robbed. Robbed of life, robbed of all those experiences.

Nell's loss was nothing compared to what the monster had stolen from Jill.

And she was lying here, doing nothing about it.

Rage.

Burning, destroying, clarifying rage.

The crystal vase of tiger lilies the young man was carrying should have looked absurd in his big hands, but somehow it didn't. He was vaguely familiar; he had been there during that period of shadows. She searched for a name. "You're Phil Johnson," Nell said slowly.

He whirled to face her. "Hey, you remember me." He moved eagerly toward the bed. "How you doing? Can I get you anything? How about some orange juice?"

She shook her head. "No, thank you. Not now." She looked down at her arm. She was surprised it was still in a cast. It seemed a hundred years since she had awakened that first time to find Tanek sitting by her bed. Tanek. She stifled a rush of blinding anger. Tanek didn't matter. She had to be calm and think clearly. "How long have I been here? And where is here?"

"Ten days at Woodsdale."

"Woodsdale?" She dimly remembered Dr. Lieber mentioning moving her to his clinic.

Phil nodded. "Do you remember the operation?"

She reached up and touched her face. Bandages.

"Dr. Lieber wants them on until you're fully healed. There are always bruises with plastic surgery, and he thinks you've had enough shocks to—" He broke off and then said, "I'm sorry. I wasn't supposed to talk to you about anything that could upset—" He made a face. "Here I go again. Foot in mouth. Should I go away?"

She shook her head. "I feel very weak. Am I going to be in this bed a long time?"

"You'll have to ask Dr. Lieber. But you'd probably get stronger if you'd eat." He smiled coaxingly. "Those IVs in your arm can't be much fun."

"I'll eat," she said. "I have to speak to Dr. Lieber. Will you ask him to come to see me?"

"Sure. He's at the hospital in the city this morning, but he should be here soon." He nodded at the flowers on the table. "Pretty. Do you want me to check and see who they're from?"

They're pretty, Mama, Jill had said. *Prettier than when they were in the garden.*

Pain twisted through her, intense, taking her breath. Block it. She couldn't function if she let pain blind her like this.

"You okay?" Phil asked, concerned.

"Yes, I'm fine," she said steadily. "Read the card."

"Just a name. Tania Vlados. A friend?"

She shook her head. "I've never heard of her."

"Well, she must have heard of you." He put the card

back. "Nice choice. Different. They look like jungle flowers."

"They're tiger lilies." The strain of behaving normally had been enormous. She wanted to close her eyes and go back to sleep. No, she would not allow herself to do it. She had done very well so far. This nice man, Phil Johnson, didn't seem to notice any hollowness in her manner. "I must thank her . . . when I find out who she is."

Phil nodded. "You probably have lots of flowers over at St. Joseph's. It takes a little time for them to send stuff over."

He was wrong. Richard could no longer send her flowers and she had no one else. "It doesn't matter." She studied him. "You look very strong. Did you play football?"

"Yep, I was a tight end at Notre Dame."

"Then you know all about exercise."

"Some."

"I hate feeling this weak. Do you suppose you could find me some sort of equipment to help me strengthen and tone while I'm lying here?"

"Maybe later."

She smothered her impatience and said carefully, "I'd really like it now. You can tell me how I should begin. I don't intend to hurt myself by trying to do too much. I'll be very careful."

He nodded understandingly. "I know how you feel. I'd be going nuts if I had to lie there doing nothing. I'll ask Dr. Lieber if it's okay."

"Thank you."

She watched him leave the room. Don't close your eyes. Don't go into the darkness. It's going well. He would try to help her and then she would help herself. It would be easier when she had to rely only on her own resources. She shifted her gaze to the flowers on the nightstand. Tania Vlados. Was she one of the guests at the party that night? She couldn't remember anyone but Elise Gueray. The party. She vaguely remembered Nadine being there after she had fallen. What of Martin and Sally? She supposed she should feel concerned.

No, she shouldn't. She had never liked either one of them, and she was done with pretense.

Richard had been killed at the party. Why couldn't she feel more sadness? He deserved to be mourned. But Jill was dead and there seemed no sorrow left to give to anyone else.

"I hear you're feeling much better," Joel Lieber said as he came into the room. He smiled as he sat down beside her. "It's about time. I've been worried about you."

She believed him. She doubted if Joel Lieber ever said anything he didn't mean. "How sick am I?"

"You're healing nicely. You have a broken arm and clavicle. The other wounds were nasty, but I made sure you wouldn't have any scars. We should be able to take the cast off in another three weeks."

She touched the bandages on her face. "And these?"

"I did some minor surgery around the eyes, but those stitches will be ready to be removed any day now."

"What is this on my face? I talk funny."

"You have a brace to keep your jaws aligned. You'll soon be able to do without it. There's still bruising, but I could take the bandages off now and you'd get an idea what you'll look like."

"No, it doesn't matter. I'll wait. I just wanted to know how long before I'll be released. A month?"

"Maybe. If all goes well and you do what I tell you."

"I will." She paused, steeling herself. "I wonder if I could see a copy of the newspapers that came out the day after . . . Medas."

His smile faded. "I don't think that would be wise. Wait awhile."

"I've waited too long already. I have to face it sometime. I promise I won't fall apart."

He studied her a moment. "I don't believe you will. All right, I'll dig one up and have it brought to you. Anything else?"

"No, you've been very kind, Dr. Lieber."

"Joel," he corrected her.

"I promise I won't trouble you much longer, Joel."

"You're troubling me now," he muttered.

"I'm sorry." Her regret was genuine. He seemed a decent man and he had worked very hard to help her. Unfortunately, he was also perceptive and could sense the remoteness that pervaded every cell of her body. Well, she could do nothing about that. "But I'll be well soon, and then you won't have to bother with me."

"I hope so." He stared at her a moment before turning and leaving the room.

Terrorists.

Nell lowered the newspaper and stared at the cream and peach striped wall. It made sense. No one would want to kill Richard or the others mentioned in the article. They must have been after Kavinski.

But why seek her out? Why would one of the terrorists attack her, when she had not even been near Kavinski? Jill's death might have been done spur-of-the-moment, but that murderer must have come after Nell.

He never makes it easy.

Tanek had spoken as if he knew the man who had killed Jill.

And if he knew who he was, he might know where he could be found.

"Where the hell have you been?" Joel said as soon as Nicholas picked up the phone. "I've been trying to reach you for the last month."

"I've been out of the country." Nicholas reached down and stroked Sam's ears. The German shepherd rubbed against his thigh.

"She wants to see you," Joel said. "Right away."

"That's a surprise. How is she?"

"Making amazing progress. She's been eating, talking to Johnson. She even got him to get her some exercise bands and she's been working on her legs and her good arm."

"Then why do you sound so peevish?"

"Peevish? I'm not peevish. Great men are never peevish."

"Sorry. Why are you concerned?"

"She's too controlled. Too remote."

"Perhaps that's best during this period. At least her health is improving."

"By leaps and bounds, and so is her determination. She's like an arrow released from a bow. It won't go anywhere but toward the bull's-eye."

"And where's the bull's-eye?"

"You tell me." He paused. "What did you say to her?"

"I gave her a purpose."

"What purpose?"

"Revenge."

"Christ."

"I had to work with what I had. I assure you I wouldn't have managed to rouse her if I'd tried to inspire her to be a brain surgeon. Revenge was the only motive that would have worked."

"And what happens now?"

"Now you divert her. Perhaps you're exaggerating the problem. She's a nice, gentle woman. Find a way to appeal to her basic nature."

"I don't think you have any idea what her basic nature is. She's sure as hell not how you described her to me." He hesitated a moment. "The first day after you left, she asked for the newspaper account of Medas."

"Did it upset her?"

"Yes. Johnson said she was pale and shaking but she was still in control. That's when she asked to see you. She's asked to see you every day since then. I think, if you don't come to see her, she'll be on your doorstep the minute she's released."

"Then I suppose I'd better get back there. Sam doesn't like visitors."

"How's his leg?"

"Stronger than ever."

"Sometimes it happens like that. You break someone and put them back together and find you have a completely new person. I'll tell her you'll be here tomorrow."

Joel's warning wasn't necessary. Nicholas had known the risk he ran. There had just been no other option. You couldn't sear and not have scars. Nicholas replaced the phone and sat down in the leather mission chair. Sam promptly tried to crawl onto his lap. Nicholas absently patted his head before pushing him down. The dog gave him a resigned look and curled up at his feet.

And there was more searing to come if he couldn't ward her off, he thought wearily. He just hoped to God he wasn't the one who had to do it.

Here we go down, down, down . . .
No!

Nell jerked upright in bed, her heart beating wildly.
It had been a dream. Only a dream.
Jill hadn't been there at the door, staring at her. . . .
She wiped her wet cheeks with the back of her hand.
Please, don't let it come again. She couldn't bear it.
Don't let it come again.

Four

"You wanted to see me?"

Nell looked up to see Tanek standing in the doorway. She felt a stirring of anger she had difficulty suppressing. She *would* suppress it. She said curtly, "Come in."

He came toward her. He was wearing jeans and a cream-colored sweatshirt, and they looked as natural on him as the tuxedo when she had first met him. You would always notice Tanek and not his clothes.

He dropped down in the chair beside her bed. "I thought you'd be rid of those bandages by now."

"Day after tomorrow. The brace is gone, but Joel wanted the stitches to be healed first." She went on the attack. "You know the man who killed Jill, don't you?"

He didn't pretend to misunderstand. "I thought you might pick up on that. Yes, I think I know who he is."

"Are you a terrorist?"

A smile tugged at his lips. "If I were, do you think I'd admit it?"

"No, but I thought I might get a response."

He nodded. "Very good."

She didn't want his approval, she wanted answers. "I don't think it was a terrorist attack at all."

"Really? Everyone else seems to think so."

"I wasn't in the ballroom. Why would a terrorist come after me?"

His eyes narrowed slightly. "Why would anyone come after you?"

"I don't know." She gazed at him challengingly. "Do you?"

"Perhaps you offended Gardeaux."

She looked at him in bewilderment. "Gardeaux? Who's Gardeaux?"

She hadn't realized he was tense until she saw him relax. "A very unpleasant individual. I'm glad you don't know him."

He had thrown out the name to see her response, she realized. Gardeaux. She stored the name in her memory. "Why did you insist on going with me to my room that night? Was it to make sure that the murderer would know where I could be found?"

"No, I imagine he had a complete diagram of the house and knew who was in every room before he reached the island." He met her gaze. "And the last thing I wanted was to have you hurt or killed."

She had to tear her gaze away. He was willing her to believe him, and that will was very strong. But she shouldn't believe him. She should suspect everyone, particularly him. "Who killed my daughter?"

"I believe it was a man named Paul Maritz."

"Then why haven't you told the police?"

"They're satisfied that it was a terrorist attack aimed at Kavinski."

"And this Maritz isn't a terrorist?"

He shook his head. "He works for Philippe Gardeaux. But the police won't go after Maritz for killing your daughter."

Gardeaux again. "Are you going to tell me what this is all about, or are you going to make me pull it out of you?"

He smiled faintly. "You were doing so well, I thought I'd let you go for a while. Gardeaux is a distributor. He's the direct link between Europe and the Middle East, for a division of the Colombian drug cartel headed by Ramon Sandequez, Julio Paloma, and Miguel Juarez."

"Distributor?"

"He distributes drugs to dealers and money to smooth the way. Maritz is one of his people."

"And Gardeaux sent Maritz to kill me? Why Jill?"

"She got in his way."

Such a simple sentence. A child was in the way, so she was killed.

His gaze was on her face. "Are you okay?"

Her composure went up in flames. "No, I'm not okay." Her eyes blazed up at him. "I'm angry and sick and I want him dead."

"I thought you would."

"And you say the law won't even try to convict him?"

"Not for your daughter's death. Perhaps they'll find another reason to arrest him."

"But you have your doubts."

"Gardeaux protects his men because it would endanger him to do anything else. A good portion of the money he distributes goes to police officials and judges."

She gazed at him, incredulous. "You're saying he can commit murder and no one will care."

"You care," he said quietly. "I care. But what we're talking about is billions of dollars. Gardeaux can lift his hand and a judge will suddenly have a home on the Riviera and the money to retire and live like a king.

Even if you found someone who's willing to bring Maritz to trial, Gardeaux would see that the jury was fixed."

"I can't believe that's true."

"Then don't believe it, but it is true."

It was the indifference in his tone that convinced her. He was stating a fact, not trying to persuade her. "Then you're telling me to forget about Maritz?"

"I'm not a fool. You'll never forget. I'm asking you to leave it in my hands. I'll make sure that Maritz is brought down with Gardeaux."

"Brought down?"

Tanek smiled.

"You're going to kill him," she whispered.

"At the earliest opportunity. Does it shock you?"

"No." It would have before Medas, she realized. Not now. "Why?"

"That doesn't matter."

"You seem to know everything about me, but I'm not to know anything about you?"

"That's the picture. What should concern you is that I've been committed for over a year and I'll devote myself to that goal with the same passion you would."

"You couldn't." There was not that much hatred or passion left in the world.

"You say that because you have tunnel vision right now. Once you're able to see other points of view, you may—"

"Where is he?"

"Maritz? I have no idea. Hiding under Gardeaux's wing."

"Then where's Gardeaux?"

"No," Tanek said firmly. "Gardeaux and Maritz are a package deal, and you don't touch that package. You go blundering into Gardeaux's playground and you'll end up dead."

"Then show me how not to blunder."

"The way to avoid blunders is to stay away from them both. Look, Maritz was a Seal. He knows more ways to kill than you can count. And Gardeaux has men murdered just for stepping on his toes."

"But you think you can get them."

"I *will* get them."

"You haven't done it yet. Why has it taken you so long?"

She had struck a nerve. His lips tightened. "Because I want to live, dammit. I won't kill Gardeaux and then be killed myself. That's no victory. I have to find a way to bring him down that won't—"

"Then you won't go after him with the same passion." She met his eyes and said simply, "I don't care if I die after I kill him. I just want him dead."

"Christ."

"So show me, use me. I'll do it for you."

"The hell you will." He stood up and headed for the door. "Stay out of this."

"Why are you angry? We both want the same thing."

"Dammit, listen to me. Gardeaux wants you dead." He opened the door. "I don't stake out goats to attract the tiger."

"Wait."

"Why? I think we've said it all."

"How did you find out so much about me?"

"I had a dossier drawn up. I had to know why Gardeaux might want you dead."

"But you didn't find out." She gestured in frustration. "How could you? There *is* no reason. None of this makes sense."

"There's a reason. We just don't know what it is yet. I'm still working on it. May I go now?"

"No, you still haven't told me why you insisted on coming to my room that night."

His expression didn't change, but she was aware of a sudden underlying tension. "What does it matter?"

"Everything matters. I want to know."

"I was given information that you might be involved."

"Involved in what?"

"The information wasn't clear. I decided it wasn't valid in your case."

"But it was?"

"*Yes*, goddammit. Are you satisfied now? I made the wrong decision and I left you to Maritz."

She studied him. "You're blaming yourself. That's why you've gone to all this trouble and brought me here."

He smiled without mirth. "Isn't it comforting to know you have someone to blame besides Maritz?"

It would be comforting. She wished with all her being she could lay the fault at his feet. "I don't blame you. It wasn't your fault."

She saw the surprise in his expression. "That's very generous."

"I'm not being generous. You didn't know. You weren't there when Maritz came."

"But I could have been."

"Yes, you could have been. If you want to feel guilty, then go ahead." She added fiercely, "I *want* you to feel guilty. Maybe then you'll help me find Maritz."

"Forget it."

"I won't forget it. I'm going to—"

He had already left the room.

Her heart was beating hard and she could feel the blood pounding in her veins. He had broken through the icy shell of composure that had protected her, but that didn't matter.

He knew Maritz. He could point the path to him. She would find a way to make sure he did just that.

She reached for the elastic exercise bands on the nightstand and slipped the stirrup over her left foot. She was getting stronger every day. She even used the bands when she couldn't sleep at night.

Sleep was no longer welcome now that the dreams had started to come.

Joel smiled slyly when he saw Nicholas's expression. "You seem a tad upset. Was I exaggerating?"

"No," he said shortly.

"As I said, I don't like that control."

"What?" He recalled the coolness with which Nell had greeted him. But that composure hadn't lasted after she had gone on the attack. He had been aware only of that single-minded determination and unrelenting will.

Then you won't go after him with the same passion.

Oh, yes, she had passion, the same blind passion that had driven Joan of Arc to the stake.

Joel shook his head. "I said that I don't like that—"

"I heard you. I don't think we need to worry about that. How long before she gets out of here?"

"Another two weeks."

"Delay it."

"Why?"

"She's not ready." And he wasn't ready. There was no question she wouldn't give up and he would have to find a way to deter her. "Can't you discover a complication?"

"No, I won't lie to a patient. She's already been here almost two months." His smile held a faint shade of malice. "What's wrong, Nicholas? After all, you told me she was no powerhouse, just a nice, gentle woman."

Nicholas wasn't sure what Nell Calder had become, but she had changed enough to make him uneasy as hell. "Knock it off, Joel. I need help here."

"Not by compromising my professional ethics."

"Then don't lie to her. She's still got broken bones. Tell her you want her to stay here until they're fully healed. It's not as if you need the bed."

Joel thought about it. "I suppose I could do that."

"Has she met Tania?" Nicholas asked.

"Not yet."

"Throw them together as soon as possible."

"Another woman's influence?"

"Another survivor's influence." He turned and motioned to Phil. "Keep a close eye on her."

Phil looked hurt. "I'm taking good care of Nell, Nick."

"I know you are." Nicholas smiled. "Just make sure she doesn't slip away without anyone knowing about it. Okay?"

Phil nodded. "I like her. I told her I majored in computer science in college and she's real interested. She's been asking me all kinds of questions about computers."

An interest in computers would guarantee Phil's affection. "What kind of questions?"

Phil shrugged. "Just questions."

Maybe her interest was without any hidden purpose. Or maybe she had instinctively zeroed in on a way to gain Phil's friendship. He wouldn't have thought such machinations were possible for the woman he had met on Medas, but Nell was now an unknown quantity. "Just keep close watch on her."

"You know I will." Phil went back into Nell's room.

"Nice guy," Joel said. "And a good nurse."

"You sound surprised. I told you that you'd like him." He shifted back to the original subject. "You'll bring in Tania?"

"Why not? She's been wanting to meet Nell." He paused. "You're worried about what she'll do when I release her and she's no longer under protection. She knows someone tried to murder her. Surely she won't be rash."

"Rash? Yes, I think you might use that word. Although *suicidal* is probably more accurate."

"You know who tried to kill her," Joel said slowly. His eyes widened. "You *told* her?"

"Domino effect. I had to give her something. Besides, she deserved to know."

Joel shook his head. "Big mistake."

"Maybe. I've made a few." He started toward the elevators. "But now the only important thing is damage control."

"Wait. You had a telephone call." Joel searched in his jacket and found the message. "Jamie Reardon. He's in London and wants you to call him back right away."

Nicholas took the message. "May I use your office?"

"By all means." Joel gestured to a door down the hall. "I live only to be of use to you, Nicholas."

"I'm glad you've finally accepted that," Nicholas said, poker-faced, as he strode toward the office. "You were a little slow in the beginning."

He heard Joel's muttered curse behind him.

He was still smiling when he reached Jamie. "You've found something?"

"Conner got the name of Kabler's informant in Gardeaux's camp. He's here in London. One Nigel Simpson, an accountant. Do you want me to try to negotiate to get him in our pocket as well as Kabler's?"

A surge of excitement flickered through Nicholas. "You're certain it's him?"

"Conner says it's him and that rabbit would be too scared to commit himself unless he was damn sure. Do you want me to approach Simpson?"

"No, I'll catch the next plane. Don't let him out of your sight."

"No problem. He's spending the night at his favorite call girl's apartment. I don't think he'll be on the move." Jamie chuckled. "Well, except inside the woman. I imagine she'll inspire a bit of movement. She's reputed to be a very kinky lady. I'll be at 23 Milford Road. I'll be driving one of the old black Rolls-Royce taxis." He sighed. "They're gradually disappearing, you know. They're being replaced by sleek monstrosities with no sense of history. Sad."

"Just so Simpson doesn't disappear."

"He won't. Have I ever failed you?"

"Ah, you are sitting up. That is good."

Nell looked up to see a tall, leggy brunette in the doorway.

The woman was dressed in jeans, a man's striped shirt with sleeves rolled up to the elbow, and a leather vest. She smiled. "May I come in? You don't know me, but I feel as if I know you. I'm Tania Vlados."

The name was familiar. "You sent me the flowers."

The woman nodded and came forward. "Did you like them? I grew them myself."

Tania Vlados had a faint accent at odds with her very American attire. "They were lovely, Miss Vlados."

"Tania." A smile lit her face. "I feel we are going to be great friends, and I'm always right."

"You are?"

"My grandmother was a Gypsy and she used to tell

me I did not have the sight but I have the sounding." She dropped down in the chair. "That I hear echoes of the soul."

"How . . . interesting."

Tania chuckled. "You think I'm crazy. I don't blame you. But it is true."

"Do you work here at the clinic?"

"No, I work for Joel. I'm his housekeeper." She stretched her legs out in front of her. "And before you ask, that doesn't mean I occupy his bed as well as his house."

She stared at her, shocked. "I would never ask a question like that."

"No? You'd be surprised how many people do. There's no privacy left in the world." Her eyes glinted with mischief. "Most of the time I tell them I do. It drives Joel insane. He's old-fashioned, you know."

"No, I didn't know."

She nodded. "You do not notice much during the first weeks. You are too full of sadness. It was so with me."

Nell stiffened. "You're no housekeeper. You're another one of those psychiatrists Joel's been sending in here. Well, you can just leave. I don't want to talk to you."

"Psychiatrist?" She smiled with amusement. "I have no use for them either. When I was here healing, Joel tried to get me to see one and I sent him packing."

"You were a patient here?"

"I was pretty badly scarred when I was brought here from Sarajevo, but Joel fixed me." She grinned. "Now I intend to fix him. Is he not splendid?"

Splendid was not a word she would associate with Joel Lieber. "I guess. I think he's very nice."

"He's more than that. He has a great heart. This is very rare. He is like a rose. It is wonderful seeing—"

"Well, are you ready for the great unveiling?" Joel asked as he strode into the room.

"Yes," Tania said eagerly.

Joel gave her a quelling look. "I was addressing my patient."

"I'm ready," Nell said.

"I hope you don't mind Tania being present when I take off the bandages. She's been badgering me to let her come to see you since the operation."

"I feel a vested interest," Tania said. "Joel let me help plan your new face. I told him to keep the mouth. You have a great mouth."

"Thank you." Her lips twitched with amusement. "But I gather you told him to scrap the rest?"

"More or less."

Joel shook his head. "Tactful, always tactful."

Why, she was actually smiling, Nell realized, shocked. A genuine smile, not like the ones she had forced to show she was returning to normalcy.

Tania's shrewd gaze was fastened on Nell's face. "It is all right," she said quietly. "You will learn that laughter is no betrayal." Before Nell could answer, Tania turned to Joel. "She thinks you are very nice but not a rose."

"A rose?" he repeated.

"You *are* a rose. I've thought so from the moment I met you. You have facets and inner beauty unfolding all the time."

He looked at her in horror.

"Of course you do not smell like a rose. More like eucalyptus, but I—"

"I'll get a wheelchair." He fled the room.

Tania stood up. "He was funny, yes? It is strange how men cannot bear being compared to flowers. I don't see why flowers should be thought only feminine."

"I admit I found the simile a little unusual." She was still smiling. "But interesting."

"Joel needs to be shaken up regularly." Tania helped her slip on a pink bed jacket and buttoned the top button. "Brilliant doctors become accustomed to awe and adulation. It is very bad for them." She nodded approvingly. "I like this bed jacket. All bed jackets should be pink. We all need color when we wake in the morning. It is a good choice."

"I'm afraid I can't take any credit for it. It just appeared."

She grinned. "I was praising myself. I chose it."

"Perhaps you thought I'd look like a rose?"

"Ah, a little humor. This is good." She shook her head. "No, Joel is my only rose. I will decide later what—"

"Here we are." Joel entered the room with Phil in attendance, pushing a wheelchair. Joel cast Tania a stern glance. "Do you suppose you can conduct yourself in a decorous manner?"

"No." Tania watched as Phil gently transferred Nell to the wheelchair. "I'm too excited."

"Are you?" Joel smiled indulgently.

Why, he loves her, Nell thought suddenly. The look they were exchanging was warm and loving and as full of understanding as if they had been married fifty years. She felt a wrenching pang as she realized that she and Richard had never exchanged a look like that. Perhaps, given time, they might have—

"There, now we are ready." Tania tucked a blanket around Nell's knees and waved to Phil. "Take her. We will follow."

"Do you like it?" Tania asked eagerly.

Nell stared at the stranger in the mirror, stunned.

"You *don't* like it." Tania's face fell.

"Hush," Joel said. "Give her a chance."

Nell reached up and gingerly touched her cheek.

"If you don't like it, it's my fault," Tania said. "Joel did beautiful work."

"Yes," Nell said. "Wonderful work. The line of the cheekbone is magnificent." She realized she was speaking as impersonally as if she were complimenting a sculpture. It was the way she felt. The face in the mirror was a work of art, totally fascinating, almost . . . bewitching. Only her brown eyes and mouth were the same. No, that wasn't true either. The faint tilt at the corners made her eyes seem larger and the color more vibrant. And her mouth looked startlingly vulnerable and sensual in comparison to the high planes of her cheeks and jaw.

She touched her eyelid. "What did you do here? It's darker."

"A little cosmetic surgery." Joel grimaced. "Tania thought you should have permanent eyeliner on the upper lid and underneath the eye in case you went swimming. Heaven forbid you don't look perfect in the water."

"It's only the faintest line. It looks very natural," Tania said quickly. "I thought we might as well go the whole way."

"I see." They were both looking at her expectantly. "I look quite . . . glamorous. I never dreamed—"

"I showed you the computer printout," Joel said.

She only vaguely remembered. "I didn't really think—I don't suppose I thought about it at all."

"It will take time to become accustomed to it. If you need counseling, I'll—"

Tania made a rude noise.

Joel ignored her. "As I said, this drastic a change can be a bit traumatic. You may need help dealing with it."

"Thank you, I won't need help." It was not as if this were going to change her life. Yet before Medas, it might have done just that, she thought suddenly. The face Joel had given her was the stuff of dreams for any ugly duckling. Beauty translated to confidence, and she had been miserably lacking in that quality. Not now. Rage also empowered. She had no doubt she could do whatever was necessary. "Though I may do a double take whenever I pass a mirror."

"So will every man within a hundred yards," Joel said dryly. "You may need a bodyguard for more reasons than Nicholas thinks."

"Bodyguard?"

"I imagine Phil is doing double duty. Nicholas wanted you protected."

She frowned. "Phil was hired by Nicholas Tanek?"

Joel nodded. "Phil used to work for Nicholas. You should feel very safe. Nicholas doesn't make mistakes in that area."

"And he's paying Phil's salary?"

"Don't worry, he's picking up the tab for all your medical bills."

"He most certainly is *not*. Send the bills to me."

"Let Nicholas pay," Tania said. "Joel is very expensive."

"I can afford it. I have a little money my mother left me." She shifted her gaze to Tania. "You know Tanek?"

Tania nodded. "For years," she said absently, her gaze on Nell's hair. "We must go downstairs to the salon tomorrow and get rid of the gray."

"What gray?" Nell looked back at the mirror. She stiffened as she noticed the gray that threaded the hair at her left temple.

"You did not have it before?" Tania asked quietly.

"No."

"It happens sometimes. My aunt's hair turned entirely white after her husband was killed in front of her." She smiled. "It's only a few threads. I think a light frosting will look wonderful in that brown hair, and everyone will think you're *très chic*."

"It doesn't matter."

"Of course it does. I won't have that face I designed in a poor frame." She turned to Joel. "It is all right?"

"You're consulting me? I thought it was all decided." He nodded. "I suppose it will be okay."

Tania turned back to Nell. "Ten tomorrow? I'll make the appointment."

Nell hesitated. She had no urgent desire to cover a few gray hairs. Yet it was clear Tania would be disappointed if her creation was marred in any way, and Nell liked the woman. What was more unusual, she felt comfortable with her. "If you like."

"Oh, I do." She beamed. "And you'll like it too. I promise."

"Your taxi, Mr. Simpson." Jamie opened the door with a flourish. "And isn't it a fine day, sir?"

Nigel Simpson frowned. "I didn't call for a taxi."

"No, I believe it was a lady who called."

Perhaps Christine had called while he was in the shower. She was always accommodating after their sessions. She believed in honey poured as a balm to soothe the sting. He smiled as he remembered how exciting she'd proved last night. The woman was bloody magnificent. He got into the taxi.

Tanek!

Nigel's hand flew to the doorknob.

Tanek put his hand on Nigel's arm. "No disturbance," he said gently. "It would make me most unhappy. I take it you recognize me? How? I don't think we've ever met."

Nigel moistened his lips. "You were pointed out to me last year when you were in London."

"By Gardeaux?"

"I don't know any Gardeaux."

"I think you do. Jamie, why don't we take a little drive through the park and perhaps Mr. Simpson will remember."

Jamie nodded and got in the driver's seat.

"I won't remember," Nigel said. He forced a laugh. "You've mistaken me for someone else."

"Was it Gardeaux who pointed me out to you?"

"No, I told you—" He broke off as he met Tanek's eyes. He was sitting motionless and his tone had been soft, almost casual, but Nigel was suddenly terrified. "I don't know anything. Pull over, I want out of this taxi."

"You're an accountant, I believe. You must be very valuable to Gardeaux . . . and to Kabler."

Nigel froze. "I don't know either of those names."

"I'm sure Gardeaux knows Kabler's name. Suppose I called him and told him that you're Kabler's informant."

Nigel closed his eyes. It wasn't fair. Everything had been going so well for him, and now this bloody bastard appeared and sent everything crashing.

"You look a little sick," Tanek remarked. "Shall I open the window?"

"You can't prove it."

"I won't have to prove it. Gardeaux won't take the chance, will he?"

No, Gardeaux would just smile and shrug and the next morning Nigel would be dead.

Nigel opened his eyes. "What do you want?"

"Information. I want reports regularly and accurately. I want to see everything first and then I'll decide what you can sell to Kabler."

"Do you think I'm the only accountant Gardeaux has? He'd never trust everything to one man. We're given bits and pieces of the records of the money that goes out, and most of that is in code."

"The list of names for the Medas hit wasn't in code."

"The action to be taken was."

"What was the reason for the hit?"

"I sent Kabler all I knew."

"Then find out more. I want to know everything about it."

"I can't probe. It wouldn't be safe."

"Do you know, Nigel"—Tanek smiled at him—"I really don't care."

"It looks . . . strange." Nell shook her head, and the pale gold streaks shimmered beneath the soft lights of the salon.

"It looks wonderful," Tania said firmly. "And the cut suits you. Casual but sophisticated." She turned to the hairdresser. "Magnificent, Bette."

Bette grinned. "It was a pleasure to put a little frosting on the cake. Now you need a new wardrobe to go with the new look."

"I agree," Tania said. "I'll take her to the city tomorrow." She frowned. "No, Joel might not like it. I'll wait until next week."

"That's not necessary," Nell said. "I can notify my housekeeper in Paris to ship over some clothes."

"You can do that too, but Bette is right. You need new clothes for the new woman."

New woman. Tania's phrase resonated in Nell's mind. In a way, she *had* perished the night Jill and Richard died, and had been born again in the agony of learning of Jill's murder. But the woman was not complete; she was hollow inside. Perhaps not entirely hollow, she realized suddenly. She had felt warmth, amusement, even envy in the past few days since Tania had appeared.

"Am I pushing too hard?" Tania asked. "It's a habit of mine. Not necessarily a bad habit. Just annoying."

"You're not annoying." Nell turned to Bette. "How much do I owe you?"

Bette shook her head. "I'm hired by the clinic. No fee, no tip."

"Then thank you." She smiled. "You're very talented."

"I did my best, but, as I said, it was only icing. With that face, you'd even look good bald."

"So, will you let me take you shopping in town?" Tania asked as they left the salon.

Nell had been thinking about it. It might be a very good idea for her to go into the city. "If Joel will let me."

"Good. I'll tell Joel we'll be charging everything to Nicholas and that will make him more likely to let us take a little day trip."

"Why? Doesn't Joel like him?"

"Yes, but their relationship is complicated. Joel is a very competitive man."

Nell looked at her blankly.

"Nicholas is . . ." Tania shrugged. "Nicholas."

"But Joel is a brilliant surgeon."

"And Nicholas is larger than life. There are some men who tend to cast a long shadow. Joel doesn't like to stand in anyone's shadow." She grinned. "So he takes out his irritation in the way that is most pleasing to him. He was very disappointed when you said you wanted to pay his fee yourself."

Nell hadn't wanted to stand in Tanek's shadow either. "The debt was mine."

Tania's gaze was fastened on her face. "You resent him."

She did resent him. She resented his ability to pierce through the barriers she had erected and the cruelty of the way he had jerked her back to life. She resented the fact that every time she saw him, she remembered Medas. She resented the fact that he wanted to close her out when he could help her. "I know he's your friend, but he's not my cup of tea. I prefer your Joel." She changed the subject. "Does this clinic have facilities other than a beauty salon?"

"Everything from a spa to a five-star restaurant. Some of Joel's patients choose to stay until they're entirely healed and require all the amenities. What did you have in mind?"

"A gymnasium."

"Yes, but I doubt if Joel will let you do much exercising for a while. He'll want to make sure the bones have healed."

"I'll do what I can. I have to get stronger."

"You will. It's only a question of time."

But she didn't want to wait. It was maddening to be this weak and ineffectual. She wanted to be ready *now*. She repeated, "I'll do what I can."

"We will see what is possible."

"Tomorrow?"

Tania raised an eyebrow. "I'll talk to Joel. Maybe if I go with you and make sure you don't hurt yourself."

"But that will interfere with your job. I don't want to impose on you. You've done too much already."

"It's no imposition. I'll enjoy it. I need to work out myself, and being Joel's housekeeper doesn't require a good deal of time." She chuckled. "Besides, he'll be pleased that it keeps me off the phone."

Nell gazed at her doubtfully.

"Truly," Tania said. "You'll need workout clothes. You can borrow some of mine until we go shopping."

Nell shook her head. Tania could not be more than a size eight. "They wouldn't fit."

"Well, they may be a little big, but that's no problem. Workout clothes should be loose."

Nell looked at her in bewilderment.

"Unless you object to wearing someone else's clothes?"

"No, of course not but I—"

"Good." They had come to Nell's door, and Tania said to Phil, "I brought her back safe and sound. How do you like her hair?"

Phil whistled admiringly. "Nice."

Tania turned to Nell. "I'll be here at nine tomorrow and help you dress." Tania smiled and waved before walking down the hall.

"I'll help you back to bed," Phil said. "You must be tired."

She was exhausted, she realized in frustration. "Thanks, but I have to learn to do for myself. I can't rely—"

Phil had scooped her up with ease and was carrying her toward the bed. "Sure you can. You don't weigh more than a feather. That's what I get paid for." He tucked her into bed. "Now take a nap and I'll bring you your lunch."

They may be a little big.

You don't weigh more than a feather.

She slowly lifted her arm, and the sleeve of her bed jacket fell away. She stared at her arm for a moment and then opened the bed jacket and pressed the loose cotton gown against her. She must have lost twenty-five pounds in the past month.

Instant diet, she thought bitterly. Fall from a balcony, lose your whole world, and you'll be svelte as a greyhound. All those years she had labored to lose those extra pounds and now, when it mattered so little, they were gone.

But perhaps it did matter. She would gain strength more quickly without those excess pounds holding her back.

Vanity wasn't important, but strength was everything.

Five

"I'm not sure I like this," Joel said in an undertone to Tania as he watched Nell and Phil come toward them down the hall. "And I know Nicholas wouldn't."

"We'll be back by three," Tania said. "And Phil is driving us to the city and from store to store. What could happen on a half-day shopping trip?"

"Tell that to Nicholas."

"I will," Tania said. "Trust me. This will be good for her."

"I don't think shopping for clothes is high on her list of priorities."

"No, but it's a simple, normal function. Doing normal things is important for her."

"Like exercising?"

Tania frowned. "There's nothing normal about the way she exercises. It's as if she's driven. She'd be in that gymnasium twenty-four hours a day if you'd let her."

"It's not hurting her." He paused. "You don't have to baby-sit her, you know. She's not your responsibility."

"I like her. I want to help her." She added slowly, "I suppose I see myself in her."

"One of you is quite enough." He turned to Nell, who was now beside them. "Don't overdo it. When you get tired, give it up and come back."

"We will."

He thrust a roll of bills at her. "Here. I didn't know how much cash you had on hand."

Nell looked at him in bewilderment. "I don't need this. I don't have my credit cards here, but I'm sure I can call and make some arrangement."

"It will be easier if Tania charges everything to the clinic and we bill you later." He opened the back door of the car. "And remember, this Lincoln turns into a pumpkin at three."

"This is Dayton's department store. We'll be able to get most of the basics here. We'll go to boutiques for the specialty items." As she got out of the car, Tania said to Phil, "Will you give us three hours and meet us here at one?"

Phil frowned uneasily. "I don't think that would be a good idea. Suppose I park the car and meet you inside?"

"Okay," Tania said. "Come to sportswear. We'll go there first."

Nell followed Tania into the department store and was immediately enveloped in mellow lighting and glittering commercialism. "We don't have to go anywhere else. All I need are the basics, Tania."

"Need and want are two different things." She stepped on the escalator. "You may not want to see yourself in—Where are you going?"

"I have something to do. I'll meet you out front at one." Nell glanced back as she moved quickly toward the side entrance.

Tania was halfway up the escalator but turned and started down. "The hell you will."

Nell reached the side door and jumped into a cab parked at the taxi stand. "Public library. Central branch."

Tania ran out the door as the taxi sped away from the curb. "Nell!"

Nell felt a twinge of remorse. Tania had been kind, and she hated deceiving her. But she was also Tanek's friend, and Nell couldn't risk her interfering.

Ten minutes later she walked brusquely into the reference room of the library and up to the woman at the desk. "I understand you have Nexis?"

The woman glanced at her. "Yes."

"I've never used the program. I wonder if I could have someone help me find some information?"

The librarian shook her head. "We supply the program for our patrons, but we've no time to give lessons." She added, "And there's a charge for each subject you research."

Nell glanced at the woman's name tag. Grace Selkirk. "I'll be glad to pay for the service as well, Ms. Selkirk."

"I'm sorry, we have no time to—"

"I'll help you."

Nell turned to see a tall, lanky young man smiling at her.

"I'm Ralph Dandridge. I work here."

She smiled. "Nell Calder."

The librarian said, "You know the rules, Ralph."

"Rules are meant to be broken." Ralph turned to Nell. "If you're not computer literate, the program is a little confusing. I'll guide you through it."

"You've no time for this, Ralph," Grace Selkirk said. "I've something else for you to do."

"Then I'll do it after lunch," Ralph Dandridge said.

"And I'm taking my lunch hour right now." He gestured for Nell to precede him. "The computers are over in the next bay."

"I don't want to get you in trouble."

"No big deal. This is only a part-time job. I go to college at night. Besides, Grace is usually pretty cool. She just likes things by the book."

"Well, I appreciate you helping me." She smiled. "I don't know what I would have done if you hadn't come along."

He stared at her in bemusement a moment before tearing his eyes away. "Well, let's see how much I can do for you. Nexis is basically an information system. It keeps a record of thousands of newspapers, magazines, and periodicals. All you have to do is type in the subject and it will bring up every reference to it during the past ten years."

"But can I access a name?"

"Sure. But you may have to weed through a bunch of similar names. Whom are you looking for?"

"Paul Maritz."

He accessed two stories about a Paul Maritz and pulled them up on the screen for her to scan. One of them concerned a screenwriter who had won an award, the other Maritz was a fireman who had rescued a child. Definitely not her Maritz.

She hadn't really expected there to be any references about Maritz, but it had been worth a shot.

"Anything else?"

"Philippe Gardeaux." The name was unusual and she doubted if she'd run into the same trouble. Which didn't mean that she would have any more luck. But according to Tanek, he was a criminal on the grand scale. Surely there would be references to arrests, trials . . . something.

Jackpot. After trying two other spellings, three references to Philippe Gardeaux. One in *Time* magazine. One in *Sports Illustrated*. One in *The New York Times*.

"They look pretty long. Do you want to scan them?" Ralph asked.

"No. Can we print them all out?"

"Sure." Ralph highlighted the references, hit the print button, and leaned back in his chair. "Are you going to write an article on him?"

"What?"

"We get a lot of writers doing research."

"It's a possibility." She eagerly watched the paper scroll out of the printer.

He picked up the bundle of sheets and handed them to her.

"How much do I owe you?"

"Nothing. I'll take it off my fringe-benefit time. My pleasure."

She couldn't let him do that; she knew what a struggle it was for most college students to just survive. "I can't accept—" But she couldn't hurt his pride by refusing either. Dammit, she wanted to read those articles *now*. She sighed. "Well, do you at least have time to run to a nearby restaurant and let me buy you lunch?"

His eyes lit up behind the tortoiseshell-rimmed glasses. "You bet I do."

She stuffed the printout into her purse and stood up. "Let's go, I don't want you to incur your boss's wrath by coming back late. Is there someplace nearby?"

"Yes." He hesitated. "But do you mind going to the Hungry Peasant? It's only a few blocks farther."

"Is the food better?"

"No, but a lot of my friends hang out there." He grinned. "I'd like them to see me with you."

He wanted to show her off as if she were some kind of trophy, she realized with distaste. The face Joel had given her had probably influenced this nice kid to help her, but it had also triggered this response. A mixed blessing.

But Ralph was looking at her wistfully, and she owed him. She said resignedly, "We'll go to the Hungry Peasant."

Nell arrived back at Dayton's at five minutes to one.

Tania was waiting outside the store.

Nell instinctively tensed when she saw her expression. "Tania, I'm sorry it was necessary for me to—"

"Don't say a word," Tania cut her off. "I'm so angry, I want to push you out in front of a car." She stepped forward to the curb and waved. "There's Phil. We'll talk when we get back to the clinic."

Phil gave her a reproachful glance as they got into the car. "You shouldn't have done that, Nell."

"Let's get back to the clinic, Phil," Tania said curtly, her expression cold.

And Tania was never cold, Nell thought. She would probably never want to see Nell again after today.

She had not expected to feel this sense of loss.

Back at Woodsdale, Tania strode into Nell's room and pulled back the sheet on the bed before turning to Phil. "I'm parched. Could you get us some lemonade? I'll see that Nell lies down to rest."

Phil nodded. "Sure."

As soon as the door closed behind him, Tania whirled on Nell. "You will *never* lie to me again."

"I didn't lie to you."

"You deceived me. It's the same thing."

"I suppose you're right. I had something to do and I was afraid you'd disapprove."

"You're damn right I disapprove. Joel didn't want to let you leave the clinic and I persuaded him. You used me."

"Yes."

"Why? What was so important that you had to lie?"

"I needed information. Tanek wouldn't give it to me. I went to the library."

"And you couldn't tell me?"

"You're Tanek's friend."

"That doesn't mean he owns me. Didn't it occur to you that I was your friend too?"

Nell's eyes widened. "No," she whispered.

"Well, it should have. I first came to see you because Nicholas asked me, but from then on it was my decision." Her hands clenched into fists at her sides. "I knew why Nicholas wanted me to come. He thought you needed me. We both had losses and he wanted me to show you how well I'd healed. Well, I'm not healed. I'll never heal, but I've learned to deal with it. You will too."

"I'm dealing with it."

"No, Nicholas held out a carrot and you're going after it. It's a substitute for the real thing. When you don't dream anymore, then you'll know you've dealt with it." She smiled crookedly when she saw Nell's startled expression. "Do you think you're the only one who's ever had nightmares? The first year after my mother and brother died, I dreamed every night. I still do occasionally." She paused. "But I don't talk about it."

"Not even to Joel?"

"Joel would listen, he would try to help, but he wouldn't understand. He's never been there." She met Nell's eyes. "But you've been there. You could understand. I needed someone to understand. I came to you because I needed you, not because you needed me."

She was telling the truth. Nell felt a rush of despair.

"I can't help you. Can't you see? I don't have anything left to give."

"Yes, you do. You're already starting to come alive again," Tania said. "It doesn't happen overnight. It comes in ebbs and flows." She smiled faintly. "You didn't like it when I was angry with you. That's a good sign."

"But I'd do it again if it was necessary."

"Because you want to find the man who killed your daughter."

"I have to find him. Nothing else is important."

"Yes, it is, but you can't see it yet. I might feel the same if the sniper who killed my mother and brother had a face." She said wearily, "None of the soldiers had faces; they were just the enemy."

"But I do have a face and a name."

"I know, Joel told me that Nicholas gave them to you." She shrugged. "He could do nothing else. Joel was very worried about you. Nicholas saved your life, you know."

"No, I didn't know." And she didn't like it. "I'm sure he had a reason. He impresses me as a man who's not moved by sentiment."

"Sentiment? No, but he feels very deeply. Nicholas is not easy but, if he commits himself, he's a man to trust. I've never known him to break his word." She shook her head. "Nicholas brought you here and tried to help you. Why do you bristle every time I mention him?"

"He's standing in my way."

"Then you'll find he's not easy to move."

"I have to move him. I'm not like you. Time won't make me forget." She added simply, "My dreams won't go away until Maritz does."

"God help us." Tania sighed. "Well, will you at least promise not to deceive me again?"

Nell hesitated and then slowly nodded. "I didn't want to do it. I didn't see any other way."

"I don't suppose you'll tell me if you learned anything?"

"No, it would mean only divided loyalties. You're still Nicholas's friend."

Tania stared hard at her. "And?"

"Mine. My friend too." Nell smiled. "Though I don't know why."

"Then I've wasted the last fifteen minutes and great many of words." Tania held out her hand. "But a little humility does no harm. It's true that my friendship is a prize beyond compare."

Nell felt a ripple of uneasiness as she stared at Tania's extended hand. Friendship. Friendship meant commitment. Step by step she was being drawn back from the hollowness that she might need to do what must be done.

Tania's smile vanished. She said haltingly, "It is not easy for me to ask. I need someone who *knows*."

Nell slowly reached out and took her hand.

Tania didn't leave for another hour and then Nell had to eat the dinner Phil brought before she could look at the computer printouts.

A half hour later she lowered the last paper.

No trials, no arrests, no mention of criminal activities.

The *New York Times* article was only a mention of the arrival of Philippe Gardeaux in New York in connection with an auction to benefit AIDS to which he was donating a Picasso. He was referred to as a European businessman and philanthropist.

The *Time* article was more expansive. It was about the wine growers of France and their battle to keep the import tariffs high. There were two paragraphs on Gardeaux and his chateau and vineyards at Bellevigne. He was forty-six, with a wife and two children, and was described as one of the most influential of the growers. He was one of the new guard who had earned his money through investments in China and Taiwan and became a grower only five years previously.

The *Sports Illustrated* story had nothing to do with the vineyard but everything to do with the Chateau Bellevigne. It concerned the yearly fencing tournament that took place at Bellevigne during the week between Christmas and the new year, culminating on New Year's Eve. A step back in time where the guests were asked to wear Renaissance clothing for the entire week. The tournament was not only the premier social event of the Riviera, but the mecca for fencing aficionados and champion swordsmen. Plus the proceeds were disbursed to various charities. At the end of the article was a brief mention of Gardeaux's priceless collection of antique swords.

Philanthropist, influential businessman, collector, sportsman.

No mention of murder or drugs or bribery. No indication that this man would hire a man like Maritz and send him out to kill.

Was the man in these articles the wrong Gardeaux?

He made his fortune in China and Taiwan.

Tanek had grown up in Hong Kong. A fragile connection at best.

She stuffed the articles back in her handbag. It was not enough. She could not be sure. She needed Tanek.

One more minute.

She pumped harder on the StairMaster, breathing through her mouth as Phil had taught her. She had discovered if she set her goals only one minute at a time, she could go longer when she reached exhaustion. Her heart was pounding and sweat was pouring down her face.

One minute more.

"If you could give me a moment, I'd like to talk to you."

She glanced at the man standing in the door of the gymnasium. Not a nurse or doctor, she judged. He was short, stocky, with curly graying hair that had once been pale brown. He wore a gray suit, striped shirt, and loafers. Probably someone from administration checking on payment now that she was nearly well. "Can it wait? I'm almost finished."

"I've been watching you for the last fifteen minutes. I'd say you should be finished now."

Maybe he *was* a doctor. She didn't want him complaining to Joel that she was overdoing it. "You're right." She smiled and stepped off the machine. "But if you want to talk to me, you'll have to walk with me. Phil says I can't rest before I cool down."

"Ah, yes, Phil Johnson. I thought I saw him in the hall." He grimaced. "Unfortunately, he saw me too. So I won't have too much time with you."

"Oh, they're not careful of visitors any longer." She started walking briskly. "I'm almost well."

"Beautifully well." He fell into step with her. "Lieber did a wonderful job. I'd never have recognized you from your picture."

"Joel showed you my photo?"

"Not exactly."

She felt a twinge of uneasiness. Her pace slowed as she glanced at him. "Just who are you?"

"The question is, who are you?"

"Nell Calder," she said impatiently. "If you saw my picture or my file, you must know that."

"I didn't know, but I suspected. That's why I ventured into Lieber's sacred territory." He glanced around the gym. "Quite a place. Did the President's wife really have a face-lift here?"

"I have no idea. Nor do I care. Who are you?"

He smiled engagingly. "Joe Kabler, DEA."

She waited.

"Tanek never told you about me?"

"We're not on confidential terms. Are you friends?"

"We share a mutual respect and a few common goals," he said. "But I don't claim criminals as friends."

She went still. "Criminals?"

"My, my, he has kept you in the dark. What did he tell you about himself?"

"He's retired. He dealt in commodities."

Kabler chuckled. "Oh, yes, he certainly did. All kinds of commodities. Official papers, information, art objects. He headed a criminal network that was very troublesome to the authorities in Hong Kong for a number of years." He shrugged. "He didn't deal in drugs, so we never came up against each other. By the way, where is he?"

"I have no idea."

He studied her face. "I believe you're telling the truth."

"Why should I lie? He has a ranch in Idaho, perhaps you should try to find him there."

"I visited him there six months ago. Getting into the grounds there makes breaching this clinic seem easy." He added, "Besides, there's no urgency involved. Now that I know that Tanek hasn't done away with you."

The words were spoken so casually that they came as a shock. "You thought he'd murdered me?"

"I doubted it, but Tanek is never predictable." He smiled. "So I thought I'd come and see what was going on. But you're obviously doing very well."

"Very well," she said absently. "Why would you even suspect him?"

"Because he's Nicholas Tanek and he was on Medas when he had no business there. Then I hear he's whisked you away and won't let me talk to you."

"I didn't know you wanted to talk to me." She hesitated. "What do you know about Philippe Gardeaux?"

"That's the question I was going to ask you."

"Nothing. Except Tanek said that he ordered the attack on Medas and his men killed my daughter and husband."

His face softened. "You must think I'm very hard. I'm sorry, Mrs. Calder. I know how you must feel. I have three kids myself."

He didn't know. It hadn't happened to him. "But you agree that it wasn't a terrorist attack on Medas?"

He hesitated. "It's a possibility that it might have been Gardeaux."

"Why would he go after me? I've never met the man."

"I agree, it doesn't seem to make much sense. We can't find any connection between the two of you. We've concluded you must have just been in the wrong place at the wrong time. Kavinski was the logical target. He must have stepped on Gardeaux's toes at some time or other. You occupied one of the finest suites in the palace. Perhaps Gardeaux's man mistook your suite for Kavinski's."

"But Kavinski was downstairs."

"Gardeaux often has backup plans." He added gently, "I'm afraid you just got in the way."

"Is this Gardeaux the same man who owns Bellevigne?"

He nodded.

"Then why don't you do something about him? If you know what he does, why can't you stop him?"

"We're trying, Mrs. Calder. It's not easy."

"No one even seems to know what he is." She said jerkily, "Tanek said that even if those murderers were brought to trial that they wouldn't be convicted. Is that true?"

Kabler hesitated. "I hope not."

It was true, Nell thought dully. Innocents could be killed and the monsters would walk free.

"I'll never give up, if it's any comfort to you," Kabler said. "I've been fighting these scum for twenty-four years, and I'll keep on fighting for the next fifty."

Kabler was clearly a decent, determined man, but that didn't alter the fact that he was losing the battle. "It's not a comfort to me. My daughter is dead."

"And Tanek has promised you that Gardeaux will pay?"

She didn't answer.

"Don't let him use you. He'll do anything to get Gardeaux."

She smiled without mirth as she remembered that she had pleaded with Tanek to use her. "He has no intention of using me."

Kabler shook his head. "The hell he doesn't. Tanek would use the devil himself if it would bring him Gardeaux." He handed her a card. "I've said what I had to say. If you need help, call me."

"Thank you." She watched him walk to the door.

He stopped and looked back at her. "Oh, and I can understand how he wangled the records at St. Joseph's. Phil Johnson's skillful enough to tap into a Swiss bank account, given enough time. But you might ask Tanek how he managed to get the Birnbaum Funeral Home to forge the documents of your cremation."

The Ugly Duckling 121

"I need to talk to you, Joel," Nell said curtly into the telephone. "Right away."

"Aren't you feeling well? You've probably overdone it. I told Tania that you take—"

"I'm feeling fine. I need to see you." She hung up the phone.

Joel walked into her room an hour later. "You need me? So here I am."

"Why the hell do my records at St. Joseph's say that I died on June seventh?"

"You found out." Joel sighed. "I had nothing to do with it. Nicholas decided you'd be safer if everyone thought you were dead."

"So he wiped me from the face of the earth. I can't even use my credit cards. I called the bank and they show me deceased." She stared at him. "And you knew it might happen. That's why you handed me that stack of bills when we went to the city last week. You didn't want me to try to use credit. How long were you going to let it go on before someone told me?"

"I was going to let Nicholas have that honor. I'm tired of taking the backlash from his actions." He was silent a moment. "How did you find out?"

"A man named Kabler came to see me."

"Kabler? Here?" He gave a low whistle. "I wonder how he got past security."

"I don't know and I don't care. Why did you go along with this? Tanek may think he's beyond the rules, but I'd think you'd be more responsible."

"I did it because he was right." He held up his hand to stop her protests. "You were very ill. I didn't want Kabler to bother you, and Nicholas thought you might still be in danger. It's not a remedy I'd have used, but it was effective."

"Oh, yes, Tanek is effective all right. What kind of paperwork do I have to do to get my life back?"

"Are you sure you want to do it?"

"Of course I want to do it."

"The danger may still be there."

"I can't even access enough money to pay you."

He smiled cheerfully. "Then let Tanek do it. Serve him right."

Drawing and quartering would serve him right. "I won't be dependent on him."

"Then I'll be your creditor until this mess is straightened out."

Her anger against him ebbed away. She had no doubt that it had been Tanek alone who had been the instigator. Joel was an honest man trying to do what was best for her. "Thanks, Joel. But you know I can't do that. I'll have to call my lawyer and see if I can get him to release some of my trust fund."

"Will you think about it for a few days? There's no hurry. You won't be ready for release until next week. I want to take a few more X rays to make sure the bones have knit properly."

"I've been here over three months. I thought you kept only your VIP patients until they were entirely healed."

"And the ones who have no place to go."

Her smile faded. No place to go. No one to go home to. Loneliness.

"Which brings me around to something Tania and I discussed last night. We'd like you to come and stay with us when you leave here. It will give you a chance to get your bearings."

She instantly shook her head. "You don't have to—"

"I don't have to do anything." Joel grinned. "But you'll keep Tania busy, and that will be a boon. She makes my life miserable when she's able to focus her entire concentration on me. We'd be grateful if you'd come."

Relief rushed over her. She had been dreading staying in an impersonal hotel room while she tried to work out a plan. "Then perhaps for a day or so. Thank you."

"Good. Then I'll tell Tania she doesn't have to come in and nag you. Nagging from Tania is enough to give anyone a setback." He stood up. "Now, get some sleep. Do I need to prescribe something to help you?"

"No." Drugs would make her sleep deeply, and sleep always brought the dreams. If she slept lightly, she could sometimes escape from them into wakefulness. "I'll be fine."

She didn't fall asleep for a long time after Joel left. Her anger was slowly dispersing. The shock of learning she was thought to be dead had generated outrage, as if Tanek had stripped her of her background, the foundation that made her who she was.

Or had that foundation already been torn away? She was no longer that woman on Medas, nor the child who had grown up in North Carolina.

Joel had asked her to think about it. All right, consider the consequences. What if everyone did think she had died? On the surface it would be a disaster. She would have no credit cards, no driver's license, no passport. She would not be able to touch the money her mother had left her, so she would be totally without funds. Personally? It was not as if she would be missed. She had no family and she had lost track of the friends she had made in college when she married Richard. He dominated her life from that moment and she'd had no time to form other bonds.

Dominated? She instinctively shied away from the word and then forced herself to come back and look at it. No more lies. No more hiding. It may have been a benevolent dictatorship, but Richard *had* dominated her. He had not wanted her to have other ties; therefore, she had none.

Now being alone might be an advantage. She would be able to move more freely if everyone thought she was dead. The threat toward her as a target should also be lessened.

If she had been a target. Perhaps Kabler was right and she had been in the wrong place at the wrong time. Nothing else made sense.

But Tanek had not thought chance had anything to do with the attack on her.

Why should she believe Tanek but not Kabler? Tanek was a criminal and Kabler was a respectable officer of the law. The answer must lie in that overwhelming aura of quiet self-confidence surrounding Tanek. She should ignore it and listen to Kabler's more reasonable explanation.

She could not ignore it. Because she *did* believe Tanek. What did she care if he was a criminal? The only thing that mattered was that he knew about Gardeaux and Maritz and could help her to get to them. It might even be better for her that he was a criminal. Tanek didn't care about the law or the rules by which Kabler was bound. He offered her what Kabler had said was impossible.

Retribution.

"Kabler was here today," Joel said into the phone. "So much for you keeping him off my back."

"He got to Nell?" Nicholas asked.

"According to Phil, he cornered her in the gym. Kabler told her that she was no longer among the living."

"And her reaction?"

"She tore a strip off me. She wants to start the paperwork to come back from the dead."

"Talk her out of it."

"I'm going to let you do that. You'd better be here in three days. I'm releasing her."

"I'll be there."

"What, no argument?"

"Why should I argue? I knew I'd have to do battle with her. I just hoped time would dull her determination."

"Then you have a surprise coming. Tania says she's—well, you'll see for yourself." He paused before adding slyly, "By the way, I may have to replace your Junot as head of security. He obviously did a piss-ant job of keeping Kabler out of the clinic."

"I told him to let Kabler in."

"What?"

"Kabler's a shrewd man. I knew there was a probability he wouldn't be convinced Nell was dead and make the connection between St. Joseph's and your clinic in Woodsdale. I told Junot if he showed, he wasn't to be intercepted."

"Why in hell?"

"We had more to lose than gain. She was well enough to survive interrogation, and Kabler has bloodhound instincts. Once he gets on the trail, he doesn't stop until he trees the quarry. By letting him inveigle his way through Junot's security, we made him feel in control. He treed Nell and got what he wanted. Now he'll leave her alone."

"And what if he'd decided to take her from the clinic?"

"Why, then Phil and Junot would have stopped him." Nicholas's tone was gentle. "Discreetly, of course."

"Of course," Joel said caustically. "I don't suppose

it occurred to you to let me know what you'd planned. It's only my clinic and my security."

"Why worry you? It might not have happened. Kabler might have taken Nell's death at face value. Besides, Junot was very disturbed at even the pretense that his system could be breached. I nobly decided to take the entire blame on my shoulders."

Joel snorted.

"I refuse to have my motives maligned," Nicholas said. "I'm hanging up. I'll see you in three days."

Six

Nell wasn't in her room when Nicholas arrived at the clinic.

"She's working out in the gym," Joel said behind him. "Come on, I'll take you to her."

Nicholas turned. "I thought she'd be getting ready to leave. Have I got the wrong day?"

"I told her I'd release her at noon. She's not about to waste time lolling about when she could spend it exercising. The gym hasn't gotten so much use since that Russian gymnast was here."

Nicholas followed him from the room. "How is she doing?"

"Physically she couldn't be better. Mentally . . ."

"Yes?"

He shrugged. "She behaves normally. She's even started to occasionally joke with Phil. If she has bouts of depression, she doesn't let anyone know about it."

"Not even Tania? You said they were close."

"Not as far as I know."

"But you're afraid she's bottling everything up inside her?"

"No question, but there's nothing I can do to prevent it. We'll just have to hope she doesn't shatter at the wrong time." He glanced at Nicholas. "You haven't seen my handiwork yet. I think you'll approve."

"I know I will. You've always done good work."

"But Tania says Nell is exceptional. Of course, she's really complimenting herself." He opened the door of the gym. "She gave me the blueprint."

Nell was alone in the cavernous room, her back turned to them as she did chin-ups on the wooden bar against the opposite wall. She was dressed in white shorts and a loose sweatshirt, and she looked taller than he remembered. No, not taller. Sleeker, leaner, stronger. She hadn't heard them come in, and he could sense a concentration that was nearly tangible as she slowly raised and lowered herself.

"Christ, is she always this intense?" Nicholas asked softly.

"No, most of the time she's more intense. She must be having an off day." Joel raised his voice. "Nell."

"In a minute," she called. She finished the set and dropped lightly from the bar. She turned to face them.

Nicholas inhaled sharply. "What the hell blueprint did Tania give you?" he muttered.

"Helen of Troy. Unforgettable but vulnerable." He smiled with satisfaction as he watched Nell come toward them. "I did good, didn't I?"

"Good? You just may have created a monster."

"I don't think it's had any detrimental psychological effect. It doesn't seem to mean much to her. Tania said she needed a face to open new doors for her."

"It depends on what's on the other side of those doors." He stepped forward to meet her. "Hello, Nell. You're looking very fit."

Nell pulled the hand towel tucked into her shorts

and wiped the sweat from her face. "I *am* fit. I'm getting stronger every day." She turned to Joel. "You didn't tell me he was coming."

"He wants to talk to you." He smiled. "And you've done enough for this morning." He turned and headed for the door. "I'll see you after lunch."

"I wanted to talk to you too," she said as soon as the door closed behind Joel. "Mr. Kabler was here."

"I know. Joel told me. Did he disturb you?"

"No, he was very polite. He didn't even ask many questions."

Nicholas felt a flicker of surprise. "No? That's odd. Kabler usually digs like a ferret."

"He seemed to wish to reassure himself that you hadn't murdered me." She paused. "And to warn me you were a criminal and not to be trusted."

He lifted a brow. "Really?"

"I don't care if you're a criminal, but it does matter if I can trust you. Tania says you always keep your word. Do you?"

"Yes." He smiled faintly. "But don't endow me with any false virtues. I've always found honesty is good business."

"Honesty?"

"My version. I keep my word and I play by the rules of the game in motion. It's important that everyone know where they are with me."

"And where am I with you?" She met his gaze. "You're no philanthropist, and yet you've taken the trouble to bring me here. You've even tried to pay my bills. It might make sense if you thought I could be of use to you, but you're refusing my help."

"I don't need your help."

"Well, I need yours," she said bluntly. "Perhaps *need* is too strong a word. If you won't help me, I'll still find a way, but it would be faster if you'd help me." Her hands clenched into fists. "I won't be a goat for the slaughter and I won't get in your way. If you won't help me any other way, tell me what I need to know. I'll do the rest."

He was again aware of that terrible intensity she was emanating. "Do you know how many men Gardeaux surrounds himself with?"

"I know that one of them is Maritz."

"Who has killed more men than he can remember. No, I take it back, he remembers every one because he enjoys it. And then there's Rivil, who killed his own mother because she forbade him to join a teenage gang in Rome. Ken Brady considers himself a great lover. Unfortunately, he not only likes to screw women, he likes to hurt them. Gardeaux had to pay a tidy sum to keep them from putting Brady away for a long time when he decided to cut the nipples off his last mistress."

"Are you trying to shock me?"

"Dammit, I'm trying to show you that you're out of your depth."

"You're only showing me that you know Gardeaux and his men very well. Will you tell me more about them?"

He stared at her in exasperation. "No."

"Then I'll have to do it myself. I've already found a little about Gardeaux and Bellevigne."

"Kabler?"

"No, I went to the library and accessed Nexis."

"So that's why you were questioning Phil about computers. He'll be disappointed that you used him. He likes you."

"I like him too. But I needed to know." She started down the hall. "I have to shower and dress. Tania is picking me up in an hour to take me to Joel's house."

Dismissed. He was no longer of use to her, so she was discarding him. He found he was experiencing a mixture of annoyance and amusement. He followed her. "You're staying with Joel? He didn't tell me."

"Only for a few days."

And then she'd be heading for Bellevigne and straight into Maritz's arms. "Can you hit a target with a gun?"

"No."

"Can you use a knife?"

"No."

"Karate? Choi kwang-do?"

"No." She whirled on him, her eyes blazing. "Are you trying to make me feel inadequate? I *know* I'm inadequate. When I was struggling with Maritz, I had to throw a goddamn lamp at him. I've never felt that helpless in my life. When we were struggling on the balcony, he had no trouble overpowering me and tossing me over the side. He'd have trouble now. I'm getting stronger every day. And if strength isn't enough, then I'll learn whatever I have to learn."

"Not from me," he said grimly.

"Then I'll find someone else."

"I wasn't suggesting that you turn yourself into some kind of commando. I was trying to show you how futile you'd be against Gardeaux."

"You showed me. Don't worry, I won't ask you for anything again." She started to turn away, and then stopped. "Except one thing. Do you know where my daughter and husband are buried?"

"Yes, I believe your husband's mother requested the remains be brought back to his birthplace in Des Moines, Iowa."

"Jill too?"

"Yes. You seem surprised."

"Edna Calder cared nothing for Jill. Richard was her whole world, and there wasn't room in it for anyone else."

"Even you?"

"Particularly me." She paused. "Do you know what cemetery they're—" She broke off and had to start again. "I want to visit the graves. Do you know where they are?"

"I can find out," he said. "But I'm not sure it's a good idea."

"I don't care what you think," she said fiercely. "This is *my* business. I didn't get a chance to say good-bye. I have to do that before I do anything else."

He studied her. "Then that's what we'll do." He turned away. "Get dressed. I'll make the airline reservations and tell Joel that I'll deliver you to Tania tomorrow morning."

She stared at him, caught off balance. "Now?"

"Des Moines is only a short hop from here. You said that you needed to go."

"But you don't have to go with me."

"No, I don't, do I?" He walked away from her. "I'll make a few phone calls and pick you up in an hour."

PEACEFUL GARDENS.

The scrolled sign arched between the stone buttresses of the entrance of the cemetery. Why did cemeteries always use arches? Nell thought dully. Probably to bring to mind heaven and pearly gates.

"All right?" Nicholas asked as he drove the rental car through the gates.

"Yes." It was a lie. She had known she had to do this and had hoped that numbness would kick in. It had not. It was like one of her nightmares. Raw. Terrible. Inescapable.

He drew up before the gatekeeper's cottage. "Stay here. I'll be right back."

He was going to find out where the graves were located.

Jill.

He was getting back into the car. "Just over the rise."

A few minutes later he was guiding her through the graves. He stopped at a bronze marker. "Here."

JILL MEREDITH CALDER.

Here we go up, up, up
Up in the sky so blue . . .

Tanek's hand grasped Nell's elbow as she swayed. "She's not here, dammit," he said violently. "She's in your heart and memory. That's your Jill. She's not *here.*"

"I know." She swallowed. "You can let me go. I'm not going to faint." She straightened her shoulders and moved a few paces to a larger, more ornate marker.

RICHARD ANDREW CALDER

BELOVED SON OF EDNA CALDER.

No mention of Nell or Jill. In death Edna had reclaimed her son. Not that she had ever lost him. He had never really belonged to Nell.

Good-bye, Richard.

"Lots of flowers," Nicholas commented.

Richard's grave was heaped with bouquets of every flower imaginable. Fresh bouquets. Her gaze shifted back to Jill's grave. Nothing.

Damn you, Edna.

Nicholas's gaze was on her face. "Not a very loving grandmother."

"She's not her grandmother." She wouldn't let that bitch claim any part of Jill. "Jill wasn't Richard's daughter." She turned and walked away from the graves.

Good-bye, Jill. I'm sorry I had to leave it in her hands, baby. I'm sorry for everything. God, I'm sorry . . .

"I want flowers on her grave every week," she said jerkily. "Lots of flowers. Will you see to it, Tanek?"

"I'll see to it."

"I don't have much money now. I'll have to contact my mother's lawyers and see if I can—"

"Shut up," he said roughly. "I said I'd see to it."

His roughness was comforting whereas politeness would not have been. She did not have to pretend with Tanek. She doubted if he would have been fooled by pretense anyway. "I want to leave here. Is there a flight back this evening?"

"I've already booked two seats on the red eye."

"I thought we were going to stay until tomorrow morning."

"Not if I could get you out of here sooner. Good-byes suck. That's why I never say them anymore. I knew this was a mistake."

"You're wrong. I had to do this."

The anger gradually faded from his expression. "Maybe you did," he said wearily as he opened the car door. "What the hell do I know?"

They arrived back in Minneapolis after midnight and were met at the gate.

"Jamie Reardon, Nell Calder," Nicholas said. "Thanks for meeting us, Jamie."

"My pleasure." His astonished gaze was fixed on Nell's face. "Ah, you're a true beauty, aren't you?"

His Irish brogue was as soothing as his craggy features. She smiled. "Not a true beauty. Courtesy of Joel Lieber."

"Close enough." He fell into step with them. "If you'd drop into my pub, it's sure the boys would be making up poems about you."

"Poems? I thought poetry was a lost art."

"Not to the Irish. Give us a dollop of inspiration and we'll create a poem to stir the soul." He said to Nicholas, "I got a phone call from our party in London. He may have something for us. He said he wants you to call him."

"Right away." He stepped through the door leading to the parking lot. "We have to drop off Nell at Joel Lieber's."

"Not tonight," Nell said. "It's too late and they're not expecting me until tomorrow. I'll check into a hotel."

He nodded. "We'll get you a room at our hotel."

"It doesn't matter." London. She should probably question Tanek about the phone call. No, she was too exhausted and she doubted if he'd answer anyway. At last the numbness had set in, but it was too late. "Your hotel will be fine. Thank you."

Jamie opened the door of the car with a flourish. "You look a bit weary. We'll have you snug in bed within the hour."

"I am tired." She smiled with an effort. "Thank you for picking us up at such an inconvenient hour, Mr. Reardon."

"Jamie," he said. "It was no trouble. I always try to pick up Nicholas. He doesn't like cabs. You never know who's driving them."

A chill went through her. What must it be like to live in a world where everyone was suspect? "I see."

Nicholas glanced at her. "No, you don't see. You have no idea."

There was so much leashed ferocity in the words that it startled her. No arguments. She didn't think she could bear conflict just then. She leaned back in the seat and closed her eyes. "I don't feel like talking, if you don't mind."

"So polite. Gardeaux has excellent manners too. He'll use all the right words and then he'll tell Maritz to cut your throat."

"Nick, she doesn't appear to be . . ." Jamie said. "Don't you think you could wait a bit?"

"No," Nicholas said curtly.

She was being a coward. She forced her lids open. "Say anything you want to say."

He gazed at her for a moment. "Later." He turned away and looked out the window.

Nicholas arranged to get her a room three doors down from the suite he shared with Jamie.

After unlocking his door, Jamie turned with a smile. "Get a good night's sleep. Unfortunately, I doubt if I will. I'll be trying out the rhymes of the poem I'll lay at your feet come morning."

"He's just a poseur," Nicholas said as he nudged her down the hall. "He'll be asleep in ten minutes."

"He has no soul." Jamie sighed as he opened the door. "It comes from living with sheep and other coarse creatures."

Nell smiled. "Good night, Jamie."

Nicholas unlocked her door and preceded her into the room. He went about the room flicking on lights and adjusting the thermostat. "Did you eat any lunch before we left the clinic?"

"No."

He went to the telephone and punched in a number. "Vegetable soup. Milk. Fruit plate." He looked at her. "Anything else?"

"I'm not hungry."

"That will be all." He smiled crookedly as he replaced the receiver. "But you'll eat it anyway. Because you'll get weaker if you don't eat properly. Isn't strength your religion these days?"

"Yes, I'll eat it. Will you go now?"

"After room service leaves."

She smiled faintly. "No one knows who's pushing the cart either?"

He didn't answer.

She looked around the large, airy room. Gray carpet, elegant gold and dark green striped couch, gold damask drapes covering the French doors leading to the balcony.

Balcony.

She heard Nicholas's indrawn breath behind her. "I forgot all the rooms on this side have balconies. Do you want me to have your room changed?"

Oh, God, she wasn't ready for this after the day she'd had. She wanted to weep and hide under the bed. But she couldn't hide. All the hiding was finished.

"No, of course not." She braced herself and walked toward the glass doors. "Do they open?"

"Yes."

"I've been in a good many hotel rooms where the doors are kept locked. I guess it's supposed to keep people from having accidents, but it used to make Richard furious." She was talking quickly, saying anything to keep from thinking about what lay beyond those doors. "He loved the view from a balcony. He said it gave him a rush."

"He probably connected them with Peron or Mussolini waving at the populace."

"That's not kind."

"I don't feel kind. Dammit, stay away from that—"

She opened the door and the sharp wind struck her face. Not like Medas, she told herself. This balcony was tiny and utilitarian. The view wasn't like Medas either. No rocks or churning surf. She stepped close to the high railing and looked down at the lights and cars streaming like lightning bugs far below.

Two minutes. She would give herself two minutes and then permit herself to leave the balcony.

The music box was tinkling . . .

Here we go down, down, down . . .

"Enough." Nicholas grasped her arm and whirled her away from the railing and into the suite. He slammed the doors and locked them.

She drew a deep, shaky breath and had to wait a moment to steady her voice. "Such violence. Did you think I was going to jump?"

"No, I think you were testing yourself to see if you could stand the pain. You had to prove how strong you were. Wasn't standing over your daughter's grave enough? Why don't you just put your hand into an open flame?"

She smiled with an effort. "There wasn't one available."

"Not funny."

"No." She crossed her arms over her chest to stop the trembling. "I wasn't testing myself. You don't understand."

"Then make me understand."

"I was afraid. I've never been a very brave person. But I can't afford to be afraid any longer. The only way to get past being afraid is to face the thing you fear."

"Is that why you went to the graves?"

"No, that was different."

Sorry, Jill. Forgive me, baby.

Panic raced through her. She felt as if she were dissolving. She turned her back to him and said quickly, "I want you to leave now. I'm not afraid of that poor waiter from room service, and I promise I won't go out onto the balcony."

He put his hands on her shoulders.

She stiffened.

He turned her to face him. "I'm not leaving."

She stared blindly at his chest. "Please," she whispered.

"It's all right." He drew her into his arms. "You feel

as if you're made of glass. Let go. I'm not important. I'm just here."

She stood rigid, staring straight in front of her.

Here we go up, up, up . . .

She slowly let her head fall on his chest. His arms went around her. No intimacy. As he said, he was just there. Close. Living. Comforting.

She stayed that way a long time before she could force herself to step back. "I didn't mean to impose on you. Forgive me."

He smiled. "Those exquisite manners again. It was one of the first things I noticed about you. Did you learn them at your mother's knee?"

"No, my mother was a math professor and far too busy. My grandmother really raised me."

"She died when you were thirteen?"

She was surprised for a minute, until she remembered the dossier he had mentioned. "You have a good memory. That report you have on me must be very complete."

"It didn't mention that Jill wasn't Calder's child."

She automatically tensed before she remembered it didn't matter any longer. No Jill to protect. No parents to please. Why not tell him? He knew everything else about her. "No, it wouldn't. My parents were very clever in covering up that fact. They wanted me to have an abortion, but when I refused, they scrambled to put on a good front."

"Who was the father?"

"Bill Wazinski, an art student I met while I was attending William and Mary."

"You loved him?"

Had she loved him? "At the time I told myself I did. I was certainly in lust with him." She shook her head. "Probably not. We were both in love with life and sex and all those wonderful canvases we were sure were going to be masterpieces. It was the first time I'd ever lived away from my parents, and I was drunk with freedom."

"And this Wazinski wasn't willing to take responsibility?"

"I didn't tell him. It was my fault. I'd told him I was on the Pill. His father was a coal miner in West Virginia and he was studying on a scholarship. Why should I mess up both our lives? I went home to my parents as soon as I found out I was pregnant."

"An abortion would have been the easier course."

"I didn't want one. I wanted to finish college and get a job." She added bitterly, "My parents didn't agree. An unwed mother was an embarrassment they wouldn't tolerate."

"In this day and age?"

"Oh, they prided themselves on being free thinkers. But they worshiped self-control. Children must be born in the family structure. Life must always be civilized and carefully orchestrated, and I'd not behaved with the proper decorum by coming back to them pregnant. I should have gotten an abortion or married my baby's father."

"But Jill was born the year after you returned to Greenbriar."

"Seven months. I told you my parents covered my indiscretion well. I married Richard two months after I returned to Greenbriar. He was working as an assistant to my father and he knew I was pregnant." She smiled without mirth. "He couldn't have escaped knowing. I'd tossed the household into a turmoil. My parents weren't used to me fighting them over anything. He came up with a solution. I could keep the baby and he'd marry me and take me away."

"And what did he get in return?"

"Nothing." She met his gaze. "Richard wasn't the

climber you seem to think he was. I was desperate and
he offered to help me. He didn't get anything out of it
but another man's child and a wife who was sometimes
an embarrassment to him. I had the right background
for an executive's wife but certainly not the tempera-
ment."

"You seemed to be doing well that first night I met
you."

"Bull," she said impatiently. "A blind man could see
I was miserably shy and as socially adept as Godzilla.
Don't pretend not to remember."

He smiled. "I only remember thinking you were a
very nice woman." He paused. "And that you had the
most extraordinary smile I'd ever seen."

She stared at him, stunned.

A knock sounded on the door.

"Room service." He turned and moved toward the
door.

The waiter was a middle-aged woman of Latin de-
scent who bustled in with the tray. She quickly set out
the food on the table by the French doors and smiled
cheerfully as Nell signed the bill.

"Not very intimidating," Nell said dryly once the
waiter had left.

"You can never tell." Nicholas started across the
room. "Keep the door locked and don't answer to anyone but Jamie or me. I'll pick you up at nine tomorrow
morning."

The door closed behind him.

His sudden departure surprised her as much as his
other actions today.

"Lock it," Nicholas said on the other side of the
door.

She felt a twinge of annoyance as she crossed the
room and shot the bolt.

"Good."

He was no longer there. She didn't hear his footsteps, but she could no longer sense his presence. It was a relief to be rid of him, she told herself. She had not wanted him to go with her today. She had wanted to face that horror by herself.

And she had certainly not wanted to confide in him. If he had shown her pity, she would have instantly rejected him. Instead, he had been as impersonal and resilient as a pillow. A dynamic man like Nicholas wouldn't be complimented by the comparison to a pillow, she thought. Oh, well, perhaps it was just as well she had broken that long silence. When the words had tumbled out, it had seemed like stepping out of the shadows into sunlight. No shame. No hiding. Release.

She moved back toward the table. She didn't want the food, but she would eat anyway. Then she would shower and go to bed. She was so exhausted, maybe she would go right to sleep. Perhaps she would not even dream.

She deliberately sat down at the table in the chair facing the balcony and started to eat.

Seven

"I've found what you want," Nigel Simpson said as soon as he picked up the phone. "I know why the hit was made."

"Why?" Nicholas asked.

"Come here and I'll tell you. And bring two hundred thousand dollars in cash."

"No deal," Nicholas said flatly.

"I have to get away. I think someone is watching me." Nigel burst out, "It's your fault. You made me do this. I've been dealing with Kabler for over a year and no one's suspected me. It's not right that I have to give up everything and run away."

"The only payment you'll get from me is silence."

"I tell you, I need the money to—"

"Jamie tells me you have a Swiss account with the money Kabler has been funneling to you. I'm sure that's enough to start a new life in some tropical paradise."

There was silence at the other end of the line. "A hundred thousand dollars, and I'll give you the books I keep for Gardeaux."

"What good would they do me? You said yourself that they weren't incriminating."

"Unless you put them together with Pardeau's records. Then the picture becomes complete."

"Who is Pardeau?"

"François Pardeau, 412 St. Germain. My counterpart in Paris." Nigel's tone became sly. "You see how cooperative I am. That didn't cost you a penny."

"The records might not do me any good. I don't want Gardeaux behind bars."

"Kabler does. I could approach him."

"Don't try to play us against each other, Simpson. If you need money right away, you know Kabler's out. It takes time to cut bureaucratic red tape and get authorization for a bribe of that size."

"Do you want the books or not?"

"I want them. For fifty thousand, false passport and identity papers and safe escort out of England. Take it or leave it."

"It's not enough. I should—"

"If you try to get your own papers, Gardeaux will find out and smash you like a cat does a mouse."

Simpson was silent. "How soon?"

"It will take a day for Jamie to get the papers. I'll fly out of here tomorrow morning and be at your flat by midnight."

"No, don't come here. I don't want to be seen with you. Drop the money and papers in the poor box at St. Anthony's Church at ten o'clock day after tomorrow."

"Without the books and information? I'm afraid my charity doesn't extend that far."

"In the box will be a key to a locker in the Thompson's holiday tour bus station in Bath. Trust me."

"Bath is more than an hour's drive from London."

"It's the best I can do. There are no lockers at any station in London because of the IRA bombings."

"How convenient."

"I'm the one who'll be taking all the risk," he said shrilly. "What if I'm followed?"

"You will be. From the moment you pick up the money until I phone Jamie that the package in the locker is legitimate. After that he'll send a man to pick you up and see that you're safely on your way."

He hung up the phone.

"Books?" Jamie asked from his chair across the room.

"Simpson's running scared. He's offering to sell Gardeaux's books and the Medas information for a lump sum and safe passage."

"Why do you want the books?"

Nicholas shrugged. "I may not. It's a wild card. I have to access Pardeau's books in Paris to even make sense of Simpson's."

"Then why pay for them?"

"Sometimes a wild card comes in handy. God knows, we've never been this close to Gardeaux before." He added, "And I do want to know why Medas was hit."

"And I suppose you want me to get cracking about Simpson's papers?" He rose to his feet and strolled toward the telephone. "Captured once more in the toils of this pragmatic world. Too bad. I was just sitting here composing a deathless ode to our beauteous Nell's eyes."

Joel Lieber's house vaguely reminded Nell of one built by Frank Lloyd Wright that she had seen in a magazine. It was all clean modern lines and glass, subtly integrated into a setting of rocks, gardens, and a small waterfall issuing from a sparkling stream.

"It's beautiful," Nell said as she got out of the car.

"It should be." Nicholas led her toward the front entrance. "It's a house that beauty built."

"Tania says that Joel does a good deal of charity work."

"I'm not criticizing him. I'm a capitalist. Everyone has a right to reap the rewards of his labor."

"Hi, Nicholas. Good to see you."

Nell turned in astonishment to see Phil coming down the garden walk. He was dressed in jeans and a Bulls T-shirt and carrying a tiller. "What are you doing here?"

He smiled happily. "Nicholas thought I should stick around just to make sure you don't have a setback. In the meantime, Dr. Lieber's letting me work in his garden. I worked my way through college selling plants in a nursery. It's kind of nice being close to flowers again." He set off down the bank by the stream. "You need me for anything, you just call."

Nell turned to Nicholas. "You know I'm not going to have a setback."

"You can never tell." He changed the subject. "Joel said you wanted to start the paperwork to nullify your death. Why haven't you mentioned it to me?"

"Because I've changed my mind."

"Good. May I ask why?"

"I've decided it might be convenient. My new name will be Eve Billings. I'll need a driver's license and a passport in that name. Can you get them for me?"

"It will take a few days."

"And I'll need money to live. Will you open an account for me and make a cash deposit to see me through until I can access my own money? Of course, I'll write you an IOU."

"You're damn right you will," he said. "I may need to collect it from your estate if you persist in trying to get yourself killed."

"Right away?"

"I'll call and transfer funds to Joel's bank in the name of Eve Billings this morning. You'll receive the IDs by mail."

"Thank you. Kabler found me too easily. Do I have to worry about Maritz tracing me to the hospital?"

"No."

He spoke with absolute certainty. He must have plugged the hole, she thought. "What about records of my surgery?"

"Destroyed except for the ones Joel keeps here. I'll ask him to get rid of them too."

"Good." She rang the doorbell. "I know I said I wouldn't ask anything of you again. I promise this will be the last. Good-bye, Tanek."

"Don't sound so final. I'll be seeing you again. If you don't end up on a slab in—"

"You're here." Tania swung open the door, smiling broadly. "And Nicholas too. This is good. Come in and see what wonders I've wrought with Joel's house."

"Another time. I'm in a hurry." He smiled at Tania. "I have a plane to catch. See you."

Nell watched him as he walked toward the car. It was the first time he'd mentioned a trip. London?

"Come in." Tania was eagerly drawing her into the foyer. "I wish to show you —"

"Wonders," Nell finished for her. "The exterior is wonderful enough."

"But cold. Joel is a surgeon, and clean, efficient lines appeal to him. But inside you must have warmth. I tell him he cannot have a house that's as neat as one of his incisions." She drew her into the living room. "There must be excitement and color."

"You certainly have that." The chairs and sofas in the room were clean and contemporary but luxuriously upholstered in camel-colored fabric. Burgundy, beige, and orange occasional pillows were tossed everywhere. Stripes and florals and tapestries that should have clashed blended for a look that was exotic yet oddly homey. A cream Berber rug covered the oak floor that gave off a soft, warm glow. "It's really lovely."

"My grandmother used to say the hardest ground can be made soft if you use enough pillows." She made a face. "Well, she couldn't be profound all the time. But you have to admit she was right."

"Your Gypsy grandmother?"

She nodded. "You should have seen the house before I came. Danish modern and very cold." She gave a mock shudder. "Not good for Joel. He's a man who won't reach out to warmth unless it's thrust at him." She smiled cheerfully. "So I thrust it at him."

"It's very unusual. Have you thought of taking up decorating?"

She shook her head. "I'm going to the university in the fall, but I intend to study writing." She moved toward the door. "Come, I will show you your room. It's over the water, and I think you'll find the sound very soothing." She ran up a spiral staircase and threw a door open at the top of the stairs. "Is it good?"

More color—golds and rusts and scarlet, a study in autumn shades. A sleigh bed draped in deep hunter green. Ivy plants in brass containers, chrysanthemums standing tall and proud in a crystal vase. Richly bound leather books in a low bookcase. "Very good."

"I thought so," Tania said with satisfaction. "Blue is supposed to be soothing, but I knew you would respond to this. I had Phil pick the chrysanthemums this morning."

Nell was touched. "You've gone to a great deal of trouble. I won't be here long, you know."

"Long enough to enjoy my house," Tania said. "I

will leave you alone to rest a little before lunch and try on the clothes in the closet."

"What clothes?"

"The clothes I had sent from Dayton's the day you decided to so rudely abandon me."

Nell stared at her in bewilderment. "You never mentioned buying any clothes."

"What was I to do?" She started for the door. "I don't believe in wasting time, and I had nothing to do until you returned."

"Why didn't you tell me?"

"Why should I? You were very bad, and I wished to heap guilt upon you. Not let you think I managed very well on my own."

Nell found herself smiling as the door closed behind her. Tania was like a warm, unexpected breeze blowing aside any obstacle in its path.

She glanced at the closet. Later.

She moved toward the window. The waterfall was only fifty yards away, and the splash of water was as soothing as Tania claimed. Phil was kneeling by the stream, digging in a bed of hybrid yellow roses.

Richard had always given her yellow roses. He knew the little touches that pleased a woman and made her feel special. Sally Brenden had doted on him. But then, everyone had adored Richard.

Now he was gone. Why wasn't she mourning his passing?

Her grief at Jill's loss had devastated her to the extent that she could feel only a pale shadow of it when she thought of Richard's death. Had she not loved him? Had she convinced herself that gratitude and need were love? Oh, she didn't know. Perhaps she hadn't been angry that Richard's mother had not mentioned her on his tombstone because she hadn't felt she deserved it.

She had tried to give Richard the love he deserved, but only Edna had truly loved him.

Phil turned his head and glanced at the house before bending over the rosebushes again. He was checking to make sure she hadn't left the house. On guard to keep her from venturing into territory Nicholas regarded as his own. He needn't have worried. As Nicholas had pointed out, she wasn't ready to go up against Gardeaux and Maritz. She must be very sure of the outcome when exacting payment.

But her plans didn't include having to stay here under benevolent guard either. She had some thinking to do. She had a kernel of an idea brewing, but she would have to have a firm plan to follow before she was ready to remedy the situation.

He was being followed. Panic soared through Nigel.

He glanced behind him. No one in sight. His step quickened on the pavement. No sound behind him. Maybe he was mistaken.

No, dammit, he'd *felt* someone there since he'd left the church that evening.

Christine's flat was just ahead. He ran up the steps and buzzed.

Was that a shadow in the doorway across the street?

"Yes?" Christine said into the intercom.

"Let me in. Now!"

The door clicked. Nigel hurried in, then slammed the door shut behind him.

"What's wrong, luv?" Christine was leaning over the banister. Her lips parted in that lovely, malicious smile. "Are you that eager?"

"Yes." He'd been eager before he'd suspected he'd been followed. Christine was not unique, but he'd found few women as talented in her field. He'd wanted one more evening with her before he left London. Now he wondered if he should have found a hole and crawled into it until it was time to go back to St. Anthony's the next morning.

"Then come up and see me. I have something special planned for you tonight. A new toy to punish my bad boy."

His cock hardened painfully. A new toy. The dildo she'd used on him last time had nearly split him in half and made him come like a geyser. He glanced at the front door behind him. He had not actually seen anyone and, if there was anyone there, it might be more dangerous to leave than to stay. Christine's place was as safe as anywhere else. There were only two flats in the building, and Christine had mentioned the other tenant was out of the country.

"Come!" Christine ordered. "Stop dawdling, or I'll punish you for it."

Excitement gripped him. It was beginning. Soon he would be on his knees before her, lost in the dark heat. He eagerly started up the steps.

She was standing at the top of the stairs, naked except for four-inch stiletto heels, tall, voluptuous, commanding. She stepped back and strode toward the door of her apartment. "How many times must I tell you that you must obey at once?"

"I'm sorry. I deserve to be punished." He followed her into the apartment. "May I see it?"

"Kneel."

He instantly dropped to his knees before her.

"Very good." She spread her legs wider and stood, looking down at him. "Now what do you want to see?"

"The toy. The new toy."

Her hands tangled in his hair and jerked his head back. Pain shot through him. "Ask me nicely."

"Please, mistress, may I see the toy?" he whispered.

"Is that all you want? Just to see it? You don't want me to use it on you?"

"Will it hurt me?"

"Very much."

He was trembling, ready. He was always like this the first time, but he mustn't come until she granted him permission. "If it pleases you, I want you to use it on me."

"You're sure?"

He nodded.

"Then that's the way it will be." She smiled cruelly. "But I don't wish to dirty my hands with you. I'll let my friend show you the toy."

"Your friend? No one else—"

Pain tore through his back! Christ, what was it? A brand? The agony was too much, he couldn't bear it.

He clutched wildly at Christine's hips.

She stepped back and he toppled to the carpet.

"Too much . . ." he whimpered. "Take—it away."

Christine was looking at someone beyond him. "You promised me it would be quick and clean, Maritz. He's bleeding all over my carpet."

"Gardeaux will replace it."

"I want him out of here now. Finish it."

"No," Nigel whimpered. No one had been following him. Maritz had been there waiting for him.

"In a moment."

"Finish it or I'll tell Gardeaux you risked the hit because you wanted to enjoy yourself."

"Bitch."

He finished it.

The key was in the poor box.

Nicholas stared at it for a moment before thrusting

it into his pocket. It looked like any key. Simpson could have given him his door key for all Nicholas knew.

He placed the packet of cash and documents in the poor box and left the church.

He waved at Jamie in the Rolls-Royce cab parked across the street and got into his rental car.

He turned the car and headed for Bath.

"I have the books," Nicholas said into his cellular phone. "Maybe. They look authentic enough. I haven't had a chance to go through them yet. I'll check them out on the plane back to the States."

"I'm surprised," Jamie said. "I thought Simpson had tried a double cross and then turned squeamish."

"Why?"

"The darlin' man hasn't shown up to claim his prize."

"What?"

"He never came to St. Anthony's. What shall I do about the money? The poor box is emptied at eight every evening."

Nicholas thought about it. It was nearly five and the chances of Simpson being this late for the pickup were slender. Unless Gardeaux had stepped in.

But if Simpson had been killed, why did Nicholas now have the books? He couldn't believe Gardeaux wouldn't have squeezed the location of the books out of Simpson before he died.

Unless Gardeaux didn't know about Simpson's deal for the books. It was possible he had just discovered Simpson's sellout to Kabler.

"Did you hear me?" Jamie asked. "I said, what shall I do about—"

"I heard you. Stay there for another hour. If he

hasn't come, retrieve the money and papers and go check out his flat."

"And then?"

"Give him twenty-four hours. Watch his apartment, and make contact if you see him."

"It's a bloody waste of time. We both know what happened to the poor bastard."

"Twenty-four hours. I made a deal."

"Coffee, Mr. Tanek?"

He smiled at the stewardess and shook his head. "Later, perhaps."

He opened the first of the account books after she had moved down the aisle. He scanned it briefly. He didn't recognize any of the company names listed; they were probably coded. Arrows pointed to blank lines throughout each account.

Pardeau's portion to be inserted?

Even if he had Pardeau's books, it would probably take an accountant guru to decipher the numbers. He saw no reason at present to run the risk of tapping Pardeau. First, he wasn't sure the contents would be of value to him. Second, Gardeaux might not realize yet that Nicholas had the books, but he would soon discover they were missing. Pardeau would be watched and it would be best to wait until vigilance slacked.

Nicholas scanned the second book, found it much the same, and replaced it in his briefcase. He pulled the final nine-by-twelve manila envelope with the name Medas scrawled on the front.

He drew out the sheaf of papers. The first was the list of names Jamie had given him that day in Athens. He tossed it aside and turned to the second sheet.

He sat up straight in his seat. "Christ."

"I have to see Nell, Tania." Tanek strode into the foyer. "Where is she?"

"Hello to you too," Tania said as she closed the door.

"Sorry. Where is she?"

"She's already out of here. Gone."

He whirled to face her. "Gone? Where?"

She shook her head. "She spent three nights here and yesterday morning she was gone. She left a note." She went over to a table and opened the drawer. "A very nice note thanking us for our hospitality and saying she'd be in touch." She handed him the note. "As far as I can tell, she took no clothes except a few pairs of jeans and tennis shoes. So she must be coming back fairly soon."

"Don't count on it." He didn't know what the hell Nell would do. He scanned the note—warm, meticulously polite, and totally uninformative. "Did she get a packet in the mail?"

"Two days ago."

The IDs that would permit her to move freely. "Where's Phil?"

"In the garden." She frowned. "And you mustn't blame him. He already feels bad enough."

"I do blame him." He moved toward the door. "But I won't shoot him, if it's any comfort to you. I'll be right back."

Phil seemed as despondent as Tania had said he was and stiffened warily as Nicholas approached. "I know. I screwed up. But I did keep an eye on her," he said before Nicholas could speak. "I even slept in my car in the driveway."

"*Slept* seems to be the operative word."

Phil nodded glumly. "I didn't expect it. She seemed so content with Ms. Vlados."

Nicholas hadn't expected it either. Not this soon. He'd thought she'd need time to recover from that traumatic visit to the cemetery. "Okay. It's done. Have you tried to find her?"

Phil nodded. "Ms. Vlados said you'd deposited money for her at First Union under Eve Billings. I tracked her to the bank, where she made a withdrawal, and then to the train station. It was pretty easy. People remember that face."

"What was her destination?"

"Preston, Minnesota. She got off there and hired a rental car. She dropped the rental car off at O'Hare Airport in Chicago. I haven't been able to track her destination yet through the airlines. Those reservation centers like to keep confidential records, and it would take time to smooze around every airline gate at O'Hare to see if she'd been seen." He paused. "Of course, if I had access to a computer, I'd find a way to tap into the airlines' computer banks and—"

"She's trying to leave a false trail. She wouldn't use her name and she'd pay in cash. She had no valid credit cards."

Phil grimaced. "Bad luck."

"But she has a passport now." He thought about it. "There may still be a way. If she had a definite destination in mind, she might have phoned from the house and made arrangements. Did she go anywhere she might have used an outside phone?"

"She and Ms. Vlados went to the supermarket, but I drove them and carried the bags back to the house. She didn't make any calls."

"Come on." Nicholas strode to the house.

Tania met them in the driveway. "Well?"

"Phil needs a computer. Joel has one in the library, doesn't he?"

"Yes." She gazed at Phil skeptically. "But he babies that computer as if it were a pet puppy. He won't like it if anything happens to any of his programs."

"I'll take good care of it," Phil promised earnestly. "And I'll need it for less than thirty minutes."

"Joel's computer will be in excellent hands," Nicholas said. "Phil worships at the shrine of Microsoft."

"Who?"

"Never mind. Trust me. Joel's programs are safe."

She shrugged and led them back to the house. She nodded toward a door down the hall. "That's Joel's study."

"Do you have more than one telephone line in the house?" Phil asked.

Tania nodded. "Joel's phone in the study and the house phone."

"What are the numbers?"

She rattled off both numbers. "Shall I write them down?"

"No, I'll remember. I'm good at numbers." He hurried down the hall toward the study.

"What's he going to do?" Tania asked.

"Tap into telephone company records and find out what numbers Nell called before she left here and to whom they belong."

"Isn't that illegal?"

"Yes."

"What if he's caught?"

"He won't be. This is a piece of cake for him. Phil could tap CIA classified records and not be caught." He changed the subject. "Where did Nell sleep? I want to see her room."

"You won't find anything. I've already cleaned it."

"I want to see it."

She led him upstairs and threw open the door. She watched him as he moved around the room. Checking the pad beside the bedside telephone.

"There wasn't any note on the pad."

He raised the pad to the light. No imprint. He went to the closet and opened the door. "You said she didn't take any luggage?"

"A small duffel. What are you looking for?"

He rifled through the clothes. "Anything." He closed the closet door and glanced around the room. A pile of magazines was stacked neatly on the shelf of the nightstand. "Were all those here when she came?"

"The magazines? Most of them. Nell picked up a few at the supermarket."

He sat down on the bed and lifted the stack. "Which ones?"

"I'm not sure. I didn't look at them." Tania moved toward the bed and watched him leaf through the magazines. "The *Cosmo* is new. I don't recognize the *Newsweek* either. I don't see any other—What's wrong?"

"I take it this is new too?" He pulled out a thin magazine from the bottom of the pile. "It's not exactly what most hostesses supply their guests."

"Soldier of Fortune?" Tania frowned. "I've never seen that magazine before. What is it?"

"A charming how-to magazine on the ways and means of becoming a mercenary. It's practically the bible of survivalists and would-be mercenaries."

"But why would Nell buy it?" Her eyes widened. "You think she wants to hire someone?"

"I don't know what the hell she wants to do." He started through the magazine page by page, checking each one for turned-down corners or written notes. He ran across nothing until he got to the list of want ads in the back. There was a slight crease in the middle of the page, as if it had been folded back.

"Have you found something?" Tania asked.

"A page that must have a hundred ads on it," he said in exasperation. It was a mixed bag of personal ads. Ex-soldiers trying to contact old buddies, weapon sales. Why couldn't the blasted woman have circled one of them?

"I think I've found it." Phil stood in the doorway with a slip of paper in his hand. "Everything that popped up on the office phone looked pretty standard, but these three numbers on the house phone seemed weird." He handed Nicholas the paper. "They're all survivalist camps. One is outside Denver, Colorado, one is near Seattle, Washington, and the last one is just outside Panama City, Florida."

"What's a survivalist camp?" Tania asked.

"It's a training camp for a group of people who think that eventually America will be attacked or become a police state and that they can survive only by being skilled with weapons and in guerrilla warfare." Nicholas was running his finger down the column in the magazine. "It's usually run by ex-mercenaries, Seals, or military types who want to pick up a few bucks training weekend warriors." All three names were on the page, but there was no indication which one she might have chosen. "Which one of these camps did she call last, Phil?"

"Seattle."

"You actually think Nell may have gone to one of these places?" Tania asked.

"Yes."

"Why?"

"Because she's a stubborn, stupid woman who's trying her best to get herself killed." And because he had opened his damn mouth and made her feel inadequate to the task she had set herself.

"I don't think she wants to die," Tania said quietly.

"Not anymore. She's beginning to come alive again. And she's not stupid. She must have a good reason for this. Is there great danger for her?"

"It depends on who's running the camp. Some of them are farces, others are run by fanatics who have no compunction about driving potbellied stockbrokers into having heart attacks to 'toughen' them."

"If they're so macho, they won't accept Nell."

"If she's lucky. But, thanks to Joel, Nell is a choice morsel and they may accept her for less than their usual reasons."

"Rape?"

"Possibly."

"Can you call these places and ask if they've seen her?"

"Membership is confidential." They would all have to be checked out. Which was the most likely? Nell was trying to get away from surveillance. Seattle was the most distant and Seattle was the last number she had called. "I'll take Seattle. Phil, you go to Denver."

Phil nodded. "Shall I call Jamie and tell him to take Panama City?"

"Jamie's still in London. Maybe we'll get lucky." He stood up and brushed a kiss on Tania's forehead. "I'll be in touch. I'll check back if she's not in Seattle and see if she's contacted you."

"Please." Tania followed him from the room and down the steps. "I'm very worried about her, Nicholas."

"You have reason to be."

Eight

Obanako, Florida

"We don't accept women in our training programs, little lady." Colonel Carter Randall's deep southern accent twanged unpleasantly on Nell's ears. "So you can get your little feminist butt out of here."

Nell brushed at the fly that had been buzzing around her face since she had entered the office. She was sweating and the humidity was like a slap in the face. Would it have endangered the man's macho image to turn on the air-conditioning? "I'm not a feminist. Or maybe I am. I don't know what that is anymore." She met his gaze. "Do you?"

"Oh, yes, I know. We've had a few of those dyke broads come down here begging us to teach them how to be real men."

"And did you teach them?"

He smiled nastily. "No, but some of the boys taught them how to be real women."

He was trying to scare her. He was succeeding, but she mustn't let him see it. He was the type of man who relished domination. She asked calmly, "You raped them?"

"I didn't say that, did I?" He leaned back in his chair. "But we have no quarters for women here at Obanako. You'd have to occupy a bunk in the barracks."

"I'm willing to do that."

"So were those dykes. They changed their mind after the first night."

"I won't change my mind." She wiped her moist hands on her jeans. She was no longer sure whether she was perspiring from nervousness or heat. "Why won't you accept women? Our money is just as good."

"But your backbone isn't." His gaze lingered on her breasts. "We accept women . . . in their place. A woman should keep to what she does well."

She smothered her resentment. She would get nowhere with this chauvinist bastard by getting angry.

But it might help if she could make *him* angry, she thought suddenly.

"I saw those big, strong men in the field outside trying to scale that wooden barrier. They didn't seem to be doing too well. Are you afraid a woman could show them up?"

He stiffened. "This is only the first week of training. By the end of the month they'll be over that wall in a flash."

"Maybe."

A flare of temper lit his face. "You're calling me a liar?"

"I'm saying I have doubts that a man who can't maintain discipline in his barracks can make soldiers out of soft recruits in a few weeks."

"I have excellent discipline here in Obanako."

"Is that why you permit women to be raped? That's not military discipline, that's barbarism. What kind of officer are you?" Before he could answer, she went on.

"Or perhaps you're not really an officer at all. Did you buy that uniform in an army-navy store?"

"I was a colonel in the Rangers, you bitch."

"How long ago?" she scoffed. "And why aren't you still in the army instead of hiding out in these swamps? Did you get too old to cut it?"

"I'm forty-two years old and I can run rings around any man in this outfit," he said through his teeth.

"I wouldn't doubt it. Those poor bastards can't even get over that barrier. It must make you feel very superior to know that you're stronger than them."

"I didn't mean the trainees, I meant—" He broke off, struggling with rage. "You think that barrier is easy to scale? It's thirty feet high. Maybe you could do better, little lady."

"Possibly. We can only see. If I get over it, will you accept me into the program?"

His smile dripped malice. "If you get over it, we'll all be very happy to accept you into our midst." He stood up and gestured to the door. "After you."

She hid her relief as she followed him from the office and down the steps. So far, so good.

Maybe.

As she drew closer, the wooden barrier loomed much taller than she had thought and appeared slick with mud from the boots of the men who had been trying to scale it.

"Step aside, men," Randall said as he grabbed one of the ropes fastened at the top of the wall. He tossed it to Nell. "Let the little lady take her turn."

She paid no attention to the hoots and grins of the men. She grasped the rope and began to climb. She realized at once it was a different proposition from clambering up the rope suspended from the ceiling of the gym. If she tried to use her knees, the rope swung her against the wood wall. The only way was to use her feet as purchase against the wall and pull herself up.

Four feet.

Her soles slipped on the muddy surface and she crashed against the wall.

Pain.

Laughter from the men below.

Pay no attention to it. Hold on. Don't let go.

She swung away from the wall and braced her feet against the wood again.

Seven feet.

She slipped again. The rough rope burned her hands as she slid down three feet before she caught herself.

"Don't worry," Randall called mockingly. "We're right here ready to catch you, sweet thing."

Laughter again.

Close them out. She could do it. Ignore the pain. One step at a time. Close it all out. There was only the rope and the wall.

She began to climb again.

Three steps up.

She slipped and rammed against the wall.

Four steps.

How many more?

It didn't matter. You could do anything if you took it minute by minute.

It took ten more of those agonizing minutes before she reached the top of the wall and straddled it. She looked down at Randall and the men. She had to wait a moment before she could steady her breathing. "I made it, you son of a bitch. Now keep your promise."

He wasn't pleased, but he was no longer laughing. None of them were laughing. "Get down from there."

"You promised to accept me if I made it. An officer always keeps his word, doesn't he?"

He gazed coldly up at her. "Why, little lady, we'll

be delighted to have you. We're going out on maneuvers tomorrow, and I know you'll just love that."

Which meant he intended to make her life miserable. She started down the other side of the barrier. He was waiting when she reached the ground. "This is Sergeant George Wilkins. He'll get your gear. Did I mention he doesn't like the idea of women in the military?"

She nodded at the short, powerfully built sergeant.

Wilkins said, "A baby could have crawled up that wall. It ain't nothing next to the swamps." He turned and strode away from her.

"Better catch up," Randall said genially. "And if I were you, I'd bandage those hands. All kind of fungus and germs live in the swamp. We sure wouldn't want you to catch anything, little lady."

For the first time, she became aware that her palms were torn and bleeding. The wounds didn't bother her nearly as much as that patronizing nickname. "I try to be a lady, but I'm *not* little." She set off after Wilkins.

Silence fell on the barracks when she followed Wilkins into the long room an hour later.

"That's your bunk." The sergeant gestured to a cot beneath one of the screened windows. "While you're here."

He turned and left.

She tried to ignore the men in the room as she dumped the clothes and gear down on the cot. *Tried* was the operative word. She could feel their eyes on her as if they were brands. What was she doing here? she wondered desperately. This was crazy. There had to be some other way to accomplish what had to be done.

Ignore them. There might be other ways, but nothing as quick as the one she had chosen. She had made a plan and must keep to it.

She sorted out the clothes and then turned to the M16 and pistol Wilkins had issued her. Wasn't she supposed to clean them or something? All the war movies she had ever seen had a scene where some poor slob was punished for not cleaning his rifle.

"Can I help you?"

She stiffened and turned around.

Why, he was only a kid. A gangly boy, not over seventeen. Freckles bridged his hooked nose, and he was smiling tentatively, almost shyly.

"I'm Peter Drake." He sat down on her cot. "I was out there watching you climb the wall. I don't think the colonel liked it when you reached the top. I liked it. I like it when people win." He smiled with childlike pleasure.

Childlike. As she stared at him she suddenly suspected how apt that term was. Randall must be some kind of fiend to accept a boy like him. "Do you?" she asked gently. "Winning does feel good."

He frowned. "I couldn't get up the wall. The sergeant was angry with me. He doesn't like me."

"Then why don't you leave this place?"

"My daddy wants me here. He was a soldier like Colonel Randall. They wouldn't take me in the regular army. He says this place will make a man of me."

She felt sick.

"And what does your mother say?"

"She's not there anymore," he said vaguely. "I'm from Selena, Mississippi. Where did you come from?"

"North Carolina. You don't sound as if you're from the South."

"I don't stay there much. He sends me away to schools." He began toying with the strap of her backpack. "I don't think the colonel likes you either. Why?"

"Because I'm a woman." She grimaced. "And because I made it up the wall."

He gazed around the barracks. "Some of these men don't like you either. Colonel Randall came here a few minutes ago and told them it was all right with him if they hurt you."

It was no more than she expected.

He smiled. "But I'll help you. I'm not very smart, but I'm strong."

"Thank you, but I can manage by myself."

His face clouded. "Maybe you think I'm not strong enough because I couldn't get up the wall?"

"That's not it. I'm sure you're strong enough to do anything you want to do." He was still staring at her with that hurt expression. She could not involve this boy in her struggles, but she felt as if she had kicked a puppy. "Perhaps you could help me by telling me about the men here. That would help a lot."

"I don't know. They don't talk to me much."

"Which ones do you think might hurt me?"

He nodded at once at a heavyset, balding man four bunks down. "Scott. He's pretty mean. He's the one who calls me Dummy."

"Anyone else?"

"Sanchez." He glanced uneasily at a small, wiry Latino who was staring at them with an unpleasant smile, and then nodded at a sandy-haired man in his twenties. "Blumberg. They started to touch me in the shower, but they stopped when Scott came."

"Scott stopped them?"

"No, but they didn't want him to know." He swallowed. "They said . . . later."

If they were homosexuals, she might not have to worry about Sanchez and Blumberg. No, rape was a crime of violence, not passion, and they had been willing to victimize a helpless boy. "I think you should leave here, Peter."

He shook his head. "Daddy wouldn't like it. He says I'm too soft. He said I needed to learn to take it."

Take rape and abuse? He must have known what Peter would face in this macho hellhole. She smothered a flare of anger. She could do nothing now to help Peter. She might not even be able to help herself. "Your daddy is wrong. This is no place for you. Go home."

"He'd only send me back." He added simply, "He doesn't want me there."

Dammit. She didn't need this. She didn't want to feel this melting pity. She stared at him in helpless frustration before turning away. "Do you know anything about guns?"

He brightened. "They taught us about the rifle the first day. We have target practice every morning."

"What about the pistol?"

"A little. I know how it's put together and how to load it."

She sat down on the bed beside him. "Show me."

"Have you heard from her?" Tanek asked as soon as Tania picked up the phone.

"Not a word. She's not in Seattle?"

"No, and Phil says she's not in Denver either. We guessed wrong."

"You think she may be in Florida?"

"I don't know." He rubbed the back of his neck. "Maybe she was laying another false trail. She could be anywhere."

"What are you going to do?"

"What else? I'm catching a plane for Florida in thirty

minutes. I should be at Obanako by midmorning. I'm
sending Phil back to your place in case she shows up
there."

"That's not necessary. I'll be here."

"It's necessary," he said grimly. "When she surfaces,
she's not going anywhere until I talk to her."

They were coming.

Nell's muscles locked beneath the blanket as she
heard the stirring in the darkness. She had been waiting
for this moment for hours.

They weren't trying to be quiet about it. Why
should they? No one would come to help her.

Except Peter. Stay asleep, Peter. Don't let them hurt
you.

They were closer. Four shapes in the darkness. Who
was the fourth man? It didn't matter. They were all the
enemy.

"Turn on the lights. I want to see her face when I
ram it into her."

Light.

Scott. Sanchez. Blumberg. The fourth man was
older, with a nondescript face and thinning hair.

"She's awake. Look, boys, she's been waiting for
us." Scott stepped closer. "We don't like dykes who
show us up, do we?"

"Go away."

"We can't do that. We want to show you how well
we can climb. I figure we'll climb off and on you so
many times, you'll be bowlegged by morning." He
moistened his lips. "Now, be real quiet and do what
we tell you. We don't like women dressed up like soldiers. It kind of turns us off. Strip."

"Leave her alone," Peter said.

He was sitting on the edge of his bunk, looking more

fragile and gawky than before in his khaki undershirt and shorts.

"Shut up, Dummy," Scott said without looking at him.

"You shouldn't hurt her. She didn't do anything to hurt you."

"It's up to her if she gets hurt. All she has to do is what we tell her and she'll have a real good time," Sanchez said.

"Go *away*," Nell repeated.

Peter was beside her bed. "Don't hurt her."

He was afraid, she realized. She could see the muscle jerking in his cheek, the slight tremor of his hands. "Go back to bed, Peter."

"Maybe Dummy wants to dip his wick too," Scott said. "Naw, he's not man enough."

"You think it makes you more of a man to rape a woman?" she asked.

"You'll see." He reached down and jerked the blanket off her.

She lifted the pistol she'd been cradling and pointed it at his crotch. "I only see that you'll no longer have a penis if you don't leave me alone."

He took an instinctive step back. "Shit."

"We'll rush her," Sanchez said. "We'll take that gun away from her and stuff it in her cunt."

"Yes, you could rush me," Nell said, trying to keep her voice steady. "Why don't you, Scott? I might not be able to shoot all of you. Of course, the first shot would make a eunuch of you and the second would be for Sanchez. After that I'd be in a hurry and have to aim for a broader target, like a stomach or chest."

"She won't do it," Blumberg said. "It would be murder."

"And murder is so much worse than rape." Nell's hand tightened on the gun. "I don't think so."

"They'd put you away and throw away the key."

"They'd try." She met his gaze and then looked at each man in turn. "But I'd do it. I won't be hurt or stopped. You're getting in my way and I can't allow that to happen. Touch me and I'll blow you away." Oh God, she sounded just like a grade-B movie.

Scott's eyes widened. He whispered, "You're fucking crazy."

"Possibly."

He backed away from her.

"You're going to let her buffalo you?" Sanchez said.

"She's not aiming at your dick," Scott said through his teeth.

"I am now." Nell shifted the barrel.

Sanchez blinked.

"You said it would be easy," the fourth man muttered.

"Shut up, Glaser," Scott said.

"You didn't tell me she was going to be like this." Glaser stalked away from the cot.

"We'll come back later. She can't stay awake all night." Scott smiled malevolently at Nell. "Close your eyes and we'll be on you."

He reached up and turned out the light.

She inhaled sharply. She suddenly felt alone and vulnerable.

Scott's voice came out of the darkness. "Took you off guard, didn't it? You can't keep up your watch forever. What you going to do once we're in the swamp? You think Wilkins is gonna care?"

"I doubt if you're going to be in the mood for rape while we're wading through the bayou."

She heard a muttered curse.

They were moving away, she realized with relief. It was too soon to relax, but the immediate danger was over. She'd been so afraid. She was still afraid, shaking in the darkness.

"I'll watch out for you," Peter said.

She had almost forgotten the boy. "No, go to sleep. Tomorrow will be hard. You'll need your strength."

"I'll watch out for you," he repeated stubbornly. He sat down on the floor beside her cot and crossed his legs.

"Peter, please don't do—" She broke off. She had no intention of going to sleep herself, but it was clear she couldn't convince him. Oh, well, it would only be a few hours until dawn.

"I was scared," Peter said suddenly.

"So was I."

"You didn't show it."

"Neither did you," she lied.

"I didn't?" He sounded pleased. "I thought Scott might know. He's like my daddy. He knows things like that."

"And your father tells you that he knows them?"

"Sure. He says a man has to face his faults. He said he'd never have become mayor of Selena if he hadn't faced his faults and corrected them."

She was beginning to detest Peter's faceless father. "Your father couldn't have been braver than you were just now. He would have been proud of you."

There was a silence. "No, he's never proud of me. I'm not smart."

The bald simplicity of the response caused pity to wrench through her. "Well, I was proud of you."

"You were?" he asked eagerly. "I was proud of you too." He paused. "That means we're friends, doesn't it?"

She wanted to push him away. She didn't want his help or the responsibility he represented. He had allied himself with her for those bullies to see and might suffer for it later. She didn't want to bear that guilt.

It was too late. She couldn't turn him away. "Yes, that's what it means."

"And we really showed them, didn't we?"

She sighed. "We really did."

"Eve Billings? I don't know anyone by that name," Randall said blandly. "And we don't accept women here at Obanako, Mr. Tanek."

Nicholas tossed down on the desk one of the pictures Tania had given him. "She might be using another name."

"Nice-looking woman." Randall pushed the photo away. "But I still haven't seen her."

"I find that very odd. She rented a car at the Panama City airport." He flipped open his notebook. "And the license number of the Ford in the parking lot in back of your office is the same."

Randall's smile disappeared. "We don't like people nosing around our camp."

"I don't like people lying to me," Nicholas said softly. "Where is she, Randall?"

"I said she wasn't here." Randall gestured expansively. "Look around. You won't find her."

"That will be unfortunate . . . for you."

Randall rose to his feet. "Are you threatening me?"

"I'm telling you that I want her back and that you won't like the trouble I cause if you don't produce her."

"We're used to trouble here. It's what we train these men to face."

"Cut the crap. The authorities in Panama City don't like you parked on their doorstep, and they'd jump at a chance to close you down for illegal activities."

"What illegal activities?" he said, outraged. "No one touched her, dammit."

"Kidnapping."

"She came to me. Hell, she forced herself on me. She'll tell you herself."

"And I'll tell everyone you kidnapped her and then brainwashed her. It will make a great story for the tabloids." Nicholas smiled. "What do you think?"

"I think you're a son of a bitch." He added sulkily, "Who is she to you? Your wife?"

"Yes," he lied.

"Then you should keep the bitch home and out of my hair."

"Tell me where she is and I'll be glad to take her off your hands."

Randall was silent and then smiled maliciously. "Why not?" He opened the desk drawer and pulled out a map and unrolled it. "She's on maneuvers. She wanted to prove how tough she could be. I can't tell you where she is right now, but she'll be here at nightfall." He stabbed his finger at a point on the map. "They always bed down at the same place. Cypress Island. You should be grateful to me. She's going to be real glad to see you after the day she'll have." His smile broadened. "But you may not be so happy to see her after you finish wading through the swamp to get to the island."

"There's no other access?"

"It's in the middle of the swamp. The closest road is two miles away." Randall tapped a line on the map. "See?"

"I see you're entirely too pleased with yourself."

"You could always stick around here and wait for them to get back. It will only be another four days."

Nicholas took the map and turned to leave.

"Have a nice trip. Give my best to the little lady."

Randall was beginning to annoy him. He stopped in midstride. No, he didn't have the time. Too bad.

He left the office.

"Keep up, Billings," Wilkins said as he pushed through the hip-deep water. "You're lagging behind. We ain't going to wait for you."

Nell ignored the jab. She wasn't falling behind; there were four men trailing her.

"Anyone who falls back gets left for the alligators."

Another fear tactic. She tried not to let him see that it was working. She had caught a glimpse of one of those horrific beasts a few hours earlier.

"I'll stay with you," Peter whispered from behind her. "Don't be afraid."

She *was* afraid. Afraid and exhausted and wanting nothing more than to be away from this eerie place. She had been in mud-clouded water for almost seven hours. The straps of her backpack were cutting into her shoulders, and she—

A silent shape undulated through the water beside her.

Snake.

She hated snakes.

"Keep moving, Billings."

She pulled her gaze away from the menace just below the surface and pushed through the water. One step at a time. One minute at a time. She could make it. No nightmare could last forever.

Except one.

Nicholas parked the rental car at the side of the road and rifled through his carryall on the seat beside him. He drew out his knife and a white handkerchief, tied the handkerchief around his forehead to keep back his hair, and stuffed the knife into the waistband of his jeans. Not exactly the approved attire for trekking through the swamp, but it would have to do.

He got out of the car and looked down sourly at the yellow water on the far side of the road. According to Randall's map, this was the closest he could get to Cypress Island without venturing into the swamp. He bent down and retied his tennis shoes tighter. He'd be lucky if he got through that mud and fetid water without losing one of them.

He hated swamps. It would have been too much to ask for Nell to have chosen a nice, clean mountain survival camp like the one in Washington. No, she had to plunge into a hot, muggy marsh crawling with mosquitoes and alligators and two-legged predators like Randall. He wanted to strangle her.

He gritted his teeth as he jumped into the water and started into the swamp.

"It seems we have a small problem." Wilkins smiled as he waded back toward them. "I need a volunteer."

Nell gazed at him dully, barely comprehending his words.

"Who's it going to be?"

She waited for him to turn to her.

His gaze fell on Peter. "You volunteer, don't you, Drake? Good. You're just right for the job. Young and quick. Go up front to the head of the column."

"What do you want me to do?"

"Just a little disposal problem. Our way is being blocked."

"Okay." He started toward the front of the column.

She stiffened warily. Young and quick. Why would he have to be quick? She hurried after Peter.

Dear God.

She stopped in her tracks.

The snake was draped like a colorful garland on the lowest branch of the cypress in front of them. They wouldn't be able to pass beneath the tree without brushing against it.

"Want to get a good view?" Wilkins asked beside her. "Get rid of the snake, Drake."

"Wait." She moistened her lips. "What kind of snake is it?"

"Just a little milk snake."

"Why don't we just go around it?"

"Good soldiers don't run away from problems, they solve them."

Milk snake. Memory was stirring. There was another snake almost identical to the milk snake. Only the layering of the stripes was different. She vaguely remembered a doggerel verse her grandfather had told her to tell them apart.

But she couldn't remember the other snake or the verse.

"Go get it, Drake," Wilkins said.

He stepped forward.

Coral snake. The other reptile the milk snake resembled was the deadly coral.

"Stop!"

Peter looked over his shoulder and smiled. "Don't worry, I used to have a pet snake when I was a kid. You just grab them behind the head and they can't bite you."

"Don't do it, Peter. It might be poisonous. The milk snake and the coral look a lot alike."

"It's just a little milk snake. See, the yellow stripes next to the red. That means it's harmless." Wilkins's gaze narrowed on Peter's face. "Go on, kid."

Peter started toward the snake.

Red next to black . . .

Why couldn't she remember that verse?

"Easy." Peter was crooning at the snake. "I'm not going to hurt you, pretty thing. I just have to get you out of the way."

His voice was almost affectionate, she realized with a chill. He'd probably be stroking the snake in another minute.

Wilkins was smiling as he watched.

The sergeant doesn't like me.

But Wilkins wouldn't deliberately endanger a child like Peter, would he? Just because he held Peter in contempt? Maybe the snake was harmless.

Or maybe Wilkins was mistaken.

Red on black . . .

"No!" She pushed Peter out of the way and lunged forward. She caught the snake behind the head and hurled it away from her with all her strength. The snake splashed into the water ten feet away.

"You shouldn't have done that," Peter said reproachfully. "The sergeant said it was my job."

"Shut up," she said through her teeth. It probably had been a milk snake, but she hadn't been able to take the chance. And now she was going to be sick. She could still feel the clammy coldness of the snake's scales on her palm. She watched dazedly as the snake cleaved swiftly through the water away from them.

"The kid's right," Wilkins said stolidly. "It wasn't your job, Billings."

"You wanted a volunteer." She tried desperately to control her shivering as she started again through the water. "I volunteered."

"You didn't have to be so rough," Peter said reproachfully as he fell in beside her. "You might have hurt it."

Was that trailing moss or another snake on the branch of the tree up ahead? Just moss. "I'm sorry."

"My snake was green. Not pretty like that one. Yellow and red and black—what's wrong?"

"Nothing."

It wasn't true. She had just remembered that bit of verse.

Red on black, venom lack
Red on yellow, kill a fellow.

Nine

They reached Cypress Island an hour before sunset. It was more of a moss-covered sandbar than an island, but that didn't matter. It was dry ground, and it looked wonderful to Nell as she staggered out of the water.

"Hello," Tanek said.

She stopped short in shock.

He was sitting beneath a cypress tree on the mossy ground. "You'll forgive me if I don't get up. I'm not feeling very polite at the moment. You might say I'm even a little irritated with you."

He was more than irritated, she thought warily. He looked muddy and wet and extremely bad-tempered. "What are you doing here?"

"I could ask the same of you."

Wilkins shoved her aside. "You ain't got no business here. Who are you?"

"It seems I'm not the only one who isn't feeling polite." Tanek rose to his feet. "You are?"

"Sergeant George Wilkins."

"Nicholas Tanek." He nodded at Nell. "I've come to get the lady."

Wilkins frowned. "Randall sent you?"

"He told me where you were."

"She's under my command. She can't go any-where," Wilkins said, to Nell's surprise. "I've no writ-ten orders to release her to you."

"Christ."

"I'm not going with you," Nell said.

Tanek drew a long breath, and she could almost see him counting. He turned and moved away from the column. "I need to talk to you."

"She doesn't have time for talk." Wilkins's jaw set belligerently. "She has to do her part to set up camp."

Tanek shot him a look. He said softly, "I'm talking to her. Don't push it."

Wilkins hesitated and then shrugged. "Talk all you like, but she's not leaving." He turned away and barked, "Scott. Come with me."

"Is everything all right?" Peter frowned uneasily.

"Fine," Nell said over her shoulder as she followed Tanek. "I'll be right back."

Tanek whirled on her as soon as they were out of earshot. "This is crazy. What the *hell* are you doing here?"

"It's necessary."

"It's dangerous."

"You said that I was no match for Maritz and Gar-deaux."

"I know what I said. And wading around in a swamp is going to make you more of a match for them?"

"Maybe it will help. I'm learning other things. I'd never touched a gun before yesterday."

He stared at her in frustration. "Look at you." He rubbed his hand on her cheek and wiped away a muddy smudge. "You're sopping wet and muddy and you're going to keel over any minute from exhaustion."

"No, I won't."

His lips tightened. "No, you won't. You'll just keep on going until there's nothing left of you."

"That's right." She stared into his eyes. "You won't help me get Gardeaux and Maritz. I have to do it myself. That's why I'm here."

He didn't speak for a moment and she could feel his anger and exasperation vibrating between them like a living entity. "Damn you," he said softly. He turned away. "Get rid of that rifle and your backpack. You won't need them anymore. You're coming with me."

"I told you that I'm staying here."

"I'll help you get them," he said harshly. "That's what you want, isn't it?"

A leap of excitement tore through her. "Yes, that's what I want. You'll give me your promise?"

"Oh, yes, even to the point of staking you out for Gardeaux. That should make you happy."

"It does." She slipped the rifle from her shoulder, tossed it on the ground, then removed the backpack. "Whatever it takes." She drew a deep breath and shrugged to ease her shoulders. She felt as if a burden had been lifted in more ways than one. "Let's go."

"What are you doing?" Wilkins was beside them. "That's no way to treat a weapon, Billings."

"I'm leaving."

"The hell you are."

"Why do you care? You didn't want me along anyway."

"It's a bad example for the other men. You've not been formally released by the colonel."

What a mental case. "I'm going." She started to turn away.

He grasped her arm. "Just like a woman. Things get bad and they take off like a—"

"Let her go," Tanek said quietly.

Wilkins glared at him, his hand tightening on her arm. "Screw you."

Tanek smiled. "Oh, I can't tell you how happy I am that you said that." He stepped forward and the edge of his hand chopped down on Wilkins's short neck. "Or how much I enjoyed doing that."

Wilkins's eyes glazed over and he slumped to the ground.

Nell's gaze was fastened on Tanek's face. "You did enjoy it."

"You bet I did." He smiled tigerishly. "The only thing I would have enjoyed more was if it had been your neck." He turned away and jumped off the bank into the water. "Come on, it will take a couple hours to get back to the car through this mess, and it will be dark soon."

"I'm coming." She started forward, then stopped. She glanced over her shoulder. Peter was staring at her in helpless bewilderment.

She had no place for him in her life. He would only get in the way. Tanek had promised her what she wanted, and she needed no impediments now.

"Where are you going?" Peter asked.

He looked poignantly alone.

And in the group of men behind him were Scott and those other bastards.

"Wait," she told Tanek as she strode over to Peter. "Come with me."

He looked at her uncertainly.

She took his hand. "It will be all right. You need to come with me, Peter."

"My daddy won't like it, will he?"

"Don't worry about him. We'll fix it. You don't want to stay, do you?"

He immediately shook his head. "It's a bad place. I don't want to be here if you're going away."

"Then take off your backpack and gun and come with me."

"The sergeant said we should never be without our rifle."

"Nell," Tanek called.

She tugged at Peter's hand. "We have to go now."

He was still staring at her with trepidation. "Why does he call you Nell? Your name is Eve."

"A lot of people have more than one name." She smothered her impatience and said quietly, "We're friends, Peter. You have to trust your friends. It would be a good thing to go with me."

A smile lit his face with sweetness. "Friends. That's right, I forgot." He laid his rifle on the ground and discarded his backpack. "Friends should be together."

She breathed a sigh of relief and moved toward Tanek. "He's going with us."

"So I gathered. Anyone else?"

She ignored his sarcasm and jumped into the water. "Come on, Peter."

He was frowning at Tanek, who was striding ahead of them through the water. "Is he mad at me?"

"No, it's just his way."

They moved swiftly for the first hour and a half, but after darkness fell, their pace slowed.

The swamp was even more eerie and frightening in the darkness. Every splash was an unknown threat, every swoop of wings startling. Nell kept her gaze fastened on the glimmer of Tanek's white shirt ahead of her and away from the moss-draped trees.

"The road's just ahead," Tanek said over his shoulder as he moved quickly out of the trees and up the bank. "The car's parked only a few yards from here."

She drew a sigh of relief. They were almost done with this ordeal.

Not quite.

Tanek was standing in the middle of the road, cursing, when she and Peter struggled out of the water and trudged toward him.

"What's wrong?"

"The car's not here."

"Someone stole it?"

He was looking around him. "No, that rain tree doesn't look familiar. I must have angled wrong." He frowned. "The damned car must be somewhere along here."

She stared at him in astonishment. "You lost the car?"

He glared at her. "I didn't lose it. You try to strike a straight line in that swamp in the dark."

She started to laugh.

"What the hell is so funny?"

She wasn't sure. She must be giddy with exhaustion, and his indignation and outrage seemed hilarious. "You made a mistake. Maybe you're not Arnold Schwarzenegger. He wouldn't have gotten lost in a swamp."

"Schwarzenegger?" He scowled. "What the hell are you talking about?" He didn't wait for an answer. "And I didn't get lost. I angled wrong." He stalked down the road.

"He's mad at you too," Peter said. "Maybe we'd better try to help him find the car."

"Maybe we'd better."

Any hint of amusement faded as she started after Tanek. Her boots squished water with every step and her clothes clung heavily to her body. The prospect of an extended walk on this deserted road was not appealing.

They found the car over a mile north of where they had exited the swamp.

"Not a word," Tanek snapped as he opened the passenger doors and got behind the wheel. "I'm wet and I'm tired and mad as hell."

Peter crawled into the backseat. "I told you he was mad."

She got in the passenger seat. She couldn't resist a final jab. "Do you have the keys?"

He stiffened. "Do you think I'd be careless enough to misplace them?"

"Well, you misplaced the—" She broke off as she met his gaze. "No, I guess not."

He started the car.

"Where are we going?"

"Panama City and a motel that'll take three people who look and smell like they were dumped in a sewage tank."

Peter laughed.

"Who is he?" Tanek asked.

"I'm Peter Drake."

"This is Nicholas Tanek, Peter." Nell huddled down in the seat and stretched her legs out before her. "Why don't you try to take a nap?"

"I'm hungry."

"We'll have something to eat when we get to the city."

"Chicken?"

"If you like."

"Kentucky Fried Chicken? That's the best."

Nell nodded. "Kentucky Fried Chicken."

Peter smiled contentedly and lay down on the backseat.

"I don't even know if there is a Kentucky Fried Chicken in Panama City," Nicholas muttered.

"Then we'll get something else. Peter isn't difficult."

"The entire situation is difficult."

"Can we talk about this later?" she asked in a low

voice. "Unless you intend to throw the boy out of the car?"

He glanced in the rearview mirror at Peter curled up in the backseat. "No."

"You were very good back there with Wilkins. Just like a martial arts movie. Karate?"

"Choi kwang-do."

"Will you teach me to do that?"

"We can talk about that later too."

She wondered if she should push it, and then decided she had gained enough that day. She leaned her head against the window and closed her eyes. The humming of the engine and smooth motion of the car were soothing. For the first time in days she felt safe.

She was almost asleep, when Tanek spoke again. "Why this hellhole?" he asked abruptly. "Obanako has to be the worst camp of its kind in the States. Did you think it was going to be a Florida vacation?"

"No."

"Then why not the one in Denver or Seattle?"

She hesitated. She should probably not answer. He was not going to like the truth. She told him anyway. "They didn't sound bad enough."

He stared at her, incredulous.

"I needed you," she said simply. "I had to show you that I'd do anything to get to Gardeaux and Maritz."

He didn't speak for a moment. "My God. A setup. You knew I'd come after you."

"No, but I hoped you would. You felt guilty enough that you'd already gone to great lengths to protect me. I thought it was likely that you wouldn't want me to go off on my own."

"The phone calls."

"Kabler said that Phil could access almost any records. I had to leave a trail."

"And position yourself in a spot that you knew

would bring pressure to bear," he said coldly. "I don't like being manipulated, Nell."

"I needed you," she repeated. "I had to do it. And I couldn't care less if you resent it."

"You might care if I decided to bow out of your plans."

"You won't do that. Tania says you keep your word."

"Tania has never tried to manipulate me." He paused. "And what would you have done if I hadn't come after you?"

"Stayed here. Finished the training. Tried to learn as much as I could."

"And get raped or die of exposure or exhaustion."

"I wouldn't have died."

"No, you think you can walk on water."

"This conversation is useless," she said wearily. "Nothing happened, and I'm not at the camp any longer. We have to move on. The only reason I told you was that I didn't want to start on a false note. I hate lies." She closed her eyes again. "I'm going to take a nap. Wake me when we get to the motel."

"Get out."

She blearily looked up at Tanek. "What?"

He reached into the car and pulled her out into a parking lot. "The door to your room is three yards away and then you can collapse."

She shook her head to clear it. "Where are we?"

"Best Western." He unlocked her door, pushed her inside, and flipped on the light. "Lock it."

"Peter . . ."

"They had only two rooms. He'll stay with me. We're two doors down."

"No, he'll be afraid. I can't—"

"I'll take care of your chick," he said roughly. "Wash off that mud and go back to sleep."

"Food. I promised him Kentucky—"

"I said I'd take care of him." He slammed the door behind him.

She stared numbly at the door before turning around. It was the usual impersonal motel room. A bed, a table, and two chairs in front of the picture window facing the parking lot. The furniture was a little worn and the gray paisley spread on the bed appeared faded but clean.

Much cleaner than she was.

She looked longingly at the double bed before she stumbled toward the bathroom.

She felt better after a hot shower and washing her hair. She glanced at the pile of filthy camouflage clothes on the floor. She had no way of cleaning them and no desire to ever see them again anyway. She rinsed out her underwear and threw it on the towel bar before leaving the bathroom and heading for the bed. Her hair was still damp when her head hit the pillow.

Her grandmother would have disapproved, she thought drowsily. She had always said Nell would catch her death of cold if she went to bed with a wet head. . . .

Here we go, down, down, down.

"Jill!"

No Jill. Just the nightmare again. Tears were streaming down her cheeks as Nell sat up in bed. Dammit, you'd think that she would have been too exhausted to dream.

She went to the bathroom and drank a glass of water. Her hand was shaking.

She should go back to bed and try to sleep. Tanek

was going to help her, and that meant she should be rested and ready.

But if she went back to sleep, she would dream again.

It was going to be a long night.

Tanek knocked on the door at eight the next morning.

She grabbed the bedsheet and draped it around herself before answering the knock.

"Very fetching." He handed her a bag with PELICAN SOUVENIR SHOP emblazoned on the side. "But I think you'll be more comfortable in these. Shorts and T-shirt. The souvenir shop down the street was the only thing open at this hour."

"Thank you." She stepped aside to let him in the room. "Where's Peter?"

"Trying on his clothes."

"Is he okay?"

He nodded. "He slept like the proverbial log. He's just had a dozen sugar doughnuts and a gallon of orange juice. The only thing that may be wrong with him is a bellyache." He held up the bag in his other hand. "Coffee. How do you take it?"

"Cream. Sit down. I'll be dressed in a minute." She hurried toward the bathroom.

She quickly put on the underwear she had rinsed out the previous night and opened the bag. Green rubber thongs. Purple Bermuda shorts, and a short-sleeve lavender T-shirt emblazoned with pink flamingos. Oh, well, at least they were soft and clean.

Tanek was sitting at the small table by the window when she came out of the bathroom. He pushed a large container of coffee toward the vacant seat across from him. "Drink it. We need to talk."

She gazed at him warily as she sat down and lifted

the coffee. "You think I need a dose of caffeine to hear what you have to say?"

"I think you need a dose of something. You look like hell. Didn't you sleep?"

She looked down into her cup. "Some." She took a sip of coffee. "Talk."

"It's going to be my way. All my way. I'll keep my word, but I'm not going to have you rushing in and getting me killed. I'll make the plans, and you'll do as I say."

"All right."

He looked at her in surprise.

"I'm not stupid. I know this won't be easy. As long as I can see a reason for you doing something, I won't argue with you."

"Astonishing."

"But I won't have you shutting me out and I won't let you deceive me."

"I said I wouldn't shut you out." He paused. "If that's what you still want when I'm ready to move."

"It's what I'll want." She took another sip of coffee. "It's the only thing I want."

"Time has a way of lessening—"

"Time?" Her gaze flew back to his face. "What are you talking about?"

"I'm not going to be ready to move until late December."

"December? This is only September."

"And I've been planning this since April."

"It's too long."

"It's the safest way."

"December." She tried to remember everything she'd read about Gardeaux. "The Renaissance Fest."

"Exactly. The perfect vehicle for infiltration."

"There's bound to be guards all over the place."

"Including Maritz." He smiled. "Maritz, Gardeaux, and several hundred guests to run interference."

"They didn't help at Medas."

His smile disappeared. "No, but we won't go in blind this time."

Her hand tightened on the cup. "I don't *want* to wait."

"My way."

"It's over three months, dammit."

"And you can spend it getting ready."

"How?"

"We'll discuss it later. You can bet it won't be crawling through the swamps." He hesitated a moment. "Or tossing coral snakes around."

She went still. "Peter told you."

"He was very informative about your short stay at the camp and the 'nothing' that happened there." He rose to his feet. "We have reservations on a flight to Boise at eleven. I called Tania last night, but I have to go and make a few other phone calls."

"Boise?"

"We fly into Boise and then get a puddle-jumper to Lasiter. My ranch is fifty miles north. I want you where I can keep an eye on you. I'm not going through this again, if you decide everything is going too slowly."

"What about Peter?"

He turned at the door. "What about him? He has a home. He tells me his father is his legal guardian."

"His father sent him to that place. He might send him back."

"And he might not. Why should you care? He'll only be in your way in this grand quest for vengeance. I thought that was all that mattered to you."

"You've been with him long enough to realize Peter isn't normal."

"You mean he's mildly retarded."

"I mean he has the mind of a child. He's . . . helpless."

He met her gaze and repeated deliberately, "Why should you care?"

She lost her temper. "Because I do, dammit. Do you think I *want* to assume responsibility for him? He just happened. He helped me and I can't leave him. His father doesn't want him. He's the mayor of a small town in Mississippi and I think Peter is an embarrassment to him. I won't let him go back there."

"I didn't think you could. I made a reservation on the plane for him."

Her eyes widened. "You did?"

"But I don't want any kidnapping charges levied at me. Peter's only seventeen. His father is one of the calls I have to make."

"Do you think you can convince him to—"

"I'll convince him. I'll tell him if he causes any trouble, we'll give a nice little story to the newspapers describing how the honorable mayor put his retarded son in Obanako to get rid of him. We might even do a photo shoot of the place." He smiled sardonically as he opened the door. "Didn't you tell the kid we'd fix it? What else do I live for but to please you?"

"Tanek."

"Yes?"

"Thank you for doing this for me. I know he may be a bother to you."

"I won't let him be a bother." He met her gaze. "And I'm not doing it for you. Most adults can take care of themselves, but it makes me mad as hell when anyone goes after kids."

"Like Tania?"

"Tania was never helpless even when she was younger." He added deliberately, "Not like Jill. If you'd let me, I'd make sure I got Maritz and that it would take him a long, long time to die."

He meant it. She felt a rush of fierce joy as she realized what he felt wasn't only guilt. He was angry and outraged and wanted Jill avenged because it was right and just. She was not alone. She shook her head. "I have to do it."

He nodded curtly and left the room.

Three months was a long time. Too long.

Yet she had to be sure. She couldn't risk being killed before Maritz died. Tanek was part of Gardeaux's world and knew the dangers. He would have moved before this if he'd thought he had a chance.

Three months.

You can spend it getting ready.

If she couldn't convince him to move before that time, that's exactly how she'd spend it—getting ready. Tanek might think he'd isolate her in the wilds until her determination lessened. But it wouldn't happen.

Peter came to her room five minutes later. He was dressed in khaki shorts and a T-shirt that bore the imprint of a grinning alligator wearing a Braves baseball cap. An identical cap perched jauntily on his head. His blue eyes glinted with excitement. "We're going to Nicholas's ranch. Did he tell you?"

"Yes, he told me."

He plopped down on the bed. "He has horses and sheep and a dog named Sam."

"That's nice."

"I've never had a dog. Daddy didn't like the barking."

"Only a snake."

He nodded. "But Nicholas said there are other dogs on the ranch. Sheepdogs that work the herds. He said Jean will let me watch them."

"And who is Jean?"

"His foreman. Jean Etch—" He stopped. "Something. I don't remember."

She smiled indulgently. "But you remember his dog is named Sam."

"No, that's Nicholas's dog, a German shepherd. He doesn't work the sheep. The Border collies work the sheep."

He already knew more about Nicholas's private life than she did, she realized in amusement. "I'm surprised you didn't ask all their names too."

"That was last night. Nicholas told me to shut up and go to sleep."

When she remembered Tanek's mood last night, she was surprised he'd answered any of Peter's questions. Or that Peter had the nerve to ask him. "I'm sure he didn't mean to be unkind."

"Unkind?" He looked at her in bewilderment. "You mean mad? He wasn't mad anymore. He just wanted to go to sleep."

And he had evidently been very patient with Peter. A quality she had not seen Tanek display. "And you don't mind leaving your home?"

His smile faded a little, and he looked away from her. "I don't mind. I'd rather be with you and Nicholas."

"Peter . . . I can't promise you that—It may not be—" She broke off as she saw his expression.

"I know," he said quietly. "You may not want me around for long. It's okay."

"I didn't say— Things are difficult. I may have to go away."

"It's okay," he said again. "Everyone goes away. Or they send me away."

She stared at him helplessly.

"But not for a while. Not before I see the dogs?"

Dammit. She swallowed hard and turned away.

"No, not for a long time after that." Three months. Time was relevant. An eternity for her might fly by for Peter. She smiled with an effort. "And maybe we can work out something for you after I go away."

"Maybe." Suddenly his smile returned. "Do you like my cap and shirt? I told Nicholas I liked the Braves."

"It's a great cap and a magnificent shirt." She turned toward the door. "Let's go find Nicholas."

"What have you found out about Simpson?" Nicholas said when Jamie answered the phone.

"He's still missing. His apartment was ransacked. I checked on his lady. She left for Paris two days ago."

"Did you get the photostats of the records I sent you?"

"Yesterday."

"I want you to verify them."

"The account books? I thought you said that it wouldn't do us any good without—"

"Not the account books, the Medas file. If it's accurate, I want you to dig."

"Are you going to tell Nell what you found out?"

"No way."

"If she finds out you're keeping it from her, you'll get a backlash."

An understatement, but he couldn't risk the explosion he knew would come if she found out what was in Simpson's file. "Just follow up on it." A knock sounded on the door. "I have to go. If you find out anything more, contact me at the ranch." He hung up the phone. "Come in."

Peter and Nell came into the room. They looked like two escapees from Disney World. Both young and so damn vulnerable he wanted to scoop them up and put them behind bars to keep them safe. What the hell had he gotten himself into?

"We're ready." Nell made a face. "Providing they'll let us on the airplane in this gear."

Nicholas's glance wandered from slim, shapely legs to breasts outlined by the soft material of the T-shirt. He felt a ripple of familiar heat.

Christ, not now. Not this woman.

He turned away abruptly and reached for his duffel bag on the bed. "Oh, I don't think there's any doubt they'll let you board the plane." He headed for the door. "But the flight attendant may want to give you a pair of Mickey Mouse ears and a coloring book."

Ten

"Another fence?" Nell asked as Tanek got out of the Jeep and moved toward the gate. "That's three. You do believe in security."

"I believe in staying alive. This is the last one." He punched a combination into the lock on the gate. The gate swung noiselessly open. "It's electric and surrounds the house and stable area." He glanced at Peter in the backseat. "Stay away from the fence, Peter. It will give you a shock."

He frowned. "Does it hurt the dogs?"

"Sam knows better than to touch it, and the livestock and outbuildings are on another part of the property outside the fences. This is only the homestead. The actual working ranch is the Bar X, several miles north of here."

"That's good." He went back to staring eagerly out the window. "It looks . . . funny out there."

Nell knew what he meant. In the distance the Sawtooth mountains towered majestically, but as far as the eye could see the land was flat and barren. Yet there was no impression of desolation. There was something . . . there, waiting. "You have plenty of room."

"Right. I dreamed about space while I was growing up in Hong Kong. All the people there nearly smothered me."

I believe in staying alive.

She studied Tanek's face as he got back in the car. He had spoken flatly, almost casually, and she was reminded of that moment at the airport when Reardon had said he didn't like to take taxis. Survival was a way of life to Tanek, and it had never been more obvious to her until she saw the fortress with which he surrounded himself. "You must feel very safe here," she said quietly. "You've made yourself impregnable."

"You're never impregnable. You just do your best." He drove through the gates which swung shut automatically behind him. "I don't think the fence or gate can be breached, but a helicopter with a missile launcher could wipe me out with no problem."

"Missile launchers?" She smiled. "That does sound paranoid."

"Maybe. But it could happen if someone was determined enough. The South American drug lords have an ample supply."

"So what do you do to protect yourself?"

He shrugged. "No one lives forever. If it's not a missile, it might be a tornado that gets me. You do the best you can, you take out insurance." He glanced at her. "And you live every moment as if it's your last."

He parked the Jeep in front of the house and jumped out. "Michaela," he called out.

"I'm here. You need not bellow." A tall, thin woman in her mid-forties came out of the house. She wore jeans and a loose plaid shirt, but her carriage lent the rough clothes elegance. "I heard the bell when you unlocked the gate." Her gaze went to Nell and then to Peter. "You have guests. Welcome." There was an almost foreign formality in her manner.

Nell stared at her. The woman's features were strong and bold and had an almost Egyptian serenity.

"This is Michaela Etchbarras," Tanek said. "I'd call her my housekeeper, but she doesn't keep it, she runs it and everything else around here." He helped Nell from the Jeep. "Nell Calder. Peter Drake. They'll be staying awhile."

"And you?" the woman asked Tanek.

He nodded.

"Good. Sam has missed you. You should not have an animal if you have to leave it alone. I'll let him out of the kitchen." She went back into the house.

"Etchbarras," Peter said suddenly. "That was the name. He has the sheepdogs."

"Michaela is married to Jean." Tanek grimaced. "She deigns to act as my housekeeper whenever Jean is upland with the sheep. Otherwise she goes back to the Bar X and sends one of her daughters to clean twice a week."

"How many daughters does she have?" Nell asked.

"Four."

"I'm surprised you let them on the property considering how careful you were with that poor room service clerk at the hotel."

"They came with the property. No danger. The Etchbarras family has been here tending the sheep since the turn of the century. They came from the Basque country of Spain to settle. Most of the people around here are Basque. It's a tight community. I'm the outsider."

"But you own this place."

"Do I? I bought it with money. They paid for it with a different commodity." His lips tightened. "But you're right, it's mine and I'll learn how to belong here and keep what's mine."

The strength of the possessiveness in his voice surprised her. This place was clearly not only a fortress to him. Nell's gaze went to the door through which the housekeeper had vanished. She said absently, "She has a fantastic face. She'd make a wonderful portrait subject."

He raised a mocking brow. "Do I detect a gentler impulse burning in that fanatic breast? Painting? What a complete waste of time."

She was surprised herself. She hadn't thought of her painting since Medas. "It was just a comment. I didn't say I was going to do it. You're right, I'll have no time."

"You never know." His gaze went to the mountains. "Time seems to slow here. You might—"

A brown and tan tornado hurtled through the front door. Tanek staggered back as the German shepherd's front feet hit his chest. He grunted.

The dog was making frantic moaning noises as he tried to lick Tanek's face.

"Down, Sam."

The dog ignored him.

Tanek sighed resignedly and knelt on the ground, where the dog could reach him. "Get it over."

Nell stared in amazement as the dog bounded excitedly around him, lunging in to lick his face.

Grimacing, Tanek lifted his arm over his mouth to avoid the dog's tongue. He scowled as he met her gaze across the porch. "What did you expect? Rin Tin Tin? I'm no dog trainer. The only command he obeys is 'Come to dinner.' "

Tanek always exuded such power and confidence, she supposed she had never thought he would permit an animal to be anything but disciplined and well trained in his presence. "He's beautiful."

"Yeah." Tanek affectionately rubbed the dog's ears. "I like him."

That was evident. She had never seen Tanek this open before.

"May I pet him?" Peter asked.

"In time. He doesn't like strangers."

That seemed impossible to Nell. The dog was now on his back in the most submissive of positions, whimpering in delight as Tanek scratched his chest. She took a step closer.

The dog was instantly on his feet, his lips drawn back in a snarl.

She stopped in shock.

"Easy," Tanek said soothingly. "They're okay, boy."

"He acts as if he's been trained as an attack dog."

"Only by life." He stood up. "I found him half starved by the side of the road when he was only a pup. He doesn't trust many people." He smiled at Peter. "Let him get used to you."

Peter nodded, but he was clearly disappointed. "I wanted him to like me."

"He will." He moved toward the front door. "I'll have Michaela drive you over to the sheep ranch tomorrow morning. The sheepdogs are much more friendly."

Peter brightened. "May I stay there for a while?"

He shook his head. "In a few days the hands will be going to the high country to bring the sheep back for the winter."

"But when they get back?"

"If it's all right with Jean."

Peter turned to Nell and said diffidently, "It's not that I don't want to be with you. You've been nice to me. It's just that—"

"Dogs." She smiled. "I know, Peter."

"Come along." Michaela stood in the doorway. "I don't have all day. I have to show you your rooms. It'll be dark in an hour. Jean is coming in from the herds tonight and I have to get home and fix his dinner."

Tanek bowed mockingly. "We'll come at once. Just show Peter his room and I'll take Nell around. We wouldn't want to inconvenience you."

"You won't. I've set a casserole in the oven for you to serve yourself. Come along, Peter." She went back into the house. Peter followed her eagerly.

Nell and Tanek entered directly into the living room. "It's larger than it looks from outside," Nell said. "It sort of rambles."

"I built on after I bought the place. I told you I liked space."

Nell looked around at the airy room furnished with camel-colored leather mission furniture grouped around a huge fireplace with a stone hearth. White flowers cascading from copper vases occupied the occasional tables, a large Chinese urn in the corner of the room brimmed with golden chrysanthemums. On the walls she had expected to see Indian rugs or cowboy artifacts, but instead there were paintings of every description.

She crossed to stand before the one over the fireplace. "Delacroix?"

"Would I be barbarian enough to hide a Delacroix here in the wilderness with no one but me to appreciate it?"

She glanced at him, remembering the possessiveness she had noticed only minutes before. "Yes."

He chuckled. "Right. Treasures are for the pleasure of those who can take and keep them."

"Take? Did you—"

"No, I didn't steal it. I bought it at auction. I'm strictly legitimate these days." He led her out the door and down a long hall. "There are five bedrooms with adjoining baths in this wing and a study and a moder-

ately well-equipped gym in the other wing." He threw
open a door. "This room is yours. There's only one
television in the house, and that's in the study, but there
are plenty of books. I hope you'll be comfortable."

She didn't see how she could help it. The room was
simply furnished but exuded comfort. A white down
comforter was thrown over the double bed. A tapestry-
cushioned rocking chair occupied the corner of the
room by a casement window. A cherrywood bookcase
on the opposite wall overflowed with books and plants.
"It's very nice. I'm surprised your guests ever leave."

"I seldom have guests. This is my place. I don't like
to share."

She turned to look at him. "Then you must doubly
resent my presence here. I promise I won't get in your
way any more than necessary."

"It was my choice. I brought you." He nodded at a
door across the room. "Bathroom. You'll want to wash
up before supper."

"What on earth is he doing?" Nell asked, her gaze on
Peter on the floor in a corner across the room. The boy
was sitting cross-legged, unmoving, his gaze fixed un-
blinkingly on Sam, who was lying beside the fire a few
yards away. "He reminds me of a snake charmer."

"According to him, you're the snake charmer,"
Nicholas said dryly.

She shook her head. "He was very upset with me.
He thought I was too rough with the snake." She went
back to the original subject. "Does he think that he can
will Sam to like him?"

"Maybe." Tanek poured her another cup of coffee
from the carafe at his elbow. "It could happen. If he
wants it hard enough. Dogs are sensitive to feelings."

"He ignored Peter all through dinner."

Nicholas leaned back in his chair. "Stop fretting. You can't make Sam like him."

"I'm not fretting. I just—I think he may have had a hard life. It wouldn't hurt the blasted dog to wag his tail at him."

"He doesn't know that. It pays to be cautious."

"Like you." She lifted her gaze. "With your electric fences."

He nodded. "Contrary to your present view on the subject, life can be sweet. I've no intention of giving up even a minute of it. I'll fight to the last breath."

She could believe that of him. Beneath that cool mask lay a passionate determination. Power, intelligence, and a passion for life; it was a riveting combination. She tore her gaze away. "But you're willing to risk it to get Gardeaux."

"Not if I can help it." He lifted his cup to his lips. "I intend to have it all."

"What if you can't?"

"I will." He paused. "And I won't let you get me killed because you want to move too fast."

"You don't understand. I *have* to do this. It's hard to wait." Her hand clenched on the coffee cup. "Do you think I don't know why I'm here? You think you can convince me not to go after them."

"That's one agenda. The other is to keep you from making me chase after you and blundering into a trap."

"You wouldn't have to chase after me."

"Yes, I would."

"Why? I told you that you weren't responsible for what happened on Medas."

"We all set our own boundaries of responsibility."

"And I'm within yours?"

He smiled. "For the time being. Boundaries sometimes shift."

She didn't want to be anyone's responsibility, much

less a man like Tanek's. Responsibility implied a certain closeness. She had already been forced to form attachments to Tania and Peter. Tanek must remain on the outside.

"You don't like that? But you used it to make sure I helped you." He lifted a mocking brow. "You have to be consistent, Nell."

Damn him. There would be no problem keeping Tanek at a distance. "I don't have to be anything I don't want to be." She changed the subject. "Why do you want Gardeaux dead?"

The mockery faded from his expression. "He deserves to die."

"That's no answer."

He didn't answer for a moment. "The same reason you want him dead. He killed someone I cared about."

"Who?" Again, she thought of how little she knew about Tanek. "Your wife? Your child?"

He shook his head. "A friend."

"He must have been a close friend."

She could sense him shutting her away. "Very close. More coffee?"

She shook her head. It was clear he was not going to talk any more about himself. She tried another path. "Tell me about Gardeaux."

"What do you want to know?"

"Whatever you know."

He smiled crookedly. "I guarantee you don't want to know everything I do about him."

"How did you come to meet him?"

"We ran into each other several years ago in Hong Kong. We were in the same business at the time. Though he was more diversified."

"You mean you were both criminals," she said bluntly.

He nodded. "But my network was more limited. I liked to keep it that way."

"Why?"

"I never planned on making it my life work." He added gravely, "I wanted to be a brain surgeon."

She stared at him, stunned.

He chuckled. "Just joking. I wanted to make enough money and then get out. You get big in the rackets and one of two things happen. Either you dip into the drug trade and the law never leaves you alone, or you get addicted to the power and you can't let go. I didn't like either prospect, so I made sure I stayed unobtrusive."

"I can't imagine you being unobtrusive."

"Oh, but I was." He added, "Relatively."

"But Gardeaux wasn't."

"No, Gardeaux wanted to be God." He thought about it. "Or maybe Cesare Borgia. I was never quite sure. Probably God. The mystique surrounding Borgia would have attracted him, but the prince came to a bad end."

She smothered a flicker of exasperation. "How did you get to know him?"

"There was a Tang vase we both wanted to 'acquire.' He told me to back off."

"What did you do?"

"I backed off."

She felt a ripple of shock.

"It was good business. He had more muscle, and a war would have cost me more than a dozen Tang vases."

"I see."

He shook his head. "No, you don't. You think I should have taken him on, been like Dirty Harry and fought the bastard in the trenches."

"I didn't say that."

"I learned a long time ago that you weigh the consequences carefully before you dive into battle. I had a fortune to acquire and people who depended on me."

"Phil?"

"He was with me then."

"And he still works for you."

"Occasionally. When I had enough money, I broke up the network. Some of my associates decided they didn't want to go to other organizations where their talents would have been welcomed."

"So you helped them make new lives."

"I couldn't walk away." He added simply, "They were within the boundaries of my responsibility."

Loyalty. She didn't want him to have any qualities she admired. When she had started to question him, she had wanted to know only about Gardeaux, but she was learning too much about Tanek. She tried to get back on track. "Backing down didn't do any good? He still killed your friend?"

"No, that was later." He stood up and stretched. "Time for bed."

He had shut the door again. She said quickly, "You haven't told me nearly all I want to know about Gardeaux."

"There's plenty of time. You'll be here awhile."

She stood up. "I don't want to waste time." She paused. "You obviously have contacts. If we can't do anything concrete, will you try to find out why Gardeaux sent Maritz to kill me?"

"Why?"

"Why? I have to know because I have to try to make sense of all this. I've been stumbling around in a nightmare for too long."

"Is it going to change your mind or your purpose?"

"No."

"Then I'd say any motive was of secondary importance."

"Not to me."

He gazed at her without speaking.

He wasn't going to do it. "All right. Then tomorrow will you start teaching me how to do what you did to Wilkins?"

"Don't you ever give up?"

"If I'd known how to fight him, Maritz would never have been able to push me off that balcony. I would have been able to defend myself."

And Jill.

The words were unsaid, but they lingered between them. He nodded curtly. "Day after tomorrow. I have to go to see Jean at the Bar X tomorrow."

She stared at him suspiciously. "You're not just trying to put me off?"

"I wouldn't think of it. I'll teach you anything you want to know about death and mayhem. But it won't be as much as Gardeaux and Maritz can teach you."

"It will be enough."

"It won't be enough. And even if it is, what will you do after it's over? It takes a certain type of character to survive murder."

"It wouldn't be murder," she said, stung.

"You see, you're shying away from it already." He repeated deliberately, "Murder. To take a life is murder. No matter what the reason, the act is the same. Nice people like you are trained from childhood to back away from it with revulsion."

"Nice people like me seldom have the same impetus I've been given."

"That's true, and you're not the woman I met on Medas. But the core is the same. As the tree is bent . . ."

"Bullshit."

"Is it? You want to be hard and cold and push everybody away, but it's not happening. Oh, I'm easy, but what about Tania? What about Peter?"

"That's different. They have nothing to do with Maritz and Gardeaux."

"But they have everything to do with who you are."

"You don't think I can do it? You're wrong."

"I'm betting I'm right." He added wearily, "I *want* to be right."

She shook her head.

"Day after tomorrow. Eight in the morning. Wear workout clothes and don't eat breakfast." He turned and left the room.

He was wrong, she told herself. He had to be wrong. It would be better if she could keep up barriers, but, if she failed, it didn't mean her determination would waiver.

"Peter." She turned toward the far corner. "It's time to go to—"

Sam's head was on Peter's knee and the boy was stroking the dog's throat. Peter's expression was lit with infinite delight.

It could happen. If he wants it enough.

She felt a wave of happiness for him sweep over her. It appeared Peter had wanted it enough.

I want to be right.

Her smile faded as she remembered Tanek's words. His will was much stronger than Peter's and he intended to focus that will on her.

Well, she was not Sam. It would do him no good.

"Come on, Peter," she said brusquely. "Time for bed. You can play with Sam tomorrow."

Dead. The woman was dead.

Maritz replaced the receiver of the telephone with a rush of satisfaction. He hadn't failed. It had taken a little time, but the Calder woman had died. He could tell Gardeaux the job was done.

Maybe.

A thorn of uneasiness pierced his satisfaction. Gardeaux had said he had failed, that the woman would recover. The bastard wasn't often wrong.

He would look a fool if it turned out the woman's death records had been fixed and she had been whisked away. Gardeaux didn't like fools.

It wouldn't hurt to make sure.

He looked down at the information on the notepad. The hospital?

Too many people.

John Birnbaum Funeral Home.

He smiled and stuffed the notepad into his pocket.

"Here." Tanek tossed a large package on the couch beside Nell. "A present."

Nell looked at him in confusion. "I thought you were going over to the other ranch to see your foreman."

"I did. I swung by town on the way back. Open it."

She fumbled with the tape on the package. "Peter hasn't come back from the ranch yet."

"He won't be coming back. Jean has taken a liking to him and gave him permission to stay a few days. If he works out, Jean may take him to the high country when he goes to bring the sheep in."

"Will he be safe?"

"Safe enough. He was crazy to go. Dogs *and* sheep."

She could see how that would prove irresistible to Peter. She began to tear off the brown wrappings. Canvas, easel, sketch pad, pencils, and a box of paints. "What is this?"

"You said you wanted to paint Michaela."

"That's not what I said."

"But you do."

"I'll be too busy."

He snapped his fingers. "Ah, yes, I forgot the mayhem. Well, I've decided to charge for lessons. I need some paintings to decorate my walls."

She asked sarcastically, "To hang beside your Delacroix?"

"Local art. My people, my mountains."

The same possessiveness she had seen in him when they'd arrived. She set the canvas on the floor. "Hire someone else to do it."

"I want you. One hour of violence and mayhem for every two you spend on my paintings. Deal?"

She turned to look at him. "What is this? Am I supposed to undergo some miraculous metamorphosis from this half-baked therapy?"

"Maybe. I figured it couldn't hurt."

"It can waste my time."

"At one point in your life you didn't think it a waste of time." He met her gaze. "I'll keep my promise. You'll get an hour of training every day from me regardless of whether or not you paint. But the only way you'll get more is to give me what I want."

"This won't do you any good."

"It won't hurt me." He smiled. "And it won't hurt you, will it?"

She slowly shook her head.

"Deal?"

Why not? It would be a way of controlling the tempo of her training without having to ask Tanek. She glanced at the canvas and felt a faint stirring of excitement. Her gaze went to the direction of the kitchen, where she could hear Michaela preparing dinner. That wonderful face . . .

"If you can persuade Michaela to let me paint her."

"I never try to persuade Michaela to do anything. You want her, go after her."

"More therapy?"

He smiled. "Terror. She scares me to death."

The Birnbaum Funeral Home glowed in the darkness like a small plantation home. Its three columns were lit by a spotlight hidden in the evergreen bushes on the sweeping front lawn.

What a waste, Maritz thought. Mansions for the dead.

Well, not only for the dead. Undertakers reaped a hefty profit from disposal of corpses. Fucking bloodsuckers. They had bled him white when he had buried his father.

But Maxwell and Son had never had a place like this. The mortuary had been on a busy street in the Detroit slums, and he had been too poor and unimportant to rate attention. He had been shuttled to Daniel Maxwell, the son. He had been filled with helpless rage as he had sat there while that acne-scarred pipsqueak tried to steal every dollar he could from him.

He had wanted to squeeze the bastard's throat until his eyes popped.

But that was before he had found the knife.

The door of the mortuary was opening and a number of people were streaming out. Swollen eyes, quiet voices, furtive relief at leaving the dead and joining the living again.

He checked his watch. Nine o'clock. Closing time. He'd give the stragglers fifteen more minutes.

He watched the mourners get into their cars in the parking lot and drive away. He had been a mourner. He had loved his father. It should have been his mother who had died, the vicious bitch. He had not meant it to happen. He had just pushed his father a little and he'd fallen down those steps. It should have been her.

A young man in a dark suit came out of the mortuary and cut across the lawn to the employee parking. A trainee to the vampire? Or maybe Birnbaum had a son too. The kid was whistling as he jumped into a blue Oldsmobile parked beside a sleek Cadillac hearse.

A new hearse, one that had been purchased in cash a week after the Calder woman's supposed cremation.

Maritz had found the record of that purchase very interesting.

The entry lights went out in the vestibule.

Maritz waited until the Oldsmobile had disappeared around the corner before he got out of the car and walked across the street. He rang the doorbell.

No answer.

He rang it again.

He waited a minute and rang it again.

The entry lights went on, the door opened. Cool air and the heavy scent of flowers surrounded Maritz.

John Birnbaum stood in the doorway—sleek gray hair, a little plump, dressed in a sober gray suit. "Do you wish to view the body? I'm sorry, we're closed."

Maritz shook his head. "I need to ask you some questions. I know it's late, but may I come in?"

Birnbaum hesitated. Maritz could almost see the wheels turning in his head and coming up dollar signs. Birnbaum stepped aside. "Have you had a loss?"

Maritz entered the foyer and closed the door. He smiled. "Yes, I've had a loss. We need to talk about it."

Nell stood watching Michaela from the doorway of the kitchen. The woman's arms were smeared with flour as she rolled out a circle of dough on the butcher block. Every movement was swift, graceful, economical.

"You want something?" Michaela asked without looking up.

Nell jumped. She said the first thing that came to her head. "What are you making?"

"Biscuits."

"The ones we had for breakfast were wonderful."

"I know."

This wasn't going to be easy. "You're very busy."

Michaela nodded.

"It's very kind of you and your husband to let Peter stay with you at the ranch for a while."

"He won't be in the way." She put aside the rolling pin and began to cut out the biscuits. "If he'd been trouble, we wouldn't have done it. Jean has no time for fools. The boy has the mind of a child, not a fool. Children can be taught." The words were spoken as crisply as the movement of the cutter in the dough. "Now, what do you want?"

"Your face."

Michaela's gaze lifted. "I'd say yours was good enough."

"I mean . . . I'd like to sketch you."

Michaela began to put the biscuits into a pan. "I've no time for posing."

"I could sketch you while you're working. I might not need you very much at first."

Michaela didn't speak for a moment. "You're an artist?"

"Not really. I don't have the time. I do it only when I'm not—" She stopped as she realized she was automatically giving the same answer she had given everyone before Medas. But there was no Jill or Richard to occupy her time now. She smothered the jab of pain. "Yes, I'm an artist." The words sounded strange and lonely to her own ears.

Michaela studied her and then nodded curtly. "Sketch away. Just don't get in my way."

Nell didn't give her a chance to change her mind. "I'll go get my sketch pad."

"I'm not going to stay still."

"I'll work around you . . ."

It was easier said than done, she realized after an hour of trying to capture Michaela's features. The woman was never still. For a woman whose face had the serenity of a Nefertiti, she was a dynamo of energy. After discarding several full-face sheets in despair, Nell decided to concentrate on one feature at a time. She started on those deepset eyes.

That was better. She was getting it. Maybe she could combine the features later. . . .

"Why are you here?"

Nell looked up. It was the first time Michaela had spoken for over an hour. "I'm just visiting."

Michaela shook her head. "Nicholas said you were staying through the winter. That's not a visit."

"I'll try not to be a bother to you."

"If Nicholas wants you here, I'll put up with a little bother."

"Nicholas said that you and Jean belonged here more than he did."

"We do, but he's getting there. He needs only a little more seasoning."

"Seasoning?"

Michaela shrugged. "I think it's hard for him to belong anywhere, but he wants it. We'll see."

"You want him to stay?"

She nodded. "He understands us and lets us go our way. The next owner might be stupid and untrainable."

She smiled. "And you're training Nicholas?"

"Of course. He's not difficult. He has great strength

of mind and will. He will meld with this country, given time."

"I'd think strength of will would keep one from melding."

"This land is strong. It doesn't like weaklings." She looked at Nell. "It chews them up and spits them out."

Her pencil stopped in mid-motion. "You think I'm a weakling?"

"I don't know. Are you?"

"No."

"Then you have nothing to worry about."

"You don't want me here, do you?"

"It doesn't matter to me if you're here." She took the biscuits out of the oven. "As long as you don't try to take Nicholas away. Talk to him. Smile at him. Sleep with him." She set the pan on the butcher block. "But when you go, leave him here."

She felt a ripple of shock. "I don't intend to sleep with him. That's not why I came."

Michaela shrugged. "It will happen. He's a man and you're closer than the women in town." She took a spatula and gently pried the biscuits from the pan. "And you're the kind of woman who would stir a man."

"He doesn't see me like that."

"All men see women like that. It's their first reaction. It's only later that they see us as people with minds as well as bodies."

"And he's the only one who has anything to say about it?"

"You like to look at him. You watch him."

Did she? Dammit, of course she looked at him. He was a man who drew attention. He had stood out like a lighthouse in that crowded ballroom. "That doesn't mean anything. There's nothing between us."

"If you say so." She turned away. "I've no more

time to talk. It's nearly lunchtime. I have to get this food on the table."

Nell breathed a sigh of relief. Michaela was entirely wrong, but the conversation had been disconcerting. "May I help? I could set the table."

"No." She opened the cabinet and took down the plates. "But you can go to the stable and get Nicholas."

Nell set her sketchbook down and hopped off the stool. "Right away."

Nicholas was grooming a bay stallion when she entered the stable. She stopped just inside the door. "Lunch is ready."

"I'll be there in a minute."

She watched him as he brushed the stallion with long, clean strokes. He did everything with that same power and clean economy, she thought. He was dressed in jeans and a sweatshirt and he looked totally at home doing the menial task. If she hadn't known better, she would have assumed he'd been born to it. It was hard to connect the Tanek on Medas to this man.

He didn't look up. "You're very quiet. What are you thinking?"

"That you do that very well. Do you know a lot about horses?"

He smiled. "I'm learning. I'd never seen any horse before I came here but the ones the British moguls at the polo club rode."

"You belonged to the polo club?"

"Not likely. I was a dishwasher in the kitchens when I was a boy."

"I can't see you as a dishwasher."

"No? I looked on it as a step up. My job before that was scrubbing floors in the whorehouse where my mother worked."

"Oh."

He looked over his shoulder. "What a polite little exclamation. Did I embarrass you?"

"No, but I—" She was stammering, she realized in annoyance. "It's none of my business. I didn't mean to intrude."

"No intrusion. I scarcely knew my mother. I was closer to the other whores than I was to her. She was an American hippie who came to China to seek the true light. Unfortunately, the only light she saw was when she was stoned. So she stayed stoned. She died of an overdose when I was six."

"How old were you when you left there?"

He thought about it. "I guess I was eight when I started at the polo club. I was kicked out of the job when I was twelve."

"Why?"

"The cook said I'd stolen three cases of caviar and sold it on the black market."

"Did you?"

"No, he did it himself, but I was a convenient target. Actually, he was very clever to choose me." His tone was coolly objective. "I was the most vulnerable. I had no one to protect me and I wasn't capable of protecting myself."

"You don't seem angry about it."

"It's over. It taught me a valuable lesson. I was never that vulnerable again and I learned to keep what was mine."

"What happened to you after you left? Did you have somewhere to go?"

"The streets." He put down the brush and patted the horse's nose. "The lessons I learned there were even more valuable, but you wouldn't want to hear about them." He left the stall and closed the half-door. "Or maybe you would. Quite a few of them dealt with dirty tricks and mayhem."

She could not even imagine what it would be like surviving on the streets, and he had been only a boy at the time.

He glanced at her and shook his head. "You're looking at me like you do Peter. Soft as butter."

She quickly looked away. "It's not soft to hate abusive treatment of children. You hate it yourself."

"I don't melt at the thought."

"I'm not melting."

"Close enough. Look, not all children are like Jill. I was a tough, self-serving, little bastard with nasty claws." He met her gaze. "You think you've changed, but you're still too soft. Soft means malleable and malleable means dead."

"Then I'll get over it." She started toward the door. "Michaela will be upset if her lunch gets cold."

"We wouldn't want that to happen." He fell into step with her. "How are you getting along with her?"

"Well enough. She's letting me sketch her." She grimaced. "As long as I don't get in her way."

"How does it feel?"

"Good." She glanced at him. "But it's not going to cause me to find a cozy little corner and forget everything."

"It may help. It's all part of the big picture."

"I spent three hours sketching today. That means you owe me."

A corner of his lip lifted in a sardonic smile as he held open the front door for her. "That's what this is all about."

She shook her head. He was a strange mixture—cool, tough, and yet possessing a code that included both a sense of responsibility and justice. It was remarkable in a man of his background.

But then, Tanek was a remarkable man.

You look at him.

Michaela's words rushed back to her, and again she felt that bolt of shock at the thought of intimacy with Tanek. It was a stupid reaction. Admitting Tanek was extraordinary didn't mean she wanted to jump into bed with him. There was no room in her life for sex with any man, and if she didn't want to be friends with Tanek, she certainly didn't want him in her bed. All he meant to her was a way to get to Maritz, and that's the way it would stay. She didn't even know why she had questioned him about his past. The less she knew about him, the better.

No, that wasn't true. She had questioned him because she had been curious about the elements that had shaped a man like Tanek. Curiosity was a normal and acceptable trait. She found she was still curious, when a sudden thought occurred to her. "The cook who got you fired. Did you ever meet him again?"

"Oh, yes, I met him again."

Tanek smiled.

Eleven

No one was following her.

It was only her imagination, Tania told herself. She was being an idiot.

But relief flooded her as she pulled into the driveway.

Home. Safety.

She sat there for a moment, her gaze on the rearview mirror. The only car that drove by was a day care van loaded with kids.

See, she was being paranoid. This was Minneapolis, not Sarajevo. She got out of the car, popped open the trunk, and took out the first bag of groceries.

"Let me carry that for you."

She jumped and whirled.

Phil was coming up the driveway. "Sorry. Did I scare you?"

"I wasn't expecting you."

Phil took the sack from Tania, grabbed the other two in the trunk, and closed the lid with his elbow. "You should have called me."

"I thought I could manage." Tania smiled at him as

she started up the driveway toward the house. "And, besides, that's not your job."

"Keep me busy. Now that the summer's over, I don't have enough to do with the garden." He grimaced. "I don't know why I'm here anyway now that Nell is in Idaho with Nicholas."

"You're a great help to us." She didn't look at him as she unlocked the front door. "Did . . . Nicholas tell you to watch out for me?"

He frowned. "What do you mean? He said to wait here until he contacted me and help out with anything you asked me to do."

"But not to follow me and keep an eye on me?"

"No." His gaze narrowed on her face. "Some creep been following you?"

"No." She entered the foyer and led him toward the kitchen. "It's probably my imagination. I haven't actually seen anyone. It's just a feeling. Why would anyone want to watch me?"

He grinned and gave a low whistle. "Who wouldn't?" He sobered. "But there are a lot of weirdos wandering around. You can't be too careful these days. Suppose I go with you next time you run your errands?"

She shook her head. "I'd feel foolish. It's my imagination."

"So what?" He set the bags on the counter. "It will give me something to do."

"We'll see." She started to unload a bag. "But I thank you for the offer."

He hesitated, staring at her, before moving toward the door. "You and Dr. Lieber have been great to me. I don't like the idea of you worrying. Just give me a holler if you want company."

She smiled affectionately as she watched the door close behind him. Phil had become an integral part of their lives in the past few weeks. He happily drifted around, chopping wood, washing the cars, puttering in the garden. It gave her a warm feeling to see him look up and wave as he worked in the garden.

Her smile faded as she tossed an empty bag into the recycling bin. She hadn't thought Nicholas would assign Phil to watch her. Why should he? Nell was the one in danger, and Nell was not here. This was America. There were no snipers waiting in the ruins to butcher the unwary.

But her instincts had been honed to acuteness by those years of wariness, and America was not the safe haven she had always thought it to be. Bombings and murders happened here too.

And she had *felt* those eyes on her.

Maybe she should let Phil come with her when she left the house.

Yes, sure, she thought in self-disgust. She would start classes at the university next week. Was she to let the poor man sit outside and wait for her, twiddling his thumbs because her instincts were screaming? Maybe she was having a flashback to Sarajevo. Memories and experiences were supposed to linger in the back of your mind. It could be she was—

She shook her head and put it firmly from her mind. She would play the situation as she saw it, as she always had done. When it was time to leave the house, she would make a decision about asking Phil to accompany her. She didn't have to worry now. She was safe in this house, where she had made a nest for herself.

She thought she was safe, Maritz thought. The Vlados woman was inside Lieber's house, feeling smug and unthreatened.

He scooched down in the seat of the car and reached

for the Big Mac he had picked up on the way to the house. It was good being in control, to set his own pace. No need to watch her every minute. Nell Calder wasn't at the house now.

But she had been there. He had questioned Lieber's neighbors and she had been seen.

At least, he thought it was her. Nell Calder had not been the beauty they had described, but Lieber was a brilliant surgeon and listed on the hospital records as Nell Calder's attending physician. Why have a plastic surgeon, if not to change your face?

He bit into the sandwich and chewed with enjoyment.

He would soon have to resolve the Calder question. Though he wasn't really worried about it. If she had been here, there was a good chance either the doctor or his housekeeper knew where she was now. What they knew, they would tell. He would have taken action sooner, but Lieber wasn't like the funeral director. It wouldn't be easy not to cause ripples if he removed Lieber and Vlados from the scene. It would do no harm to give it another week or so and see if Calder popped up at the house.

Besides, he was enjoying watching Tania Vlados. On the second day he had discovered to his joy and astonishment that she sensed his presence. He had made no mistakes, but she still knew he was there. He could read it in the line of her back, the quick look over her shoulder, the jerkiness of her stride.

It had been a long time since he had stalked a prey. Gardeaux always insisted on a quick, efficient kill. Get in, get out. He didn't understand the pleasure of the hunt, the fear of the victim that was almost as intoxicating as the kill itself.

He finished the Big Mac and tossed the wrapper in the bag. He would give it another half hour before driving by the house and checking it out. She wouldn't be leaving again anytime soon.

She felt safe inside the house.

Nell hit the floor *hard*.

"Get up," Nicholas said. "Fast. Never stay down. You're vulnerable when you're down."

Fast? She couldn't breathe, much less move. The gym was whirling around her.

"Get up."

She got up . . . slowly.

"You'd have been dead a second after you hit the mat," Nicholas said. He gestured for her to come at him again. "Come on."

She scowled at him. "Don't you think you should teach me how to defend myself first?"

"No, I'm teaching you what to do when you're down. It's going to happen sometime no matter how good you get at this. You have to learn how to relax and become boneless so that you're not hurt when you hit the ground. Then you have to roll to avert a hit and bounce to your feet."

"I want to learn how to fight back. Is this the usual method?"

"Probably not. But it's my method. Rush me."

She rushed him.

He threw her down on the mat and straddled her. "If I were Maritz, I'd drive the ball of my hand up underneath your nose and send the bone splinters into your brain."

She glared up at him. He was trying to make her feel as helpless and ineffectual as possible. "No, you wouldn't."

"You think he'd be merciful? Forget it."

"No, you said Maritz liked to use a knife. If he had me down, why would he waste the opportunity?"

Surprise flickered across his face before it hardened. "Either way, you're dead."

"Today. Tomorrow I'll do better. And the day after that I'll be better still."

He gazed down at her for a long while, his expression reflecting a mixture of emotions she couldn't define. "I know you will." His knuckles were curiously gentle as they brushed the line of her cheek. "Damn you."

She was suddenly aware of the dominance of his position, the muscular control of his thighs, the power of his hands pinning her wrists to the mat. The scent of sweat and soap surrounding him enveloped her too. It was . . . disconcerting. She glanced away from him. "Then let me up and we'll start again."

For an instant she felt a tightening of his thigh muscles against her hips. Then he was off her, on his feet. He reached down and pulled her to her feet. "Not today."

Her eyes widened in shock. "What do you mean? We've barely begun."

"We made a hell of a lot more progress than I planned." He started toward the door. "No more today."

"You *promised* me. You owe me."

He glanced over his shoulder. "Then chalk it on the debit side. I'm sure you're keeping score. Go take a hot bath to ease the bruising. Same time tomorrow."

Her hands clenched into fists with frustration as the door slammed behind him. He had made her feel helpless and then left her before she could regain a sense of her own strength. Maybe that was going to be his strategy. Maybe he thought if he constantly discouraged and undermined her, she would give up.

But his departure had been too abrupt. She had an idea he had not meant to curtail the session.

It didn't matter whether he had meant to do it or not. He was gone and the morning was wasted. She must not let it happen. She would go after him and—

What? Drag him back? Arguing wouldn't help her. She would just have to do as he said and chalk up this day as a loss and hope he would keep his promise tomorrow.

An hour later she was wondering if she'd be in any shape to face him tomorrow. She gingerly slipped into the hot water and leaned against the curved back of the tub. The muscles of her shoulders and back were sore and stiffening more with every passing minute. She had a livid bruise on her hip, another on her left thigh, and five purple marks on her right forearm, where his hand had grasped her.

No one could say Tanek didn't leave his stamp on a woman, she thought ruefully. Every time he'd touched her today, he'd hurt her.

Except that moment when he'd brushed his knuckles against her cheek. He hadn't hurt her then.

But even that moment of gentleness had been unsettling.

Forget it. She closed her eyes and let the warmth of the water flow into her. Forget everything but preparing herself for tomorrow.

"Ready to begin?" Tanek motioned for her to come at him. "Let's go."

She stood looking at him. His face was without expression. "You're not going to cut it short again?"

"No way. But you'll wish I would before it's over." She rushed him.

He flipped her over and down on the mat. "Don't stiffen. Boneless. When you hit, roll and on your feet."

Don't stiffen, she told herself as she struggled to her feet. Don't stiffen.

Easy to say. When you were flying through the air, tensing the muscles was as natural as breathing.

At the end of an hour she was so limp with weariness that she no longer tensed any part of her body.

He stood over her. "Shall we stop?"

"No." She struggled to her feet, swaying. "Again."

At the end of another thirty minutes of work, he picked her up, carried her to her room, and dropped her on the bed. He said roughly, "Remind me not to let you call the shots again. You'd go on until I killed you."

He left the room.

She would rest for a moment and then force herself to get into the tub. God, she hurt. She closed her eyes. Tomorrow she would remember not to stiffen when she fell. Tomorrow she would roll and get to her feet . . .

Something cold and wet was pressing against her hand that was hanging off the bed.

She opened her eyes.

Sam. He must have followed Tanek into the room and gotten shut in.

"Do you want out?" she asked. "You'll have to wait a minute until I can move. I'm not in very good shape."

The German shepherd looked at her for a moment and then lay down on the floor beside the bed.

Acceptance. He knew about pain and wanted to comfort her.

She reached a tentative hand down to stroke his head.

The next day, she didn't stiffen with the toss, but she couldn't force herself to spring to her feet.

The day after, she rolled during the first few falls but fell apart when the exhaustion hit her.

The third day she managed to relax, roll, and get to her feet. She felt as if she'd painted a masterpiece. It was coming together!

"Good," Tanek said. "Do it again."

She didn't do it again for another two days. He made sure the falls were harder, the pace faster.

She spent two hours a day in the gym, but it might have been twenty-four. When she wasn't there, she was thinking about it, preparing herself mentally and physically for the next time she faced Tanek. She continued sketching, she talked to Michaela, she ate, she slept, but everything was unreal. She felt as if she were existing in a cocoon with nothing in the world but the dominant figure of Tanek, the gym, and the falls.

But she was growing stronger, more agile, faster. Soon Tanek would no longer be able to totally dominate her.

Tanek heard the sound of light footsteps pass his door.

Nell had left her room. The dream again.

Tanek rolled over on his back on the bed and stared into the darkness.

Tania had told him about the nightmares, but knowing and watching Nell try to survive them was not the same. He had followed her a few times but had not let her become aware of his presence. Not after he'd caught a glimpse of her tear-stained face. She wouldn't want him to see her weakness.

She would go to the living room and curl up on the

couch and look up at the Delacroix or wander to the window and stare out at the mountains. She would stay an hour, sometimes two, before returning to her room.

Did she sleep when she went back to bed?

Precious little, he'd bet. She never appeared fully rested, always balanced on a fine, nervous thread.

Yet it never interfered with her determination or endurance. No matter how many times he hurt her, she came back for more. Strength of spirit and indomitable courage, wrapped in that beautiful fragile package. When she made a mistake, she learned from it. No matter how tired or bruised, she endured.

She endured his hardness, his brutality, his indifference to her pain.

God, he wished she'd go back to bed.

On Tuesday it finally did come together. She found the falls no longer hurt her, and she could roll away from an attacker and bounce to her feet, ready to defend herself.

"By George, I believe she's got it," Tanek said. "Do it again." He threw her, hard.

She was on her feet seconds after she hit the mat.

"Good. Now we can begin. We'll start attack and defense tomorrow."

She smiled brilliantly. "Really?"

"Unless you'd rather I kept on throwing you around the gym."

"I imagine I'll still get enough of that," she said dryly.

"But you'll be able to concentrate on what I'm teaching you and not worry about getting hurt." He threw her a towel and watched her wipe the perspiration from her face. He said, "You did well."

They were the first words of praise he'd given her,

and warmth rushed through her. "I was slow. I didn't think I'd ever learn."

"You were quicker than I was." He wiped his face and neck. "I was only fourteen and had a highly developed sense of self-preservation. I resisted every step of the way, and we didn't have any mats in the warehouse where Terence was teaching me. I nearly got my neck broken a dozen times before I learned."

"Terence?"

"Terence O'Malley."

She could almost see him closing up again. "And who was Terence O'Malley?"

"A friend."

A curt dismissal, but this time she ignored it. He knew everything about her. It was time she learned more about him. "The friend Gardeaux killed?"

"Yes." He changed the subject. "You deserve a reward. What would you like?"

"A reward?" she repeated, surprised. "Nothing."

"Name it. I subscribe to the tutorial system of reward and punishment." He added dryly, "And you've had enough punishments lately."

"There's nothing I want." She thought of something. "Except perhaps . . ."

"What is it?"

"What you said about Maritz—" She stopped. "When you had me down. Something about hitting me under the nose and killing me. Could I learn to do that? Right away?"

He stared at her for a moment and then started laughing. "No candy or flowers or jewelry. Just another lesson. I should have known." His smile faded. "Too bad. I was hoping you'd be fed up with violence by now. I've been exposing you to enough of it."

Violence? There had been pain and frustration, but he had never been violent. She had always known that the force he exerted was measured and without malice. "I don't think you were violent."

"No? It felt like it to me." He shrugged. "But then, I'm not accustomed to throwing around women who aren't even half my weight."

It had bothered him, she realized. Behind that cool mask, distaste had been festering. "I asked you to do it."

"That's right." He stepped closer and took her hand. "Just as you asked me for this pleasant little present. You asked me, so I gave it to you." He lifted her hand to his lips. "Just as I'll give you the gift of killing Maritz with one blow." He turned her hand over and pressed his lips to the palm. "With this very hand."

He had caught her off guard. She stared at him, unable to tear her gaze away from his face. Her palm tingled and she felt as breathless as the times before she had learned to properly hit the mat.

"Isn't painting a picture more satisfying than killing a man, Nell?" he asked quietly.

He dropped her hand and left the gym.

The next day Michaela brought two large cardboard boxes from the Bar X.

Nell was perched on her usual stool, sketching, when she noticed the boxes in the corner. The lids were open and they appeared to be brimming with fabric. "What's that?"

Michaela glanced at the box. "Only some old clothes I brought to take to Lasiter this afternoon. The Basque Benevolent Society is having a rummage sale this Saturday. I need to put them in the truck. I was going through them this morning to make sure they didn't need repairs." She shrugged. "Children are hard on clothes."

"Children?"

"I have two grandchildren. I didn't tell you?"

Michaela a grandmother? The idea was odd. She couldn't imagine her bouncing a grandchild on her knee.

"My daughter Sara's son and daughter," Michaela said. "Six and eight. Come put aside that pad and help me take them to the truck."

Nell obediently set the pad on the butcher block and followed her across the room.

"You take this one." Michaela thrust one of the boxes at her. "I left the pickup in the stable yard." She lifted the other box and swept out of the kitchen.

Nell made a face as she started after her. Michaela made a better general than a grandmother. She could see her rallying the troops and—

Something had fallen out of the box. She stopped to pick it up.

It was a tennis shoe, a very small, red tennis shoe.

A child's shoe. How many times had she picked up shoes like that and tossed them in the closet after she'd put Jill to bed?

She couldn't pick up this shoe.

She could only stare at it.

Jill.

"Hurry, I have to get back to my baking," Michaela called impatiently.

Nell forced herself to kneel and pick up the shoe. She crouched there with the shoe in her hand. It felt so good, so . . . familiar.

"Oh, God," she whispered. She found herself rocking back and forth with the tiny shoe clutched to her breast. "No . . . no . . . no . . ."

"What's keeping—" Michaela was standing in the doorway. She hesitated only a moment before coming forward. "Oh, you dropped a shoe." She took it from

Nell and dropped it into the box. "I can take this now. Go wash your face. You have a smudge." She picked up the box and strode out of the room.

Nell got up slowly and went to the bathroom. No smudge. Her cheeks were streaked with tears. Stupid. Falling apart over a shoe. She had no control over her dreams, but during her waking hours she had thought she was in control, growing tougher, maybe even starting to heal. Was it going to be like this all her life?

"Don't take all day." Michaela was outside the door. "I need you to help peel potatoes."

Michaela never asked for help with the meals. She regarded the kitchen as her exclusive domain. She had ignored Nell's moment of weakness and was trying to keep her busy. Kindness came in all packages.

"Coming." She opened the door. "I'm sorry, I—"

"About what? You were clumsy and dropped a shoe." Michaela headed for the kitchen. "I'm not interested in your chattering. Come and help me."

"That's good." Nicholas tilted the sketch under the lamp. "You've caught her."

Nell shook her head. "Not entirely. It's frustrating as the devil trying to sketch someone who flits around like Michaela."

"Michaela doesn't flit. That's much too airy a term."

"Whatever." She took the sketch back and put it in her portfolio. "But I think I'm ready to set up the easel and oils tomorrow." She looked at him from under her lashes. "Do I get a bonus for that?"

"Nope." He knelt by the fire and stoked the logs. "I'm giving you enough time in the gym. Any more would be overload."

She had thought that would be his answer, but it hadn't hurt to try. Actually, he was probably right. She was satisfied with her progress in the week since he had started teaching her the rudiments of attack and defense. But it would take a lot more time for the moves to become second nature.

"I didn't learn very much about guns at Obanako," she said tentatively.

"Not my area of expertise. Jamie likes guns. If he comes here, maybe you can persuade him to teach you."

"Or knives."

He looked up and met her eyes. "I'll teach you how to defend yourself in a knife attack but not how to use one. You wouldn't have a chance against Maritz anyway. You can't learn in three months what it took him years to learn." He stood up and filled her coffee cup. "You'd better have another weapon, a damn good plan, or just plain luck."

"What about Gardeaux? What would I have to have with Gardeaux?"

"Leave Gardeaux to me."

"I can't. He gave the order." She lifted the coffee cup to her lips. "Tell me about Gardeaux."

He sat down on the hearth and linked his arms around his knees. "You told me you researched him."

"I know what *Time* knows. I want to know what you know."

"He's smart. He's cautious. He wants to move up into the hierarchy of the drug cartel."

"I thought he was already in the hierarchy."

"On the lower rungs and climbing. He wants to reign with Sandequez, Juarez, and Paloma. That's where the real power lies, and he loves the taste of it. He also loves money and beautiful women and he has a passion for rare and antique swords."

She remembered a mention of the sword collection. "Passion?"

He shrugged. "Definitely a passion. Maybe it's an extension of his desire for power."

"A sort of phallic manifestation?"

He chuckled. "In a manner of speaking. Though the picture is a bit mind-boggling."

"He has a wife?"

"He's been married for over twenty years and appears completely devoted to her and their two children." He added, "Though that devotion doesn't keep him from having a mistress in Paris."

"You know who his mistress is?"

"Simone Ledeau, a model. But you can't get at him through her, if that's what you're thinking. Gardeaux makes sure that his ladies are aware of what will happen to them if they betray him."

"How?"

"He probably has them attend one of his private fencing matches at the auditorium he built at his chateau. When he wants to make a production of a punishment, he has a young fencer who disposes of threats to him. It pleases his sense of style."

"Murder?"

"Murder. Though he does give the other man a sword for self-defense."

"What if that man wins?"

"He has a promise of release from Gardeaux, but Gardeaux hasn't had to replace his pet swordsman, Pietro, in over two years. Fencing isn't exactly a skill taught in every neighborhood gym."

"But you said his man was replaced. So sometimes the other side does win." She had a sudden thought. "Was it you?"

"No, it wasn't me." He looked down at his clasped hands. "And he didn't live even though he won."

"Gardeaux doesn't release anyone?"

"He releases them." He abruptly got to his feet. "I'm going into town."

"Now? Why?" she asked, startled.

"I'm tired of questions and living with the thought of Gardeaux and Maritz every minute." He headed for the door. "I'm choking on it."

But he hadn't seemed to mind her questions before they had touched on the fencing matches. She said quietly, "I'm sorry if I upset you."

She flinched as the door slammed behind him.

A moment later she heard the sound of the Jeep roaring out of the stable yard. She stood up and moved toward the window. The taillights fading in the distance gave her a sudden sensation of loneliness. He had visited the Bar X many afternoons in the past weeks, but this was the first time he had gone into town at night. She felt oddly abandoned.

Idiotic. It was just as well he had broken the pattern. She had become entirely too comfortable with him and the evenings spent in this firelit room.

He's a man and you're closer than the women in town.

She felt a ripple of shock as Michaela's words came back to her.

The women in town. Of course, Tanek wouldn't live in the semiwilderness with no sexual outlet. She should be surprised that he hadn't decided he needed a woman before this.

One particular woman?

It was none of her business. He had his life and she had hers. Abandonment was an impossibility in their relationship.

Something soft brushed her thigh, and she looked down to see Sam looking up at her.

"Hi, boy." She gently stroked his head. "He's gone. Want to sleep in my room tonight?"

They might as well stick together.

He had been abandoned too.

"More," Melissa gasped. She lunged upward to take more of him. "That's it. *Help* me."

He dove deep. Deeper.

His release came too soon. He collapsed on top of her, shuddering.

He could feel her flex around him as she climaxed.

He rolled off her onto his back and put his arm beneath his head. He knew he should hold her. Closeness after the act was important to most women.

He didn't want to hold her.

He didn't want to be there.

"It was good," Melissa murmured as she nestled closer. "I'm glad you dropped by, Nicholas."

He stroked her hair. Sex was always good for Melissa. Melissa Rawlins was blessedly uncomplicated, asked little, and gave generously. She was a thirty-four-year-old divorcee who owned her own real estate business in Lasiter and wanted no ties. She was perfect for him.

But he didn't want to be there.

She kissed his shoulder. "I was afraid I wouldn't see you again. I heard there was a woman at your ranch. Is she still there?"

He didn't want to think of Nell now either. "Yes."

She giggled. "Well, she must not be very good." She reached out and grabbed him. "You nearly raped me before I could get my clothes off."

"Rape implies lack of consent." He kissed her temple. "Wrong word."

"Well, I didn't want to fight too hard. I missed you." She stroked him teasingly. "And you missed me."

"Of course." He couldn't leave yet. Melissa was no

whore. He couldn't take and walk away. That wasn't
according to the rules. So give her something, you bastard. He forced himself to slide his arm around her.
"I'm sorry if I was too rough for you."

"I liked it." She yawned. "I like whatever you do
to me. Different though." She released him and cuddled closer. "Do you mind if I take a nap? I had a bitch
of a day."

"Would you like me to leave?"

"No, I just want a nap." She rubbed her cheek cat-
like against his shoulder. "I know you'll want it again
soon."

"It's what you want that matters."

"Then you'll stay the night. I'm not about to let you
go now that you finally decided to pay me a visit."

He smothered a leap of impatience. She had a right
to expect it; he usually stayed the night. "Then go to
sleep. I'll be here."

"Okay," she said drowsily. She was silent a moment
and he thought she was asleep. "Who is she?"

"A friend."

"I didn't mean to be nosy," she whispered. "I was
just . . . curious. You were hurting."

"It's been a long time for me." He touched her
mouth with his forefinger. "Hush and go to sleep."

"You don't want to talk about her."

"There's nothing to talk about." He didn't want to
talk about Nell and he didn't want to think about her.
He should have been able to block her out by losing
himself in sex. He had always used sex to relax and take
the edge off, and he sure was balanced on one hell of
an edge now.

It wasn't working. He didn't want to be here. He
wanted to be back at the ranch with Nell, watching the
absorbed expression on her face as she sketched, seeing
her reach down and pet Sam.

Admit it.

He wanted to be in bed, screwing the hell out of her.

And she wasn't ready. She might not be ready to accept him for a long time, maybe never. It would probably be better if she weren't. He had worked a long time to get his life the way he wanted it, and she would disrupt it. She had already disrupted it. She wasn't a woman who could be relegated to the background and visited when it was convenient for him. Even in her quietest moments, he found himself watching her, worrying about her silences.

The solution was obviously distance, but that wasn't an option. They would continue to live on top of each other, intimately involved every day.

Christ.

"Nicholas hasn't come back from town?" Michaela asked.

Nell didn't look up from her sketchbook. "Not yet."

"It's almost dark. He usually doesn't stay this long with her."

Nell deliberately resisted the impulse to ask the identity of *her*.

"Why did you let him go?" Michaela asked.

"He does what he likes."

"You could have stopped him. He only uses her. Next time give him what he wants and he won't go."

She looked up swiftly. "What?"

"You heard me."

"I'm not sure I did. I thought you wanted me to leave as soon as possible."

"I changed my mind. I've decided I could become used to you."

"Thank you," Nell said dryly.

"And you could become used to the land. You might help to root Nicholas here with us."

"I'm glad you think I could be of service to you."

"You resent my words. I wish only the best for all of us."

"On your terms."

She smiled. "Of course. But I'm willing to make concessions to make you more content. I'll even give you fifteen minutes of stillness a day for you to paint me."

"Your generosity overwhelms me."

"It should." She moved toward the door. "I don't like to stay quiet."

"That's an understatement." Nell put aside the sketch pad as the door closed behind her.

The woman was astonishing, totally deaf to any purpose but her own.

But wasn't she the same? The pot calling the kettle black.

She stood up and moved restlessly toward the window. The sky was darkening as evening approached. She had missed the challenge of the hours spent in the gym. She had become accustomed to the routine, the rhythm of the days.

Accustomed to Tanek.

It was perfectly natural and meant nothing. She had become accustomed to Michaela and Sam too.

Where was he?

A sudden chill touched her. What if he weren't with a woman? Michaela said he never stayed this long. A man who surrounded himself with fences must be in danger when he left them behind.

Sam barked shrilly and bounded down the porch steps.

The Jeep!

She found herself out on the porch, waiting.

Sam was skittering dangerously close to the Jeep's wheels as it roared into the stable yard.

She smiled when she heard Tanek curse as he jerked on the brakes.

"You're late." She walked down the steps. "Michaela almost has supper ready. She would have been upset if you—" She stopped in surprise as she saw Jamie Reardon get out of the Jeep. "Hello."

Tanek was kneeling, quieting the dog. "I had to pick up Jamie from the airport. He came in only an hour ago."

Jamie smiled as he came toward her. "Nick called me early this morning in Minneapolis and said you needed my services. Though I hate to envision a lovely lady with a lethal weapon, naturally I flew to your side." He glanced at the mountains on the horizon and gave a mock shiver. "You can't imagine the sacrifice. No civilized man would venture into this wilderness."

Guns. He was talking about guns, she realized. She had mentioned her lack of knowledge to Tanek only last night. His offhand reference to Jamie had not led her to think he would take action. "Thank you for coming."

Tanek stood up and moved toward the porch. "Come and see the homestead, Jamie. It's not quite the hovel you expect."

"Our Nell has survived all these weeks," Jamie said. "That's an excellent sign that I might be able to tolerate it."

Nell slowly followed them as they went into the house.

Jamie turned and smiled at her. "I didn't mean to intrude. Shall I go away?"

"No, of course not. I'm just surprised," she said quickly. "I didn't expect this."

"Neither did I." He made a face. "But Nick can be persuasive. I promise I won't be in the way."

But everything would be changed. His presence injected a new note, dispelling the intimacy.

Which was what Nicholas had obviously wanted, or he wouldn't have summoned Jamie here. He was growing bored and edgy spending time alone with her.

She ignored the pang the thought gave her. All right, accept the change and make it work for her. She was using this time to learn, and Jamie had something to teach her. "You won't be in the way. I'm glad you're here."

He was wasting time, Maritz realized regretfully. The Calder woman wasn't going to come. He would soon have to put an end to it. Pity. He felt very close to Tania Vlados.

Almost affectionate.

He had watched her, knowing her fear, tasting it. After those first few days she had refused to acknowledge him, but she had felt him. She had gone about her business and he had found himself beginning to feel a tentative respect for her resistance. It made the pleasure of the hunt a hundred times more intense.

He usually had no sexual desire for the victim, but he'd been toying with the idea of joining with her before the end. Sort of a compliment to mark her difference from the others. But honoring her would necessitate doing it in the afternoon, when Lieber wasn't in the house to interfere. During the day there was only the handyman around and he could be dispensed with out in the grounds. Any struggle might involve mistakes, and Maritz needed information before the kill. He would prefer to get it from Tania, if she knew anything.

It might take a long time to get Tania Vlados to give him that information, he thought proudly. She had faced his stalking with rare bravery.

Yes, she deserved to be treated differently from the others.

Twelve

Jamie watched Nell leave the gym. "She's good."

"She's getting there." Tanek wiped his face with the towel.

Jamie grinned. "Aggressive as hell. She almost downed you once."

"Like I said, she's getting there."

"It was interesting watching you. Usually when you're on top of a woman, it's not for that pur—"

"Have you found out anything?"

Jamie shook his head. "I've a few leads, but he's sealed off most of the avenues. It will take time." He paused. "I did run across one bit of information that might interest you. I called Phil to see how he was doing, and he mentioned an article he'd run across in the back pages of the newspaper a few weeks ago. John Birnbaum has disappeared."

Birnbaum. It took a minute for Tanek to make the connection. The funeral home director he'd bribed to falsify Nell's death. "Any connection?"

"Not on the surface. No sign of foul play. A large sum of money was gone from the safe, but it had been opened by someone who knew the combination. And Birnbaum's car has disappeared with him. It appears Birnbaum is in the process of a messy divorce, so there's a possibility he did a flit to avoid paying alimony." He considered for a moment. "But his son thought one of the pine coffins used for cremation was missing."

"Cremation. Gardeaux always did insist on neatness."

"And Minnesota has lakes galore where a car could be sunk." Jamie shrugged. "Of course, it's all supposition and the theory of Birnbaum's flit could be right."

"And it could be wrong. For safety's sake, we have to assume it's Gardeaux or Maritz and that he found out what he wanted from Birnbaum. Did you tell Phil to keep a sharp eye on Tania and Joel?"

"I didn't have to tell him. He told me. He's not a fool. He says he hasn't noticed any activity, but Tania mentioned once a few weeks ago that she felt as if she had been followed. Nothing since then."

"Not good."

"I disagree. No news is definitely good news in this case."

"The house hasn't been searched?"

Jamie shook his head. "And they have an A-one security system."

"I still don't like it."

"You can't surround them with armed guards on the chance that something *might* happen."

"I promised Joel I'd protect him if he helped me. I made a mistake on Medas. I'm not doing it again." He thought about it. "Why don't you call Phil and tell him to contact us if there's anything—"

"I already did."

"Of course you did." He grimaced. "Sorry."

"And I'll go back there as soon as you let me leave

this wilderness and add my considerable intellect to searching out the truth of the matter."

So much for distancing and barriers. Well, Nicholas had tried. It must be fate. Bull, he told himself in disgust. He was only looking for an excuse and had found it. "Three days. Teach her all you can in that time. I don't want her to realize there's anything wrong, or she'd hop on a plane for Minneapolis."

Jamie nodded. "I can teach her the rudiments in that time. The rest is practice anyway." He expelled a sigh of relief. "I admit I'll be glad to get away from this place. Everything is too big and the silence is disturbing."

"How would you know? You haven't been still since you got here."

"Your ingratitude chills the heart." He headed for the door. "I'll go find Nell. She'll appreciate me."

Nell made a face. "Missed again."

"But you hit the target every time," Jamie said. "It will come."

"When?"

"You're too impatient. You can't expect to hit the bull's-eye after only a day's training." He moved forward and adjusted the target on the corral fence. "You have a good eye and a steady hand. Use them. Concentrate."

She frowned. "I am concentrating."

He grinned. "Then don't concentrate so hard. Maybe you want it too much."

That was possible. She did want it. Her hand tightened on the Lady Colt Jamie had given her. "You'd think I'd get it."

"Not everyone is a born marksman, and a man is a bigger target than a bull's-eye. If you can learn to get off quick shots at the target itself from any position, you'll be okay."

"I don't want to be okay. I want to be good."

"No, you want to be perfect."

She smiled and nodded. "I want to be perfect."

"And you'll practice until you are." He sighed. "God preserve me from the obsessed." He took the gun from her. "Come on. We'll take a break and have a cup of coffee."

"I'm not tired."

"*I* am." He took her arm and firmly led her across the stable yard. "And all this fresh air is disconcerting me. No wonder God invented pubs."

"I thought man invented pubs."

"It's a common misconception. No, they're definitely God's country." He waved a hand at the plains and mountains. "After He abandoned this wilderness."

"If you miss your pub so much, why are you still here?"

"Nick called me." He shrugged. "And I'm a bit obsessed myself. Terence and I went way back."

"Terence O'Malley?"

"Nick told you about him?"

"He told me Gardeaux killed him. They were good friends?"

"Closest thing Nick had to a father. Terence picked him up out of the gutter. He was an ignorant little savage just managing to survive, but Terence liked him. He took him in and fed him and taught him. It didn't take much. Nick was hungry. He wanted to learn everything in the world. He outpaced Terence in no time and went out and grabbed more. He started to climb and he took Terence with him." He inclined his head. "As well as my humble self."

"Climb where?"

"Out of the gutter in the only way he could."

"Crime?"

"It's all we knew. Terence and I were bumblers, small-time smugglers and occasional thefts, but Nick . . . Ah, Nick was an artist. He always knew what he wanted and how to go about getting it."

"And what did he want?"

"Out. With enough money to make sure he'd never be drawn back in the loop."

"Evidently he succeeded."

Jamie nodded. "And he tried to give us what we wanted. I took it and ran, but Terence didn't want to settle down. He'd been at it too long. He liked the life, the thrill of the score. When Nick bought this place, Terence tipped his hat and wandered away."

"And?"

"He stepped on Gardeaux's toes." His lips tightened. "He came back to Nick to die."

"What happened?"

"Gardeaux made an example of him." He opened the front door for her. "A tiny bit of *coloño* culture on a sword tip. Ninety-seven percent fatal and a death that was unimaginably cruel. Nick had to stand by and watch him die."

"*Coloño?* I've never heard of it."

"It originated in the Amazon. All kinds of new diseases are emerging since they've been hacking down the rain forests. It's communicated only through blood so it's not contagious, but it's first cousin to Ebola. I'm sure you've heard of that little nasty."

She shuddered. She had read in the newspapers about the disease that literally ate its victims' organs. "I've heard of it."

"The cartel keeps a supply of serum on hand to use on people who displease them. The threat works very well. They keep Gardeaux well supplied."

"Diabolic."

"Yes. Take warning." He met her gaze. "Do you think Nick would be acting with such care if Gardeaux were an easy target?"

No. Watching his friend die slowly and painfully must have been agonizing. "I'm here, aren't I? I'm being patient."

"Except when you don't hit the bull's-eye."

She smiled. "Except then."

"I thought he was going to stay longer." Nell watched in disappointment as Michaela maneuvered the Jeep down the road with Jamie in the passenger seat. "I haven't learned enough."

"He had some other things to do. He said you were doing well enough to continue on your own," Nicholas said. "And he finds the place too barbaric for his taste."

"It's not barbaric." She looked out at the mountains. "It's basic."

"It is that." He glanced back at the Jeep that had now reached the first gate before asking her, "You like it here?"

She had not thought about it. The homestead was just the setting for the work she had been doing. Yet now she realized that she had gradually become accustomed to the peace and ambiance of the place. She felt at home here. "Yes, I like it. It feels . . . rooted."

"That's why I bought it." He was silent a moment and then turned abruptly on his heel. "Get into jeans and a warm jacket and meet me at the stable."

She stared at him in bewilderment. "Why?"

"Do you ride?"

"I've ridden before, but I'm no cowgirl."

"You don't have to be. You're not going to be roping steers. We're just going to ride up to the foothills

to meet Jean and Peter. They should have reached the
lower levels with the herd by now."

"But why are we going?"

"Because I want to go." His smile was suddenly
reckless. "And I've decided to stop being boringly responsible and do what I want to do. Don't you want
to see how Peter has adjusted to the life of a herdsman?"

"Yes but I— How long will it take?"

"We'll be at the mesa where they usually make camp
by late afternoon. We'll overnight with the herd and
come back in the morning." He smiled mockingly. "In
plenty of time for you to practice with your new toy."

"I could take the gun with me."

"No, you can't. You're not good enough yet. You
might hit one of the sheep or dogs."

"Then maybe I should stay here and—"

"Do you want to go?" he asked with exasperation.

She did want to go, she realized suddenly. She
wanted to meet Jean Etchbarras and see Peter again. It
would do no harm to take a break. She would work
twice as hard when she came back. She walked swiftly
toward the porch. "I'll meet you at the stable."

Jean Etchbarras was no more than five foot six, stocky,
muscular, and his smile lit his lined, round face with
humor. Nell would no more have connected him to
the statuesque Michaela than to Cleopatra.

"I'm glad to meet you." He beamed. "My Michaela
says you're a fine woman."

Nell blinked. "She does?"

He nodded and turned to Tanek. "We lost one
sheep to a wolf. Still, that is good."

Tanek smiled. "Yes, that is good. Nell came to see
Peter. Where is he?"

Jean gestured to the back of the herd. "There. He did well."

Peter had seen her and was eagerly waving but did not come forward.

"See? He stays and guards the sheep. Sometimes he forgets things, but never to watch the sheep." Jean's proud smile caused the sun lines around his dark eyes to deepen. "He learned quickly."

"May I go to him?" Nell asked.

Jean nodded. "It's time to set up camp anyway. Tell him to set the dogs to watch and come in and eat his supper."

Nell handed her horse's reins to Tanek and started around the huge herd. She wrinkled her nose as she came closer to them. Sheep en masse were definitely not sweet-smelling, and their fleece was dirty beige, not white. So much for Mary's little lamb.

"Aren't they pretty?" Peter asked when she got within hearing range. "Don't you like them?"

"Well, you certainly appear to like them." She gave him a quick hug and stepped back to look at him.

He was not as brown as Jean, but he was tanner than she had last seen him. He was wearing a ragged wool poncho, boots, and leather gloves. His eyes were sparkling, his expression glowing. "I don't have to ask if you're well."

He pointed to a black and white Border collie circling a straying lamb. "That's Jonti. He's a shepherd, like me. At night, when we're not on guard, we sleep together."

"How nice." No wonder he smelled like a combination of sheep and dog. Not that it made any difference. Nothing mattered but the fact that he was happy and proud of himself.

"And Jean says that when Jonti's mate has puppies, I can have one and he'll teach me how to train it."

This was beginning to sound disturbingly permanent. "Won't that take a long time?"

His smile faded. "You're thinking I may have to leave." He shook his head. "I'm never going away. Jean doesn't want me to leave. He says I'm a good shepherd." He added simply, "I can belong here."

She felt tears sting her eyes. "That's wonderful, Peter." She cleared her throat. "Jean says for you to set the dogs to guard and come in to supper."

Peter nodded and called sternly, "Guard, Bess. Guard, Jonti." He turned and fell into step with her. "Isn't it pretty here? You should see the high country. It's all green and soft and yet you look up and see the mountains right on top of you and it's kind of scary but not really and . . ."

"He's happy." Nell took a sip of her coffee and looked over the leaping flames to Peter and Jean on the other side of the campfire. Jean was showing Peter how to whittle and Peter's brow was knotted in concentration. "He's walking on air."

"Yes." Tanek's gaze followed her own. "Nice."

"He wants to stay."

"Then he'll stay."

"Thank you."

"For what? He's earning his place. It's not easy being a shepherd. Isolation, hard work, sun, snow. I tried it for a season when I first came here."

"Why?"

"I thought it would make the place more my own."

"Did it?"

"It helped."

"Possession is important to you."

He nodded. "I didn't have anything but the clothes on my back when I was a kid, and I wanted to grab everything in the world and hold on tight. I suppose I still have the instinct."

She smiled. "No question about it."

"At least, I've modified my demands." He poked at the fire with a stick. "And nowadays I pay for what I want."

She looked up at the mountains. "You love this place."

"From the first moment I saw it. Sometimes it happens that way."

"It did for Peter. He said he belonged here." Her gaze returned to the boy's face. "I believe it. He looks . . . complete."

"Complete?"

"Finished." He was still looking at her inquiringly and she searched for words. "He's not an ugly duckling anymore."

"He looks a little tanner, but I don't see any startling improvement in his appearance."

"That's not what I meant. When I was a little girl my grandmother used to tell me about the ugly ducklings of the world and how they all became swans." She shrugged. "And then I found out that it wasn't necessarily true."

"It was for you."

"But that was a miracle. Joel's miracle. But lately I've been thinking that perhaps everyone has a shot at becoming a swan. Because it's partly inside. If you search out who you are and come to peace with yourself, maybe that's a kind of miracle too. Maybe as we grow out of all the awkwardness of immaturity and self-doubt, it all comes together. Maybe that's what we—" She stopped and made a face. "I sound so profound. Why aren't you laughing at me?"

"Because I applaud any sign that you're thinking of something besides Medas. So Peter is finished?"

"You *are* laughing at me." When he didn't reply, she said, "Maybe not finished, but he's taken a big step."

"A goose step?" He held up his hand. "Sorry, I couldn't resist. All these fowl allegories are befuddling me. Actually, I think it makes sense. So Joel created a swan in more ways than one?"

She shook her head. "Not me. I'm not finished. I'm . . . splintered. But I think you know who you are. So does Tania." Her gaze shifted to his face, and she found he was no longer smiling but was looking at her with disturbing intentness. She quickly glanced away and said lightly, "Tania may be a swan, but I'm sure you're a chicken hawk."

"Possibly." His tone was absent and she still felt his stare on her face.

She shivered as a breath of icy wind pierced the warm cocoon of the circle of the campfire.

"Button your jacket," he said.

She didn't move.

"Button it," he repeated. "It gets cold here in the hills."

She thought of disobeying him, but why cut off her nose to spite him? She buttoned her jacket. "I don't need you to tell me how to care for myself. I've been doing it for a long time."

"Not very well," he said with sudden harshness. "You let everyone within striking distance make a doormat of you. You gave up a career you loved, you let your parents stampede you into marriage to a man who didn't give a damn about you, and then—"

"You're wrong." She was caught off guard by his abrupt roughness. "Richard cared for me. I'm the one who cheated him."

"I can't believe you. He's still managing to manipulate your emotions even though—"

"Richard's dead. Stop talking about him."

"The hell I will." He turned his head and met her eyes. "Why won't you admit the bastard used you? He had a sweet little well-bred wife he could dominate to his heart's content, a wife who would never say no because she was filled with gratitude that he had lowered himself—"

"Shut up." She drew a deep breath. "What difference does it make to you anyway?"

"Because I want to go to bed with you, dammit."

Her mouth fell open. "What?"

"You heard me." His words hammered at her. "Or should I use more earthy Anglo-Saxon terms? Do you want to hear it in Chinese? Greek?"

"I don't want to hear it at all," she said shakily.

"I know that. I didn't say I was going to try to drag you into bed. I know you're not ready for that."

"Then why mention it at all?"

"Because I want it," he said simply. "And I'm tired of fighting it. And because it won't hurt to put the thought into your head. Maybe I'll get lucky."

She moistened her lips. "I wish you hadn't said anything. It will make things uncomfortable."

"Join the club. I've been uncomfortable for some time. I'm uncomfortable now."

Her gaze dropped to his lower body and quickly sidled away. "I'm sorry. I never meant . . . I wish you—"

"Would let you put your head under a pillow and ignore it?" he asked. "Just as you've been doing for the past few weeks?"

"I haven't been ignoring it. I didn't know."

"You knew. It's hard to ignore."

"You hid it well."

He smiled lopsidedly. "Not that well. It's a condition that's not easy to disguise."

Had she known and buried her head in the sand? Perhaps. It was possible she had rejected Michaela's words because she had not wanted to believe them. "I didn't want this to happen."

"No, sex would get in the way, wouldn't it? Though we could probably squeeze it in between murder and mayhem."

"You needn't be sarcastic."

"Yes, I do. Sarcasm can be very satisfying. The only satisfaction I may get from you."

"Use someone else for your verbal punching bag." She paused as a sudden thought occurred to her. "Does this mean you won't teach me anymore?"

He stared at her. "You're incredible."

"Does it?"

"No, I rule my body, it doesn't rule me." He muttered, "Most of the time."

"Good." She put her forgotten cup of coffee on the ground and lay down in her blankets. "Then it won't interfere."

"It wouldn't interfere if you decide to go to bed with me either. I'm asking for sex, not a lifetime commitment."

"You don't understand. I'm not like you." She bit her lower lip. "I can't just—I've had sex with only two men in my entire life."

"Did you like it?"

"Of course I liked it."

"Then maybe you should try a third. You say Nell Calder is dead. Why are you clinging to her sense of morality?" He smiled recklessly. "Let Eve Billings go to bed with me. She's alive and functioning, and I'm not particular."

She frowned. "Don't be ridiculous. I just wish you hadn't seen fit to tell me, since it's an exercise in futility."

"Not entirely. It made you aware of something about me besides my knack for martial arts." He spread his blanket. "You'll think about it and wonder about how we'd be together." He lay down and closed his eyes. "We'd be very good, Nell. I wasn't raised in a whorehouse without learning how to make damn sure of it."

She felt heat flood her and she instinctively sought to stem it. "You left there when you were eight years old," she said tartly.

He opened one eye. "I was precocious."

She shut her own eyes and drew the blanket over her. "Bull."

"You'll never know unless you try me." She heard the rustle of his blankets as he settled.

Go to sleep, she told herself. Tanek had propositioned her and she had refused. It was done. There was no reason to feel uneasy. He was a civilized man who would take no for an answer.

He was also a man who had fought for everything he wanted from childhood and won. He would not give up easily. He would not force her, but he was not above persuasion.

But you could say no to persuasion, you could refuse anything you didn't want. She didn't want the disturbance and hot mindlessness connected with sex. She wanted to stay cool and focused, to stand outside, apart.

She opened her eyes. Tanek was lying with eyes closed, his lax hand outstretched toward the fire. A strong hand, well shaped, capable, the nails cut short. She knew that hand well. She knew its power and lethal force. A dangerous hand. Yet now it didn't look dangerous. Just strong . . . and masculine. She had always loved to paint hands. There was something magical about them. Hands built cities and created great works of art, they could be brutal or gentle, bring pain or pleasure.

Like Tanek.

She felt as if she were melting just looking at the damn man's hand. Why the devil did this have to happen? She wanted her sexuality to stay soundly asleep.

Too late. But not too late for control. Maybe it would go away.

She closed her eyes again. She could smell the evergreens and the burning oak and feel the coldness of the air. Awareness. She was suddenly acutely sensitive to sound and scent, the rough feel of the wool blanket against her bare arms. Nothing had changed. Jill was still dead. Her body had no right to come alive again.

Damn Tanek.

"Sharper," Tanek said. "You're sluggish. I could have put you down twice this morning."

She whirled and kicked him in the stomach.

He staggered back but instantly recovered to grab her arm as she closed in to finish him. He flipped her down and straddled her. "Sluggish."

"Let me up," she panted.

"Maritz wouldn't let you up."

"I was distracted. I wouldn't be distracted with Maritz."

He got off her and pulled her to her feet. "Why are you distracted?"

"I didn't sleep well."

"You never sleep well. You wander around the house like a ghost."

She hadn't realized he knew. "I'm sorry if I disturbed you."

"You do disturb me." He turned his back on her.

"Go take a bath and a nap. Tomorrow I want you alert and razor-sharp."

Like him. Since they had come back from the mesa two days before, he had been razor-sharp and all edges. She did not know what she had expected, but it was not to have him treat her with brusque indifference.

No, not indifference. She knew he was aware of her, that was part of the problem. He *exuded* awareness beneath that cool, incisive exterior.

And she was aware of Tanek.

Christ, she was aware of him.

"Go to bed." Tanek closed his book and stood up. "It's late."

"In a minute. I want to finish this sketch." She didn't look up. "Good night."

"I thought you were done with the sketches for Michaela."

"Another few won't hurt before I start painting."

She could feel his eyes on her, but she didn't look up.

"Don't be late. You were so groggy, you weren't worth my time this morning."

She flinched. "I'll try not to disappoint you."

"If you do, you'll go a week without a session. I told you I believed in reward and punishment."

She said quietly, "Are you sure you're not looking for an excuse?"

"Maybe. Don't give me one."

She drew a breath of relief as he left the room. When he was with her, she had to fight to keep herself from looking at him. She didn't want to see his lean body lounging in the chair or his hand turning the pages of the book. She didn't want to smell the scent of soap and aftershave that surrounded him.

She traced in the last few strokes of the hairline. Her hand was shaking, she realized. She hated to feel this weak. She didn't want to respond like an animal in heat as she watched the way he moved across the room. It hadn't been like this with Richard, or even Bill. What the hell was wrong with her?

She put down her pencil and studied the sketch of Tanek. She had thought if she used him as a subject it would act as a catharsis. She had caught his likeness very well. The quiet intelligence, the strength, the intensity that lay beneath the surface, the faint hint of sensuality in the curve of his lower lip . . .

Sensuality. Had the sensuality been there or had she let her own obsession color the sketch? She didn't know. She knew only that it was there, stark and raw before her.

She jumped up and stuffed the sketchbook into her portfolio. She was hot, her cheeks flushed and feverish. Stupid. Stupid. Stupid. She should never have sketched him. It hadn't helped. Where was the control she had been going to exercise? She wasn't a young girl with hormones raging, panting for her first encounter.

But she felt as vulnerable and unsure as that girl. She had thought she'd passed through that valley of uncertainty. What was the use of being confident in other aspects of her life if she let herself be swayed by—

Forget it. Go to bed. Go to sleep. Start again tomorrow.

If she could sleep. She had lain there for hours last night, frustrated, wanting—

She *would* sleep.

She was dreaming again.

Tanek stopped in the hall as he heard the soft, whimpering sounds coming from behind Nell's door.

Dreaming. Hurting.

He should go to his room and forget it. It wasn't as if it didn't happen almost every night. He couldn't help her. He didn't *want* to help her.

To breach those dreams would be to draw closer to her, and he was too close already.

He wanted to screw that strong, lovely body, not soothe her tortured soul.

Hell, he would go to bed and forget her.

Down, down, down, touching the rose . . .

Nell fought her way out of the heavy layers of sleep and away from the dream.

She lay there shaking, trying to control the sobs.

I'm sorry, baby. I'm sorry, Jill.

She sat up and thrust her feet blindly into her slippers.

Get away from the bed, the room, the dream . . .

The living room. Space, fire, windows . . .

She moved quickly down the dark hallway. She could see the glow of the firelit walls of the living room ahead. It was going to be all right. She would stay there until she was calm and then go back to bed and—

She stopped abruptly in the doorway of the living room.

"Come in." Tanek was sitting on the leather couch before the fire, wrapped in a white terry robe. "I've been waiting for you."

She whispered, "No, I don't . . ." She backed away. "I didn't mean—I'll go."

"And leave me to sit here, worrying about you? Why? Do you brood more efficiently alone?"

"I wasn't brooding."

"The hell you—" He broke off and said wearily, "Sorry. I know you weren't. I'm the one who's brooding. You're just trying to survive. Come on in and we'll try to do it together."

She hesitated. Her feelings for him were confused enough, she didn't want to be exposed to him when she was this vulnerable.

He looked up and smiled faintly. "Come on. I won't bite."

No edge. No sharpness. She came slowly toward him.

"Good." He gazed back at the fire, ignoring her.

She perched on the edge of the stool beside the fire.

"You needn't be so tense. I'm not going to jump on you. Neither physically nor verbally. I don't fight dirty with the walking wounded."

"You don't fight dirty at all."

"Sure I do. You just haven't seen me in the right arena." He reached into the pocket of his robe, drew out a handkerchief, and threw it to her. "Wipe your face."

She dabbed at her cheeks. "Thank you."

A silence fell, only the sound of the crackling wood and their breathing in the air. She began to relax. His silent presence was oddly comforting. This was better than being alone to face the demons. He couldn't share the dreams, but he kept them at bay.

"You can't go on like this, you know," he said quietly.

She didn't answer. There was no answer.

"Tania told me about the dreams. Sometimes it helps to talk. Would you like to tell me what they're about?"

"No." She met his gaze and then shrugged. "Medas."

"I know they're about Medas. What else?"

"Jill," she said jerkily. "What else could there be?"

"I can understand sorrow. I can't understand torment."

"Jill is dead and Maritz is still out there."

"Anger, not torment."

She felt cornered. She wasn't in any condition to accept probing. "I told you I didn't want to talk about it."

"I think you do. I think that's why you didn't run away when you saw me here. What happens in your dream, Nell?"

Her hands opened and closed nervously. "What do you think happens?"

"Are you struggling with Maritz?"

"Yes."

"Where is Jill?"

She didn't answer.

"Is she in the bedroom?"

"I don't want to talk about it."

"Are you on the balcony?"

"No."

"Can you hear the shots from downstairs?"

"No, not anymore. All I hear is the music box."

Down, down, down, we go, touching the rose so red.

Why wouldn't he stop? She was being drawn back into that dark, hazy world.

"Where is Jill?"

Damn him, why wouldn't he stop?

"Where is Jill, Nell?"

"She's in the doorway," Nell burst out. "She's standing in the doorway, crying, and watching us. Is that what you want to know?"

"That's what I want to know. Why didn't you want to tell me?"

Her nails dug into her palms as her hands clenched. "Because it's none of your business."

"Why?"

Here we go down, down, down.

"Why, Nell?"

"Because I *screamed*." Tears were running down her cheeks. "I didn't think . . . they always tell you to scream to frighten off an attacker. I screamed and she came out of the bedroom. It was my fault. If I hadn't screamed, she might have stayed in bed. He might not have known she was there. She might have been safe."

"My God."

She was rocking back and forth on the stool. "It was my fault. She came out and he saw her."

"It wasn't your fault."

"Don't tell me that," she said fiercely. "Didn't you hear me? I screamed."

"A terrible sin when a man is trying to stab you to death."

"It was a sin. She was my daughter. I should have thought. I should have protected her."

He grabbed her shoulders and shook her. "You did what you thought was right. Maritz would have found her anyway. He doesn't leave any ends untied."

"He might not have known she was there."

"He would have known."

"No, I screamed and he—"

"Stop it. The music box." He jerked her into his arms, his hand burying her head in his shoulder. "You said the music box was still playing. He would have known someone was in the other room. He would have checked."

She pushed back and stared at him in shock.

"You didn't think of that?"

She shook her head.

"It doesn't surprise me." He stroked her hair back from her face. "I wondered why you didn't blame me for what happened. You were too busy blaming yourself."

"I still blame myself. Do you think remembering the music box is going to make everything all right?"

"No, not until you forgive yourself for being alive when Jill is dead."

"When Maritz is dead, I'll forgive myself."

"Will you?"

"I don't know," she whispered. "I hope so."

"So do I." He drew her back into his arms and rocked her back and forth. "So do I, Nell."

She could smell his scent, feel the roughness of the terry-cloth robe against her cheek. No passion, not that heated awareness, just a golden peace. She stayed there for a long time, letting the peace enfold her, heal her.

Finally, she raised her head. "I should go back to my room and get to sleep. You'll say I'm sluggish tomorrow."

"Probably." He drew her down on the couch and pushed her head back on his shoulder. "Worry about it then."

She relaxed against him and let the peace flow into her, around her. Strange that Tanek, who wasn't at all peaceful, could bring her this serenity. She would stay just a little longer and then go. . . .

She was nestled against him as trustingly as if he were her mother, Tanek thought in rueful disgust.

It wasn't what he'd had in mind.

He'd wanted casual sex and emotional distance.

He'd gotten no sex and a greater intimacy than he'd ever experienced with a woman.

His own fault. He hadn't been forced into the role of surrogate mother.

Except by Nell's need.

His arm was cramped and painful, but he didn't move it from around her. He looked down at her hand lying lax on his thigh. Tiny half-moon marks indented the palm where she'd dug her nails. He gently touched

one red circle. Scars. These marks would fade, but the
unseen ones would linger. They were as ugly as his
own, and the wounds bonded them together.

She stirred against him and murmured something inaudible.

"Shh." His arm tightened around her.

That's what a mother should do, right? Give comfort
and hold the nightmares away.

He sighed resignedly. This definitely wasn't what
he'd had in mind.

Thirteen

Nell sleepily opened her eyes when he put her down on her bed.

"It's okay. Just tucking you in." He pulled the cover over her. "Go back to sleep."

She met his eyes, beautiful light eyes shimmering in the dimness of the room. "Good night."

"Call if you need me."

"I won't need you. Thank you for—"

He was gone. No, not really gone. She still felt his presence . . . comforting, sensual. How strange that the two could exist side by side. At the moment, comfort was a bigger part of their relationship than sex, but she knew that would shift. The prospect no longer disturbed her, she realized. Something had changed that night.

How stupid she'd been to resist, she thought drowsily. The man who had held her while she slept was no threat. Sex was no threat. It could be controlled like anything else, and the release would be good for her. They would be thrown together for weeks to come, and there was no sense in making it difficult for both of them. She would go to him tomorrow night.

A tiny stir of anticipation rippled through her, and she quickly suppressed it. She must not dwell on it and make it more important than it was.

It was only sex.

"You haven't found her yet?" Gardeaux asked softly. "What the hell have you been doing?"

Maritz's hand tightened on the telephone receiver. "I have a lead. She and the doctor's housekeeper were pretty chummy. The housekeeper might know where she is or if she might come back. I've been watching the doctor's house."

"Just watching?"

"I'll get her."

"Alive. We need her alive now. Things have changed. She may be the key."

"I know. I know. You told me."

"But did you listen?"

Bastard. Maritz gritted his teeth. "I said I'll get her."

"You seem to be having trouble with this little problem. Should I send someone else?"

"No," he said quickly. "I have to go now. I'll be in touch."

He hung up the phone. Send someone else? he thought, outraged. Spoil the end of the hunt, when he'd devoted so much time and effort to it.

No way.

Tanek looked up from his book when Nell opened the door. "Yes?"

She stood in the doorway. The lamplight fell on his bare shoulders and the triangle of dark hair that thatched his chest. He was obviously naked beneath the sheet. She took a deep breath. "May I come in?"

He closed the book. "Do you need to talk?"

"No." She moistened her lips. "Thank you."

"You're welcome."

"I wondered if you . . . do you still . . ." She said in a rush, "I'd like to go to bed with you, if you don't mind."

He went still. "Oh, I don't mind. May I ask why?"

"I thought—There's too much tension between us. It will be better when—"

"Oh, it's therapeutic?"

"Yes. No." She drew a deep breath. "I want it," she said baldly.

He smiled and held out his hand. "Hallelujah."

She tore off her nightshirt, flew across the room, and dove beneath the covers and into his arms. "I don't know what to do," she said fiercely. "I hate this. I thought I'd never feel this uncertain again. Everything seemed so clear."

"Everything is clear." He stroked her hair. "What's the problem?"

"What's the problem? One, I don't know if I'm doing the right thing. Two, I tried to tell myself that taking what I want is strength, but it might be weakness. And three, I've had two men and you've probably had two million women."

He chuckled. "Not quite."

"Well, you get the idea."

"I get the idea." He kissed her temple. "If you're nervous, we'll just lie here for a while and be together."

She relaxed against him. She could hear the steady pounding of his heart beneath her ear. It was like last night and she suddenly felt safe. "Maybe just for a little while."

"And if it will give you more confidence, I've never gone to bed with Helen of Troy."

"What?"

"Didn't Joel tell you he was aiming at giving you a face more memorable than Helen of Troy's?"

"No." She was silent a moment. "Is that why you're willing to—"

"Willing is the wrong word. Eager. Frantic."

"Stop trying to distract me. You want me because of this face that Joel gave me."

"I want you because you're Nell Calder and all that implies."

"But you would never have gone to bed with the old Nell Calder. You wouldn't have even noticed me."

"I did notice you. I noticed the smile and your eyes and the—"

"But you wouldn't have wanted to go to bed with me."

He lifted her chin and looked into her eyes. "What do you want me to say? Am I attracted to beauty? Yes, but it's not all I look for in a woman. If you suddenly reverted to that woman on Medas, would I still want you? Yes, because I *know* you now. I know your potential, your stubbornness, your strength. . . ."

She grimaced. "Very sexy."

"Strength is sexy. Intelligence is sexy. You always had those qualities beneath that meek exterior." A rueful smile quirked the corner of his lips. "Now, will you stop making comparisons? I feel polygamous trying to seduce both of you."

"Sorry, I only wondered. It just occurred to me." She buried her face in his chest again. "Sometimes I do feel like two people. Not often. That other woman is fading away."

"No, she's not. She's just blending into the person you are now." He touched her lower lip with his finger. "As I'm aching to do. Have you had enough time? I promise I'll go slowly."

She suddenly realized his heart was beating harder

against her ear and his muscles were taut and tense against her. It had been hard for him to wait, but he had given her the space she needed, the words she needed.

She lifted her head and kissed him. She whispered, "You don't have to go slowly."

"Go get cleaned up," Tania ordered Joel as soon as he came into the house. She perched a fuchsia party hat on his head and slipped the elastic band beneath his chin. He looked tired. Not a good sign. "Tonight we celebrate."

"I look stupid in party hats."

She stopped him from taking it off. "Nonsense. You look wonderful. The color is just right for you. It goes with your hair."

"My hair is not fuchsia." He glanced at her peach georgette dress. "That's pretty. I like all those flowers. You look like a garden. What are we celebrating?"

"I got an A on my English exam. This is very good, when you think of what a horrid language English is." She kissed him on the cheek and gave him a push toward the stairs. She put a green party hat on her own head. "I'm very smart, yes?"

He smiled. "Very smart."

"I've made pot roast and potatoes and a new dessert with lemon sauce. Low fat for your heart. Healthy. Since you think yourself so old, I thought this would make you happy."

"I never said I was old," he said, stung. "You're just . . . young."

She shrugged and hurried to the dining room. "Hurry." She checked the flower arrangement on the table, lit the candles, and headed for the kitchen. She set the platter with the pot roast on the table as Joel came into the dining room. He was still wearing the party hat, she saw with approval. "Sit. Eat."

She kept the conversation light throughout dinner and coffee afterward in the living room. "I did well. Wonderful, yes?"

He smiled. "Wonderful."

She had always loved his smile. From the first moment he had walked into her hospital room those many years ago. "I even gave you caffeine in your coffee. You know, of course, that I'm buttering you up."

"I suspected it. You didn't get an A on the test?"

"Oh, yes, but I knew I would. It was no triumph."

"Then why am I wearing this extremely stupid party hat?"

She grinned. "Because it is good for you." Her smile faded as she moved across the room and stared out the window. "And if you would be sensible, we would have reason to celebrate."

He immediately stood up. "I've had a rough day. I'm not up to arguing with you, Tania."

"You don't argue. I could win an argument. You just say no."

"And I'm saying it again. What made you think tonight would be different?"

She whirled on him. "Because you're a fool," she said shakily. "You behave like that stupid Galahad. Why can't you be like other men and take and be happy?"

"Self-defense. I'd be miserable when you decided that I was—What's wrong?" His gaze narrowed on her face. "You're really upset."

"Of course I'm upset. Do you expect me to keep on laughing about this? Every minute of life is so precious, and you're letting it ebb away from us." She folded her arms across her chest to stop them trembling.

"How do you know—" She whirled away from him. "Oh, go away. You don't understand anything. You're a stupid, stupid man."

"I'm doing what I think is best, Tania," he said gently. "Life *is* precious, and I won't have it spoiled for you."

"Go away." She stared blindly out the window, fighting back the tears.

"Tania . . ."

She didn't answer, and a few moments later she heard him leave. She hadn't thought she could persuade him. The night had been a complete blunder. She had picked a time when he was tired and probably feeling every one of his years. She should have stopped the moment she had seen his face when he had walked in the door.

She couldn't stop. She'd had to try. Lately, she'd had the feeling that time was running out. . . .

She stared into the darkness. She was crazy. He couldn't be out there. Surely she would have seen some sign of him during these weeks.

You bastard, why won't you go away?

She was only talking to a delusion from her past. There was no one out there.

She looked cute in that silly party hat, Maritz thought. But her expression was the tense, wary one he'd come to know, the one he brought to her face.

Thank you for inviting me to the party, Tania.

Yes, I'm still with you.

She turned away from the window and he lowered the Russian-made binoculars.

Yes, it would definitely have to be in the house.

She felt so safe there.

Nell avoided Nicholas's rush, kicked his legs out from under him, and pounced. She was astride him in an instant.

"I did it," she panted, her face glowing with delight. "You're down!"

"Stop crowing." But Nicholas's smile belied the injunction. "It took you long enough."

"But I did it." She scowled with mock ferocity. "I have you at my mercy."

"Totally."

"Stop patronizing me."

"Never satisfied. I was merely giving you your due."

"Admit it, you're proud of me."

"Enormously."

She was so pumped with triumph, she felt giddy. "Penalty and reward. What do I get?"

His smile deepened indulgently. "What do you want?"

"The homestead. Sam. The world."

"For one fall?"

"It was a great fall, a splendiferous fall."

"True. But you can't have the homestead or Sam. Anything else."

"Okay." She lifted his sweatshirt to bare his chest and ran her hands through the dark hair on his chest. "You. Here. Now."

"My, how aggressive you've become."

She delicately licked his nipple and saw the pulse in the hollow of his throat jump in response. "Now."

He didn't move. "It's not good discipline to interrupt a session."

"I want my reward. Fair is fair."

"Well, if you put it that way." He sat up, tore off his sweatshirt, and threw it aside. "What else can I do but yield meekly?"

She snorted. Nothing Nicholas did to her was done meekly. Sometimes it was smooth, sometimes rough, but it was always decisive and bold . . . and full of joy. She hadn't expected that almost-pagan sensuality in him.

Or herself. It was as if the floodgates had opened and freed her to pleasure. With Richard she had always felt obligated to make sure he was pleased and felt guilty if she demanded anything of him. Sex with Nicholas was between equals, brimming with erotic experimentation.

"I'm glad you see that you've no choice in the matter." She pulled the jersey over her head and took off her bra. She leaned forward and rubbed against him. A shudder went through her as the soft hair of his chest brushed her nipples.

"No choice at all. You have me at your mercy." He suddenly bent his head and caught her breast in his mouth, sucking strongly.

She inhaled sharply, her hands blindly reaching out to tangle in his hair. But he had moved away to shed his clothes.

"Hurry," he told her.

He didn't have to. She was already tearing off her clothes, throwing them in all directions.

He was back on the mat, parting her thighs. He sank deep, deeper. Her fingernails dug into his shoulders as he started moving, fast, hard.

Suddenly he rolled over, bringing her on top.

She looked down at him. "What is—"

His eyes twinkled. "I thought you'd prefer a dominant position today." He bucked upward and smiled as she caught her breath. "This way I'm totally at your disposal."

He was holding her sealed to him so that she would feel every inch as his hips moved upward.

"That's not the way it feels," she gasped.

"How does it feel?"

"Like I have a club—" She gasped again as he lunged upward.

"Move." He whispered, "Ride me. Make me feel you."

She moved, hard, frantically, joyously.

When the climax came she collapsed on top of him in total exhaustion.

She was shaking, coated in perspiration, clinging helplessly to him. He was laughing, she realized dazedly. "What's so funny?"

"I don't know if I'll ever be able to look at this mat in the same way again. Every time I have you down, I'm going to want to tear the clothes off you." He kissed her. "I told you it was bad discipline." He pulled her to her feet. "Come on, let's hit the shower."

"I can't move." She leaned against him, her arms linked about his waist. He felt good. Lean and tough and wonderful. "Being rewarded takes all the stuffing out of me. I think I'm going to melt."

"Can't have that. Michaela would never consent to clean up the mess." He lifted her and carried her from the gym to his bathroom before setting her down to adjust the water in the shower. He drew her beneath the warm spray, standing behind her, his hands gently rubbing her belly. Those wonderful hands . . . She never got tired of looking at them or feeling them on her body. She had discovered he was a very tactile person. Even when no sex was involved, he liked to touch her, caress her.

Standing here was wonderfully soothing, she thought dreamily. She felt cosseted, soothed, safe.

"I heard you last night," he whispered in her ear. "The dream again?"

A tiny ripple disturbed the serenity she was experiencing. "Yes."

"It hasn't happened for a while." He pulled at the lobe of her ear with his teeth. "I was hoping they were gone."

She shook her head.

"I want you to move in with me tonight."

"What?"

He took the soap and began to rub it over her shoulders. "I want you to sleep in my bed. I want to wake up in the night and be able to reach out and touch you."

She understood at once. "You want to be able to wake me when I have a bad dream."

"Among other things." He ran the soap under her breasts. "What's the harm? You spend a good portion of the night here anyway."

She didn't know why the idea made her uneasy. To have him there to bring her out of that horror would be unbelievable relief.

Too much relief, she realized. Nicholas was wrapping her in a web of pleasure and serenity with moments like these. She was becoming too comfortable. The dream was agony, but it was a reminder of what she still had to do. "No."

He went still against her and then his hand resumed its soothing motion on her body. "Whatever you say. I'll be here if you change your mind."

No argument. No pressure. Everything easy and without effort. Did he realize that by that very acquiescence he drew her deeper into the web? Probably, he was very clever. "You're still trying to convince me not to go after Maritz, aren't you?"

"Of course." He chuckled. "I've even sacrificed my body to your lust. Do you think I enjoy this?"

She relaxed back against him. Honesty. Nice to have humor and sex and honesty in one package. No need to be wary of him. "I suspect you do."

His hand moved up and rubbed the nape of her neck. She could have purred as the knotted muscles relaxed. "Damn right," he said cheerfully. "I'm glad all the abuse I've handed out lately hasn't totally damaged your brain."

"No sign of Maritz," Jamie said. "I've even shadowed Tania myself, and I haven't been able to mark him."

"But that doesn't mean he's not stalking her," Nicholas said.

"Hell, no. He's good and he likes this part of it. I'm keeping a close eye on the situation. I've even had Phil key in Lieber's security alarm number into my pager. That's all we can do right now." He paused. "But I got a call from Conner in Athens. Bingo."

Nicholas stiffened. "You've got it?"

"Verified and detailed. I'm faxing you a full report."

"Good."

"You're still not telling Nell? You're piling up serious trouble."

"Tell me about it. I'll be waiting for your fax." Nicholas hung up the phone.

"There is a man coming. He's waiting at the third gate. Should I let him in?" Michaela stood in the doorway of the gym, gazing disapprovingly at Nell, who was on the mat on her stomach with Tanek on top of her. "I don't like this rough play. You should have better things to do than roll around on the floor."

"What man?" Tanek got off Nell and stood up.

"It is that Kabler. The one who was here before."

Nell tensed, her gaze flying to Tanek.

"Is he alone?" he asked.

"So he says," Michaela answered. "Make up your mind. I have work to do."

"Let him through." Tanek moved toward the door. "Session's over, Nell. Go take a shower while I see what he wants."

"No."

He glanced at her over his shoulder.

"I won't be kept out of this. I told you when I came here that I wouldn't allow you to keep secrets from me."

"I'm hardly keeping secrets when I don't know why the man's here," he said dryly.

She went to her room, washed her face, took off her sweaty jersey, and put on a clean blouse.

Kabler was driving into the stable yard when she joined Tanek on the porch.

The air was biting cold, and huge snowflakes were beginning to drift slowly to the ground.

"You're not wearing a coat," Tanek said without looking at her. "Would you consider it Machiavellian if I suggested you wait inside?"

"I'm fine."

Kabler was getting out of the car. "Paying you a visit is like getting into Fort Knox," he complained. His gaze went to Nell. "Hello, Mrs. Calder. Are you the gold he's trying to keep to himself?"

She inclined her head. "Mr. Kabler."

"Come in, Kabler. Let's get this business over." Tanek went into the house.

"How are you?" Kabler asked Nell in a low voice as he passed her.

"Fine. Don't I look fine?"

"You look damn gorgeous."

She felt a ripple of shock. Since she had arrived in Idaho she had almost forgotten the change in her appearance. "Well, I'm also healthy and strong. You can see Nicholas hasn't been keeping me walled in a dungeon. Is that why you're here?"

"Partly."

"Kabler," Tanek called.

"Impatient bastard, isn't he?" Kabler murmured, and entered the house.

She followed him and closed the door to shut out the chill.

"Nice place," Kabler said as he wandered around the room. "Luxurious but comfortable. I like that." He stopped before the Delacroix. "New?"

"No, you saw it the last time you were here." He paused. "You even commented on it."

"So I did." He grinned. "As a matter of fact, after I left, I checked to make sure you'd obtained it legally."

"Why? Art theft isn't your bag."

"I hoped it might give me an edge with you. No telling when I might need one." He shook his head resignedly. "Unfortunately, I found everything was aboveboard. You're a hard man, Tanek."

"Why are you here?"

"Mrs. Calder disappeared after she left the hospital. Since I doubted the earth had swallowed her, I thought you might have." He met Tanek's eyes. "Why is she here? Are you setting her up as bait?"

"You said the attack on me was pure chance," Nell said quickly. "If that's true, then there would be no reason for Tanek to think I'd be good bait."

"How quickly she jumps to your defense," Kabler said. "You were always good at winning people's confidence. Have you forgotten that Tanek does believe there was a reason for your attack, Mrs. Calder? Tell me, did he tell you about Nigel Simpson?" He smiled. "No, I see he didn't."

"Tell her yourself," Tanek said impassively. "You're obviously salivating to do it."

"Very perceptive of you. Nigel Simpson was one of Gardeaux's accountants, who was obligingly feeding me certain information, Mrs. Calder. But he disappeared." He shook his head. "Around the time our Mr. Tanek paid a visit to London. What a coincidence."

London. Nell tried to hide her shock as she remembered the call from London and Tanek's trip the next day.

"Do you think I've got him hidden here too?" Tanek asked.

"No, I think the poor bastard's probably hidden at the bottom of the ocean."

"And I did it?"

"Maybe." He shrugged. "Or maybe you moved in on my source, tapped him for too much, and Gardeaux decided to chop him. What did he tell you, Tanek?"

"Nothing. I didn't see him."

"I could bring you in for questioning."

"You don't have grounds. The only thing that you know is that I was in the same city at the same time."

"That's enough with you." He hesitated briefly. "Okay. I can't pressure you. Have you shared your findings with the lady?"

"But we haven't established that I found out anything."

"Then why was Reardon sniffing around?"

Tanek gave him a blank stare. "Sniffing around what?"

"Athens."

Nell stiffened.

Tanek smiled. "Greece is a beautiful place. Maybe he needed a vacation. Is that what you came to ask?"

"No, I think I know the answer." His expression became grim. "I just came to tell you not to step on my toes again or I'll nail you. I needed Simpson."

"So did I." Tanek strode toward the door and opened it. "Good-bye, Kabler."

Kabler's brows rose. "Thrown out into the cold? How inhospitable. Is that the code of the West?" He strolled toward Tanek. "You're still a hoodlum at heart, Tanek."

"I never denied it. We are what we are . . . or were."

Kabler glanced around the room again, his gaze pausing on a Chinese vase in the corner. "And you were paid very well. That vase alone would send my kids to college." His tone was suddenly bitter. "You live high, don't you? You and that filth Gardeaux. Doesn't it ever bother you that—"

"Good-bye, Kabler."

Kabler opened his mouth to speak and then stopped as he met Tanek's gaze. He turned to Nell. "Will you walk me to my car? I'd like a word with you alone. Providing Tanek will let you out of his sight."

"By all means," Tanek said without expression. "Take a jacket, Nell."

Nell grabbed a jacket from the coatrack by the door and followed Kabler.

The snow was falling faster, harder. The windshield of Kabler's car was now covered. "I'll be lucky to get back to town before this becomes a blizzard," Kabler muttered as he opened the car door.

"You could stay the night."

"After Tanek threw me out? I'd rather risk the blizzard."

"He's not an ogre. If there's really a danger, he'd let you stay."

"He's not an ogre, but I wouldn't bank on his store of the milk of human kindness." He added wearily, "Besides, I couldn't stay anyway. I have to get back to

Washington. I've got a sick kid. My wife needs me to help out with him."

For the first time, she noticed that he looked older, more worn than the last time she had seen him. "I'm sorry." She impulsively put her hand on his arm. "I know it's worse than being sick yourself. What's wrong?"

He shrugged. "Flu, maybe. But he can't seem to shake it."

"I hope everything will be all right."

"It will." He smiled with an effort. "We've been through it before with the other two. Kids bounce back."

She nodded. "Jill had pneumonia one week, and two weeks later she was running in the park. It was as if—" She stopped. "He'll be all right."

"Sure. Thanks for understanding. I guess I needed someone to say what I already knew." He glanced back at the house. "Don't trust him. Once a crook, always a crook."

"You're wrong. People change."

"He's not like us, none of them are. Can you imagine him tearing his guts out over a sick kid? They walk in the mud and the mud hardens and nothing gets through."

"That's not true."

He shook his head. "I've seen it for twenty-four years. They're not like us." His hand clenched into a fist. "But they're kings of the earth. The money rolls in and there are no rules for them. They just take and take and take."

"Is that what you wanted to tell me?"

"He's got you fooled. I could see it. I don't want you to get hurt."

"I won't get hurt and he's not trying to fool me. Not anymore."

"Then why didn't he tell you about Nigel Simpson?"

"I have no idea. But he will when I ask him."

His lips tightened. "He's really got you, hasn't he? Are you sleeping with him?"

"That's none of your business," she said coolly.

"Sorry. You're right. I only wanted to help. Do you still have my card?"

"Yes."

"I'll be around." He started the car. "Don't wait until it's too late to use it."

She watched him drive out of the stable yard.

He's really got you.

He was wrong. Tanek had no hold on her. He was wrong about everything. Except, perhaps, about Nigel Simpson.

She walked slowly back into the house.

Nicholas was standing by the fire with his hands outstretched. "Come and get warm. You were out there a long time."

She shed her jacket and came forward. "It's snowing hard. I asked him to stay the night."

"But he chose not to risk it?"

"I told him you wouldn't object."

"But you're not certain I wouldn't have staked him out in the snow for the wolves?"

"Don't be ridiculous."

"I wouldn't." He smiled at her. "Not if you asked him to stay."

She noticed he didn't mention that he'd refrain from doing it if she had not invited Kabler. "I like him."

"I know. Why not? Family man, upstanding, protective . . ."

"But you don't?"

"He's too righteous for me. Since I'm the one who's

being bombarded by stones, I don't embrace a man prone to cast the first one."

"What happened to Nigel Simpson?"

"Probably what Kabler thinks happened to him." His eyes narrowed. "But if you're going to ask if it was my doing, it—"

"I wasn't going to ask you that," she interrupted.

"Because you think me too pure and incapable of such barbarity?" he asked mockingly.

"I don't know. Maybe you're capable, but I don't think—You wouldn't do it unless—" She stopped and finally said, "I just don't think you killed him."

"Well, that's clear."

"But I do want to know what you found out from him."

He was silent a moment. "He gave me his set of Gardeaux's account books and the name of the other accountant in Paris who could complete them."

"Will that be valuable?"

"Possibly."

"How?"

"Information is always useful. I dealt in it extensively while I was in Hong Kong. Some I passed on, some I kept in reserve. When I got out, I used it for an insurance policy."

"Insurance policy?" she asked, puzzled.

"I've made a lot of enemies over the years. I couldn't be sure I wouldn't be targeted after I left the Network. So I stashed a piece of high-voltage information about Ramon Sandequez in various safety deposit boxes around the world with instructions to leak the contents to the appropriate parties if I disappeared or turned up dead."

The name sounded familiar. "Who is Ramon Sandequez?"

"One of the three heads of the Medellin drug cartel."

That's right, Paloma, Juarez, and Sandequez, Nell remembered. Gardeaux's bosses, the hierarchy.

"Sandequez isn't a man to cross. He sent out word that if I was touched, he would not be pleased."

She felt a rush of intense relief. "Then you're safe."

"Until Sandequez thinks he's found all the safety deposit boxes. He's already located two. Or until Sandequez is killed himself. Or until some crazy like Maritz decides that he doesn't care about the risk."

"But if you kept a low profile and stayed here, you'd be safer?"

"Pull in my head and hope?" He shook his head. "I'm willing to take precautions. I'm not willing to stop living a full life. That's not why I came here."

He had come here to put down roots. But those new roots were so terribly fragile. "Don't be a fool," she said fiercely. "You should stay here out of sight. You love it here. There's no reason for you to go anywhere else."

"There's a reason."

"Not worth risking—"

Gardeaux. Maritz. Of course there was a reason. What had she been thinking?

She had been thinking only of keeping him safe.

Guilt rushed through her. Closeness and intimacy had crept into her life, and now they threatened to interfere with what she had to do. She quickly turned away from him. "I have to take a shower."

"Running away?" he asked quietly.

"No, I just— Yes." She wouldn't lie to him. "I think I should go away. Things are becoming too complicated."

"I thought it would come to this," he said. "*Damn* Kabler."

"It's not his fault. It's just—"

"Complicated," he finished sarcastically. "With Kabler as the catalyst." He reached out and grasped her shoulders. "Listen to me. Nothing has changed. You don't have to run away."

Something had changed. For an instant she had forgotten what was important because of her concern for him.

And he knew it. She could see it in his expression.

"All right. I won't touch you again," he said. "It will be like it was before."

How could it be? She had grown accustomed to him both physically and emotionally.

"You're not ready." He cupped her face with his hands. He whispered, "Stay."

He kissed her lightly, gently. He lifted his head. "See? As sexless as a brother. What's so complicated?"

She leaned against him. How she wanted to stay. She *needed* to stay. He was right, she wasn't ready to leave him. Maybe it would be all right now that she realized what was happening. "Okay. For a little while."

She could feel the tension leave him. "Smart."

She wasn't sure how smart it was. She wasn't sure of anything at the moment but the fact that his arms were strong and caring and she wanted to be there. "Let me go."

"In a minute. You need this now."

She did need it. He knew her so well. He had studied her and learned what she needed, what she wanted. When she needed comfort, he gave her comfort. When she wanted sex, he gave her all she could handle. He was the one who was clever. It should frighten her instead of giving her this sense of solid security. She finally pushed him away and moved toward the door. "I'll see you at lunch."

"Right."

She stopped at the door as a sudden thought occurred to her. "You didn't tell me why Jamie was in Greece."

"He was checking out a couple of leads about the raid on Medas."

"Did anything come of it?"

"Too early to tell." He spoke indifferently; his expression was equally casual.

Too casual, perhaps. She had meant to question him about Jamie immediately, but he had skipped from Simpson to Ramon Sandequez and she had somehow lost the thread. Had he purposely tried to deter her from pursuing that particular thread? "Are you telling me the truth?"

"Of course."

She said haltingly, "It's very important to me. I need to trust you, Nicholas."

"You've made that crystal clear. Have I ever done anything that might make you distrust me?"

She shook her head.

His smile lit his face. "Then gimme me a break, kid."

Beautiful smile, full of warmth. She found herself smiling back at him, as she usually did these days. "Sorry." She turned to leave and then hesitated as she glanced out the window. "It's snowing harder."

He sighed. "And you're worried about Kabler. Do you want me to trail after him and make sure he makes it back to town?"

"Would you?" she asked, startled by his offer.

"If that's what you want."

She felt a rush of glowing warmth. "No, then I'd worry about you."

"It's nice to know I rate above the virtuous Mr. Kabler."

"Maybe the snow will stop."

"I doubt it. The weather channel said that there would be snow all along the Canadian border all this week." He glanced at the white flakes pelting the window. "Even Joel and Tania should be getting it in Minneapolis in a few days."

Fourteen

"Do you need anything from the store?" Phil stood in the doorway of the kitchen. He sniffed. "That smells good. What is it?"

"Goulash." Tania smiled at him over her shoulder. "I'll put some aside for your dinner."

"Great." He came over to the stove. "Could I have a bite now?"

He was nothing more than a big boy, Tania thought indulgently as she dipped the ladle into the pot and proffered it to him. He tasted the goulash, closed his eyes, and sighed. "Delicious."

"It's an old family recipe. My grandmother taught it to me." She turned down the heat on the stove to low. "It will be better after a few hours of simmering."

"It couldn't be." Phil glanced at the window. "The snow's coming down pretty hard. It may be impossible to get out in a few hours. I wondered if you might need some milk or bread or something."

"Milk. I used the last at breakfast." Her gaze followed his to the window. "But don't go just for groceries. The streets must be slick as glass."

"I was going out anyway. Something's wrong with my car. I have to take it into the garage."

"What's wrong?"

"Beats me. It worked fine day before yesterday, but last night it was hiccuping." He shrugged. "Could be I got hold of some bad gas." He started for the door. "I'll be back in a couple of hours. Come to the front door and set the security system behind me. What's the use of having security if you don't set it? I walked right in."

"I always set it. Joel must have forgotten to do it when he went out this morning." She followed him to the foyer and pressed the armed button after he opened the door. She glanced out at the swiftly swirling snow, now so thick she could barely see two feet ahead. "This is nasty. Do you have to go?"

"Can't do without my wheels." He grinned. "I'm used to driving in weather like this." He waved as he carefully went down the ice-filmed steps. "And I'll remember the milk."

He was lost behind the veil of snow.

She shut the door and started back toward the kitchen. She stopped, frowning, before she'd gone more than a few steps. Water had pooled on the oak floor of the foyer. Phil was usually so careful to wipe his feet. He must have been really worried that he'd been able to just wander into the house. She'd have to go to the kitchen and get a towel and wipe it up before it damaged that beautiful wood.

She didn't sense his presence, Maritz realized with disappointment.

He watched her bend down and carefully wipe up the water that had dripped from his shoes when he had followed the caretaker into the house. He'd have wiped it up himself, but he hadn't been sure how much time he had before the guy left for the garage. He'd opted to play it safe, taken his wet shoes off, and run up the stairs to the second-floor landing.

I'm right here, pretty Tania. If you look up, you'll see me.

She didn't look up. She finished wiping the floor and went back to the kitchen.

He supposed he shouldn't be so disappointed. He had run across this blindness before. Sensitivity was dulled when you were in a place you considered safe.

But he'd thought she would be different.

Maybe it was just as well. The surprise would be greater, the fear all the more intense.

Where would he take her?

He heard her humming in the kitchen. She was happy this morning.

The kitchen, center of the home, foundation of family life.

Why not?

He started down the steps.

Phil turned the wheel in the direction of the skid and came out smoothly. He enjoyed the feel of control driving a car gave him. It was almost like surfing the Internet, negotiating in and out of computer programs, dipping and skimming until he came to something that interested him.

If he knew as much about what went on under the hood as he did any computer, he might be in better shape, he thought ruefully. It was probably going to cost him an arm and a leg to have the car fixed.

Maybe not. He'd had his oil changed at the Acme Garage and the guys seemed to be pretty regular. He'd stayed around and shot the breeze with Irving Jessup, the owner, and he'd—

Acme Garage.

The sign on the tall column leapt out at him. He carefully pulled into the station.

One car ahead of him even on this snowy day. He'd probably have to wait. He didn't mind. Good business was always a sign that a company produced. No problem.

He was in no hurry.

The goulash needed a little more pepper, Tania decided. She set down the spoon and reached for the crystal pepper mill on the countertop. Phil had said it was perfect, but he had never tasted her grandmother's goulash. It always made her happy when she cooked one of her family's recipes. It brought back memories untainted by those last years. Grandmother sitting at the table peeling potatoes and telling her tales of the old days when she had toured the countryside, her mother coming in from the office with her father, laughing and telling her—

"It's time, Tania."

She whirled toward the door.

A man stood there, a knife in his hand. He was smiling.

Her heart jumped and then froze.

Him. It had to be him.

He nodded as if she had said the words out loud. "You knew I'd come. You were waiting for me, weren't you?"

"No," she whispered. He looked so ordinary, like anyone. Brown hair, brown eyes, a little over medium height. He might have been the grocery clerk at the supermarket or the insurance salesman who'd come to the door last week. This wasn't the faceless menace who had haunted her.

But he had the knife.

"You don't want to do this." She moistened her lips. "You don't even know me. Nothing has happened yet. You can walk out of here."

"I do know you. No one knows you better." He took a step closer. "And I do want to do this. I've wanted it for a long time."

"Why?"

"Because you're special. I knew it the first time I followed you."

The door?

No, he was blocking it as he came toward her.

She had to keep him talking while she tried to think.

"Why were you following me?"

"Because of the Calder woman. I was hoping she'd come back or contact you." He took another step. "But then I realized how special you were and I began to enjoy you for yourself."

"I don't know where Nell is."

"I expected you to say that. I'll find out whether you do or not." He smiled. "Actually, I hope you don't tell me for a long time. I'll be sorry to have this end."

The drawer with the butcher knives?

By the time she reached it and pulled open the drawer, he'd be on her.

"Who are you?"

"I forgot we hadn't been introduced. I feel so close to you, Tania. I'm Paul Maritz."

Oh, God. Nell's monster was now her monster, and he was coming closer every minute. What could she do? "I lied. I do know where she is, but you'll never find out if you kill me."

"I told you, I'd rather it be later instead of sooner." He was only two yards away from her. "But we can talk about that when I—"

She shattered the glass pepper mill on the edge of

the counter, hurled the pepper into his eyes, and the jagged shards after it.

He cursed, flailing blindly with the knife.

She picked up the pot of goulash and threw the contents in his face.

He screamed and clutched his scalded cheeks.

She ran past him through the door to the foyer.

He was cursing behind her.

She reached the front door and fumbled at the lock.

His hand fell on her shoulder, whirling her away from the door.

She staggered back against the wall, caught herself on the hall table before she fell.

"Stupid bitch." Tears were running down his red, swollen face. "Do you think I'd let you—"

She hurled the brass vase on the table at him and ran for the door.

She got it open, hit the emergency alarm on the panel as she rushed outside.

Her feet slipped out from under and she tumbled down the stairs.

She had forgotten the ice on the front steps.

He was coming down the steps slowly, deliberately, careful not to make the same mistake.

The security alarm wailed as she frantically struggled to her feet. Someone would hear it. Someone would come. Pain shot through her left ankle as she hobbled across the lawn toward the street.

"Where are you going, Tania?" he called from behind her. "The neighbors? You'll not make it with that ankle, and no one can see you in this storm. The security company? They can't get here in time."

She kept on going.

"I'm right behind you."

Shut up, you bastard.

"Give up. It will be the same anyway."

She lurched as she slid again on the ice.

She could hear his heavy breathing almost in her ear.

"You know it's going to happen. You've known all these weeks."

Her ankle gave way and she fell to the ground.

She rolled over in the snow and looked up at him.

"Pretty Tania." He knelt beside her, his hand caressing her hair. "I didn't plan it like this for you. I wanted something nicer than you groveling out here in the snow. But you set off the alarm and now I have to hurry."

"But I didn't tell you about Nell," she said desperately.

"Then tell me."

"She's in Florida. Let me go and I'll tell—"

He shook his head. "I think you're lying. I can always tell. I don't believe you'll tell me. I'll have to ask the good doctor."

"No!"

"But you leave me no choice." His hand closed tightly on her hair and he raised the knife. "I won't hurt you like you did me. One quick stroke and it will be over."

She was going to die. Think. There had to be an escape. She had not stayed alive in that hellhole of Sarajevo to die here.

There was no way, she realized in horror.

The knife was arcing toward her throat.

No way at all to save—

Jamie Reardon was at his hotel when his beeper picked up the alarm call from the Lieber house.

It took him twenty minutes to get there. A patrol car with Radar Security was parked at the curb, but it was unoccupied. The siren was still wailing from the open door of the house. Why the hell hadn't they turned it off?

He got out of the car and started up the driveway.

He saw the first bloody footstep when he reached the top of the driveway. Outlined against the snow, the dark liquid was encrusted with ice crystals.

He felt his stomach lurch.

Drops of blood peppered the snow, leaving a trail.

He followed the trail through the swirling snow.

Two uniformed security guards stood with their backs to him, looking down.

He knew what they were looking at.

He was too late.

"I need to talk to Nick. Right away."

"He's over at the Bar X this afternoon, Jamie." Nell glanced at her watch. "But I doubt if you can reach him there. He's probably on his way back by now, but there's no telling how long it will take him in this snow. Shall I have him call you?"

"Yes. The minute he gets in."

"Are you at a hotel?"

"No, I'll give you the number."

She took down the number on the pad by the phone. "What's wrong? Can I take a message?"

There was silence on the other end of the line. Then, "No message."

She stiffened. She felt as shut out as that time Jamie had given Nicholas the cryptic message about Nigel Simpson. But that was before Nicholas had promised her there would be no secrets between them. "I want to know what's wrong, Jamie."

"Then ask Nick," Jamie said wearily. "He'd have my head if I told you."

He hung up the phone.

She slowly sank down in the chair by the phone. She felt sick. The inference was clear. Deceit. Nicholas had told Jamie not to reveal something to her. How much was Nicholas still keeping from her?

She glanced down at the number on the pad. The number was vaguely familiar. What city was that area code?

Minneapolis.

And she had called that number before and knew to whom it belonged.

Her hand was shaking as she dialed the number.

"Hello."

"What are you *doing* at Joel Lieber's house, Jamie?"

"Christ. I should have given you the beeper number."

"What are you doing there?" When he didn't answer, she demanded, "Let me talk to Tania."

"That's not possible."

Fear leapt through her. "What do you mean, it's not—"

"Look, I can't talk anymore. Tell Nick to call me."

She crashed down the phone when she heard the disconnect.

She jumped to her feet and ran toward her bedroom. "Michaela."

She didn't arrive at the Lieber house until almost eight hours later. Yellow tape. It was barricaded with yellow tape. They always did that with crime scenes, she remembered frantically as she paid off the taxi. How many times had she seen that yellow tape on the evening news? But that was always somebody else's house, not the house Tania had made her own.

There was a burly policeman standing in front of the barricade. He looked cold. Almost as cold as she felt.

"Nell."

Jamie was getting out of a car parked at the curb. "You shouldn't have come," he said gently. "This was what Nick was trying to avoid."

"What happened here?"

"Maritz. He's been stalking Tania, waiting for you to come back."

She felt as if she had been punched in the stomach. Her fault. She had brought this down on Tania. She and Joel had tried only to help her, and she had brought the monster into their lives. "She's dead?"

He shook his head. "She's in the hospital with a broken ankle."

The relief that surged through her made her limp. "Thank God." She looked back at the yellow tape and a wave of fear washed down her. "Joel?"

"He wasn't here." He took a deep breath. "But Phil was. Maritz had disabled his car and Phil took it to the garage. The mechanic told him someone had tampered with one of the intake lines below the carburetor. He borrowed the service station's truck and barreled back here in time to save Tania." His lips tightened grimly. "But not himself. Maritz killed him. But they struggled long enough to give the security company men time enough to get here. Maritz had to leave before he could finish Tania."

Phil. Sweet, sunny Phil. She felt tears rise to her eyes as she remembered how gentle he had been with her in the hospital. She whispered, "I liked him so much."

"So did I." Jamie cleared his throat, but his eyes held a suspicious moisture. "He was a great guy."

"I want to see Tania. Will you take me?"

"That's why I've been waiting around." He took her elbow and led her toward the car. "Nick told me not to let you out of my sight until he could get here."

"You talked to him?"

"Three hours after you left for the airport. He was ready to strangle me . . . and you."

"You were here already? You *knew* they were in danger."

He shrugged. "The funeral director had disappeared. We wanted to be certain Joel and Tania were safe."

"But they weren't safe." She got in the passenger seat. "And neither was Phil."

"Do you think I don't feel bad enough?" he said roughly. "Phil was my friend."

"I don't care how bad you feel. Maritz killed Phil and tried to kill Tania because he wanted to get at me. And Nicholas didn't even tell me."

"Because we knew you'd come back here. Nick wanted to keep you safe."

"What right did he have to—" She broke off. There was no sense in arguing with Jamie when it was Nicholas who was to blame. "I don't want to talk anymore. Just take me to Tania."

"She's on the fifth floor," Jamie said as he drew up in front of the hospital. "Do you want me to come with you?"

"No." She got out of the car and slammed the door.

Joel was in the hallway outside Tania's room.

"You look terrible," Nell said. "How's Tania?"

"Broken ankle, lacerations, shock," Joel said. "She saw Phil stabbed to death." He smiled bitterly. "Other than that, she's just fine."

"It's my fault."

"I'm the one who forgot to turn the alarm on when I left for the day. The bastard just walked into the house." He shook his head. "He just walked in."

"I'm sorry, Joel."

"She almost died." He gave her a stony stare. "Stay away from her. I don't want you near her."

She flinched. She couldn't blame him for his resentment, but it still hurt. "After today I promise not to see her until all this is over. I just want to tell her how— May I see her?"

He shrugged. "After Kabler is through talking to her."

Her glance flew to the door. "Kabler is here?"

"He got here a few minutes ago. He said he had to question her about Maritz."

"Do they have a chance of catching Maritz?"

"Kabler says he's probably already on a plane out of the country."

"But Tania saw him do it. What about extradition?"

"Extradition is good only if they can find him."

"He'll go back to Gardeaux for protection."

He shook his head. "I don't know. I just want him to stay away from Tania."

"So do I." She touched his arm. "Surely he wouldn't dare come back now that he's been identified."

"No? The bastard's crazy. He could do anything. He's been watching her, stalking her, and he just walked into the house and—" He broke off. "Just have your say and get away from her. She's had enough of—"

"I expected you, Mrs. Calder," Kabler said as he closed the door of the hospital room behind him. "Where's Tanek?"

"I came alone." She asked Joel, "May I go in now?"

"As soon as I check to make sure Kabler hasn't done any damage." He went into Tania's room.

"Too bad about young Phil," Kabler said. "You knew him well?"

"Yes. No, I guess not. What are you doing here?"

"I've had a man monitoring the situation here in

Minneapolis since we heard about Birnbaum's disappearance. You remember I was curious about his involvement?"

She leaned against the wall. "Evidently your man didn't monitor it close enough."

"You weren't aware that Maritz was stalking Ms. Vlados?"

"Of course I didn't know," she said impatiently. "Do you think I'd let her run the risk of—"

"Easy." He held up his hand. "I'm just asking. Since Reardon was on the scene, it appears that Tanek knew." He shook his head. "I told you he couldn't be trusted. If he used Ms. Vlados for bait, do you think he wouldn't use you?"

"He didn't use her for bait."

"Then why didn't he tell you?" He shook his head in despair when she didn't answer. "You still believe him."

"He wouldn't put Tania in danger."

"Did he tell you what he found out from Nigel Simpson?"

"Yes."

"No, he didn't. You wouldn't be so calm about it." His lips tightened as she turned away. "I'm not going to let this happen again. Meet me downstairs in the lobby when you're finished talking to Ms. Vlados."

"Why?"

"I'm going to show you proof that Tanek can't be trusted. Not for a minute."

She watched him walk away. She was furious with Nicholas, but she had instinctively defended him. What a fool she was. Clutching at her trust in him as if it were a lifeline.

She had never felt so alone.

"You can go in now." Joel stood in the open doorway. "But only for a few minutes. She needs to rest."

Tania looked pale and terribly fragile propped up against the white pillows.

Her words, however, were brusquely characteristic. "Stop looking like that. There's nothing much wrong with me. My ankle will be fine."

"I guess you know how sorry I am." Nell came forward. "I never dreamed this would happen. It should have been me. I was the one he was after."

"Don't flatter yourself. Maybe at first, but he found me a very appealing victim." She smiled without mirth. "He thinks I'm special. Isn't that nice?"

"How can you joke?"

Tania's smile vanished. "It's the only way I can cope," she whispered. "I don't think I've ever been that frightened. He just kept coming at me. I couldn't stop him. It was like that with you, wasn't it?"

Nell nodded.

Tania's eyes filled with tears. "He killed Phil."

"I know."

"Phil saved me and Maritz killed him. I saw one of those horror movies once about a bogeyman whose sheer evil kept him alive. No matter what happened." Tania's hand tightened with bruising force on Nell's. "He just kept on going, killing. It wasn't like that in Sarajevo. They didn't have faces. Maritz has a face. But he looks so ordinary, like anybody else."

"I'm upsetting you. I'd better go. Joel will have my head."

Tania tried to smile, but it was a weak effort. "Yes, he's being very protective, isn't he? Maybe you'd better go. I'm not very good company right now. Keep in touch."

"I will. I promise." She bent down and brushed a kiss on Tania's cheek. "Get well."

Tania nodded.

"Nell."

Nell stopped at the door.

"Be careful," Tania whispered. "He really is the bogeyman."

Tanek stood waiting outside the door. "How is she?"

"Not good," Nell said coldly. "How did you think she'd be? She was almost killed and saw Phil stabbed to death in front of her eyes." She started down the hall.

"Where are you going?"

"Now? I need a cup of coffee. Seeing Tania like that wasn't pleasant." She needed more than coffee. She was shaking and she mustn't let him see it. She knew how good Nicholas was at attacking any weakness. She turned into the waiting room and fumbled in her purse for change for the coffee machine. "Not that it's any of your business."

"The hell it isn't." He punched quarters into the machine and watched as black liquid poured into the paper cup. "Why didn't you wait until I got back? I would have brought you here."

She took the cup from him. "I couldn't be sure, could I? You didn't even tell me that Maritz was stalking her."

"We didn't know. Not for sure."

"You were sure enough that you sent Jamie here."

"It was just a safety measure. I didn't want another Medas."

She sipped the black coffee. "Well, you got one. Phil's dead."

He nodded. "And how do you think that makes me feel? I'm the one who brought him here."

"Frankly, I don't care how you feel."

His lips tightened. "All right, I didn't tell you everything. I didn't want you to come running back here."

"That wasn't your choice."

"I made it my choice. I didn't want you dead, dammit."

"If I'd have been here, Maritz would have gone after me instead of Tania."

"Exactly."

"And who made you God, Nicholas? What right do you have to make decisions like that?"

"I did what I had to do."

She finished the coffee in two swallows and tossed the cup in the wastebasket. "And I'm doing what I have to do." She left the waiting room and walked toward the elevator.

He followed her. "Where are you going?"

She didn't answer.

"Look, I can see why you're upset, but what happened doesn't alter the basic situation. Maritz may be under Gardeaux's wing by now. We should stick to the plan."

She punched the elevator button. "I don't think that plan will work anymore. It requires a certain amount of trust."

He met her eyes. "You may not believe it now, but you'll trust me again."

"I hope I'm not that much of a fool." She went into the elevator and stopped him as he started to follow her. "No, I don't want you to come with me."

He nodded and stepped back. "Okay, I can understand how you'd need some space."

She felt a flicker of surprise. She hadn't thought he'd give up so easily. The door shut between them, and she leaned back against the side. She felt as bruised and exhausted as if she'd been in a battle and there was still Kabler to face.

Kabler was coming out of the gift shop when she got off the elevator. "Mighty Morphin, the Red Ranger," he said when he saw her glance at the sack he was carrying. "For my kid. They're hard to find in the stores in my neck of the woods."

"I don't think this is what you were going to show me," she said.

"I saw Tanek go up. What did he—"

"You said you had something to show me."

He took her arm. "It's not here." He led her out of the hospital to the parking lot. "You look tired. Just relax and trust me."

Why not? She supposed she did trust him. She had to trust someone. She got into his car, leaned back in the seat, and closed her eyes. "I'll relax, but you'd better not. Nicholas let me leave too easily. I'd bet Jamie Reardon is somewhere around. He's driving a gray Taurus rental car."

"He's five cars back. It doesn't matter. He can follow only so far."

"She's with Kabler?" Nicholas swore beneath his breath. "Keep on their tail. What the hell's he doing with her?"

"I can't keep on their tail. I'm calling from the airport. They just boarded a private jet that's taxiing down the runway."

"Can you find out their destination?"

"A DEA charter? Given a little time, maybe. Spur-of-the-moment? No way."

Nicholas had known that was not an option, but he was grasping at straws. Besides, he had a good idea where they were going. He hadn't thought Kabler would go that far. "I'm on my way. See if you can charter a flight and be gassed up and ready when I get there."

"I guess I know what flight plan we're going to file."

"Bakersfield, California."

The large Victorian house was set back from the street, surrounded by spacious lawns and towering oaks. It looked timeless, gracious, and dignified in the deepening twilight.

"Go on," Kabler said.

"I don't believe you," Nell whispered. "It's not true."

Kabler came around and helped her out of the car. "See for yourself."

Nell slowly walked up the steps of the huge wraparound porch and rang the bell.

Through the etched flowers on the glass door, she could barely see a woman coming down a staircase.

The carriage lantern beside the door suddenly lit the porch and the woman peered through the barely transparent glass.

The door swung open. "May I help you?"

Nell was frozen. She couldn't speak.

A tiny frown marred the perfection of the woman's forehead. "Are you selling something?"

"What is it, Marla?" A man was coming down the steps.

She was going to faint. No, she was going to be sick. Oh, God. Oh, God.

The man put his arm affectionately around the woman's shoulders. He smiled. "What can we do for you?"

"Richard." She barely managed to get the name past her lips.

The man's smile vanished. "You're mistaken. You must have the wrong house. I'm Noel Tillinger, and this is my wife, Marla."

Nell shook her head as much to clear it as to negate

the man's words. "No." Her stunned glance shifted to the woman. "Why, Nadine?"

Nadine's gaze suddenly narrowed on her face. "Who—"

"Stay out of this, Marla. I'll handle her."

"I think she's been handled enough," Kabler said from behind her. "And not too kindly."

Richard's eyes widened. "Kabler? What the hell are you doing here?"

Kabler ignored him, his gaze on Nell. "You okay, Mrs. Calder?"

She wasn't okay. She wasn't sure anything would ever be okay again. "I didn't believe you."

Richard's gaze swung back to her. "Nell?"

"I think we'd better go inside," Kabler said.

Richard stepped aside, his eyes never leaving Nell. "He told me you'd had surgery, but—I can't believe it. . . . You're stunning."

She almost laughed hysterically. Was the change in her appearance all he could think about?

Kabler nudged her gently over the doorstep. "We should get off this porch. The first rule in a witness protection program is not to attract attention."

Nadine forced a smile. "You might as well come into the parlor." She led them from the foyer through an arched doorway into a room that looked as if it had been plucked from an Edith Wharton novel, all huge ferns and palms and dark, carved wood. She gestured to the tapestry-cushioned couch. "Sit down, Nell."

She was perfectly at home, as beautiful and confident as Nell remembered her. "Why, Nadine?"

"I love him. When he called me, I came," Nadine said simply. "I didn't want it to happen. I liked you. No one wanted to hurt you."

She moistened her dry lips. "How long?"

"We've been lovers for over two years."

Two years. He had been sleeping with Nadine for years and she had never suspected. He had been so clever. Or maybe she had just been stupid.

"Why did you bring her here, Kabler?" Richard asked. "You said she'd never know. You said no one would know."

"I had to prove a point. She was moving toward deep trouble. I thought she'd had trouble enough."

"What about me?" Richard asked. "What if she tells someone?"

"I seriously doubt if she'd confide in the people who killed her daughter, don't you?"

Richard flushed. "No, I guess not," he muttered. "But you shouldn't have brought her."

"I don't understand any of this," Nell said hoarsely. "Tell me, Kabler."

"The attack on Medas was aimed at your husband," Kabler said. "He's been laundering money through his bank for Gardeaux for some time. When the Kavinski opportunity came along, he told Gardeaux he wanted out. Not very bright. No one gets out until Gardeaux wants them out. Gardeaux needed him, so he decided he would send him a warning."

"What warning?"

"The death of his wife. You were the initial target."

"They were going to kill me to punish *him*."

"It's not an uncommon practice in their circle."

"And Jill?" she asked jerkily. "Were they going to kill Jill too?"

"We don't know. We don't think so. It could be that Maritz took it upon himself. He's not too stable."

Not too stable. He kept coming. The bogeyman.

"If I was the target, then why was Richard shot?" Then the answer occurred to her. "But he wasn't shot, was he? You faked it."

Kabler nodded. "A few hours before the party we

found out that the information we'd received targeting you was authentic." He paused. "But there was an addendum also targeting Calder. It seems Gardeaux had discovered why Calder was so comfortable about giving up the fat percentages from the money laundering. He was skimming funds and funneling them into a Swiss bank account. I didn't have time to do much more than send a few men to the island."

"Then why weren't you there to save Jill?" she asked fiercely. "Why weren't you *there*?"

Richard smiled mockingly. "Yes, tell her. Let her know where your priorities were." He turned to Nell. "That's why you're here. That's why he seems so worried about you. They had orders to contact me first, to offer me a deal. My neck and a new life if I agreed to testify against Gardeaux when the time came."

"I thought we had time," Kabler said to Nell. "I thought you'd be downstairs in the ballroom with everybody else. I'd assigned a man to cover you."

"But getting Gardeaux was your number-one priority," Richard pointed out. "You even had a plan in place. You'd sent a doctor with the team, pretending to be one of the guests. I was to have a heart attack and be whisked off the island." Richard's lips twisted. "But you miscalculated, didn't you?"

"We got you out," Kabler answered.

"And sent me to this Podunk of a town. I wanted to go to New York."

"It wasn't safe."

"You promised me a new face. That would have made it safe."

"All in good time."

"It's been almost six months, dammit."

"Shut up, Calder." Kabler turned back to Nell. "Have you heard enough?"

Too much. Lies. Ugliness. Betrayal.

She turned to leave.

"Nell." Richard's hand closed on her arm, stopping her. "I know this has upset you, but it's important that no one know I'm here."

He was smiling at her, that charming, boyish smile that had smoothed his way through life.

"Let me go."

"I loved Jill too," he said gently. "You know I wouldn't have done anything to hurt her or you."

"Let me go."

"Not before you promise to keep silent. You know I'm right. Just—"

"For God's sake, let the poor woman leave, Richard," Nadine said.

"Be quiet, Nadine," he said without looking away from Nell. "This is between the two of us. It's not my fault Jill is dead. I was downstairs. I wasn't there to protect her like you were, Nell."

She stiffened, staring at him in disbelief. He was trying to use guilt to manipulate her. Why not? she thought bitterly. He had done it all through their marriage. "You son of a bitch."

He flushed, but his hand tightened on her arm. "I just wanted to get ahead. I was moving too slow. I took good care of you and Jill."

"Let me go," she said through her teeth.

"You know I—"

She punched him in the stomach, and when he bent over in pain, she gave him a chop to the neck. He dropped to the floor and she pounced on top of him. He had started it all, the chain that had led to Jill's death. One well-placed blow and he would be dead. She raised her arm. One blow and—

"No." Kabler was lifting her off Richard. "You don't want to do this."

She struggled wildly. "The hell I don't."

"Well, I can't let you. I need my witness." Kabler grimaced. "Though I can't say I blame you."

He was holding her firmly, but Nicholas had taught her ways of getting out of most holds. But to do it would mean hurting Kabler, and he didn't deserve to be hurt. Not when he had been trying to help her. She drew a deep breath. "You can let me go. I won't hurt him . . . now."

Kabler instantly released her.

Richard sat up dazedly, gingerly touching his abdomen. "What the hell has happened to you, Nell?"

"*You* happened to me. You and Maritz and—" She turned on her heel. "If you want him in one piece, you'd better get me away from him, Kabler."

"It's not what I want, it's what I have to have. If I had my choice, I'd run a bus over him." He took her arm and tried to lead her away.

She shook him off and looked back at Richard. "I want to know only one more thing. Why did you marry me?"

He smiled maliciously. "Why do you think? That I'd marry a plain little nobody who'd been stupid enough to get herself knocked up? Your father gave me a fat check and a glowing letter of introduction to Martin Brenden."

He thought he'd found a way to hurt her. He didn't realize that his words cut the last fragile tie between them, freeing her.

"You didn't have to tell her that," Nadine said even as she carefully helped him to his feet. "You can be a real bastard sometimes, Richard."

Kabler gently guided Nell out of the room. "I'm sorry I had to put you through this," he said as he held the front door open for her. "I didn't see any other way to prove Tanek was lying to you on all fronts."

"He knew about this?"

"Nigel Simpson gave him the information."

"How can you be sure?"

"Reardon was in Athens, talking to the doctor we had on Medas who certified Calder was dead. He's been snooping, trying to find out where we'd stashed Calder."

"Nicholas knew he was alive and he didn't tell me?"

"I told you, when you get into that circle, they're all the same." He looked back at the house as they walked toward the car. "You were pretty impressive back there. Tanek's work?"

She barely heard the question. "Why didn't he tell me?"

"My guess is that he had plans for you that didn't include you being distracted by such a minor thing as a live husband."

He was talking about Nicholas using her for bait again. For the first time, she wondered if he was right. Nicholas was very clever. Could he have manipulated her and made her think she was the one in control? She didn't think she could be that stupid, but—

Later. She was too shocked and angry to think clearly now.

"Can I trust you to keep quiet about this?" Kabler asked. "I've put my job on the line by bringing you here. You won't be dropping any anonymous notes to Gardeaux about Calder's whereabouts?"

"What makes you think Gardeaux knows he's alive?"

"Reardon isn't the only one who's been asking questions, and Simpson didn't get his information from us."

She felt another flare of sheer rage. "I promise I'll not communicate with Gardeaux." She added coldly, "I don't promise I won't kill that bastard myself."

"I was afraid of that." He sighed. "That means I'll have to move Calder to another—"

"Are you ready to leave now?"

She whirled to see Nicholas walking toward her down the street.

"You wanted proof he knew about Calder. Here he is," Kabler murmured. "You're too late, Tanek. I don't think she's going to go with you."

"You did know," she whispered. She hadn't realized until that moment how desperately she had wanted to believe he hadn't lied to her about this too. "You knew everything and you didn't tell me."

"I would have told you eventually."

"When? Next year? Five years?"

"When it was safe." He turned to Kabler. "You had to bring her here, didn't you? You knew Calder was still targeted and you brought her to him. She shouldn't be anywhere near him."

"He's well hidden here in Bakersfield. It's you she shouldn't be near. She knows that now. You can't use—"

Nell was knocked to the ground with the force of a giant fist!

Nicholas had been knocked to the ground too, but was now on top of her, protecting her from flying debris.

Debris from where? she wondered in bewilderment. What had happened?

Then over Nicholas's shoulder she saw the house.

What was left of the house. No windows. No porch. The south wall was blown away and the entire ruin was on fire. Licking, roaring flames.

"What happened?" she asked blankly.

"A bomb." Kabler was on his knees, his face cut and bleeding. His hands clenched into fists as he gazed in helpless fury at the house. "Dammit, they *got* him."

He was talking about Richard. Richard had been in that house. Richard was dead. Nadine was dead.

She had just been talking to them and now they were dead.

She was vaguely aware that Nicholas was standing up, pulling her to her feet. "Come on. We've got to get out of here."

Kabler was getting to his feet slowly, painfully, staring at the ruin. "Damn them. Damn them to hell."

Nicholas grasped her arm and was pulling her down the street toward his car.

"Where do you think you're going?" Kabler asked, whirling toward them.

"Away from here. Or do you want them to get her too?"

"Maybe it wasn't Gardeaux. You showed up very conveniently. Maybe it was you."

"You'd like to think so. Then you wouldn't be blamed for leading them to Calder." He met Kabler's eyes. "But you don't think it was me. You know you made a mistake when you brought her here. She was probably watched from the time she showed up at Lieber's house. They followed you here and set the bomb up next to the gas main while you were in there talking to Calder."

"They couldn't have followed us here. I've ordered that all DEA flight plans are sealed."

"They wanted Calder. Offer anyone enough money and seals can be broken. You know that as well as I do."

Kabler opened his lips to protest and then closed them. "Yes, I know that," he said. He suddenly looked old, beaten.

"Now, are you going to let me take her out of the battle zone before they kill her too?"

Kabler didn't speak for a minute and then nodded

jerkily. "Get out of here." He turned to Nell. "I have to do damage control, but I'll catch up with you later. If you're smart, you'll remember what you saw here tonight and not let him use you." He glanced back at the burning house. "Or you'll be as dead as Calder."

"I've kept her alive for five months." Nicholas half pulled, half nudged her toward his car.

People were coming out of the neighboring houses, she noticed numbly. A siren wailed in the distance.

Nicholas opened the passenger door. "Get in."

She hesitated, looking back at Kabler.

He was no longer staring at the house. He was bending over the open door of his car, talking rapidly into the car phone.

Damage control, he had said.

What could be controlled in that inferno? Richard and Nadine were both dead.

She got into the car and Nicholas slammed the door shut.

Fifteen

"Are you okay?" Nicholas asked quietly as he maneuvered the car through the residential street.

She didn't answer directly. "Will Kabler get into trouble for this?"

"Maybe. He made a big mistake. But he wields a lot of power in the agency. They're not going to jettison him."

"It's not his fault. He couldn't know we'd be followed."

"I don't want to talk about Kabler. I don't give a damn about him. How are you?"

"Fine." Her hands tightly clutched the leather strap of her shoulder bag. She had to hold on to something, anything. Everything seemed to be sliding away from her. "Where's Jamie? Did he come with you?"

"He's waiting at the airport. That's where we're heading."

"I'm not getting on any plane with you."

"Christ, do you think I'm going to kidnap you?"

"I don't know what you'll do."

"I just want to get you out of this town."

"How do I know that? How do I know anything you say is true?"

He muttered a curse and suddenly pulled over to the curb beneath a streetlight and shut off the engine. "All right. Let's talk."

"I don't want to talk." God, she felt as if she were falling apart.

"Look at me."

She stared straight ahead.

He took her chin and turned her to face him. "It's all right. I'm not going to force you to do anything you don't want to do."

"You couldn't."

"It's true I might have trouble. I've taught you too well." His finger traced the line of her cheek. "But I couldn't teach you how to handle this. You just have to breathe deep and wait until the shock passes."

"Why should I be shocked? Because I saw two people blown up? I might have considered setting the fuse myself. Richard started all this."

"Very hard. Very tough."

"Shut up." She was starting to shake. "Start the car. I told you I didn't want to talk."

He tried to draw her into his arms.

She stiffened. "Let me go. Don't touch me."

"When you stop shaking."

She backed to the edge of the seat.

"Okay, I'm a liar and you don't trust me. Then use me. Take from me. That should make it all right."

"Get your hands off me."

His hands dropped away from her. "All right. Talk. Sometimes that helps."

"I don't want to talk."

"Tell me about Calder."

She shook her head.

"I wouldn't have thought the bastard's death would have upset you this much."

"I *hated* him," she said, stung. "Jill wouldn't have died if he hadn't been dealing with Gardeaux. I would have killed him if Kabler hadn't stopped me. I wanted him dead."

"Did you want her dead too?"

"Nadine? No. I don't know. I don't think she meant to hurt. . . . I don't know."

"But it was taken out of your hands."

"Yes."

"And that scares you because it makes you feel helpless. It will happen again. You can't control everything all the time. Sometimes you can only react."

"Start the car."

"Where are we going?"

"You're going to drive me to the airport."

"Will you let me take you back to the ranch?"

"You've got to be kidding."

"I didn't think so. What are you going to do?"

"My plans haven't changed."

"But I'm not involved in them any longer."

"I can't trust you."

"But you need me. That hasn't changed. You're letting your emotions get in the way of your reasoning." He glanced at her. "All right, I lied to you. Principally by omission, but that's a cop-out. I lied. Do you believe Kabler that I'm trying to use you as bait?"

"I believe you're capable of anything."

"You're not answering me."

"No," she said curtly.

"Have I done anything to endanger you?"

"No."

"Then what have I done that's so heinous?"

"You *robbed* me. You shut me out," she said fiercely.

"This is my life. I had a right to know about Richard. I had a right to go to Tania when she was in danger."

"Yes, I robbed you of those rights and I'd do it again."

"And you expect me to just go on as if nothing had happened?"

"No, I expect you to realize that I'll lie and cheat if it means keeping you safe. And I expect you to learn to adjust and defend yourself against it. But I also expect you to use me the way you planned to in the beginning. Why shouldn't you? Think calmly and logically. Aren't I right?"

She wanted to yell and hit out at him. She didn't feel like being logical. She felt alone and betrayed, and she wanted him to suffer for it.

"It's my ballpark. I know the way around the bases. Didn't Calder's death teach you anything?"

She shuddered as she remembered her last glimpse of that blazing inferno. The explosion had come out of nowhere. She had never dreamed—But Nicholas had known at once what had happened. All right, put aside the hurt and anger. She did need him. Everything else might have changed, but that had not.

"I won't go back to the ranch."

"That's already a given."

"And I won't wait until the end of the year. I'm going to leave for Paris immediately."

"If that's what you want."

She stared at him suspiciously. He was being too accommodating.

"I'll make the reservations as soon as we get to the airport. Do you mind if Jamie comes with us? He can be very helpful."

"I don't mind," she said slowly.

"Good. Then lean back and leave everything to me."

"That's the last thing I intend to do. I won't make that mistake again." She met his eyes. "There are a lot of mistakes I won't make. Don't think that anything is going to be the same, Nicholas."

"You don't have to tell me that." He started the car. "Like you, I'll learn to adjust."

"Where are we going to stay?" Nell asked as she got into the dark blue Volkswagen Jamie had rented at Charles de Gaulle airport.

"I keep a flat on the outskirts of the city. Nothing pretentious, but it has the advantage of privacy. We'll stay there tonight."

"As private as you can get in Paris." Jamie climbed into the backseat. "You can't count on Gardeaux not knowing about the flat."

"I don't count on anything." Nicholas negotiated the car out of the parking lot. "That's why I want you to scout around and find something in the country tomorrow. I don't want to risk one of Gardeaux's men seeing Nell. They know she's alive, but they don't know what she looks like. That could work to our advantage."

She looked at him inquiringly.

"If I decide to send you into the cage with the tigers." Nicholas added, "Maybe I'll do what Kabler told you I'd do and stake you out."

She shook her head. "No, you won't."

"Why should I bother, when you're willing to do it yourself?" He shrugged. "But, despite Kabler's concern, your value as bait has diminished. You should no longer be a prime target."

"Why not?"

"You were targeted first as a punishment to Calder.

Maritz went after you a second time to try to squeeze information about Calder's whereabouts."

"But you saw that I didn't know anything about it, didn't you?" she said bitterly.

"They didn't know that. It was logical that a wife would know where her husband was."

"Then you think she's safe?" Jamie asked.

"Maybe. She shouldn't be on Gardeaux's list anymore." He shot her a look. "But you may still be on Maritz's. He tends to get obsessive."

He really is the bogeyman.

"I know." She shook off the chill the thought brought. "But that may work to our advantage too."

"On the other hand, he may regard you as just another job and leave you alone."

"I might as well start looking for a place today," Jamie said. "When we get to the flat, I'll drop you off and take the car and see what I can come up with."

Nicholas unlocked the door of the flat and stepped aside for her to enter.

"Very nice." She looked around the living room. Comfortable, elegant, spacious. She should have expected the latter. Nicholas always liked plenty of room. "Which is my room?"

Nicholas gestured to a door to the left. "There's a bathrobe in the closet. We'll buy whatever else you need tomorrow."

"Okay." She moved toward the door he'd indicated.

"Come to the kitchen when you're finished freshening up. The landlord keeps the refrigerator stocked with the basics. I'll make an omelette. You didn't eat on the plane."

"I'm not—" She stopped. She was hungry and there

was no use starving herself to avoid Nicholas. "Thank you."

"Yes, you have to keep up your strength," Nicholas murmured. "After all, the game's afoot."

She ignored the hint of irony and carried her bag into the bedroom. Lord knows, she didn't have much strength at the moment. The effort to maintain control of herself was taking its toll.

She went into the bathroom and washed her face. She didn't look as haunted as she felt. The face staring back at her in the mirror was pale and a little haggard but the same beautiful image Joel had given her those many months ago.

Joel. She felt a sharp pang of regret as she remembered how bitter he had been at the hospital. Not that she could blame him. He cared about Tania and she had almost gotten Tania killed. But if Nicholas was right and Nell was no longer a target, then Tania should also be safe now. She could only hope.

She dried her face and went to find the kitchen.

"Pour the coffee and sit down at the bar." Nicholas was taking plates down from the cabinet. "Food will be ready in a minute."

She poured coffee from the automatic maker on the counter and carried the two cups to the breakfast bar.

Nicholas set the omelettes down on the bar and sat down on the stool across from her. *"Bon appétit."*

She picked up her fork. The omelette was filled with mushrooms and cheese and surprisingly tasty. "It's good. Did you learn to cook in that kitchen in Hong Kong?"

"I picked up what I could. Omelettes are easy." He began to eat. "What are you going to do?"

"Get Maritz."

"You have to have a plan, dammit."

"I know that. I'll have one. I haven't had time to think yet."

"Will you listen to mine?"

"Not if it means waiting."

His hand tightened on his fork. "It's only a little over a month, dammit."

She didn't reply.

"Look, Gardeaux is a very cautious man, but he has a passion for swords. What do you think he'd do to get a chance at Charlemagne's?"

"Charlemagne?" She vaguely remembered seeing the sword on display at a museum. "You're going to steal it?"

He shook his head. "But I'm going to tell Gardeaux I did and that I replaced the real one with a fake."

"He wouldn't believe you."

"Why not?" He smiled. "He knows I've done it before."

She stared at him. "Have you?"

"Well, not a sword." He took a drink of coffee. "But the principle is the same. Since last April I've had a swordmaker in Toledo working on duplicating and aging the sword. I'll send Gardeaux pictures and offer to have one of his experts look at the sword before he sees it. Without chemical tests he won't be able to tell the difference. If I demand a meeting alone with him to show him the sword, I don't think he'll be able to resist."

"Doesn't he know you intend to kill him?"

"Yes."

"Then he'd be a fool to meet you."

"Not on his own territory, surrounded by a chateau full of guests and his own people."

"And then you'd be killed."

"Not if Gardeaux can help it. His associates would be very upset."

He was talking about Sandequez, she realized. His insurance policy.

"It's still dangerous."

"But it can happen . . . if you'll agree to wait."

"What about Maritz?"

He hesitated. "There's a possibility he might not be at Bellevigne. Gardeaux may think harboring him there is too risky after his attack on Tania."

Her gaze flew to his face. "Then where would he send Maritz?"

"Jamie will contact a few people and see if he can find out."

"You *knew* I thought Maritz would be here."

"And he may be. I just don't know." He finished his coffee. "And you're the one who told me we were off to Paris."

"I don't want Gardeaux without Maritz."

"Then we'll try to find him for you."

"I won't be stalled again, Nicholas. I want him now."

"Credit me with a little intelligence. I wouldn't try something as crude as stalling you." He leaned back on his stool. "I take it you refuse to wait?"

"You haven't given me a reason."

"I gave you an important reason. It would be safer."

"You just told me Gardeaux would do anything to keep you from being killed."

"Except to keep from being killed himself. And Sandequez's umbrella doesn't extend to you."

She pushed back her stool and rose to her feet. "I've waited too long already. Find me Maritz, or I'll go out and find him myself."

She left the kitchen and went straight to her room. She couldn't argue with him any longer. His argument might have merit, but this had to be over. Everything was shifting, splintering around her. Black was white.

White was black. Nothing was the same. It had gone on too long.

She needed it over.

She took a long, hot shower and then placed a call to Tania at the hospital. She was told Tania had been released that morning. She called the house.

"How are you feeling?" she asked as soon as Tania picked up. "How's your ankle?"

"Annoying. I can only hobble along with a cane. Where are you?"

"Paris."

There was silence on the other end of the line before Tania asked, "Maritz?"

"If we can find him. Nicholas says that he may not be at Bellevigne, that his attack on you might make him persona non grata with Gardeaux. I may have to find a way to make him come to me." She grimaced. "Which may not be easy. Nicholas says I could have been just a job to Maritz and my status as a target has recently gone down."

"Thank God." There was a pause before Tania asked curiously, "Why?"

Nell's hand tightened on the telephone as a vision of the burning Victorian house came back to her. "I'll tell you some other time. We'll be moving tomorrow, but I'll call you when we're settled and see how you are."

"Not tomorrow." Tania's voice was suddenly throaty. "Tomorrow we go to Phil's funeral. He's being buried in his parents' hometown in Indiana and we won't be back until late tomorrow evening."

"Are you well enough? Phil would understand."

"He saved me. He gave his life. Of course I'm well enough."

It had been a foolish question, Nell thought. Tania

would have crawled there on her hands and knees if necessary. "Take care. Give my best to Joel."

"Nell," Tania said hesitantly. "Don't blame him for being angry. He'll get over it. He strikes out at everyone because he blames himself."

"I'm not blaming him. He's right. I should have been the one hurt, not you." She added, "We left so quickly, I didn't get a chance to send flowers to Phil. Will you do that for me?"

"As soon as I hang up."

"Which will be now. I'll let you get your rest. Good-bye, Tania."

Tania replaced the receiver and turned to Joel. "She's in Paris."

"Good. Shall I send her a ticket to Timbuktu?"

"You're not being fair. Nell was not at fault here."

"I don't feel like being fair. I'm mad as hell."

"At yourself for not switching on the security system. I do not blame you."

"You should," he said jerkily. "I was criminally careless."

"You didn't know there was any danger. I didn't know myself. It was only a feeling."

"That you didn't share with me."

"You're a busy man. Was I to waste your time on what might have been foolishness?"

"Yes."

She shook her head.

"Dammit, you almost *died*."

"And you've been hovering over me ever since. You canceled all your appointments and I cannot even go to the bathroom without you there." She smiled ruefully. "It is most embarrassing."

"It shouldn't embarrass you. I'm a doctor." He stood

up and crossed the room. "And, as your doctor, I'm telling you that it's time you got off that ankle and into bed." He lifted her in his arms and carried her toward the stairs. "And no arguments."

"I will not argue. I am weary." She buried her face in his shoulder as he started up the stairs. "It's strange that heaviness of the heart makes the body weary. That poor boy was—"

"Don't think about it."

"I've thought of nothing else since it happened. Such evil . . ."

He laid her down on her bed and drew the crocheted coverlet over her. "It will never touch you again," he said fiercely.

A ghost of a smile touched her lips. "You're going to keep it away by missing all your appointments and taking me to the bathroom?"

He sat down on the bed beside her and grasped her hand. "I know I'm not Tanek." His words came haltingly. "I'm Paul Henreid, not Humphrey Bogart, but I swear I'll never let anything hurt you again."

"I don't know what you're talking about. Who is Paul Henreid?"

"*Casablanca*. The movie. Never mind." He stroked her hair back from her face. "What's important is that you know I'll make sure you'll be safe for the rest of your life."

She went still. "I believe you're saying something very important here. But you're being most clumsy. Are you telling me that you no longer intend to nobly cast me out of your life?"

"I should do it. I'm probably being a bastard not to—"

"Hush." Her fingers covered his lips. "Don't spoil it. Tell me the words I want to hear."

"I love you," he said simply.

"Oh, I know that. Tell me the rest."

"I want you to live with me. I don't want you to ever leave me."

"Good. And?"

"Will you marry me?"

A joyous smile lit her face. "It will be my pleasure." She drew him down into her arms. "And yours. I promise you, Joel. I will make you so happy."

"You already do." He held her closer and mumbled, "I don't know why you want me, but here I am."

She kissed him exuberantly. "You must continue with such humility. I believe it to be a very good thing." Her smile faded. "But you pick a very bad time for such declarations. I've been trying so hard to get you to go to bed with me, and now it's not—"

"I know you're ill. I wouldn't—"

"It's not my ankle, it's that it's not fitting. We mourn a good friend."

He nodded and gently kissed her cheek. "I'll leave you and see about supper."

She shook her head. "You will do no such thing. This time is special for us. You will stay here with me and we will hold each other and tell each other our thoughts." She scooted to the other side of the bed and pulled him down to lie beside her. She cuddled close. "See, this is good too, isn't it?"

His voice was uneven. "Yes, this is good."

"And after we run out of words, we will turn on the television set."

"Television?" he echoed, surprised. "You want to watch television?"

"And the VCR." She kissed his throat. "And you will put on the *Casablanca* tape. I must study this Paul Henreid."

"I want you out of here, Maritz," Gardeaux said. "You've done nothing but blunder since Medas." He moved toward the sideboard and poured himself a glass of wine. "And then you compound your error by coming here when I've expressly forbidden it."

Maritz flushed. "I had to see you. You weren't taking my phone calls."

"That should have told you something."

"I need protection. The police are after me. Tania Vlados saw me. She knows who I am."

"Because you blundered. I've no use for blunderers."

"I can still be useful to you. If you hadn't told me to get out of the country, I would have taken care of Richard Calder for you. You didn't have to call someone from outside to take care of him."

"Yes, I did. I had to be sure. I can't trust you anymore, Maritz."

"All I have to do is go back and get Tania Vlados. Then there won't be a witness."

"You'll not go near her. I can't chance you being caught. You know too much. You'll stay here in France and lose yourself."

"And then you'll call me when it's safe?"

"Eventually. Keep in touch."

He was lying, Maritz thought. Did the bastard think he was stupid? He would go into hiding and then one day someone would show up to make sure he would never be arrested and become a threat to Gardeaux. "I'll need money."

Gardeaux just looked at him.

"I'm not begging. You owe me."

"I pay for success, not failure."

"I've worked for you for six years. It's just bad luck that this job didn't pan out."

"I've no work for you to do."

"The Calder woman."

"She's not important any longer."

He sought wildly for another target. "Tanek. Rivil told me that Tanek's name is on a passenger list for a flight that came in to Paris today. I'll go after Tanek."

"I told you he isn't to be touched."

"You hate him. It doesn't make sense. Let me go after him."

"It makes perfect sense . . . right now. He's protected." He smiled. "But his protection may be weakening even as we speak."

"I can wait. Just let me have the job."

"I'll consider it." Gardeaux walked to the door and opened it. "Give Braceau your address and wait for my call."

Or a visitor with a garrote, Maritz thought sourly. He moved toward the door. "I'll do that."

The door shut behind him with finality.

Gardeaux was through with him, and he was a dead man. Nothing could be clearer. But he wouldn't lie down and wait for it. He could still come out of this if he could get back in Gardeaux's good graces.

He would go into hiding, but there would be no call to Braceau.

He would be too busy trying to find a way to save himself.

"A call on the private line, Monsieur Gardeaux." Henri Braceau was smiling as he proffered the telephone. "Medellin."

Gardeaux took the phone. "Is it done?"

"Ten minutes ago."

"Any problem?"

"Smooth as glass."

Gardeaux replaced the receiver.

Braceau looked at him inquiringly.

"Call Rivil. Tell him to take care of that matter I discussed with him. Immediately."

"I t was a nice funeral." Joel unlocked the door and flicked on the lights in the foyer. "I liked Phil's parents."

"No funeral is nice." Tania hobbled as quickly as she could into the house, averting her eyes from the snow-covered lawn. The yellow barricade was gone but not the memory of blood on the snow. "They are all terrible."

"You know what I meant," Joel said.

"I'm sorry. I didn't mean to be sharp with you." She limped over to the window. "Today was difficult."

"For me too. Sit down and rest. I'll make some coffee. We both need it."

She didn't sit down. She stood staring out at the snow where she had huddled and tried to escape Maritz's knife, where Phil had died. . . .

"Here." Joel was back, handing her a cup. She must have been staring out the window longer than she had thought. She took the cup.

"You're pale as a tombstone," Joel said. "You shouldn't have gone. It was too much for you."

"He's still free," she whispered.

"He can't hurt you. They don't even think he's in the country."

"Nell isn't sure where he is. She says she may have to draw him to her."

"She should leave it to the police."

"Police can't stop people like him. He'll just keep killing and killing . . ."

"He's not some supernatural demon, Tania. He's a man."

He had seemed like a demon to her. Joel didn't understand. But Nell did. She had faced the demon and knew its power.

She turned back to the window. "I hate him."

His hand pressed her shoulder. "Phil was a good man."

"Not only because he killed Phil. He made me afraid. I thought I'd been afraid before, but it wasn't like that." She shuddered. "I'm still afraid."

"Do you want to leave here? We'll sell the place and go away."

"And hide for the rest of my life? He'd like that. It would be a victory for him."

"Then what do you want to do?"

It seemed as if the winter chill outside had suddenly invaded the room. She crossed her arms across her chest to ward off the cold. "I don't know." She was silent a moment. "Nell isn't sure she can get Maritz to come to her."

He stiffened. "I don't like where this conversation is going."

"He'd come for me."

"No," he said flatly.

"With Nell it was a job, but he became 'involved' when he was stalking me. You should have seen his face when he realized he didn't have time to kill me before the security men got here. I've never seen an expression of such frustration." She smiled bitterly. "Oh, yes, he'd come for me."

Joel jerked her around to face him. "I said no."

"I don't like being afraid. As long as I fear him, he'll always be with me."

"Did you hear me? You're not going. I won't let you out of my sight."

"What if he disappears? I'll be looking over my shoulder for the rest of my life." Her expression hardened. "He's not going to win, Joel. I won't let him win."

"For God's sake, this isn't a game."

"It was to him."

He jerked her close. "Shut up. I won't lose you. Do you hear me? You're not going anywhere."

She relaxed against him. *That's right, Joel, keep me here. Keep away the cold. Keep me safe.*

Don't let me go.

The house Jamie found for them was a small cottage on the coast. It was perched on a high cliff overlooking the Atlantic and a boulder-strewn shoreline.

"Does it bother you?" Nicholas asked her. "Jamie probably didn't think."

Jamie muttered an exclamation of surprise.

"It doesn't bother me." It was true; standing there on the windswept cliff didn't disturb her. It was completely different from the enclosed balcony at Medas. Maybe enough time had passed so that the pain was dulled. She turned and went into the cottage. Clean and cozy, it was decorated in an unpretentious style.

Jamie followed her. "I'm an idiot. Forgive me?"

"There's nothing to forgive. The cottage is very pleasant."

"Well, you'll have to enjoy the sea air by yourself for a few days. Nick and I have to go up to Paris."

She whirled to face him. "Why?"

"Pardeau, Gardeaux's accountant. Nick wants to see what we can do in that quarter."

You can never have too much insurance, Nicholas had said. "What about Maritz?"

"We'll tap a few sources while we're there," Nicholas said from the doorway. "You'll be safe here. No one can recognize you and Jamie was careful to make sure this location is secure. I've written the car phone number on the pad on the counter."

"Why can't I go with you?"

"For the same reason we moved here. I don't want you recognized. Once we start probing, Gardeaux will know I'm in Paris. If you're seen with me, he'll draw conclusions and the advantage is blown. Make sense?"

"Yes," she said slowly. "When will you be back?"

"In a day or two. Can I trust you to stay here?"

"What good would it do me to leave until I know where Maritz is?"

"Promise me."

"I'll stay here. Satisfied?"

He smiled crookedly. "Hell, no. I've forgotten what it is to be satisfied." He turned away. "Come on, Jamie, let's get going."

"Be careful," she said impulsively.

Nicholas raised an eyebrow. "Concern? Does this mean I'm forgiven?"

"No, but I never said I wanted you hurt."

"Then I'll have to be grateful for small favors."

She went to the door to watch them leave. The Volkswagen barreled down the winding two-lane road and was out of sight in minutes.

She was alone.

The solitude would be good for her, she told herself. It would give her time to think, to plan. She hadn't really been alone in months. Nicholas had been there, talking to her, teaching her, making love to her. . . . No, not love, sex. Love had never been mentioned between them.

But sometimes it had seemed like love.

Which was why it was good she had been jarred out of that relationship. She and Nicholas were different as night and day. He had made it clear what he wanted from her, and it was not commitment. There could be no future with a man like him.

Future?

For the first time she realized she was thinking beyond Maritz. Was that a sign she was beginning to heal?

Possibly. It was too soon to tell, but, if she was healing, she owed it as much to Nicholas as time itself.

He had lied to her, he had hurt her, he had healed her.

She was thinking too much about Nicholas. It was safer not to think of him at all.

Sixteen

"Pardeau is scared to death," Jamie said as he got back in the car at 412 St. Germain. "He won't be easy."

"Money?" Nicholas asked. He started the car and drove toward the Seine.

"He's tempted, but he heard what happened to Simpson. He says that Gardeaux knows I've been in touch with him and he doesn't want me to come there anymore." He shook his head. "I thought I might have him the last time I talked to him, but something's changed. He's jumpy."

"Which means?"

Jamie shrugged. "I'm not sure. All he'd say was that there was no way he could give up the records now. No matter where he hid, Gardeaux would never stop searching for him."

"So what's different?" Then Nicholas answered himself. "He's been given information that could hurt Gardeaux more than just the exposure of his usual business transactions."

"That's my guess." Jamie smiled. "But I was able to purchase one bit of information that might interest you.

Two days ago Pardeau was ordered to delete the Maritz account. Gardeaux said that he was no longer on the payroll."

Gardeaux had cast his principal demon into outer darkness. Or maybe he had deleted Maritz in more than the numerical sense. No, Maritz wasn't a great intellect, but he had instinct and cunning. Nicholas would bet that he'd gone underground. "I want to know where—"

"We're being followed," Jamie interrupted. "Two cars back."

Nicholas stiffened as he glanced in the rearview mirror. He located the two headlights, but in the darkness he couldn't determine the make or color of the car. "How long?"

"Since we left Pardeau's flat. A dark green Mercedes. It pulled out from the curb a half block behind us."

"A tail on Pardeau?"

"Maybe. But why leave his surveillance to follow us?"

No reason. Unless Pardeau was right and Gardeaux was waiting for him to be contacted again. Nicholas wasn't worried. Gardeaux liked to keep tabs on him, and he'd been followed before. Usually it didn't matter, but now that he'd learned what he came to find out, he wanted to get back to Nell.

"Do we try to lose them?" Jamie asked.

Nicholas nodded. "They'll know the city better than we do, but there are a lot of side roads in the hills outside the city." He pressed his foot on the accelerator. "Let's go see if we can find one."

He was five miles into the hills when he realized that the Mercedes was not tailing him.

It was pursuing him.

The Mercedes was practically on top of them and bearing down at full speed.

It rammed into their rear bumper.

"Christ."

"Not a good place," Jamie said grimly as he glanced around the hilly terrain. "If we go off anywhere along here, we'll end up bouncing two hundred feet down an embankment. Where are those side roads when you need them?"

The Mercedes rammed them again.

Nicholas floored the accelerator and the Volkswagen leapt ahead.

"You can't keep ahead of them," Jamie pointed out. "The Mercedes has more power. Not to mention it's built like a tank."

"I know that." The attack was pointed and lethal. This wasn't supposed to happen, dammit.

The Mercedes was overtaking them. There was no escaping it. Nicholas could fight it off for a few more times, but eventually the Mercedes would blast them off the road.

All right. If they were going off the road, it was better for him to choose the spot than leave the option to them.

"Unfasten your seat belt."

Jamie unsnapped the seat-belt catch.

The Mercedes's front bumper hit their left side.

The Volkswagen skidded and Nicholas narrowly avoided leaving the highway. Jamie cursed as his head struck the side window. He rubbed his temple. "If you're going to do much of that, I'm going to fasten my seat belt again."

"Not if you want to get out of here alive. We're going over the side."

"I gathered that. Where?"

"The next curve. The incline doesn't seem as steep there. I'll aim the car for the edge of the road and we jump. Get your hand on the passenger doorknob. I'll try to slow down as much as possible, but they'll be right behind us and I don't want them to know we're not in the car."

The curve was just ahead.

Nicholas floored the accelerator and the car leapt forward. The Mercedes was left behind.

"I'm not sure this is such a good idea," Jamie murmured.

Nicholas released his seat belt. "Neither am I."

They were rounding the curve. He jammed on the brakes and the car fishtailed.

"Now I *know* this isn't a good idea," Jamie gasped.

Nicholas turned the steering wheel toward the edge of the road and flung open his car door. "Jump!"

The Volkswagen careened off the road and hurtled down the incline.

The first bump threw Nicholas out the open door.

So much for jump—

He couldn't breathe. The fall had knocked the air out of him. He was rolling down.

Where was Jamie?

He could see the headlights of the Volkswagen as it bounced down the hillside toward the valley.

He grabbed a bush and held on tight. His gaze fastened on the road above.

He could see the lights of the Mercedes. It was parked at the edge of the road.

Three men were looking down.

At the car or at him?

It was too dark for them to see him. They had to be looking at the Volkswagen.

The car had come to rest at the bottom of the hill. Would they go down and check it out?

He caught the glint of light on the barrel of an automatic weapon.

The sound of the bullets was drowned out by the

explosion of the Volkswagen. The car was instantly enveloped in flames.

Very clean. Mission accomplished.

Follow-up?

No, they were getting back in the Mercedes.

Not clean at all. Lazy.

Thank God.

A few minutes later Nicholas could no longer see the beam of the headlights.

Where the hell was Jamie?

"Nick?"

Relief surged through him at Jamie's cautious whisper. Jamie was above him on the incline.

"Here." Nicholas released the bush and began wriggling up the hill. "Are you okay?"

"My right side hurts like hell. You?"

"I'm alive. I wouldn't have given very much for our chances of that ten minutes ago."

"Now you tell me."

Jamie was lying under an overhanging rock formation only ten feet from the road. Nicholas reached him. "I didn't want to discourage you. Were you close enough to see who they were?"

"I recognized the one with the automatic. Rivil."

One of Gardeaux's hit men, one of the elite who would never be given such a menial task as surveillance of a lowly bookkeeper. He was sent out for one task only.

"I think you're in trouble," Jamie said.

Nell woke in the darkness, fully awake and in a panic.

There was someone in the cottage.

The sounds in the living room were soft, secretive, but undoubtedly footsteps.

Maritz?

How could he know they were here?

Tania would not have been surprised.

He really is the bogeyman.

Nell reached over to the bedside table and closed her hand on the Lady Colt.

She stood up and glided toward the door.

He was still moving. Was he coming toward the bedroom?

She couldn't wait to find out.

Her hand tightened on the Colt as she threw open the door and flicked on the light.

Nicholas was standing at the sink.

His head and face were covered with blood.

"Would you mind pointing that gun somewhere else? I'm still not very confident of your ability in that area." He turned on the faucet. "I tried not to wake you, but I suppose it was—"

"What happened to you?"

"We were run off the road." He was splashing his face with water. "I'm afraid Hertz is going to have to buy a new Volkswagen."

"Jamie?"

"I think he's all right. He got a bad knock in the ribs. I stopped a car on the highway and dropped him off at the closest hospital for X rays."

"Why the devil didn't they keep you too? You look like you need a new head."

"I wanted to get back. Everything was crazy tonight. It shouldn't have happened. I wanted to make sure they hadn't found out where I'd moved you."

"They?" she whispered. "Gardeaux?"

"Jamie recognized his man Rivil. I don't know who else was in the car."

"Sit down and let me look at your head."

"You don't have to bother. I'm used to patching myself up."

"Oh, then if it needs stitches, I'll just hand you my sewing kit."

"Is it kind to be sarcastic when I rushed here to—"

"Sit down." She crossed the room and shoved him into a chair at the table. "Let me clean it properly." She filled a basin at the sink and grabbed a kitchen towel. "If the car was destroyed, how did you get here?"

"I hitched a ride with a farmer at the hospital." As she started to clean the blood from his face, he added, "All this isn't necessary, you know. I'm not badly hurt."

"You're right. It's nothing," she said as she finally reached the cut on his hairline. Lord, her hands were shaking. "You must bleed easily."

"Actually, it's not blood at all. I bought a bottle of catsup on the way back. Terence always used to tell me that the best way to get a woman's sympathy was to bleed a little."

"He was wrong. I don't feel at all sorry for you."

"Sure you do. You're paler than I am." He smiled up at her. "Works every time."

She was beginning to feel sick, suffocated. "You obviously don't need my help." She threw the towel down. "And I need some air."

She slammed the door shut behind her, then stopped to take a deep breath. The air was cold and she welcomed its bite.

"You've chosen the wrong place to be if blood makes you sick." Nicholas came toward her.

She took a step back. "I just needed some air. Blood doesn't make me sick."

"You could have fooled me."

"I thought you said you were safe from Gardeaux."

"It appears I was mistaken."

"Why were you attacked? What happened to that fine insurance policy?"

"Maybe someone canceled it."

"You mean Sandequez is dead."

"It's the logical conclusion."

"Why are you so calm about it? Gardeaux tried to kill you tonight." She started walking faster. "And he'll try again, won't he?"

"At every opportunity."

"You'll never be safe again."

"That's not necessarily true. It just means that I have to be careful until I solidify my position."

"If you live that long."

"I stand corrected. There's always that qualification."

"Stop smiling," she said fiercely. "I don't see anything funny about this."

"Neither do I. But you're being serious enough for both of us."

She wanted to strike him. "That's right. You believe in enjoying every minute to the fullest. Dammit, don't you realize they've just blown up all your blasted gates and they're going to roll right over you?"

He was studying her. "I realize you're very upset at the thought of my demise. I like it."

She didn't like it. She didn't want to feel the panic that had torn through her when she had first seen Nicholas that night. "What are you going to do?"

"The same as before. But with a great deal more care."

"You shouldn't even be in the same country with him." She looked away from him. "It's not—I don't mind—if you don't go through with it."

His smile vanished. "Have you forgotten I didn't start this to help you? I have no intention of opting out."

She didn't know if she was more frightened or relieved. "I just wanted you to know." She paused. "Of course, you wouldn't want to—"

"Nell," he said quietly. "It's going to be all right. I just have to do some damage control."

Damage control. That was what Kabler had said as he looked at the burning house. Death and destruction and the ever-popular damage control.

"Whatever you say." She moistened her lips. "But under the circumstances I don't think we'll move forward as quickly as I'd like. We'd better wait for New Year's Eve."

A slow smile lit his face. "If that's what you want."

"It's not what I want at all." She turned her back on him and moved toward the cottage. "It's what we have to do to keep you from getting killed."

Jamie showed up the next morning with fresh croissants and a newspaper. He gave the croissants to Nell and tossed the paper down on the table in front of Nicholas. "I told you that you were in trouble."

"Sandequez?"

"Dead as a doornail. He was killed at his hacienda in the hills by the Colombian drug enforcement forces. The entire compound was wiped out."

"When?"

"About three hours before we left Pardeau's. Since there was no public news release for another eight hours, I'd say Gardeaux had advance information."

"Or furnished it to the authorities. Sandequez was well guarded. The police have been trying to get him for years."

Jamie whistled. "You mean Gardeaux served Sandequez up to them. My, my, what a nasty man."

"Why would he do that?" Nell asked. "Didn't you

say that Sandequez was one of the men Gardeaux works for?"

"But I've been a thorn in Gardeaux's side for a long time, and Sandequez's removal might serve him in other ways."

Jamie nodded. "He might move up on the corporate ladder, so to speak, and the Colombian government had put a five-million-dollar bounty on Sandequez. That would nicely pad one of Gardeaux's Swiss bank accounts. You think he tipped off the Colombian authorities?"

"Possibly." Nicholas shrugged. "At any rate, it's a moot point. Sandequez is dead. Which means I'll have to stay out of sight with Nell until we're ready to move."

Nell felt a rush of relief, which she quickly tried to hide. "Remarkably sensible of you." She carried the croissants to the microwave. "But I've no intention of staying out of sight. As you've pointed out, no one can recognize me."

She could feel Nicholas's gaze on her back.

"May I ask where you intend to go?"

"Paris."

"And what do you intend to do there?"

"Work."

"Where?"

"I'm not sure. You'll have to tell me." She turned to face him. "Which modeling agency does Gardeaux's mistress work for?"

"Chez Molambre." Nicholas was studying her face. "What do you have in mind?"

"I need to get into the Renaissance Fest. I doubt if Gardeaux is going to issue me an invitation, and it would be risky for you to steal or forge them. The *Sports Illustrated* story said that there's a fashion show every year as part of the festivities. Jacques Dumoit does a special collection, and it's almost a certainty Gardeaux would ask him to use his mistress's agency to furnish the models."

"He does."

"And you intend to apply at the agency." Jamie smiled. "Ah, bright girl. We could have used her in the old days, Nick."

"You have no experience," Nicholas said.

"I've been to dozens of fashion shows. I'll fake it." She turned to Jamie. "If you can fake my credentials and arrange to have photographs taken for a portfolio."

"I know a photographer in Nice I can trust," Jamie said. "Give me three days."

"I don't like it," Nicholas said.

"I didn't expect you to like it." She met his gaze. "But will they hire me?"

"You know damn well they will." His smile was grim. "Who wouldn't hire Helen of Troy?"

"Good. I thought it would work. And I like the idea. There's a sort of . . . justice to it."

"Justice?" Jamie asked.

"She means that she got that exceptional face courtesy of Maritz and Gardeaux, and it's only fair that she use it to gut them."

She should have realized that Nicholas would know exactly what she meant. Nicholas knew her so well. Too well. She took the croissants out of the oven and put them on the table. "I'm not as tall and thin as most runway models. You'll have to make those credentials impeccable, Jamie."

"Trust me. Besides, they'll be so in love with your face, I'll bet they'll never notice."

She wasn't so sure. "We'll see."

"You must have been thinking about this for a while," Nicholas said quietly.

"You left me alone for two days. What was I supposed to do? Twiddle my thumbs?"

"Heaven forbid." He stood up and moved toward the door. "Remind me not to leave you alone again."

The Charlemagne sword was hand-delivered the next morning by a dark-haired young man who looked little older than Peter. He wore a black leather jacket, arrived on a motorcycle, and his smile was supremely confident.

He presented the leather-wrapped package to Nicholas with a flourish. "Here it is, Señor. The finest piece of work my father has ever done."

"Thank you, Tomas." When he remained standing there, staring at Nell, Nicholas added, "Tomas Armandariz, Eve Billings."

Tomas beamed at her. "I am also a great craftsman. I will someday be very famous."

"That's nice," she said absently as she followed Nicholas back into the cottage.

The boy followed her. "I did a great deal of work on the sword myself."

Nicholas was drawing the sword from its leather sheath.

"As a reward for my work, my father says I can go on to Paris for a few days' holiday." Tomas smiled beguilingly at Nell. "I don't suppose you would want to go with——"

"Good-bye, Tomas," Nicholas said, his gaze on the sword.

Tomas didn't seem to hear. "I attended school at the Sorbonne, and I know many cafés that——"

Nicholas pointed the sword at the boy. "Good-bye."

Tomas blinked and began backing toward the door.

Nell didn't blame him. She had not seen this Nicholas since that moment in Florida when he had struck down Sergeant Wilkins.

Tomas said, "Only a small joke, Señor Tanek."

"I thought as much." Nicholas smiled gently. "Tell your father I'm very pleased with the sword. And now you have to be on your way to Paris, don't you?"

"Yes, yes. At once." He bolted out of the cottage.

"You didn't have to frighten him," Nell said. "All I had to do was say no."

"He was cocky." He was looking at the hilt of the sword again. "And he annoyed me."

She dismissed the subject and looked at the sword. She had seen the genuine sword only once, but this forgery seemed amazingly similar. "Is it close enough?"

He nodded. "It's a work of art."

"You're still going to use it?"

"With Sandequez dead, it's literally and figuratively the only weapon I have."

"You'll be walking into the lion's den." She hesitated. "I've been thinking. If I can get into Bellevigne undetected, why don't you stay here and let me handle everything?"

He stared at her, waiting.

She rushed on. "It's only sensible. Forget the sword. You'd be recognized and there's no way you'll get out alive."

"Has it occurred to you that you're trying to close me out?" he asked quietly. "That you're robbing me."

The words were familiar, the ones she had used to him. "This is different."

"It's always different when applied to yourself." He smiled. "I understand perfectly. But have you stopped to wonder why I was so determined to keep you at the ranch and protect you?"

"Because you're an arrogant man and think you're the only one in the world who—"

"I think you know that's not the reason." He met her gaze. "But maybe you're not ready to take your head out of the sand yet."

Her hands clenched in frustration. "I don't *like* this."

"I know. But you'll have to adjust to it. I did." He turned back to the sword. "And I'll just have to get a few tricks up my sleeve to keep the situation level."

"Damage control?"

"Exactly." He took a pile of photographs out of a kitchen drawer and began to compare them to the sword. He murmured, "Amazing work."

He had clearly ended the conversation. She turned to leave.

"Maritz won't be at Bellevigne."

She whirled back to face him. "You're sure?"

He nodded. "Gardeaux has given him his walking papers. We'll have to deal with them one at a time. We'll concentrate on Gardeaux and then worry about Maritz."

Disappointment compounded her fear and frustration. "But can we find him?"

"We'll find him." He put a photograph of the hilt next to the actual sword hilt. "After you go to Paris, I don't want you coming back here until we're ready to move."

"Why not?"

"It's too dangerous. If you're going to be Eve Billings, be Eve Billings. Make friends with the other models. No mysterious disappearances on weekends. Spend them in Paris."

"I see." She felt oddly bereft. He was right, of course. Going to Paris had been her choice, and she must follow through with it. "But we'll have to make plans."

"Not until I get in touch with Gardeaux and find out the lay of the land. I'll come to your apartment the night before you leave for Bellevigne. Until then, no contact unless there's an emergency."

She tried to smile. "That seems sensible."

"You'll go to Nice tomorrow with Jamie for the photo shoot. He's already arranged for you to sublease a small apartment in the Sorbonne area. Nothing fancy. Something a student or struggling model could afford."

"Jamie is very efficient."

"More than you know."

He was right. She was not really part of their lives and certainly not their past. The closeness she felt toward them would vanish as soon as she left them.

"You'll be careful?" She hadn't meant to ask that question; it had tumbled out.

He looked up and smiled. "Of what? The sea gulls? Want to ship me back to the ranch?"

Yes, she did and lock all the gates behind him.

And he knew it.

"With all the pollution around these days, you can never tell what germs sea gulls carry," she said lightly. "I'll go pack."

The sword was as alluring as a siren song.

Gardeaux studied the color photographs with a magnifying glass.

If it was a fake, it was a brilliant one.

And it could be real. Tanek was very talented in the area of acquisition.

The excitement that rippled through him made his hand tremble. The sword of a conqueror. Perhaps the greatest conqueror who ever lived.

That feeling was what Tanek had planned on. He was being manipulated.

Charlemagne's sword.

Would Tanek dare to offer him a fake?

It was a trap to lure him to his death.

Attempts had been made on Charlemagne's life too, but strength and brains had made him tower above those foolish enough to try to kill him.

As he, Gardeaux, towered above Tanek.

His forefinger gently touched the hilt of the sword in the photograph. Incredible. Magnificent.

His.

"I'm sorry, Mademoiselle, we cannot use you." Molambre tapped the open portfolio in front of him. "These pictures are very impressive, but we handle only runway models and you don't meet our qualifications."

"I'm not tall enough?"

"Five foot seven? You lack power and presence. You must have presence to show clothes. Perhaps you would do for the New York runways, but our designers are more particular." He shrugged. "Stick to print. You have a great future there."

"There are only so many magazines. I need to do both."

He closed the portfolio and held it out to her. "As I said, I'm very sorry."

His tone was final. She stood up and took the portfolio. "Good day, Monsieur Molambre."

Brick wall.

Well, she would just have to go around it.

"And what can I do for you, Mademoiselle Billings?" Celine Dumoit asked indifferently.

Well, Nell couldn't expect anything but indifference. Jacques Dumoit was one of the leading designers in the world. These people dealt in beauty, used it, discarded it when it faded. "I need to speak to your husband, Madame."

The woman bristled. "That's not possible. I run this salon. You speak to me. Everyone wishes to speak to Jacques. He's a busy man. My husband is putting together a special collection."

"For the Renaissance Fest." Nell nodded. "I want him to use me as a model at the fest."

"He uses the Chez Molambre agency. Apply to them."

"I did. They refuse to consider me. They say I lack presence."

Madame Dumoit studied her. "I disagree. You do have a certain presence, but that is neither here nor there."

"I need this job."

"And that is supposed to influence me?"

Nell doubted if any human need would influence this iceberg. "I'm trying to break into modeling here in Europe. The Renaissance Fest would be a perfect showcase for me."

"And for a thousand other models here in Paris."

"Your husband always does a collection influenced by the Renaissance for the fests. I'm right for it."

"What makes you think so?"

"Put me in a gown and let him judge."

"We have all the models we need." She hesitated and then nodded. "But your face does have an unusual quality and Jacques wants to please Monsieur Gardeaux. We will see how you look in number eight."

Number eight turned out to be a magnificent burgundy gown with long, tight sleeves and a square neck.

It was also a very small size six, and the waist was so tight, Nell could barely breathe.

"You are abominably fat," Celine Dumoit said. She put the pearl-trimmed cap on Nell's head, stepped back, and tilted her head. "But there is definitely . . . something." She turned to a tall man coming into the room. "Ah, there you are, Jacques."

"Why did you send for me?" Jacques Dumoit's tone was peevish. "I'm very busy, Celine."

"I know, my love." She gestured to Nell. "What do you think?"

"Fat. She will have to lose at least ten pounds before the show."

"Then you think she will do?" Celine asked.

"Of course she will do. Stunning. Renaissance courtesan. That face looks like it might have been painted by da Vinci. May I go now?"

"Of course, my darling. I promise I'll not bother you again."

"Assign her the green gown too." He was striding out of the dressing room. "And make sure she gets rid of that hideous fat."

"Yes, Jacques." She turned to Nell. "Give the receptionist your phone number. You'll come for fittings whenever you're summoned, and if you miss one, you're out."

"Yes, Madame."

"And you have two weeks to lose the weight."

"Yes, Madame."

"You should be grateful. We're giving you a great opportunity."

"I'm very grateful, Madame Dumoit."

"Naturally, we will not pay you for your services in this case. You should be paying us."

Why, the ice-coated skinflint! "I'm very grateful," Nell repeated.

Celine Dumoit nodded with satisfaction and left the dressing room.

As the dresser undid the buttons of the gown, Nell turned to the mirror and the face that had gotten her a ticket to Bellevigne. Renaissance courtesan was every bit as good as Helen of Troy. She had told the woman the truth.

She was grateful.

Thank you, Joel.

"Tanek, how good it is to hear from you," Gardeaux said.

"Yes, Rivil conveyed your enthusiasm. You received the photographs?"

"Exquisite bait, but, of course, I'm not fool enough to think the sword is authentic."

"You won't know until you examine it yourself. I was going to let you have an expert inspect it, but I believe now that any contact will be hazardous to my health."

"You heard about Sandequez? Sad."

"It depends on your position."

"My position is very solid. Yours is very precarious." He paused. "I don't want you at my fest, Tanek. Choose another place and time."

"You might have had a chance at persuading me if you'd not made my position that precarious. I'll wait until I can come into the courtyard with a crowd of your very prestigious guests. I want people around who would make it embarrassing for you if you decide to rid yourself of me."

"But you intend to do the same to me." He fell silent and then said, "You're going to a great deal of trouble and bother for O'Malley, Tanek. He really wasn't worth it."

"He was worth it."

"I disagree. The man wasn't in the least interesting.

Now, *you'll* be much more entertaining. Pietro would find you fascinating."

"He won't get the chance. I wouldn't play your game."

"Yes, you will."

"Do you want the sword?"

"I'll call you back. Give me your number."

"I'll call you." Tanek hung up and turned to Jamie. "He wants it. He's salivating, or he wouldn't be trying to negotiate."

Jamie looked at the sword. "It's truly a beautiful weapon. But not worth the risk."

"Gardeaux thinks it is," Tanek said. "Thank God." It was coming to an end. A little over a month, and all the waiting, all the frustration would be over.

"What do you want me to do next?" Jamie asked.

"Stay here at the cottage in case Nell calls. Keep away from her unless there's trouble. Your face is as recognizable as mine. I'll try to phone and give you a number where I can be reached."

"You won't be here?"

He shook his head. "I'm taking the first flight out of Paris tomorrow morning."

Seventeen

"No, I won't *have* this, Tania." Nell's hand tightened on the phone. "Stay home, where you're safe."

"But Maritz took care that I'd know I wasn't safe, even at home," Tania said. "He destroyed that for me."

"I won't use you for bait. What do you think I am?"

"I'm not asking you, I'm telling you. You can help me or not—your choice."

"You know I wouldn't leave you to—Tania, don't do it. I'd never forgive myself if you were hurt again."

"I'm not doing it for you. I'm doing it for me."

"What does Joel say?"

"That I'm crazy, that he won't let me go, that he'll go after Maritz himself. He's going to be a problem."

"He's right, you're crazy."

"No. Maritz is crazy. This is sane. I won't let him control my life." Tania paused. "I have to do this, Nell. I don't have any more options than you do. I'm not going to argue anymore. I'm hanging up now."

"Wait. When are you coming?"

"Oh, you'll know when I get there."

December 23
Marseilles

She had come to him.

And she looked so happy.

Maritz gazed at the picture on the front page of the feature section of the Paris newspaper. Tania was wearing a white suit and she was gazing up at Joel Lieber with a radiant smile.

But then, all brides were radiant.

He scanned the text under the picture.

Joel Lieber, world-renowned surgeon, and the former Tania Vlados arriving at Charles de Gaulle airport on the first leg of an extended honeymoon. The couple will be traveling to Cannes and staying at the Carleton Hotel until after the New Year.

He had thought his luck was gone.

But then pretty Tania had walked back into his life.

If he could remove her as a witness, Gardeaux might accept him back into the fold.

But that wasn't what was causing the excitement coursing through him.

The hunt was about to begin again.

Jamie gave a low whistle when he saw the article.

Nick wasn't going to like this. He wished to hell he could get in touch with him. He had tried two days before, but Nick had moved on and was no longer at the number he'd given him.

He called Nell instead. "Did you see the newspaper?"

"Yes, I'm very happy for them. Didn't she look beautiful?"

"What's she doing here?"

"Honeymooning, the paper said."

"She didn't tell you?"

"She mentioned nothing about a wedding the last time I talked to her."

"You can't see her. Joel's too much in the spotlight."

"I know that. I had no intention of going to see her." She paused. "How's Nicholas?"

"Fine." He changed the subject. "And how do you like your new vocation?"

"Boring."

"Well, day after tomorrow is Christmas. It won't be much longer. But I don't like Tania being here."

"Neither do I. Good-bye, Jamie."

Nell shook her head as she hung up the phone. She hadn't lied, but, as Nicholas had once said, omission was a cop-out.

The picture in the newspaper had scared her to death. She hadn't expected Tania to issue that bold an invitation. She had even given the bastard her address.

The phone rang again.

"Did I not look beautiful in the picture?" Tania asked. "The suit is by Armani. Joel decided to stop in New York and buy me a complete wardrobe."

"Gorgeous. You didn't tell me you were going to be married."

"Joel insisted we be married before we came. He seems to think it will control me in some way." Nell heard a derisive grunt in the background. "Well, you do, Joel."

"Where are you?"

"At the Carleton. It's very elegant. Do you know that movie stars stay here during the film festival?"

"You sound happy."

"Ecstatic. But not as happy as Joel. Which is only proper. I only got a testy, aging doctor. He got me." She was giggling. "I must hang up. I think he's going to attack me. I'll keep in touch."

She meant that she'd tell Nell when Maritz surfaced. Nell hadn't the slightest doubt that the last sentence was the only one in the conversation that counted.

But Tania had sounded wonderfully happy, Nell thought wistfully. Gloriously happy, so happy that the cloud that hung over her had made no difference. Tania knew how to seize the moment.

And so did Nicholas.

She hadn't heard from Nicholas in the three weeks she'd been in Paris, and he obviously hadn't considered it important to talk to her when Jamie had called.

Well, what was there to say?

They were in waiting mode.

Nine days more.

"Shall we go out to dinner and show off one of my new gowns?" Tania asked Joel as she turned away from the phone, after the conversation with Nell. "The pink one, I think. I shall look so splendid, the waiters will think I'm a movie star."

"If you like." He watched her as she crossed the room and threw open the French doors of the balcony. "How is Nell?"

"I gave her no chance to tell me. I love my pink gown. I love this hotel." She breathed in the air. "I love the ocean." She glanced over her shoulder. "And I love you, Joel Lieber."

"Big deal. I'm last on the list." He followed her out to the balcony and took her in his arms. "I think I should at least precede the pink gown."

"But then you would have nothing to work for." She nestled closer. "I wouldn't want to rob you of purpose."

"I have a purpose." He buried his face in her hair. "To keep you from getting killed."

Her arms tightened around him. He loved her. What a blessing. But he must not be involved, and it was going to be difficult to keep him out of it. "No talk of that. He may not come." She kissed his cheek. "And you must now make wild love to me and convince me that I love you more than the pink gown."

December 27

"I'll let you come to the fest, Tanek," Gardeaux said. "You will, of course, bring the sword."

"I'll have it."

"That's good. Because you won't be permitted inside the front door until I see it."

"You're checking swords at the door? You sound like the sheriff of an old cow town."

"Only your sword."

"You can see it in full view of your guests. You can't have it."

"I'm to brandish a priceless stolen sword in front of four hundred people?"

"Tell them it's an excellent copy. No one would suspect it's authentic. You have such a sterling reputation."

"And how will you stop me from taking it?"

"By embarrassing you in front of the prime minister and all the people you're trying to impress with your respectability." He narrowed his eyes. "By telling them just what you are."

There was a silence. "You're not going to succeed in this, you know, Tanek. You've overreached yourself and should be punished. I've decided you should end up like your friend O'Malley. Do you remember how he suffered?"

He couldn't forget. "I'll see you in a few days, Gardeaux. Eleven o'clock."

He hung up the phone and turned to Jamie. "It's set."

"I hope you know what you're doing."

"So do I."

Gardeaux sat looking at the telephone. He shouldn't be worried; he had all the cards in his hands.

But Tanek was a man obsessed, and if he couldn't find a way of destroying Gardeaux totally, he would do whatever damage he could. His threat of embarrassing Gardeaux in front of his guests had made him uneasy. He had built a life of power and prestige for himself at Bellevigne. If Tanek decided to attack him by unmasking him, his position might be made intolerable.

Nonsense. If his plan worked, he'd whisk Tanek away before he could say anything. Even if it didn't, Gardeaux could deny Tanek's words, laugh about them. Say Tanek was drunk or crazy.

But Tanek was a very plausible man and even a hint of trouble would displease those paranoid bastards in Medellin. They would say he'd indulged himself at their expense. As a front man, his image had to be pristine.

He would have to protect himself. He would make sure he had a way to nullify the damage Tanek might do his reputation.

He picked up the telephone and quickly dialed a number.

December 28

"Look, Joel. Is that not a lovely scarf?" Tania said. The silk scarf printed with an Egyptian motif hung in the window of a small boutique. "I like Egyptian things. They have a sort of lasting grace."

"Well, our reservations won't last if we don't get to the restaurant in five minutes." Joel smiled indulgently. "You've stopped at every shop along the street and not let me buy you a thing."

"I don't have to own. Looking is good too." She linked her arm through his. "I think you would have done very well in ancient Egypt. They knew a great deal about surgery, you know."

"I prefer modern instruments and medicines."

"Well, I wouldn't like to have brain surgery without a potent anesthesia, but there's something—"

Joel looked at her inquiringly when she stopped speaking. "What is it?"

She smiled at him. "I think I really must have that scarf. Would you run in and buy it for me? I want to look at the purses in that store next door."

Joel shook his head resignedly. "We'll never make it on time."

"Yes, we will. I promise I'll not look in another window until we get to the restaurant."

"Promises. Promises." He went into the shop.

Tania's smile vanished.

He was here, watching her.

No question. Her instincts were screaming and she wouldn't make the mistake of doubting them again.

She permitted herself one look over her shoulder.

She hadn't expected to see him. Maritz was good at this.

But he liked to know she was aware of him. He liked to watch her sweat, to know she was afraid.

She had to strike a balance. She must let him have his fun and not let Joel know Maritz had surfaced.

She moved to the handbag shop next door and looked in the window.

She quickly glanced over her shoulder again.

Does that please you, bastard?

Get your kicks. It's going to be different this time.

"You're scaring me to death," Nell said.

"Nothing to be afraid of yet. I'm being careful and he's in no hurry. He wants to savor it," Tania said. "Do you have a place?"

"The seaside cottage Nicholas rented. It's isolated and would be very tempting to Maritz. Jamie and Nicholas are still there, but that will change soon." She gave her the address and directions. "You're sure Maritz is on the scene? You didn't see him."

"I'm sure. I don't have to see him. We're closer than Siamese twins. I'll call you when he's ready to be drawn into the net."

"I leave for Bellevigne day after tomorrow."

"That's right, it's almost the new year. Happy New Year, Nell."

December 30
Paris

"You're thinner," Nicholas said as soon as she opened the door. "Have you been ill?"

She shook her head. "It seems I was 'abominably fat'

and had to shed a few pounds. Madame Dumoit should have seen me before Medas." He looked the same—hard, fit, keen-edged.

He lifted a brow. "May I come in?"

"Oh, of course." She hurriedly stepped aside. She had been staring at him as if she'd never seen a man before. "I wasn't sure you'd be here tonight."

He shrugged out of his coat and threw it on a chair. "I told you I'd be here."

"That was a month ago."

"We've both been busy. But I'd hardly let you go in without a plan." He raised a brow. "Coffee?"

"It's already made." She went into the kitchenette and poured the coffee. "Have you heard from the ranch?"

"I called Michaela last week. Peter is fine. He's moved into the Bar X permanently. I told Michaela to give him your best."

"How's Jamie?"

"Well."

"Is he still at the cottage?"

"No, he came with me to Paris. He's at the Inter-Continental Hotel."

She handed him his cup. "Will he be going with you to Bellevigne?"

He shook his head. "That wasn't in the deal with Gardeaux. I go to Bellevigne alone." He inclined his head to her. "Except for you, madam."

He took the coffee and carried it into the sitting room. He walked over to the mantel and peered down into the fireplace. "Gas?" She nodded, and he bent down and lit the logs. "That's better. I hate wet, chilly nights."

She nodded again. What was wrong with her? She couldn't take her eyes off him. "Sit down." She took her cup and followed him to the couch in front of the fireplace. She knew what was wrong with her. She had missed him.

"Jamie told me Tania is here."

She stiffened. "Not in Paris."

"You haven't seen her?"

"Hardly. She's on her honeymoon."

He gazed at her, and she instinctively tensed. There had been moments when she had felt as if he could read her mind. He must not read it now.

He dropped the subject. "When is Dumoit's fashion show?"

She tried to keep the relief from her expression. "At one in the afternoon. We're being driven down to Bellevigne early tomorrow morning. After the show we're supposed to mix with the guests and show off Dumoit's gowns."

"All day?"

She nodded. "And we change to other gowns in the evening for the party."

"Good." He knelt before the fireplace, took a folded piece of paper from his coat pocket, and spread it out on the floor. "This is the layout of Bellevigne." He pointed to the central floor plan of the detailed schematic. "This is the main house, where most of the action will be going on during the fest. I'll be arriving at eleven at night. The party should be in full swing by the time I get there." He tapped a long rectangle to the side. "And this is the private auditorium where the fencing matches take place. The last one is at three in the afternoon, and the awards given out at six, so it will be deserted by evening."

The auditorium. Fear rippled through her as she remembered Jamie's story about the deadly virus applied to swords as part of Gardeaux's macabre retribution. Her gaze lifted to his face. "Why are you telling me about the auditorium?"

"Because that's where Gardeaux will take me."

She almost spilled her coffee. "No."

"Yes," he said quietly. "It's the only place my plan will work. If he picks up on the lead I gave him, he'll take me somewhere he won't be surrounded by people."

"But he'll have his people there. It will be a trap."

"But I think I can spring it. Gardeaux will make sure I'm not armed, so sometime in the early evening I want you to slip back into the auditorium and tape this .44 Magnum under seat A15." He pulled the gun out of his pocket and handed it to her. "It's the first row middle aisle."

"You *think* you can spring the trap? What will you do?"

"Manipulate Gardeaux into a position where I can bring him down."

"How?"

"After I get him to the auditorium I'll have to play it by ear. I've done it before."

"He'll kill you."

He smiled. "We always knew that was a possibility, didn't we? But I don't think it will happen this time. Not if you help me."

"It happened to your friend O'Malley."

"Nell, this is the only way. Help me."

He had made up his mind. "Is that all you want me to do?" she asked jerkily.

He tapped another spot on the map. "The drawbridge. It will be guarded, but I doubt if it will be up, since guests will be coming and going. You'll have to get rid of the guards before eleven forty-five. Because at eleven forty-five, you need to be at the fuse box about five yards left of this door." He pointed to the south side of the auditorium on the floor plan. "I want you to douse the lights in the auditorium and then run like hell for the drawbridge. Jamie will be waiting in the woods on the other side of the moat with the car. And I'll be right behind you."

"Maybe."

He ignored the comment. "Gardeaux will probably post a guard outside the auditorium when we go inside. You may have to take care of that guard before you go in the south door. Try to do it quietly, or you might get me killed. How's that for responsibility?"

"More than I thought you'd want to give me." More than she wanted to think about right now. "I expected you to be more selfish."

"I am being selfish. I'm taking Gardeaux." He met her eyes. "And I'm surprised you're not fighting me for the privilege."

She shook her head. "He has to die and I have to be a part of it, but I'm content to let you do it. He's . . . remote to me. I've never seen him, never heard his voice. I know he's as much to blame as Maritz, maybe more, but he's not as alive to me. Not like he is to you." Her lips tightened. "But don't try to cheat me of Maritz."

"Let's take one at a time."

"Is that an evasion?"

"You're damn right. I don't want to think about Maritz. I'm terrified at throwing all of this at you."

"Are you? You don't think I can do it?"

"If I didn't think you could do it, I'd have drugged your coffee and locked you up until after tomorrow night." He smiled. "You're smart and you're good and Jamie is right. We should have had you around in the old days." His smile faded. "That doesn't mean I want you within a hundred miles of Bellevigne."

"I have a right to be there."

"You have a right." He winked. "But keep an eye on that coffeepot."

She relaxed and smiled back at him. "Every minute."

"Maybe not every minute." He took her coffee cup away and set it down on the hearth. "It might get in the way." He slowly drew her into his arms. He whispered, "Okay?"

More than okay. Passion. Comfort. Home. Her arms tightened around him. "Okay."

"This was too easy. Maybe I should go away more often." He kissed her. "Or are you providing aid and comfort to one off to the wars?"

"Shut up," she whispered. "I'm going to war too." She needed this. She needed *him*. She leaned back and started to unbutton her blouse. "I think you should be the one to provide aid."

"Not here." He pulled her to her feet. "Where's your bedroom? I refuse to be seduced in front of a fireplace. It's much too campy."

He was getting dressed, a dim, pale shadow in the predawn grayness of the room.

"Be careful," she whispered.

"I was trying not to wake you." He sat down on the bed. "Why, Nell?"

She took his hand. "I told you, I needed aid and comfort."

"You gave more than you took tonight. Where did all the anger go?"

"I don't know. All I knew was that I missed you. I guess I'm not thinking very clearly right now."

"Well, your head's still in the sand." He gently caressed her hair. "But maybe you're thinking more clearly than you believe. Sometimes it's best to trust instinct." He smiled. "In this case it was a hell of a lot more enjoyable."

Her grasp tightened on his hand. "This isn't a good plan, Nicholas. Too many things can go wrong."

"There will never be a better time or plan." He added heavily, "And I'm tired to death of this. I'm sick of that scum Gardeaux living like a fat cat in his castle. I'm tired of thinking about Terence and the futility of his death. I'm tired of worrying about you. I want to get the job done and go home." He kissed her forehead. "Last chance, Nell. Is all this worth it to you?"

"What a time to ask me that. You know the answer."

"Nevertheless, I'm asking it."

"You're giving me a way out. I don't want it." She met his gaze. "They killed my daughter, deliberately and with malice. They took her life as if she were worth nothing, and they got away with it. They'll keep killing and hurting innocent people as long as—" She stopped. "No, I'm not doing it because I'm afraid they'll hurt someone else. I'm not that public-spirited. It's Jill. It's always been Jill."

"Okay, I thought that would be your answer. But if you see everything going downhill, cut and run. Do you hear me?"

"I hear you."

"But you're not committing. Let me put it another way. If you're killed at Bellevigne, Gardeaux and Maritz will live and no one will ever pay for Jill's death."

She flinched with pain.

"I thought that would strike home." He stood up and moved toward the door. "Eleven forty-five. Don't be late."

Eighteen

Gardeaux looked like an affable politician, sleek, mature, beautifully well groomed in his green and gold Renaissance garb. He was smiling courteously down at his wife, ignoring the horde of influential people surrounding him.

Charming.

To look at him, Nell would never have guessed his mistress was just across the room . . . or that he was a child murderer.

"What are you staring at?" Madame Dumoit hissed as she passed Nell. "We didn't bring you here to stand in a corner and gawk. Move around. Show off Jacques's gown."

"I'm sorry, Madame." Nell set her glass of wine down on a passing waiter's tray and moved into the throng. In her Renaissance gown she blended perfectly with the costumed crowd, and the crush was so thick, she would be lost in its midst in seconds and could escape back to obscurity.

Twenty-five more minutes and Nicholas would be there.

The room was too warm, the music deafening.

Watch Gardeaux. Watch the child killer. How could he smile like that when he intended to kill Nicholas within the hour?

Oh, God, she was afraid.

Gardeaux was turning away from his wife, holding out his hand, a smile of welcome lighting his face.

A man was coming toward him. A small man, looking a little uncomfortable in his black tuxedo.

Nell froze in shock.

Kabler?

Kabler was smiling too. He took Gardeaux's hand and shook it. He said something jokingly before slapping him on the back.

Not Kabler. Kabler hated him. Kabler would not be here.

He was here, and treating Gardeaux as if they were best friends.

But he was a policeman. He had to be undercover or something.

She drifted closer, her gaze fixed on the two men.

Gardeaux was introducing Kabler to his wife. His good friend, Joe Kabler, head of the Drug Enforcement Agency in America.

He knew who Kabler was. Kabler, his good friend.

Money can buy almost anyone, Nicholas had said.

She hadn't thought it could buy Kabler.

He was smiling at Gardeaux's wife and murmuring something about a nice party and how nice it was for them to invite him. His gaze casually wandered around the room. Oh, yes, he belonged to Gardeaux.

And he could recognize her.

Her heart jerked with panic. What was she doing

standing here? She quickly wheeled away from them and headed for the door.

Had he seen her?

She was afraid to look over her shoulder. The most he would have been able to see was the back of her head and her profile.

The most? That would be enough. They had spent hours together.

She bolted through the door into the foyer.

Please. Don't let him have seen me.

She tore down the front steps to the courtyard. She risked a glance over her shoulder.

Kabler, his expression grim, was weaving through the crowd in the foyer.

He caught her as she reached the bottom of the steps and spun her around.

"Let me go." She glared up at him. "There are people not twenty feet from us. I could call out."

"But you won't. You don't want to blow whatever you're here for. I warned you to stay away from Tanek. Look what he's done to you." His tone was pained. "I don't want you hurt. Give it up. I can still save you."

"By interceding with your friend Gardeaux?" she asked bitterly.

"That filth is not my friend, and he'd pay no attention to any intercession if he knew who you were."

"You didn't tell him?"

"I said I thought I saw someone I knew. I don't want you dead, Nell. Let Tanek be put down. He's just filth like the rest."

"And what are you?"

He flinched. "I couldn't fight them anymore. It had gone on too long. I came home from Idaho that day and Gardeaux's man was waiting for me again. So was my kid's doctor. My son has leukemia. He deserves the best and now I can give it to him. You can't beat them.

They have too much money and too much power. No one can beat them."

"So you joined them. How much does he pay you, Kabler?"

"Enough. My wife is getting some of the things she deserves at last. My kids will go to good schools and have a future. I'll be able to give them anything they need or want."

"How nice for you. I don't have a child. Gardeaux killed her."

"But you're alive. I want you to stay alive. You're not like them."

"I'm like you?"

He nodded. "It doesn't matter what happens to them. I didn't care about Calder or that woman. They were as dirty as Gardeaux."

She stared at him in shock. She had not made the connection. "*You* killed them."

He shook his head. "I just told Gardeaux where to find them. He wanted me to take you there first so that I could claim I was followed." He smiled wryly. "I'm in a very valuable position. He didn't want it jeopardized."

"You used me. You did the same thing you accused Nicholas of doing."

"You had a right to know about Calder."

"And how will you explain your presence here tonight? Your people know what Gardeaux is."

"I'm only trying to gather information. Just doing my job." He glanced over his shoulder. "We've been out too long. Tanek should arrive any minute and I don't want you in the way."

"You're going to help him kill Nicholas."

"I don't have to help him. That's not why I'm here. Gardeaux wanted me to come, slap him on the back and nix any harm Nicholas might inflict on his image."

He took her arm. "I'm going to take you to my room and stay there with you. When it's over, I'll let you go on your way."

When it was over. When Nicholas was dead. "What if I won't go with you?"

"Then I'll have to tell Gardeaux who you are. And he'd kill you as well as Tanek." He said gently, "I don't want to do that, Nell. I want you to get out with your skin intact. Will you come with me?"

He wasn't bluffing. He would tell Gardeaux. He wanted to save her, but he would let her die rather than endanger his affiliation with Gardeaux. "I'll come."

He was immediately beside her, cradling her elbow as they entered the foyer.

"I have a gun holstered beneath the jacket of this monkey suit. Just thought I'd let you know." He led her toward the staircase. "Smile," he murmured.

She glanced at the grandfather clock next to the doors to the ballroom. Her hand clenched on the banister.

Ten fifty-five.

11:10 P.M.

Four people got out of the limousine as it stopped just inside the courtyard. Two women in rich Renaissance dress under velvet cloaks, their escorts in tuxedos. Talk. Laughter.

The perfect opportunity for Nicholas to blend in with the crowd. He stepped out of the shadows of the trees and quickly crossed the moat.

He fell in close behind the four guests as they strolled across the courtyard.

"Ah, Tanek, there you are." Gardeaux stood on the

front steps. He wasn't looking at the guests, but at Tanek. "I've been waiting for you."

Nicholas stopped short and then moved closer to the group of guests. "I can never resist a party."

"I'm afraid you'll have to miss this one." He gestured and the four partygoers parted like the Red Sea. "You seem to be lacking your advance guard."

Nicholas watched the four hurry back toward the limousine. "Your people?"

"Obviously. Did you think I couldn't counter such a simple ploy? You gave me the time of your arrival and I had only to set up the trap. I really couldn't allow you to go into the ballroom. You might have made things awkward for me." He looked over his shoulder. "Rivil, we're going to escort Mr. Tanek to the auditorium. You remember Rivil, Tanek?"

"How could I forget?" He watched Rivil come down the steps. "He made a big impact on me." Rivil was followed by a smaller man. Marple, Nicholas recognized, vicious, good with a garrote, excellent reflexes. Gardeaux had called out the top guns.

"Terrible pun," Gardeaux said. "But I'm glad you're not too disconcerted. It will make things more interesting if you don't fall apart." His gaze fastened on the leather-wrapped sword Nicholas was carrying, and a flicker of excitement appeared on his face. "That's it?"

Nicholas nodded.

Gardeaux hurried down the steps and took the sword. "All this trouble for nothing. You're out of your league, Tanek." He started to unwrap the sword and then stopped. "Let's get him out of this courtyard."

"Suppose I decide not to go?" Nicholas said.

"Then Rivil hits you on the head and we take you." Gardeaux started toward the auditorium. "Simple."

It was enough of a protest. Gardeaux knew him well enough not to expect a futile struggle.

He let Rivil and Marple usher him toward the auditorium.

11:20 P.M.

Gardeaux ripped off the leather wrappings as soon as he got inside the auditorium. He held the sword up to the light. "Glorious," he whispered. "Magnificent. I can feel the power."

He fondled it lovingly before starting down the long aisle toward the stage and runway. "Bring him. You've never seen my auditorium, have you? The greatest swordsmen in Europe competed here this afternoon. But not Pietro. Though he probably could have beaten them all." Gardeaux stopped in front of the runway and gestured to the tall, slim fencer standing there. "May I present Pietro Danielo." The man appeared totally anonymous in the white fencing garb and mesh mask. "I've been wanting you two to meet for a long time." He offered the Charlemagne sword to Nicholas. "I'm even giving you the sword of the conqueror to fight him. That should bring you luck."

Nicholas ignored the sword. "I'm not fighting him. I won't entertain you, Gardeaux."

"Pietro, come here."

The fencer jumped down from the runway and bounded toward them, his sword held before him. Rivil and Marple shied away from him.

"Show Tanek your sword. He's developed an interest in such weapons of late."

Pietro extended the sword until it was only an inch from Nicholas's chest.

"Notice the tip, Tanek."

The steel tip gleamed wet under the strong overhead lights.

"*Coloño.* I had a fresh supply flown in from Medellin when I knew you were coming. All Pietro has to do is break the skin. Do you remember how small O'Malley's wound was? But that didn't last, did it? Almost immediately, a tiny blister formed around the cut. He was a mass of blisters and sores when he died. The virus ate him from the inside out."

Nicholas couldn't take his gaze off the tip of the sword. "I remember."

"If Pietro slices you now, you've no chance. Take the sword. It's a weapon. You're a clever man. Make the opportunity work for you."

"And if I win, Rivil and Marple hold a gun on me and you prick me with Pietro's sword anyway."

"I didn't say it was a golden opportunity."

"While you sit like a god and watch your will be done."

"There's no thrill like it," Gardeaux said. He offered the sword again to Tanek. "Take it."

Pietro moved the tip of his sword the tiniest bit closer until it almost brushed the front of Nicholas's shirt.

"Take the sword," Gardeaux said softly.

It was moving too fast, Nicholas thought. He had another twenty-five minutes before Nell doused the lights.

"You don't want to die like this," Gardeaux said.

A vision of Terence writhing in pain came back to Nicholas. He stepped back away from Pietro's sword. "No, I don't." He reached out and took the sword Gardeaux was extending. He turned and jumped on the runway. "Let's get to it."

11:35 P.M.

Nell jerked open the velvet drapes at the window. A light was on in the auditorium.

Her hand clenched on the drape. Nicholas was there now. Gardeaux had taken him there to kill him.

"Come away from the window," Kabler said from across the room.

She whirled around to face him. "You can't do this. He's *there*. Do you know what they're going to do to him?"

"I didn't ask for details." He studied her for a moment. "I'm sorry, but you appear to be a little desperate. I'm afraid I'll have to take precautions." He drew the gun from his holster and pointed it at her. "Now come back and sit down. I'm not like Calder—I know your capabilities. You won't catch me by surprise."

"You're ready to kill me yourself?"

"I don't want to do it."

"But you'd do it. Doesn't that make you the filth you call Gardeaux?"

His lips tightened. "I'll never be like him."

"You will, if you kill me." She deliberately moved toward the door. "But I don't think you will."

"Stay away from that door."

"You might let Gardeaux kill me, but you won't do it yourself. We're alike, we're not like them." She deliberately played on his rationalization. "There's no way you could justify killing me to yourself."

"Stop where you are. I can't let you go."

She couldn't stop. Panic was racing through her. Her hand closed on the knob.

He muttered a curse and launched himself across the room.

She spun and caught him in the abdomen with a flying kick. He cried out and bent double.

Another kick to the groin. A slash to the back of his neck with the edge of her hand. He was disabled but still conscious. He had to be taken out of the picture.

She took the gun he'd dropped at the first kick and crashed the butt down on his head.

He crumpled to the floor.

She unlocked the door and flew down the hall and down the steps. Her eyes flew to the clock. Eleven-fifty.

No time to take out the guard at the auditorium.

No time to cut the lights and give Nicholas the darkness he needed.

She was too late.

11:51 P.M.

Where the hell was she?

Pietro lunged at him, almost touching him with the tip of the sword and then dancing away.

The fencer was just teasing him. Putting on a good show for Gardeaux's amusement. He could have driven the point into him a dozen times in the past ten minutes. Nicholas was as clumsy as a bear brandishing a sword, dodging and trying not to get stung.

He chanced a glance at the auditorium clock.

Eleven fifty-two.

"Getting tired, Tanek?" Gardeaux asked from the front row.

Nicholas blocked Pietro's next lunge and backed away.

"I thought you were stronger," Gardeaux called. "Pietro can go on for hours."

Eleven fifty-three.

He couldn't wait any longer.

He lowered his sword.

"Giving up? I'm disappointed. I thought—"

Nicholas lifted the sword and threw it like a spear at

Pietro. The man screamed as the sword struck his upper thighs and bounced to the floor.

Nicholas dove from the runway, hit the ground running toward the aisle seat where Nell had hidden the gun.

A bullet whistled by his head.

"Stop him. Don't shoot him, you fool."

No, Gardeaux wouldn't want to be cheated at this point.

He reached under the seat and ripped out the Magnum.

They converged on him before he could raise the gun. Rivil tackled him, knocking the gun out of his hand. Gardeaux was standing before him. Smiling.

He had probably smiled like that at Terence's helplessness too, Nicholas thought. A surge of hate tore through him. "You son of a bitch." He lunged upward and drove his fist into Gardeaux's face.

Rivil kicked Nicholas in the stomach. Marple crashed the butt of his gun against his temple. He fell to the floor, fighting darkness.

Gardeaux's face was above him. His lip was cut and bleeding and he wasn't smiling any longer. "One of you get Pietro's sword."

Rivil moved toward the stage.

Nicholas struggled to get up and Gardeaux put his foot on his chest to hold him down.

"Do you feel helpless, Tanek? Are you so scared you want to vomit?" He took Pietro's sword from Rivil. "It's nothing to what you'll feel in a day or so." He poised the sword above Nicholas's left shoulder. "Not too deep. I don't want you to die too soon."

Nicholas could see the sword point glisten as it came toward him.

Gardeaux plunged the sword into his shoulder.

Nicholas gritted his teeth to keep back a scream as agony shot through him.

Gardeaux pulled the sword out.

Nicholas closed his eyes as warm blood streamed out of his shoulder.

"Happy New Year!"

Gardeaux whirled toward the doorway across the auditorium.

People were streaming in. Gardeaux stared, stunned, as the orchestra began playing "Auld Lang Syne" while moving down the aisle toward the stage.

"What the hell is happening?"

Confetti was being tossed in the air, noisemakers were being blown.

"Happy New Year!"

"My God, there's the Prime Minister." Gardeaux glanced down at Nicholas. "Rivil, get him the hell out of here! Out the far door. They haven't seen him yet." He carefully wiped Pietro's sword and slid it under the row of seats next to him. Then he took a handkerchief out of his pocket and dabbed at his cut lip. "Marple, the Charlemagne sword is on the runway. Tell Pietro to get it before one of those fools finds it." He pasted a smile on his face and moved toward the waves of guests flowing into the auditorium.

Rivil lifted Nicholas to his feet and half carried him toward the exit.

Nell was suddenly there before them. "I'll take him."

Rivil tried to brush her aside.

"I said, I'll take him." She lifted a gun from the folds of her gown. Her voice was shaking. "Let him go, you bastard."

Rivil shrugged and took his arm from Nicholas's shoulders. "Take him. Gardeaux only said he wanted him out of here. He's through with him. He won't care now who gets him out." He strode toward the crowd that had surrounded Gardeaux.

She put her arm around Nicholas's rib cage and slung his arm over her shoulder. "Lean on me."

"I don't have much choice. I'm not feeling too well."

"I'm sorry," she whispered. Tears were running down her cheeks. "I tried—Kabler—I couldn't—"

"I'm too woozy to make much sense of what you're saying. You'd better tell me later." He looked over his shoulder. "But why the hell are all these people here?"

She opened the exit door. "I was too late," she said jerkily. "I couldn't think of any way to get rid of the guard outside the auditorium and get to you in time. So I ran to the bandstand in the ballroom and announced that Gardeaux wanted to celebrate the new year in the place where the athletes had their greatest triumphs. The crowd just swept the guard in with them. It was all I could think of doing."

"Good."

"It wasn't good," she said fiercely. "I came too late. They hurt you. How bad is it?"

"Blow to the head. Sword through the shoulder."

She inhaled sharply. "Sword? Whose sword?"

"A very nasty one. Pietro. I think you'd better get me to a hospital."

"Oh, God."

He was getting dizzier by the moment. "Just get me to Jamie. Okay?"

She nodded and helped him across the courtyard. The guards at the drawbridge didn't even challenge them as they started across it.

"You said I'd have to get rid of them," she said dully. "They don't seem to care."

"Neither does Gardeaux."

Her arm tightened around him. "Damn him to hell."

She was hurting and he wanted to comfort her. He couldn't do it. Later. He would do it later.

The emergency room of Our Lady of Mercy Hospital was full to capacity, and Dr. Minot, the resident in charge, was in no mood for Nicholas's demands. "The wound is not deep, Monsieur. We'll treat it with antibiotics and a tetanus shot. There's no need to put a blood sample under a microscope."

"Do it for me anyway," Nicholas said. "You know how we hypochondriacs are."

"We have no time for pampering here. If you like, we'll send a sample out to the lab. It will come back in a day or so."

"I need it now."

"Impossible. I can't do—"

Nell stepped forward until she was only inches away from the resident. "You'll do it." Her eyes were blazing at him. "You'll take that sample now. Not tomorrow. Now."

The young resident took an involuntary step back and then forced a smile. "But of course, anything to please so lovely a lady."

"How long will it take?"

"Five minutes. No more." He beat a hasty retreat.

Nicholas gave her a weary smile. "What would you have done to him?"

"Anything. From neutering him to going to bed with him." She sat down on the bed. "How do you feel?"

"Protected."

"I didn't protect you very much at Bellevigne."

"Things happen. You didn't expect Kabler. Neither did I. Where's Jamie?"

"Still in the waiting room. They let only one of us come in with you. Will Minot be able to tell how badly you're infected?"

He nodded. "The microbes are pretty bizarre. You can't miss them under a microscope."

"And what do we do then?"

He avoided the question. "Let's not count our microbes before—"

"Shut up." Her voice was trembling. "Don't you dare joke right now."

"Okay." He smiled. "We'll just wait."

The resident didn't come back in five minutes. He made them wait fifteen, and when he walked back into the room he was frowning. "Done. Nothing abnormal. A complete waste of time. I hope you're satisfied."

Nell stared at him, stunned.

"Completely normal?" Nicholas asked.

"Completely."

Nicholas sank back against the pillows. "Thank God."

"Now I'm going to prescribe some antibiotics and a mild sedative for possible—"

"I need a telephone," Nicholas said, sitting up again. "There's none in here."

"You can use one after I've—" He glanced at Nell and said, "I'll have the nurse bring one in to you." He left the room.

"How could it be?" Nell whispered. "What happened? It's a miracle."

"It's no miracle." He grabbed the receiver and punched in Gardeaux's number as the nurse plugged in the phone. "It's much baser than that."

When Nicholas was connected to Gardeaux he was still in the auditorium. The party had gone on for hours and there were no signs it was slacking.

"You'll excuse me?" Gardeaux asked when he was handed the portable phone. "Anyone who would call at this time of night may be in need of help."

"Or another drink." The Prime Minister laughed. "Tell him to come to the party. You have the finest wine in France."

Gardeaux smiled as he moved to a quieter area. He could have ignored the call from Tanek, but he wouldn't deny himself the pleasure. "What is it, Tanek?" he asked. "Getting panicky? There's no use begging. You know there's no antidote."

"I just wanted to tell you that the Charlemagne sword is a fake."

Anger flared through Gardeaux. "You'd say that even if it were authentic."

"It was crafted by Hernando Armandariz in Toledo. You can check on it."

Gardeaux drew a steadying breath. "It doesn't matter about the sword. I still won. You're a dead man. Now, if you'll excuse me, I have to get back to my guests."

"I won't keep you much longer. I just wanted to tell you to expect a report from Our Lady of Mercy by courier tomorrow." He paused. "And to tell you to go look in the mirror."

He hung up.

Gardeaux frowned as he stared at the phone. Tanek was entirely too cryptic. Of course he wasn't going to go look in the mirror. Was he supposed to see himself as some kind of monster because of what he'd done? He was the one who had triumphed. No reason why he—

In the bathroom mirror his reflection was everything

it should be. The picture of a successful, powerful man, a conqueror. He started to turn away and then wheeled back.

The light had fallen on the cut in his lip that Nicholas had made when he had lunged up and struck him.

Encircling the cut were the tiny beginnings of a blister.

Gardeaux screamed.

"*Coloño?*" Nell shook her head in bewilderment as she helped Nicholas into the car outside the hospital. "Gardeaux has *coloño*? That's crazy. I don't understand."

"It worked?" Jamie looked back at them from the driver's seat. A delighted smile lit his face. "You brought the bastard down?"

"I'd lay odds on it." Nicholas leaned back in the seat. "We'll check tomorrow, but I'd wager he's on his way to the nearest hospital right now."

"How?" Nell asked.

Nicholas took out his handkerchief and carefully removed the signet ring on his middle finger. "A modern version of the Renaissance poison ring. I thought it fitting since Gardeaux is so intrigued with the period." He laid the ring in the handkerchief and tied the four corners before placing it in the car ashtray. "On impact the initial in the center compresses and allows the poison to flow out."

Nell shivered as she realized Nicholas had been wearing that ring the whole time he had been struggling with Gardeaux's men.

"I was careful." Nicholas's gaze was on her face, reading her thoughts.

"You were lucky," she said. "But where did you get the *coloño*?"

"The same place Gardeaux got his. Medellin. From Paloma and Juarez."

Paloma and Juarez. Sandequez's partners in the drug cartel. "They gave you poison to kill their own man?"

"Not at once. I spent two weeks in Medellin waiting on the hot seat for their decision. It could have gone either way. Up to the last minute tonight." He wearily leaned his head back against the seat. "Everything had unraveled and I had to get an edge. I thought Sandequez's death might be the key. So I went to Paris and put pressure on Pardeau. He'd recorded the reward money that had changed hands from the Colombian Drug Enforcement Forces to Gardeaux. I told him that I was on my way to Medellin and he either had to worry about Gardeaux or the entire Colombian drug cartel. He let me have the books."

"And you took them to Paloma and Juarez to prove Gardeaux had murdered Sandequez."

"They didn't like it. Unity is everything to them. It's the way they survive. If Gardeaux killed Sandequez, who was to say he wouldn't nibble at the power structure by killing another one of them? On the other hand, it's bad policy to admit disruption in the ranks, and Gardeaux had been valuable to them. It might have been worth the danger he represented to keep him on."

"But they decided not to do it?"

"I told them that I'd take care of the matter for them. If an outsider killed Gardeaux, it would solve their first problem. After two weeks they told me that they'd decided to go along with me. Gardeaux had requested a new batch of *coloño* and they would make sure the serum was switched and a harmless liquid substituted. They gave me the poison ring and their best wishes and sent me on my way."

"Then why didn't you tell me?" Nell asked bitterly.

"Because it could have been a lie. There was a possibility that they had sent me to Bellevigne to die, that they didn't switch the serum to give me a chance. That there was no *colono* in the ring. Or that there was poison in the ring but also on Pietro's sword. That might get rid of both of us. There were too many variables."

"Why did I plant the gun if you had the ring?"

"Insurance. I knew his men wouldn't let me near Gardeaux. That's why I wanted you to douse the lights. I thought I'd make the move then."

But she hadn't given him that chance. "I didn't make it there in time."

"I still had the gun you planted. I used it as a threat to get him close enough." He shook his head. "I almost didn't make it."

"But you did," Jamie said. "What next? Will Gardeaux be after you?"

"Within twenty-four hours he'll cease to care about anyone but himself."

"Where do we go? The cottage?"

"No," Nell said quickly. "Not the cottage. I want to go back to Paris."

Nicholas nodded. "It's just as well, Jamie. I want you to get Pardeau away from Paris for a day or two until we're sure about Gardeaux. I promised to protect him."

"Yes, by all means, let's protect all the beasts and idiots in our midst," Nell said.

Jamie gave her a cautious glance and started the car.

"I'm in deep trouble?" Nicholas asked in a low tone.

Nell didn't answer.

He closed his eyes. "Then I suppose I'd better rest and gather my strength. Wake me when we get to Paris."

Nell slammed the door of her apartment behind them. "Go to bed. I'll go to the pharmacy and have your prescription filled."

"That's not necessary."

"It's necessary. Or don't you think I'm capable of doing that either?"

Nicholas sighed. "Here we go."

"You should have let me help you."

"I did let you help."

"You could have told me about the *coloño*. You could have brought me into it."

"Yes, I could have done that."

"But you let me run around the edges while you—" She stopped and said wearily, "Maybe you were right. I couldn't even do that right. I almost got you killed."

"You did what you could."

"It wasn't enough. I should have moved on Kabler more quickly. I should have been there to douse the lights." Tears were flowing down her cheeks again. "I failed you, dammit."

"You've never failed me. So you're not superwoman. Things happen," he said roughly. He moved across the room and grasped her shoulders. "And the reason I didn't set up a way for you to help me with the *coloño* was that I didn't want you around the stuff. I saw what it did to Terence. I couldn't stand the thought of you even being near it."

"You'd rather take a chance yourself. How do you think I felt when you told me the wound was—"

"How did you feel, Nell?"

"You know how I felt."

"I want you to tell me. For once, tell me, Nell."

"I felt guilty and scared and—"

"You didn't want to lose me."

"All right, I didn't want to lose you."

"Why?"

"Because I'm used to you, because you—"

"Why?"

"Because I love you, dammit." She buried her head in his chest. "And it hurts. I never wanted this to happen. It shouldn't have happened. I fought it so hard. You're the last person— You with your damned gates. You'll die, like Jill died. I can't stand the thought of it happening again."

"We all die. I can't promise to live forever." His arms tightened around her. "But I can promise to love you as long as I live."

"That's not good enough. I won't *have* it. Do you hear?" She pushed him away. "Oh, go to bed. I don't want to look at you anymore. I'll go get your prescription." She snatched her purse up from the table and headed for the door. "And it doesn't mean anything. I won't let— I'll get over it."

"Don't count on it." He smiled. "I think the best thing we can do is accept it and roll with the punches."

She slammed the door behind her and stopped outside to mop her wet cheeks with the back of her hand. Accept it? She couldn't accept it. She had been torn apart when she had seen Nicholas hurt, when she had thought he might die. All the pain that had almost destroyed her when she had learned of Jill's death had rushed back, almost overwhelming her. She couldn't go through that again.

She could never accept it.

Nineteen

"Gardeaux checked into the hospital yesterday morning," Jamie said as he came into the apartment waving a newspaper. "He's suffering from an undisclosed ailment and his condition is considered critical." He grinned. "So sad after the success of his most memorable Renaissance Fest."

"And what about Kabler?"

He shrugged. "No word on him. My bet is that he's on his way back to Washington, trying to figure out how to cover his ass."

"He must know what happened to Gardeaux. Can he hurt you?" Nell asked Nicholas.

"He'd be a fool to try now that I have Pardeau's books. He figures prominently in them."

"Another insurance policy?"

"Combined with Simpson's books, a platinum-plated one."

"And Kabler will just continue with the DEA?"

"He's shrewd. I doubt if they'll even know he turned dirty. He may end up by retiring with a gold watch."

Nell shook her head.

"We can't have everything," Nicholas said quietly. "I can't bring him down. We need his silence."

"But we may have Maritz," Jamie said. "I've heard through the grapevine that he may be in the South of France. Someone saw him in Monte Carlo."

Nell turned to face him. "When?"

"A few days ago. I'm checking on it."

"You'll let me know?"

Nicholas's gaze narrowed on her face. "You're not very excited."

"I'm fresh out of excitement," she said dryly. "I've had too much in the last few days." She got up and went to the closet. "Which reminds me, I have to return Dumoit's gown. Celine has left three messages on the answering machine. She's about to call out the gendarmes." She took out the bedraggled and bloodstained gown and made a face. "She may do it anyway when she sees how I've ruined it." She draped the gown over her arm, grabbed her purse, and headed for the door. "I'll be back in a few hours."

"He's not in Monte Carlo. He's here," Tania said flatly when Nell reached her by phone from a booth near her apartment. "We're not far from Monte Carlo. Joel and I went there for the day."

"And he followed you."

"Everywhere. He's getting anxious . . . and careless. I saw him yesterday."

"Where?"

"On the waterfront. Just for a second, a reflection in a shop window."

"You heard about Gardeaux?"

"Yes. Is he really ill? It wasn't what I expected."

"It wasn't what I expected either. A surprise from Nicholas." Nell paused. "Soon?"

"Very soon. I want to be sure he's ready to pounce. I'll call you. Stay close to the apartment."

"You weren't long," Nicholas said when she walked in the door.

"No." Long enough to call Tania. Long enough to rent a car and park it near the apartment. Soon. It would be soon.

"Was she roaring?" Nicholas asked.

"Who? Oh, Madame Dumoit?"

"Who else?"

The question was casual, but she cursed herself for not being more alert. Nicholas didn't miss anything. "She was furious." Nell smiled. "She says she'll ruin me. I'll never model again."

"Pity. I guess you'll have to take up sheep raising."

Nell's smile faded.

"It's all right. Don't get jumpy," he said quietly. "I'm letting it lie for the time being." He stood up. "Why don't I take you out to lunch? We've never eaten a meal in a public place before. It will be an experience."

Stay close.

She shook her head. "I'm tired. I'd rather eat in. There's a store down the street. Will you go and pick something up?"

He raised his brows. "Whatever you like."

Soon.

Maritz had been in their suite.

Tania looked down at the jewelry box. She'd put it on the dresser. Now it sat on the counter in the bathroom.

The white Armani suit she'd worn in the picture that appeared in the newspaper had been taken out of the closet and draped across a chair.

He had been here and he wanted her to know it.

He was ready.

January 4
7:10 A.M.

When the phone rang, Nell was out of bed in seconds, running into the sitting room.

"Today," Tania said. "I'm leaving for the cottage at six this evening. I should be there by eight. Don't be late."

"I won't be late." She had been late at Bellevigne and had almost lost Nicholas. Nothing would stop her this time. "But after you draw him into the open, he's mine."

"We'll see."

"No. You've no right. He's mine. You've done your part. You're out of it."

"I don't like—"

"He killed my daughter."

There was silence on the other end of the line. "All right, I'm out of it." Tania hung up.

Nell went back to bed and slipped beneath the covers.

"Who was it?" Nicholas asked.

She didn't answer. She had lied to him before. She didn't want to do it again.

"Wrong number?"

She nodded and cuddled close. He didn't think it was a wrong number, but he was giving her an out. He suspected something, but he would never force it out of her. That wasn't his style. He would watch and wait.

"I'd like to make love, Nicholas," she whispered. "If you don't mind."

"You said that the first time you came to me." He turned over and took her in his arms. "I don't mind. I'll never mind. Not now." He kissed her. "Not for the next fifty years. Always ready to oblige."

Her arms tightened fiercely around him.

"If you leave my ribs intact."

"I love you, Nicholas."

"Shh, I know you do." He pulled down the cover and moved over her. "It's all right. I know . . ."

6:35 P.M.

"Nell's heading south," Jamie said.

"Don't lose her. I'll be right behind you." Nicholas put down the phone and left the apartment. He had known the excuse Nell had given him for leaving the apartment was bogus and it had taken all his restraint to let her go.

South. Monte Carlo?

He got into his car and pressed on the accelerator.

Who the hell knew where she was going?

Wherever it was, she thought Maritz was at her destination.

And it scared him to death.

6:50 P.M.

Pretty Tania had decided to put an end to it.

Her brown hair blew in the breeze as the red convertible Triumph roared down the highway.

She was alone.

Maritz's car kept pace, but he didn't try to overtake her.

She knew he was behind her.

She knew she couldn't escape him.

She knew it was the time of the kill.

He felt a rush of pleasure as he remembered the struggle she had given him before. It would be even more interesting now that she was fully aware of the danger.

Stop soon, pretty Tania.

"She's heading for the cottage," Jamie said when Nicholas picked up the car phone. "Maybe it's all right, Nick."

It wasn't all right.

If she was going to the cottage, it was because Maritz was there.

Or would soon be there.

Christ.

"Shall I drive right up to the cottage?" Jamie asked.

Yes. Drive up, stop her, save her.

"Nick?"

He drew a deep breath. "No, park at the bottom of the hill and wait for me."

7:55 P.M.

It was dark when Nell drove the car around to the back of the cottage.

No lights. No other car.

She wasn't late tonight.

She got out of the car and quickly walked around to the front door. She unlocked it, set her Lady Colt on the doorstep, and turned on the porch light. There was bright moonlight, but she wanted every advantage. She strode over to the edge of the cliff and looked down at the crashing surf. She took several deep breaths and shook her shoulders to loosen the muscles.

She had expected to be nervous or frightened or angry. Instead, she felt a sense of inevitability and calm purpose.

Maritz was coming. This was the task for which she had worked and trained.

She tensed as she saw the lights of a car coming up the road.

She couldn't be sure it was Tania until she was a hundred yards away.

The small red convertible drew up before the front door, and Tania got out.

"He's behind you?" Nell asked.

Tania looked back over her shoulder. "There."

A car was coasting slowly, almost leisurely, up the road.

"Go into the cottage. I unlocked the door."

Tania hesitated. "I don't want to leave you. Do you have a gun?"

"It's on the doorstep."

"What good is it going to do you there?"

"If I don't stop him, he'll come after you."

"For God's sake, take the gun."

She shook her head. "It's too quick. He didn't make it easy for Jill. I want to hurt him. I want him to know he's going to die."

Tania strode over to the door, picked up the gun, and thrust it at Nell. "Take it. Or I won't go inside."

Nell took the weapon. There was no time to argue. The headlights were only yards away. "Hurry."

Tania ran toward the cottage.

Nell was suddenly bathed in a pool of light.

The car stopped in front of her. A man got out and stood by the open door.

"Where's Tania?"

Maritz. He was in shadow, but she would never forget that voice. It echoed in her nightmares.

"Tania's inside. You'll not get to her."

He came forward, his gaze traveling from her tennis shoes and jeans to the gun in her hand. "She called in the cops? I'm disappointed in her."

"I'm not the police. You know me, Maritz."

He peered at her. "I don't know— Calder? The Calder woman?"

"I knew you needed only to be prodded."

"Lieber did quite a job. You should thank me."

Searing rage blazed inside her. "Thank you? For killing my daughter?"

"I forgot about the kid."

He was telling the truth. It had meant so little to him that he had forgotten he had murdered Jill.

He took another step forward. "But I remember now. She was crying, trying to get to the balcony."

"Shut up."

"She saw me in the cave. I told Gardeaux I was afraid that she'd recognize me. But that was a lie. Killing a kid is special. They're soft, and the fear is so keen, you can taste it."

Her hand holding the gun was shaking. She knew it was what he wanted but he was destroying her composure, killing her with words.

"The knife went in once, but it wasn't enough. She was too—" He leapt forward and jerked the gun up, backhanding her cheek with his other hand.

She fell to the ground.

He was on top of her, staring maliciously down at her. "Don't you want to know how she screamed when I—"

Her fist struck him in the mouth. She rolled to the side, dislodging him.

Moonlight glittered on the edge of the blade in his hand.

The knife. She sprang to her feet and backed away from him. Memories whirled back to her.

Medas. I'm helpless. Don't hurt me. Don't hurt Jill. Why won't he stop?

"You can't stop me." Maritz came toward her. "You couldn't do it then. You can't do it now."

He really is the bogeyman.

He just kept coming.

"Come on," Maritz murmured. "Don't you want to hear some more about how I stabbed the little girl? How many times it took?"

"No," she whispered.

"No guts. You're the same sniveling woman. New face but just the same. It won't take me a minute to finish you and go after Tania."

The words struck her like a dash of ice water. Tania would be the victim here. Not Jill. This wasn't Medas and she wasn't that woman anymore.

"The *hell* you will." She whirled and back-kicked him in the stomach.

He grunted with pain and doubled over. Before she could follow through, he'd recovered and spun away.

She moved toward him. "You won't kill Tania. You'll never kill anyone again."

"Good." He was smiling. "Fight me."

She kicked at his arm and the knife went flying.

He muttered a curse and dove for the knife.

She ran toward him.

He was up, slashing with deadly accuracy.

Blinding pain. Her upper arm . . .

He was coming, always coming, smiling.

She backed away, fighting the pain.

She was on the edge of the cliff and he was coming toward her. The sea was crashing below her.

Medas.

No, never again.

She waited for him.

"Are you ready?" he whispered. "It's coming. Do you hear it whisper to you?"

Death. He was talking about death. "Oh, yes, I'm ready."

He dove toward her. She stepped aside and twisted the arm holding the knife.

The ball of her hand shot up and struck him beneath the nose, shattering bones and sending the fragments into his brain.

He swayed and tumbled backward off the cliff.

She took a step closer and watched the waves washing over his broken body.

Down, down, down, we go . . .

She sank down on the ground.

It's done, Jill. It's over, baby.

"Nell."

It was Nicholas, she realized dazedly.

"He's dead, Nicholas."

He took her into his arms. "I know. I saw it."

"For a while I didn't think I could—" She looked up at him. "You saw it?"

His voice was uneven. "And I never want to go through anything like that again."

"You watched it and didn't interfere?"

"You went to a lot of trouble to make sure I didn't step in. I knew you'd never forgive me if I cheated you of Maritz." He paused. "I almost did anyway."

"I had to do it alone, Nicholas."

"I know." He stepped back and looked at her arm.

"It's stopped bleeding, but we'd better get to the cottage and get that bandaged."

Tania was coming toward them. "We did it?" she asked quietly.

Nell looked back at the cliff before starting toward the cottage. "We did it."

Joel's expression was forbidding as he stalked out of the emergency room.

Tania sighed. She had known he would be angry.

"Her arm is all right?" Tania asked.

"Fine. She lost some blood, so they're keeping her overnight."

"You wish to divorce me?"

"I'm considering it."

"You must not do it. I've learned all about alimony from your ex-wife. I'm sure I could do it better. You would be beggared."

"I'm not in a mood for jokes."

"I had to do this, Joel." She moved into his arms and laid her head on his chest. She whispered, "I know you wished to protect me, but I could not allow it. You are too dear to me. But I promise I'll let you slay the next mugger who approaches me. I'll even go looking for one. I hear Central Park has them lined up for inspection. Suppose we stop off in New York and—"
He was chuckling and she looked up at him. Good. The storm was over. "You don't think that's a good idea?"

"You'd do it, wouldn't you?" He looked down at her. "I can't handle this. It can't ever happen again, Tania."

"I promise. But I was not really in danger."

He snorted derisively.

"No, truly." She smiled up at him. "I was only Paul Henreid. Nell was Humphrey Bogart."

Nicholas sat down in the chair beside Nell's bed and took her hand. "How are you?"

She knew he was asking about more than her physical condition. "I don't know." She shook her head. "Peaceful. Numb. Empty."

"Joel did a good job stitching your arm. You won't have a scar."

"That's good."

"I've made reservations for a flight tomorrow. I'm taking you back to the ranch."

She shook her head.

"You'd like us to stay here for a while?"

God, she was finding this hard to say. "I want you to go back to the ranch."

He went still. "Without you?"

She nodded jerkily. "I need some time alone."

"How much time?"

"I don't know. I'm not sure. I'm not sure about anything anymore."

"I'm sure. I'm sure you love me."

"I'm afraid, Nicholas," she whispered.

"That I won't live forever? I can't solve that for you." He touched her cheek with a finger. "You'll just have to decide if the time we have together is enough."

"Easy to say. What if I make the wrong decision? It could happen." She thought a moment before continuing. "Do you remember what I said about the steps people take to become complete? I told you then I was stunted, splintered. I'm no better now."

"I can help you."

"You can shelter me. You can't help me. I have to do it alone."

He smiled lopsidedly. "So you're going away to become a swan?"

"I'm going away to heal and grow up and get my life together."

"What will you do?"

"Paint, get a job, talk to people. Whatever it takes."

"And I'm not included?"

"Not yet."

"But you'll come back to the ranch when you're ready?"

"If you still want me."

"Hell, yes, I'll want you." He stood up and gazed into her eyes. "I'll give you your space, but I don't promise I won't come after you." He kissed her quick and hard. "Hurry it up, dammit."

He left her.

Her eyes filled with tears. She wanted to call him back, to tell him she'd get on that plane with him and never look back.

She wouldn't do it. She wouldn't cheat him by giving him less than a whole person.

And she wouldn't cheat herself.

Epilogue

"There's someone at the gate," Michaela said.

Nicholas looked up from his book. "Who? Peter? Jean was supposed to bring him over to show me Jonti's puppy."

"It's not them." She turned away. "Go down and see for yourself."

"Why should I go down? Why don't you just buzz whoever it is through?" He suddenly realized Michaela looked entirely too satisfied; there was almost a smirk on her usually impassive face. Nicholas slowly rose to his feet. "Who is it?" He didn't wait for an answer. He was out on the porch, shading his eyes from the autumn sun with a hand.

She was standing by the gate intercom, dressed in jeans and a plaid shirt. The sunlight picked up the shimmer of gold in her hair.

He started walking toward her. It seemed to take him a long time to reach the gate.

He stopped and stared at her. God, she looked wonderful; beautiful and strong and free. "You took your time about it. More than a year."

"I'm a slow learner. It took me a while to get it right."

He tilted his head. "Madame Swan, I presume?"

"You're damn right." A radiant smile lit Nell's face. "Open that gate and let me in, Tanek."

About the Author

IRIS JOHANSEN has received many awards for her achievements in writing. She lives near Atlanta, Georgia.

Iris Johansen returns with a novel of even more shattering suspense . . . a chilling tale of murderous greed and deadly passions.

LONG AFTER MIDNIGHT

At twenty-nine, Kate Denby believes she's finally carved out a safe and secure life for herself and her nine-year-old son. But the gifted scientist couldn't be more wrong. . . . Deep in a research laboratory, Kate is very close to achieving a major medical breakthrough. But there is someone who will stop at nothing to make sure she never finishes her work. Someone not interested in holding out hope, but in buying and selling death. Now Kate is waking up to a nightmare world where a dangerously unpredictable killer is stalking her . . . where the people closest to her are considered expendable . . . and where the research to which she has devoted her life is the same research that could get her killed. Her only hope is to put her trust in a stranger, a man whose intentions are nearly impossible to fathom, a survivor used to putting his neck on the line. For no matter what happens, Kate must find a way to protect her son, and make that breakthrough. Because destroying her enemy could mean saving millions of lives . . . including the lives of those who mean the most to her.

Turn the page for an exciting preview of this thrilling novel.

Available now

The rays of the late afternoon sunlight dappled the path in front of Ishmaru as he ran swiftly through the woods. He always chose a motel that opened onto a wooded area. It was necessary for the preparation for the kill.

He ran faster. His heart was pumping with fierce pleasure.

He was fleet as a deer.

He was unstoppable.

He was warrior.

But warriors should not be guided by fools like Ogden. The kill should be made in a burst of glory, not cool calculation. He had lain awake a long time last night thinking of the kill tonight, the disturbance growing within him.

He reached the summit and stood there, gasping for breath. Below him spread a subdivision with neat, small houses like the one in which Kate Denby lived. If he shaded his eyes, he could see her subdivision just on the horizon. He had been pleased that her house was so close to the others in the neighborhood. It was an exciting challenge for him to move like a shadow among these sheep, to strike boldly.

But Ogden did not want him to strike boldly. Ogden wanted him to hide the act behind lies and deception.

Since it disturbed Ishmaru, there must be a reason. His instincts had told him from the first moment that Kate Denby might be special. Was she Emily sent to challenge him? He would meditate and wait for a sign.

He fell to his knees and dipped his finger into the dirt of the path and painted streaks on his cheeks and forehead. Then he threw out his arms. "Guide me," he whispered. "Let it become clear."

The ancient ones used to pray to the Great Spirit, but he was wiser. He knew the Great Spirit was within himself. He was both the Giver of Glory and the Punisher.

He stayed kneeling, arms thrown wide for one hour, two, three.

The rays of the sun paled. Shadows lengthened.

He would have to give up soon. With no sign he would have to submit to Ogden's will.

Then he heard a giggle in the shrubbery to his right.

Joy tore through him.

He didn't move. He kept his head facing straight ahead, but he slanted a glance toward the bushes from the corner of his eye.

A small girl was watching him. She was no more than seven or eight, wearing a plaid dress and carrying a backpack. His joy increased as he realized she had fair hair. Not the same ash blond as Kate Denby's but pale yellow like Emily Santos's. It could be no coincidence; his power must have pulled the child to him.

She was the bearer of the sign. If he could count coup on her, then that must mean he could ignore Ogden and follow the true path.

He slowly stood up and turned to the little girl.

She was still giggling. "You have a dirty face. What are you—" She broke off and her eyes widened. She took a step back.

She felt his power, Ishmaru exalted.

She whimpered, "I didn't mean— Don't—"

She whirled and ran down the path.

He started after her.

It would do no good for her to run.

He was fleet as a deer.

He was unstoppable.

He was warrior.

"Did you pack my laptop and my video games?" Joshua asked.

"They went in the trunk right after your bat and

catcher's mitt," Phyliss said. "And don't ask us to stuff one more toy in this car. There's barely enough room for the suitcases."

"All we've got in there are clothes," Joshua said. "Who needs clothes for sleeping? We could take out my pajamas and—"

"No," Kate said firmly and shut the trunk. "Now go into the house and take your bath. I'll be in as soon as I check the tires and oil, and you'd better be in bed."

"Okay." Joshua made a face at her before loping toward the front door.

"He's perking up," Phyliss said. "I think this trip will be good for him."

"I hope so. Will you hold the flashlight for me? It's getting too dark to see."

"Sure." Phyliss took a step closer and aimed the beam of the flashlight as Kate opened the hood and took out the oil stick.

"It's a quart low. We'd better stop at a gas station before we get on the road tomorrow."

"You made up your mind in a hurry," Phylliss observed. "It's not like you."

Kate grinned at her. "Slow, boring, methodical Kate?"

"You said it, I didn't."

"I have a right to an impulsive moment now and then."

"Maybe." Phyliss paused. "And it's not like you to run scared just because some young hoodlum decided to rob us."

"I thought we'd all had enough."

Phyliss's gaze searched Kate's expression. "Is something wrong, Kate?"

She should have known Phyliss was too perceptive not to be aware of Kate's tension. "Of course there's something wrong. We're a house of mourning." She knelt and began checking the air in the left front tire. "Will you go in and see if you can keep Joshua from smuggling his tennis racquet into his pillowcase? He was entirely too sentimental about taking his very own pillow along."

"I thought so too." Phyliss chuckled. "What a schemer." She went into the house.

Joshua was always a good distraction, Kate thought. Or maybe Phyliss had merely allowed herself to be distracted. She had a great respect for personal privacy, both her own and—

"What you got there?"

Kate's heart leaped to her throat and then quieted when she looked up and saw the man who had spoken wore a blue police uniform. She hadn't seen the police car draw up to the curb, but there it was.

"I didn't mean to scare you." He smiled. "I'm Caleb Brunwick. You're Dr. Denby?"

She felt foolish. No one could look less frightening. Caleb Brunwick was a heavyset man, with gray-flecked dark hair and a lined face. She nodded. "You weren't the one on duty last night."

"No. I just got back from vacation. I took my grandkids to the Grand Tetons. Beautiful country, Wyoming. I've been thinking of retiring there." He squatted beside her and took the tire gauge. "I'll finish this for you."

"Thank you." She stood up and wiped her hands on her jeans. "That's very kind of you. May I see your ID?"

"Oh, sure." He handed her his badge. "Here's my shield. Smart of you to check."

"I'll return this to you after I call the precinct."

"No problem." He moved to the next tire. "Sorry I'm late. There's a little girl missing from the Eagle Rock subdivision about ten miles from here. Since I was going to pass it on the way here, they asked me to stop and make out the report."

"A little girl?"

He nodded. "She missed the school bus."

My God, what a terrible world when a child could be put in danger because she missed a bus. It came too close to home. Joshua took a bus from school everyday. "Why didn't one of the teachers take her home?"

"She didn't ask. The subdivision where she lives is right over the hill from the school." He glanced at her. "I know how you feel, but they're searching for her now. She might have just gone to a friend's house. You know how kids are."

Yes, she knew how kids were. Thoughtless. Trusting. Impulsive. Defenseless.

"You taking a trip?" he asked.

She nodded. "Tomorrow morning."

"Where are you going?"

"I haven't decided."

"You ought to try Wyoming." He bent his head over the tire. "Great country . . ."

"Maybe I will." She smiled and held up his badge. "I'll bring this back in a minute."

It took more like ten minutes to check with the precinct and return his badge to him.

Joshua was in his pajamas and looking extremely disgusted when she entered his room. "I need my tennis racquet."

"You're taking enough equipment to open a sports store."

"My tennis racquet goes wherever I go."

"I'll make you a deal. Leave your baseball glove and you can take the tennis racquet."

Joshua's eyes widened in horror. "Mom!"

She had known he would never leave that treasured beat-up glove. "No? Then give it up, kid."

He studied her and then nodded. "Okay, now I'll make a deal with *you*. If I need a tennis racquet, we'll go to a store and you can buy—"

She threw a pillow at him. "Brat."

He grinned. "I had to give it a try." He hopped into bed. "Grandma says we have to get up at five."

"Grandma's right . . . as usual." She drew the covers over him and brushed her lips on his forehead before straightening. "Joshua, what would you do if you missed the school bus that brings you home?"

"Go back in the school and call Grandma."

"You know we wouldn't be mad at you. You *would* call us?"

He frowned. "Sure, I told you I would. What's wrong?"

"Nothing." She prayed for the sake of that little girl's parents that she spoke the truth. "Good night, Joshua."

"Mom?"

She turned back to him.

"Will you stick around for a while?"

"You can't put off—" She broke off as she saw his expression. "What's wrong?"

"I don't know— I feel— will you stick around for a while?"

"Why not?" She sat down on the edge of the bed. "You've been through a lot. It's natural to be a little nervous."

"I'm *not* nervous."

"Okay, sorry." She took his hand. "Do you mind if I say that I'm nervous?"

"Not if it's true."

"It's true."

"It's not that I'm scared. I just feel kind of . . . creepy."

"Do you want to talk about the funeral now?"

His brow immediately furrowed. "I *told* you I wasn't thinking about that anymore."

She backed off. It was clearly still too soon to approach him. It was just as well. She was probably too raw herself to maintain any degree of control. All he needed was to see her break down. "I was only asking."

"Just stick around for a while. Okay?"

"As long as you want me."

She didn't look like a warrior, sitting there on the boy's bed, Ishmaru thought in disappointment. She looked soft and womanly, without spirit or worth.

He peered through the narrow slit afforded by the venetian blinds covering the window of the boy's room.

Look at me. Let me see your spirit.

She didn't look at him. Didn't she know he was there, or was she scorning his threat to her?

Yes, that must be it. His power was so great tonight, he felt as if the stars themselves must feel it. Coup always brought added strength and exultation in its wake. The little girl had felt his power even before his hands had closed around her throat. The woman must be taunting him by pretending she was not aware he was watching her.

His hands tightened on the glass cutter in his hand. He could cut through the glass and show her he could not be ignored.

No, that was what she wanted. Even though he was quick, he would be at a disadvantage. She sought to lure him to his destruction as a clever warrior should do.

But he could be clever too. He would wait for the moment and then strike boldly in full view of these sheep with whom she surrounded herself.

And before she died, she would admit how great was his power.

Joshua remained awake for almost an hour, and even after his eyes finally closed, he slept fitfully.

It was just as well they were going away for a while, Kate thought. Joshua wasn't a high-strung child, but what he'd gone through was enough to unsettle anyone.

Phyliss's door was closed, Kate noted when she reached the hall. She should probably get to bed too. Not that she'd be able to sleep. She hadn't lied to Joshua; she was nervous and uneasy . . . and bitterly resentful. This was her home, it was supposed to be a haven. She didn't like to think of it as a fortress.

But, like it or not, it was a fortress at the moment and she'd better make sure the soldiers were on the battlements. She checked the lock on the front door before she moved quickly toward the living room. She would see the black-and-white from the picture window.

Phylliss, as usual, had drawn the drapes over the window before she went to bed. The cave instinct, Kate thought as she reached for the cord. Close out the outside world and make your own. She and Phyliss were in complete agree—

He was standing outside the window, so close they were separated only by a quarter of an inch of glass.

Oh God. High concave cheekbones, long black

straight hair drawn back in a queue, beaded necklace. It was him . . . Todd Campbell . . . Ishmaru . . .

And he was smiling at her.

His lips moved and he was so near she could hear the words through the glass. "You weren't supposed to see me before I got in, Kate." He held her gaze as he showed her the glass cutter in his hand. "But it's all right. I'm almost finished and I like it better this way."

She couldn't move. She stared at him, mesmerized.

"You might as well let me in. You can't stop me."

She jerked the drape shut, closing him out.

Barricading herself inside with only a fragment of glass, a scrap of material . . .

She heard the sound of blade on glass.

She backed away from the window, stumbled on the hassock, almost fell, righted herself.

Oh God. Where was that policeman? The porch light was out, but surely he could see Ishmaru.

Maybe the policeman wasn't there.

Didn't Michael tell you about bribery in the ranks?

The drape was moving.

"Phyliss!" She ran down the hall. "Wake up." She threw open Joshua's door, flew across the room, and jerked him out of bed.

"Mom?"

"Shh, be very quiet. Just do what I tell you, okay?"

"What's wrong?" Phyliss was standing in the door-way. "Is Joshua sick?"

"I want you to leave here." She pushed Joshua toward her. "There's someone outside." She hoped he was still outside. Christ, he could be in the living room by now. "I want you to take Joshua out the back door and over to the Brocklemans."

Phyliss instantly took Joshua's hand and moved toward the kitchen door. "What about you?"

She heard a sound in the living room. "Go. I'll be right behind you."

Phyliss and Joshua flew out the back door.

"Are you waiting for me, Kate?"

He sounded so close, too close. Phyliss and Joshua

could not have reached the fence yet. No time to run. Stop him.

She saw him, a shadow in the doorway leading to the hall.

Where was the gun?

In her handbag on the living room table. She couldn't get past him. She backed toward the stove. Phyliss usually left a frying pan out to cook breakfast in the morning. . . .

"I told you I was coming in. No one can stop me tonight. I had a sign."

She didn't see a weapon but the darkness was lit only by moonlight streaming through the window.

"Give up, Kate."

Her hand closed on the handle of the frying pan. "Leave me *alone*." She leaped forward and struck out at his head with all her strength.

He moved too fast but she connected with a glancing blow.

He was falling. . . .

She streaked past him down the hall. Get to the purse, the gun.

She heard him behind her.

She snatched up the handbag, lunged for the door, and threw the bolt.

Get to the policeman in the black-and-white.

She fumbled with the catch on her purse as she streaked down the driveway toward the black-and-white. Her hand closed on the gun and she threw the purse aside.

"He's not there, Kate," Ishmaru said behind her. "It's just the two of us."

No one was in the driver's seat of the police car.

She whirled and raised the gun.

Too late.

He was on her, knocking the gun from her grip, sending it flying. How had he moved so quickly?

She was on the ground, struggling wildly.

She couldn't breathe. His thumbs were digging into her throat.

"Mom." Joshua's agonized scream pierced the night.

What was Joshua doing here? He was supposed to

be— "Go away, Josh—" Ishmaru's hands tightened, cut off speech. She was dying. She had to move. The gun. She had dropped it. On the ground . . .

She reached out blindly. The metal of the gun hilt was cool and wet from the grass.

She wasn't going to make it. Everything was going black.

She tried to knee him in the groin.

"Stop fighting," he whispered. "I've gone to a great deal of trouble to give you a warrior's death."

Crazy bastard. The hell she'd stop fighting.

She raised the gun and pressed the trigger.

She cold feel the impact ripple through his body as the bullet struck him.

His grip loosened around her throat. She heaved upward, slid out from under him and struggled to her knees.

He was lying on his back on the ground. Had she killed him? she wondered numbly.

"He hurt you." Joshua was beside her, tears running down his face. "I was too far away. I couldn't stop him. I couldn't—"

"Shh." She slid an arm arund him. "I know." She started coughing. "Where's Phyliss?"

"She's using the Brocklemans' phone. I ran out of the house—"

"You shouldn't have done that."

"And you should have come with us," Joshua said fiercely. "He *hurt* you."

She could hardly deny that when she couldn't muster more than a croak. "It's not as bad as it—"

"It's bad enough." She turned at the voice to see a lean, darkhaired man running up the driveway.

She instinctively raised the gun and pointed it at him.

"Easy." He held up his hands. "Noah Smith sent me."

"How do I know that?" How could she believe anything? she wondered dazedly.

"You don't. Just keep the gun pointed at me and you'll feel better. I'm Seth Drakin."

Seth. Noah had mentioned a Seth. "What are you doing here?"

"I told you, Noah thought you might need some help.

I was protecting you." He added, "Though I seem to be a little late." He turned Ishmaru's body over with his foot. "This was the same man who was here last night?"

She nodded.

"I don't think there's any doubt it's Ishmaru."

"Is he dead?"

He bent down and examined the wound. "No. Nasty flesh wound in the right side. It doesn't look like you've cut an artery. Extremely painful but not serious. Pity. Do you want me to finish him?"

"What?" she asked, shocked.

"Just a thought." He turned to Joshua. "Go get your grandmother, son."

Joshua looked at Kate.

She nodded. "Tell her to call an ambulance."

Joshua streaked across the lawn.

"An ambulance for a man who just tried to kill you?" Drakin asked.

"No, for me. I don't want to be responsible for killing a man if I can help it."

"Noble," he said. "I'm afraid I wouldn't be as generous." He glanced away, his gaze raking the dark houses along the block. "Nice supportive neighbors you have. Someone must have heard that shot."

"Most of them know how Michael died, and they've seen a police car here for the last two nights. Naturally they're afraid." She shuddered. "I would be too."

He studied her and then smiled. "But I don't think you'd be hiding behind closed doors if you thought a neighbor was in trouble. I'll be right back." He disappeared into the house and returned with a length of drapery cord. He swiftly tied Ishmaru's hands behind him.

"What are you doing? He's helpless."

"You won't let me kill him. I need to make sure of him. Ishmaru has the reputation of being always more than expected." He pulled her to her feet. "Come on, we have to get out of here before the police and ambulance come."

"Run away?" She shook her head.

"You just shot a man."

"It was self-defense. They won't hold me."

"Maybe not for an extended time, but do you want to leave your son alone and unprotected while you make explanations down at the police department?"

"He's safe now."

"Really? And where's the officer who was supposed to be protecting you?"

She glanced at the black-and-white. "I don't know."

"Probably somewhere spending Ogden's money. Suppose the police send your officer to protect Joshua while they're holding you?"

"Stop it. I'm not going anywhere with you. You could be lying. I don't even know you." She ran her fingers through her hair. She couldn't think. "And you're confusing me."

"You don't have to go with me. Go to Noah at the motel. Now's not the time to make a mistake. You wouldn't be the one to pay for it."

Joshua would pay. Joshua must be protected. Maybe Drakin was right. At any rate, she needed time to sort things out. She nodded jerkily. "I'll go to the motel."

"Good. I'll phone Noah and tell him you're coming. Do you need anything from the house?"

"No."

"Don't change your mind." His gaze searched her face. "Don't get halfway there and decide to take off. You need all the help you can get."

"I'll go to the motel," she repeated. She turned and watched Joshua and Phyliss coming across the lawn toward her. She was still clutching the gun, she realized. She picked up her purse and stuffed the weapon inside. "That's all I'll promise."

"Hurry. You've got to move fast." He glanced at Ishmaru. "And don't untie him. I have a hunch he's playing possum. Are you sure you don't want me to send him to the happy hunting grounds?"

So casual. So cool. What kind of a man was he? She shivered. "I told you no."

"Just asking." He hesitated. "I don't want to leave you alone. Suppose I wait until you take off before I go."

"And what will you do to him after I leave? Kill him? You go first. I don't trust you."

He nodded approvingly. "Good, you shouldn't."

"Leave."

"Promise you won't untie him."

"I promise," she said through clenched teeth.

"Then I'm on my way." He strode down the driveway.

She stared after him. The appearance of this stranger had been as bewildering as everything else this evening. Bewildering and terrifying. He had seemed to know just what buttons to push to get her to do what he wanted.

"Emily . . ."

At the whisper she went rigid and then swung around to look at the man on the ground.

His eyes were open and he was staring directly at her. How long had he been conscious?

"I knew it was you, Emily."

"My name is Kate."

"Yes, that too." He smiled. "You're . . . wonderful, Kate. You did . . . well."

A chill went through her. He was lying there with a wound she'd inflicted and there was genuine admiration in his voice. Noah was right, the man had to be insane. "Why did you do this?" she whispered.

"Coup . . . I will have three when you are all dead." He closed his eyes. "But you alone will bring me great honor, Kate. I can hardly . . . wait."

She took a step back before she realized what she'd done. There was no reason to be afraid. He was no threat. He was wounded, bound, and soon the police would be here. She could hear the sirens now. She would call Alan from the motel and tell him what happened, and he would make sure this scum was kept in jail, away from them.

She turned her back on him and went to meet Phyliss and Joshua.

Ishmaru opened his eyes and watched the taillights of the Honda move down the street away from him.

Happiness flooded him, warming him. The woman had brought him down but he felt no shame. The women were always the coldest, the fiercest. That's why warriors always gave their prisoners to the women for torture. This wound she had given him was great torture. Every breath he took was pain, and she had known it. When the man had asked if he should finish him, she had said no and the man had thought her merciful.

Ishmaru knew better. She had wanted him to suffer. She wanted him to lie here and know she had done this to him. He had been right about the strength he had sensed in her.

Sirens . . . far away . . .

It made no difference what she had said. She had called an ambulance to heal him so that he would be well enough to face her again. She had realized that he was her destiny.

But the police would also come. A gauntlet for him to run before he could get to her.

Clever, Kate. She was testing him to see if he was worthy of meeting her again.

He was worthy.

He rolled over and began to crawl up the driveway toward the open front door. He would get a shard of glass from the window he'd cut and slice through these bonds, then go out the back door and lose himself in this suburban wilderness of tract houses.

He was bleeding and each movement was agony. It didn't matter. He was used to pain, he welcomed it.

He was in the shadows at the side of the house.

The sirens were closer.

He must move faster. He pressed his back against the brick wall and pulled himself up to a standing position.

Dizziness swamped him and he swayed.

He fought it back and staggered toward the front door.

You see, Kate. I'm coming.

I'm worthy of you.